The
Version
of Me
You Loved

Eight Years. Eight Versions. One Story.

THE VERSIONS SERIES, BOOKS 1-2

Brandon LeMar Bass

BLB Productions
An imprint of DoubleB Publishing, LLC
Springfield, Massachusetts, USA

Library of Congress Cataloging-in-Publication Data
Bass, Brandon LeMar, author.
The Version of Me You Loved: *Eight Years. Eight Versions. One Story.* Books 1-2 of The Versions Series / Brandon LeMar Bass
Includes Index.
LCCN: 2025923033
ISBN: 979-8-9997044-9-8 (Hardcover) 979-8-9997044-8-1 (Paperback) 979-8-9997044-7-4 (eBook/Digital)

Website: https://linktr.ee/smoothdoubleb

$34.99
ISBN 979-8-9997044-9-8
53499>
9 798999 704498

$24.99
ISBN 979-8-9997044-8-1
52499>
9 798999 704481

Message to the Reader

Dear Reader,

This story isn't just fiction. It's a mirror.

It's about a girl who lived eight lives in one. Who changed because she had to. Who loved deeply, fell apart quietly, and kept going even when the world shifted beneath her feet.

Some versions of her were fearless. Others were broken. Some ran. Some stayed. But every version mattered — even the ones she tried to forget.

As you turn these pages, you won't just meet her. You'll meet the parts of yourself you've lost, found, hidden, or never dared to name.

This book is about memories. About identity. About love, and what it costs to hold onto it. But most of all... It's about becoming.

So, wherever you are, whatever version of yourself you're in right now — I hope this story finds you. And I hope, in some small way, it helps you remember the version of *you* that once dreamed a little louder. See you on the other side.

With heart,
Brandon LeMar Bass

Introduction

The Version of Me You Loved. Eight years. Eight versions of her. And one question that never stopped echoing:

If you met every version of yourself... would you still recognize the one they loved?

It began with a $100,000 social media blackout that went terrifyingly wrong. Then came the confession app that tore friendships apart, a cloned identity that blurred her reflection, and a love that was never entirely human. From there, the versions only multiplied.

College brought a stranger who changed everything, a forbidden door that should've stayed locked, and a fall through the floor of reality itself. Senior year became a battle against memory and time—a desperate race to piece herself back together before the world forgot who she was.

Each year rewrote her. Each version unraveled another truth. And somewhere in the chaos was the version of her that dared to love, to fight, and to remember—the one she had to become to survive them all. But something new has begun to wake inside her reflection.

Contents

Book

1

ONE

Freshman Year

*Off the Grid – The Version
of Me That Went Silent*

The world didn't end when Nova Temples woke up late—but it definitely felt like it should've.

My eyes were crispy like the food I ate last night. My ears were ringing after I took off my headphones. I rubbed my eyes, barely awake.

My bedroom glowed with the soft, electric hue of ten different devices blinking at once. Phone. Tablet. Smart mirror. Alarm clock. Voice assistant. Smart light. Smart googles. Smart watch. Robot vacuum. Headphones. Each one pinging, lighting up, or talking over the other like digital birds competing for my attention.

I reached for my phone first, thumb already instinctively hovering over my favorite app. The blue glow of my phone was the first thing that greeted me, as always. My screen flickered to life—flashes of filtered perfection: a dance trend I'd missed, a viral skincare hack, two hundred unread messages, and a fresh stream of notifications tagging me in memes, stories, and duets I didn't remember filming. Comments stacked like bricks. The screen was my mirror, my battlefield, and sometimes, when I let myself think too hard, my only window to the world.

I hadn't even brushed my teeth yet and already felt behind.

Followers: 84,213.
New likes: 1,182.
DM from: @Ivy_AfifyOfficial: "Cute post. I see you copied my aesthetic tho 😽 ."

I sighed. Morning had begun.

Everything in my room buzzed and blinked, except for me. I sat still at the edge of my bed, overwhelmed by my own curated world. Legs were shaking with nerves. A part of me liked the chaos—liked being *seen*—but lately, it felt more like drowning than performing.

Across the hall, my younger brother, Milo, shouted at a headset mid-game. "You literally stole my kill, bro! I will hex your gaming dog!"

Downstairs, my mom's voice chimed through the intercom, "Nova, honey? The smart fridge says we're out of almond milk. Can you order some?" No good morning. No hug. Just a grocery request from a machine.

Still tired, I got up. I looked at my smart mirror, trying to smile at myself, but I'm still drained. It felt forced, edgy, not real. I made silly faces, trying to cheer myself up, and said, "I got this," but it felt weird because the voice assistant was hearing every word.

I brushed it off and went to my closet.

I got dressed in silence—sliding into my carefully chosen first-day outfit: pastel layers, clear lip gloss, hair tucked into loose twin buns. I looked like someone who had their life together. Maybe today I could convince myself of that, too.

As I headed downstairs, my mom came on the intercom again, "Nova, honey, I have an early meeting and I'm already late, please take the bus today." Once I stepped downstairs, I saw her mom relaying the message. "I heard you, Mom," I stated.

My dad Eli was already on the phone saying his goodbyes. He works in the tech field, so he's always busy. My mom tried to tell him he forgot his lunch, but after he hugged her and said goodbye, he was already near the door.

He yelled, saying bye to Milo, but he was too busy playing his game. He needed to get ready for school, but he was too focused on playing his game.

As my dad walked past me, he hugged me and said he loved me. It felt cold, maybe because he was in a rush or because he wasn't there all the time. I had love for him, but I don't know if I truly loved him. It felt like a person you care for because they were around your presence, but also far away, like a new stranger who's your roommate.

After he left, my mom said that my grandparents (Adina and Dion) were coming over to stay for a while. They were going to celebrate their anniversary, and it always felt like they cared for me more than my actual parents. I knew my parents meant well, but I could talk to my grandparents about anything. No judgment. Pure wisdom. And always listened.

As my mother talked, I grabbed a bowl of cereal, totally forgetting that we're out of almond milk. I'm excited that my grandma is coming because she made the best breakfast. As I fantasized over her famous breakfast, someone kept calling my name. "Nova. Nova. Nova."

As I gained my consciousness back, it was my mom telling me the cereal was overflowing. Good thing we had robot vacuums.

I didn't know my mom wanted me to help Milo get ready for school. He had to take a different school bus since he went to the middle school. I had no clue because I was imagining her grandma's breakfast. It slipped right past my head.

My mom, Eliana, walked out the door, saying "Bye," and left like that. She had a presentation for work, and this could determine whether or not she gets the promotion. She was up against strict competition, but I believed in her even though it felt like no one believed in me, besides my grandparents.

I realized all the cereal I poured. Being the first day of school, I may need the extra calories. My smart watch was pinging. I didn't care because I felt like it was telling me to watch my calorie intake. Not knowing, it was a ping letting me know that I was late and needed to hurry up. Our dog Micah came by, and I gave him the rest of my cereal.

I went upstairs, and Milo was hogging the main bathroom. "Oh, now you want to get ready," I stated. "There's another bathroom," he said. "I took a sniff and immediately turned away. I love my brother, but he can be a pain to deal with. But I love that kid.

I got all my shower gear, skincare, hair products, etc., for my daily routine. I try to stay on my routine to keep myself sane. I grabbed my speaker, listened to my favorite music, and got ready.

Once I was done, Milo was already downstairs. He yelled out, "Love you, sis, see ya later." Right after I said it back, he was out the door. No time for a hug. No time for a kiss on the cheek. I guess he knew where he was going. I don't know if he even showered. That's none of my business. My parents did treat him like a baby. I'm just happy I have this alone time by myself. No one to bother me. Right when I closed my eyes, my door opened. As I opened my eyes, it was Micah.

As I rubbed his fur, I remembered all the fun times we had. The times we played at the park. The times he looked outside the window during our family trip. He was my peace in any storm. He was my warmth whenever I needed it.

Knowing that I was late, I rushed downstairs and quickly ran out the door with my stuff. I forgot to lock the door, but when I was halfway down the street, I used my phone to lock the door.

We lived in a nice neighborhood here in Wildermere, Calvonna, because my parents' main focus was working. The slogan for this town is "*Where the lake meets the legend.*" I'm grateful for everything we have, but sometimes having a dynamic unit is much better than having a lavish lifestyle.

Luckily, since it was the first day of school, there was traffic. So, I didn't miss the bus as it turned down our street right after I approached the bus stop.

As the bus opened, it was Ms. Linda, who was a great and fun bus driver, but today she wasn't as excited. Maybe since it was the first day, something happened at home, I don't know. She did give me a nice smile, but as I walked on the bus, I knew why she wasn't feeling it.

The school bus ride was louder than usual—people filming livestreams, vlogging "first day" content, or snapping shots of each other's fits.

At the front of the bus, Ivy Afify—hair slicked, outfit sharp—took selfies with a ring light suction-cupped to the window. Her hashtag? #FirstDayFlex.

"Nice top," Ivy said, loud enough for me to hear. "Totally retro. Is polyester back?"

I rolled my eyes. Ivy had been my digital frenemy since sixth grade: always smiling in public, always slithering behind the scenes. Nice to people's faces, but a snake behind their backs.

I sat next to my best friend, Amina Dankworth, who was already holding court on a group FaceTime with three other girls.

Amina blew a kiss at the screen. "Okay, but Nova's fit? ATE. Okay? Y'all not ready."

I smiled, grateful. Amina was like a glitter bomb in human form—loyal, chaotic, and occasionally exhausting.

Behind us was Zayden "Zay" Roan, who leaned forward, earbuds in, mumbling, "Y'all are so loud I forgot what silence sounds like." Zay was the type to wear the same hoodie every week and still somehow look cool. He edited indie videos for fun and claimed social media was "rotting our collective consciousness," but had 50K followers for his conspiracy theory videos.

As we pulled into Ravenlock High, the school shimmered under the late summer sun—sleek, modern, and wired to the gills. Giant LED banners flashed updates: lunch menus, schedule changes, social reminders. Drones hovered, scanning IDs. The school mascot, Ravenlock shadows—oddly, a mechanical owl—blinked as students passed through security.

I took a breath. All of my friends were around me, but why did I feel this way? One last scroll before school started. My finger hovered over the app... then froze.

The LED screen above the school doors glitched.

Then it changed.

A small crowd had already formed outside the school doors. Two giant banners hung over the entrance, printed in bold blue:

"OFF THE GRID."
Win $100,000.
Thirty Days. No Phone. No Social Media. No Exceptions.
Sign-Up Opens Today.

Other students stopped in their tracks. Confused murmurs rippled through the courtyard. Zay's earbuds dropped from his ears.

"What kind of twisted tech nightmare nonsense is this...?" he muttered.

As we walked off the bus, "You see the school board announcement?" Amina asked, blowing her bangs out of her eyes. "It's literally *insane.*"

"I just got twelve different texts about it now," Nova said, opening up the app and still scrolling.

Amina leaned in, smirking. "You think they're actually gonna do it? Like—$100K? For staying off social media for a *month*? It sounds fake."

"It sounds like a trap," muttered Zay. "Like some dystopian TV pilot."

"Or genius," Nova said slowly, locking her phone and staring at the screen. "I mean... think about it. We live online. What if this is our chance to prove we can survive without it?"

Amina blinked. "Girl, you scheduled a post for every day this week."

"I said, *prove we can*. Not *want to.*"

Inside, students were herded into the auditorium, and a silence fell across the group. Then came the buzz—soft at first, then louder. Students whisper, gasp, and laugh nervously, all buzzing with questions.

"Is this even legal?" someone muttered.

"Wait, wait—do we *have* to do it?" a sophomore asked.

"No," came the voice of Principal Heath, stepping through the doors as her hair wisped through the air, light and effortless. "It's voluntary. But for those who join... the rules will be strict. We'll be monitoring everything."

A ripple of murmurs spread through the auditorium.

Onstage stood Principal Heath in a black power suit that screamed, "I don't have time for your excuses."

Her voice echoed. "Welcome, students. This year, Ravenlock High is partnering with the DoubleB Foundation to launch an experiment—an opportunity. A chance to prove you can survive without constant validation. Without filters. Without the grid."

Behind her, a holographic logo shimmered.
OFF THE GRID: The Blackout Challenge.
Prize: $100,000 Scholarship.
Rule: 30 Days. No Phones. No Social. No Exceptions.

The auditorium exploded.

Amina gasped. "Oh, she's testing my spirit. No scrolling for a *month*?"

Zay laughed. "Finally. My time has come."

Ivy raised a hand. "Will there be accommodations for influencers with active contracts?"

I sat frozen. No phone? No filters? No followers?

But $100,000. That was real. That could mean a future. College. Escape.

My stomach fluttered—not from fear, but from...something else. Excitement, maybe. Hunger.

I looked down at my screen. All those likes. All those messages. They couldn't hold me anymore.

This phone, the one thing I never leave home without. For the first time in a long time, I imagined what life would feel like without it buzzing constantly in my hand.

Freeing?

Or terrifying?

Maybe both.

In my head, I told myself that I'm in.

By the time the bell rang, the school was already divided.

Throughout the day, debate buzzed like static electricity. In the hallways. In the bathrooms. In whispered circles and loud lunch tables.

Amina was already spiraling. "What am I supposed to do? Actually, *talk* to people between classes?"

Zay made a fake gagging sound. "Imagine reading a book for fun. Couldn't be me."

A whiteboard near the front office listed sign-ups—only a few names so far.

I was at the top. They passed out this device we had to lock our phones with.

Amina trailed behind me. "Girl, are you okay? You just... signed up for death."

Zay smirked. "No. She signed up for freedom. I respect it."

Ivy scoffed. "This is going to be *so* entertaining. Watch her crack by Day Three."

I didn't say anything.

This will disrupt my "normal, mundane" life. For the first time in years, the silence rang louder than the noise.

That night, I sat on the edge of my bed, phone cradled in both my hands.

On my screen: curated memories. Follower counts. Perfected filters. So many people who think they know me.

My reflection in the black screen looked tired. Honest.

I clicked open the school challenge page they sent and hovered over the registration form.

My fingers shook slightly.

I wasn't doing this for the money. Not really. I was doing it to see who I was without a screen telling me who to be. I clicked submit.

The screen dimmed.

I turned off my phone.

Then went black.

And so did my connection to the world.

The next morning, I sat cross-legged on my bed, staring down at my phone like it was a dying friend. I turned on my phone for the last time. The lock screen blinked up at me—an old photo of me, Amina, and Zay squished into a sun-drenched selfie at the beach last summer. Our arms tangled. Sand stuck to our cheeks. The kind of photo that normally lives in my story highlights.

Now, it felt like a relic.

Downstairs, my mom's voice floated up. "Nova, let's go, baby! You're gonna be late!"

I'm not ready.

I pressed the power button. The screen went black.

I slid my phone into the official school-issued magnetic pouch and watched the light on it blink red—locked. I couldn't open it for 30 days. Couldn't text Amina. Couldn't check the news. Couldn't doomscroll. Couldn't even Google if the sky looked weird because of a storm or the apocalypse.

I dropped it into her backpack and grabbed the strap, muscles tense.

Thirty days. Just thirty days. One month without the noise. For one hundred thousand dollars.

Downstairs, the smell of toast and Adina's perfume mingled as my grandma buzzed around the kitchen like she had three places to be.

Dion stood leaning against the sink, coffee in hand, his eyebrows already raised like he was mentally preparing for teen drama.

Surprised to see them, I gave them both a big hug. The thought of this challenge still weighed heavily on me.

"I thought y'all were coming in next week," I said.

"We wanted to surprise you, Nova!" Excitement ran through their body.

Milo popped a waffle into his mouth while scrolling freely on his tablet, making exaggerated faces.

"You're not doing the challenge?" I asked, glaring at him.

"I'm *eleven*," he said with a mouth full of syrup. "No one's offering me a hundred thousand dollars to log off."

My grandma didn't make her famous breakfast, so I shoved a banana in my bag, trying to ignore the weight in my chest.

Micah wagged his tail and flopped at her feet like a doorstop.

"Be good today," Adina said, walking me to the door. "Don't overthink it. You've got this. Your mom told me about the challenge."

Nova hesitated.

"I already miss everyone."

My grandma smiled, brushing a strand of hair behind my ear.

"They'll still be there. But your future's waiting too."

The front of Ravenlock High looked like someone had tried to turn a prison into a mall. Concrete, brick, metal — softened only by a few desperate trees and the school's raven-shaped flag snapping in the wind.

As I approached the gates, a group of students was already crowding around the school steps. Above them, a *massive holo-projection* glitched in and out on a curved billboard screen attached to the building's overhang.

OFF THE GRID: THE BLACKOUT CHALLENGE
Starts Today. No Phones. No Social. No Exceptions.
Prize: $100,000. Winner(s): To Be Determined.

Principal Heath stood on the top steps with a megaphone in one hand, and her eyes scanning the crowd like a coach at tryouts.

"Welcome to Ravenlock's newest tradition," she announced. "Thirty days. Zero digital distractions. You've locked in your devices, now it's time to unlock the real world."

Murmurs rippled through the students like wind over water. Some rolled their eyes. Some looked terrified. Others—mostly the non-participants—watched with amused detachment, already texting about it in group chats I could no longer see.

No phone, no social media, no lifeline. My face was raw, awkward silence of the real world... and the first signs that something isn't quite right at Ravenlock High.

Inside, the halls buzzed like they always did — but Nova noticed it immediately.

The change.

No music leaking from backpack speakers. No half-whispered video audios playing behind someone's hair. No flashes from phone cameras. Just... voices. Lockers slamming. Shoes squeaking. Coughs. Creaks. Laughter that sounded too loud in the digital silence.

She spotted Amina down the hall, giving her a smile. No phone. Just a real smile.

Zay was next to her, tapping the side of his head like, *"You got this."*

I gave them both a thumbs-up, but my fingers curled halfway. I was already reaching for my pocket out of muscle memory.

There's nothing there. Just air. And silence.

In the cafeteria, the division between participants and non-participants was palpable.

I wandered with my tray, scanning. The OFF THE GRID kids mostly stuck together — some nervous, others acting too cool about it. Amina waved her over, but Nova noticed Ivy first — sitting at the far end of the room with her followers, screen out, laughing at something no one else could see.

Nova sat down beside Amina and Zay, pretending not to look.

"Don't worry, we won't pull out our phones near you, but are you feeling it yet?" Amina asked, popping a grape in her mouth.

"Like I've lost a limb," I muttered.

Zay leaned in. "I heard one guy dropped out in the second period. Had a panic attack when he realized he couldn't check his streaks."

Nova laughed — too loud. It felt good, but it didn't last.

From across the room, Ivy caught her eye. She smirked, held up her phone, and made a dramatic fake "recording" motion.

Then mouthed:

"Missin' me yet?"

Nova's stomach flipped. Amina scowled. "Ignore her. She's probably live-posting her entire meal."

"She's not gonna let up," I whispered.

"That's what makes her Ivy," Zay said.

Just as I took a bite of my sandwich, someone dropped a tray across from me with zero warning.

The tray clattered.

"God, finally. Have you ever tried eating alone in the library? I think the dust was judging me."

I looked up to see a boy with shaggy dark curls, techy rings on his fingers, and a "404 ERROR" patch sewn onto his denim jacket. He had a sharp smile and lazy confidence. I decided to help him out.

"You're Knox, right?"

He gave her a mock salute. "Knox Flanker. Hacker. Anarchist. Alleged conspiracy theorist. Allegedly."

He sat next to us.

Amina raised an eyebrow. "You're in the challenge?"

"Had to," he said, grinning. "This whole thing smells like a behavioral experiment. I want front-row seats."

I blinked. "So, you're not in it for the money?"

Knox leaned back in his chair. "Please. Money's a distraction. I'm here for the meltdown."

By the last period, my thoughts were fractured.

Every time someone whispered behind me, I imagined a post. Every laugh I wasn't part of felt like a thread I couldn't click. I didn't feel *offline*. I felt invisible.

In my notebook, I scrawled a list:

- What is Ivy posting?
- What if someone posted about me?
- What if I miss something important?
- What if I get forgotten?

I tapped my pen. Then stopped. Then tapped again.

Knox, two rows back, was watching me with quiet interest. He lifted his pen, then drew a square in the air — like a phone — and crossed it out.

I smirked. It was stupid. But it helped.

That night, my mom took all my smart gadgets away, so I wouldn't lose the challenge. At first, I was mad, but I see why now. She was looking out for me.

I sat on my bed, a blanket over my shoulders, and my phone pouch on the nightstand like a locked treasure chest. I imagined it glowing. Buzzing. Pulling me back.

One day down. Twenty-nine to go.

Micah snored at the foot of my bed. I lay open across my knees as I journaled.

I wrote:

Day 1 – Felt like I was underwater. Quiet. Cold. Off balance.
Ivy's still loud. The world didn't pause.
But I didn't give in. And maybe tomorrow I'll feel a little less... gone.

I capped my pen.
Let's see who cracks first.

By Day 4, things were already cracking.

Phones might have been locked away, but Ravenlock High was leaking rebellion through its seams.

I noticed it first in History when a folded piece of paper slipped across my desk.

I paused before touching it — like it might explode. But it was paper. Real paper. Folded three times and torn at the top. It read, in all-caps block letters:

BLACKOUT MEETING — ROOM 107 AFTER SCHOOL. COME IF YOU'RE SERIOUS. NO SNITCHING.

No name. No explanation. Just black ink and tension.

Across the room, I caught Knox's eye. He gave me a small nod, then tapped his pencil against the desk four times in a rhythmic pattern. It felt like a code.

After school, I ducked out of the usual route. Room 107 was one of the unused classrooms in the old science wing — cold and dusty, half the lights flickering.

Inside were nine other students, some she recognized, others she didn't. Zay sat on a desk, swinging his legs. Amina leaned in a chair backward. Knox must've invited them to participate. They must not be in it for the money, then.

Knox was already writing on the whiteboard with a Sharpie:

THE BLACKOUT GROUP

"When the world shuts off, we switch on."

I snorted. "You practicing for the slogan contest?"

"Branding matters," Knox said, dead serious.

They went around the room, establishing the rules:

- No digital devices.
- In-person meetings only.
- Analog communication only — notes, codes, locker signals.
- Help each other stay in. No one cracks.

It felt ridiculous... and brilliant.

"They're watching us," one junior girl said. "Teachers. Admins. Principal Heath. There's something weird about this whole setup."

Zay nodded. "And no one's talking about Devon."

"Who's Devon?" Nova asked.

The room went still for a second too long.

"Guy from Track. Was in the challenge. Stopped showing up yesterday. No explanation. No calls. No online posts. Just... gone."

"What do you mean, *gone*?" someone asked.

"No one's seen Devon since Tuesday. His locker hasn't been touched. He was doing the challenge."

I whispered to Amina, "Did you know Devon from Track?"

Amina whispered back with a frown, "Yeah. Tall. Quiet. Lived on my street before they moved. You think he broke and ran?"

I shook my head. "Something's off. Knox thinks the school's hiding something. That it's more than just a scholarship stunt."

"Like... what? Behavioral tracking?"

I didn't answer.

That made five people now. Five names. Five kids who had deleted their socials dropped their phones and vanished. No status updates. No story posts.

Not even a goodbye.

Back at home, I pushed open the front door and dropped my backpack harder than necessary.

Micah greeted me with his lazy tail wags from the couch.

In the kitchen, my dad stood with an iPad in one hand, a Bluetooth in his ear, and a half-burnt grilled cheese on the counter.

"Hey, kiddo," he said distractedly. "Can't talk, Q3 report's behind— you can eat, right? There's soup."

I stared. "You know I'm literally starving to death in there without a phone, right?"

He raised an eyebrow but didn't look up.

"Eliana said you volunteered."

"She also said you'd be around more."

That landed. Briefly. But the Bluetooth buzzed again, and he turned away, muttering into it.

Upstairs, Milo shouted through her door before she even opened it.

"Hey! Still no phone? That scholarship better come with therapy!"

I slammed the door.

Friday. Day 5.

The hallway air buzzed louder than usual. I kept my head down, but as I passed the lockers near the gym, a chorus of laughter followed me.

I turned. Ivy stood dead center, holding up a blown-up printout of my old social profile picture, taped to a stick like a protest sign.

"In loving memory of Nova Temples' social life," Ivy announced like a town crier.

The crowd howled.

I blinked — my mouth opened, but nothing came out.

"You miss the dopamine yet?" Ivy asked, stepping forward. "You know what they say — once you go offline, you become obsolete."

Zay appeared at her side. "Don't you have a mirror to talk to?"

Ivy didn't even blink. "Don't worry, Temples. I'll post enough for both of us."

I wanted to snap back. I wanted to win. But the words were caught in my throat.

I walked away, fists clenched.

That night, I lay awake, the red light of the pouch blinking softly on my desk.

A part of me burned to rip it open. Just to check. Just one post. Just one headline. Just proof that the world hadn't shifted without me knowing.

But then I remembered Ivy's voice. Devon's empty desk. The silence in my house. The eyes of the Blackout Group. And the small, stubborn voice inside her that said: *If something weird is happening... I want to be awake when it does.*

I grabbed her notebook and wrote:

Day 5 –

Ivy's louder. Milo's a brat. Dad's a ghost. Devon is missing. A network is forming. I could quit. But I won't. Not yet.

Day 8

It started with a sticky note. Bright yellow. Bent at the corner. Slapped crooked onto locker #618 — a locker that had been empty for a week.

I paused as I walked past it. Something about it buzzed in my chest.

At first, I thought it was a joke, but when I peeled it off and unfolded it, the air shifted.

☠ 01001100 01101111 01101111 01101011 ☠

Some eyes never close.

Binary. A skull symbol. No name. No context.

Knox appeared behind me so quietly that it made me jump.

"Binary's sloppy," he muttered, reading over my shoulder. "Anyone with a browser and five minutes can crack that. It says: *LOOK*."

I turned to him. "Is this from Devon?"

Knox frowned, his expression tightening. "Or someone who wants us to think it is."

Over the next two days, more cryptic messages showed up.

Etched lightly into bathroom stall doors. Scribbled on gum wrappers slipped into OFF THE GRID students' backpacks. Tucked under desks. Even written in condensation on the mirror in the second-floor girls' bathroom:

WE'RE NOT ALONE.
DO NOT TRUST THE MONITORS.
LOOK UP.

It was enough to unnerve even the calmest kids. A sophomore dropped out mid-day. A senior screamed during AP Lit when she found something scrawled on her textbook:
YOU'RE NEXT.

I started to notice strange near-encounters.

Once, I passed a janitor's cart and saw a cellphone beneath a towel — the screen blinking with a video paused on what looked like a classroom feed.

Another time, I swore someone followed me after school — footsteps behind me, stopping when I turned. But when I whipped around outside the gates, no one was there.

And worst: Amina was acting weird.

Distant. Short. Glancing over her shoulder in class, chewing her pencil raw. She hadn't spoken much in the last two Blackout meetings, and when I asked if she was okay, she brushed me off.

"Just tired. Tests. You know."

But I didn't know. Because my *best friend* was lying to me.

I cornered Knox in the library during a group project I had no intention of finishing.

I slid the latest note across the table — torn from a lined notepad and written in faint ink: The Grid isn't the only thing that can be locked.

Knox read it three times. Then pulled out a tiny flip notebook full of scribbles and hand-drawn diagrams.

"Okay," he said. "Time to break into Ravenlock's brain."

We waited until after school.

Room 107. Lights off. Chairs pushed aside. Knox came in with a thumb drive, a roll of red tape, and a screwdriver.

I kept watch while he popped open the back of a teacher's spare laptop, booted into something that looked like code but smelled like rebellion.

"They said no phones. Didn't say I couldn't use an old-school USB."

He smirked. "They locked our eyes. Not our brains."

After ten minutes, Knox blinked at the screen.

"Nova... look at this."

The screen lit up with a *list*. A master list.

Student names. Status indicators. GPS pings. But half the names weren't live — they were greyed out, labeled "disconnected."

Devon's name was there. Grey. Two others they hadn't heard about yet, also grey.

"Why would the school be tracking us like this?"

Knox's voice dropped.

"Because we're in the beta test. And something's already wrong."

Monday morning.

I walked into school and nearly dropped my bag.

Ivy — queen of constant commentary, flawless posts, and dagger smiles — was sitting alone in the courtyard. No phone in hand. No entourage.

Just... quiet.

I slowed.

Ivy glanced up. Her eyes were rimmed in red. Not from makeup.

"You win," Ivy muttered, barely audible. "You were right."

I blinked. "Are you okay?"

Ivy let out a small, humorless laugh.

"My cousin goes to East Creek. They ran the same challenge there last year. But their winner never showed up to graduation. Or college. Just vanished."

My stomach dropped.

"I thought you weren't a part of the challenge. You're telling me you joined the challenge... knowing that?"

Ivy looked up. "No. I joined because I thought I was untouchable. Beat you and rub it in your face, but what if something happens to me now? It won't matter how many followers I have."

That night, I found Amina on her porch swing, hood up, arms crossed, face hard.

"Hey," I said. "I've been texting you... except, you know. In analog."

Amina didn't smile.

"Stop pushing this, Nova."

I sat beside her, unsure. "Pushing what?"

"The Group. The codes. Devon. Everything. This was supposed to be a *challenge*, not a conspiracy."

My throat tightened. "Amina, someone's tracking us. People are disappearing. We need to stay ahead of this."

Amina turned to her, eyes sharp. "Or maybe we need to quit before we *can't*."

The air between them went cold.

My voice cracked. "You really think we can just leave and pretend it's all fine?"

Amina stood. "I think I want my life back. And if you cared about me, you'd stop trying to play detective and let us *be normal*."

She walked inside.

I stayed on the swing, alone in the dark.

In my room, I sat at her desk, heart pounding.

On her notebook page, I scrawled:

Day 8

Amina's out. Ivy's afraid. Devon's name is grey. They are watching. The messages aren't stopping. I won't either.

I flipped to a blank page.

Operation Look Up begins tomorrow.

Outside, somewhere across town, a red light blinked.

Day 12 — Journal Entry, Nova Temples

I don't know how to write this without sounding like I've lost it, but someone's gone. And this time... everyone knows it.

It was supposed to be a normal Tuesday.

Third period. Biology. I was half-asleep, still annoyed that Knox said the cafeteria chicken nuggets might be made from *"lab-grown disappointment."* And then I noticed it: Tariq's desk. Still empty. Fourth day in a row.

At first, no one said anything. I figured maybe he dropped the challenge. Maybe his parents pulled him. Maybe he got sick or just gave up. Lots of people have.

But then Mr. Ellison looked at his attendance sheet and... paused.

And stared. For a little too long.

"Tariq won't be returning this semester," he said. "Focus on your notes, please."

No explanation. No follow-up. Just... *won't be returning.*

And that was it.

Like, Tariq was a line of code someone deleted.

I cornered Knox after lunch. He didn't look surprised.

"There are rumors," he said. "Someone's watching the participants who start getting... too curious. Or close to breaking."

He showed me a grainy photo he'd printed in the library — old-school, like it came from a security feed. It showed someone in a black jacket crouched on the rooftop of the gym.

Holding binoculars. At night.

"Could be school security," he said.

"Or not."

He thinks there's a network behind this. Some surveillance system outside the school, maybe tied to the company that funded OFF THE GRID in the first place.

"You don't give teenagers a $100,000 prize and lock them away without eyes on the test."

I stared at the photo until my skin crawled.

Because here's the thing: *That rooftop?*

It looks directly into my third-period classroom.

Back home, I tried telling my mom.

I thought maybe if she knew someone was *actually* missing — that this wasn't just me being dramatic — she'd take it seriously.

But she barely looked up from her tablet.

"Nova, you're letting this game get in your head."

Game.

She said *game.*

Dad wasn't home (as usual), my grandparents were busy planning their anniversary, and Milo just threw popcorn at me and said, "If this is a horror movie, can I be the comic relief?"

I wanted to scream.

Instead, I locked myself in my room and stared at my phone pouch until I wanted to throw it across the room.

I feel like I'm the only one actually awake right now. Everyone else is asleep with their eyes open.

We met again last night. Blackout Group. Room 107. No lights. No phones. Just notebooks, old-school flashlights, and whispered theories.

Ivy was there this time. Which still messes with my head. I never thought I'd see Ivy sit in the back of Room 107. No smirk. No phone. Just her knees drawn up on a chair, her fingernails scratching at a chipped corner of the desk like she wanted to claw her way out of her own skin.

When I walked in, her eyes darted to mine, then down again. Not a word. It was like seeing a raven lose its feathers.

She looked rough. Her eyeliner smudged, her words softer. She didn't even throw a single jab at me.

"Tariq was my lab partner in Chem," she said. "He told me last week someone was watching him after school. Thought it was a prank. Now he's gone."

Zay's knee wouldn't stop bouncing.

Amina sat beside me — quiet again, but her fingers brushed mine under the desk. Just once.

Maybe she's still in this. Maybe she hasn't quit on me yet.

We started mapping everything we've seen — notes, sightings, hallway cameras that move, hall monitors who linger too long near challenge participants.

And there was this moment — not loud or dramatic — just a feeling in the room. Like we were all finally facing the truth.

This isn't just a challenge anymore. It's something bigger. And none of us feel safe.

I used to think the scariest thing would be losing my phone.

Now?

I think the scariest thing is knowing that someone out there is watching... and no one's stopping them.

Not the school. Not the parents. Not the world.

And if we don't figure it out soon... One of us might be next.

Zay shut the door. Knox taped a sheet of paper over the window — a habit now, automatic. The room smelled like chalk and dust and a little like panic.

"We're not safe here," Ivy said finally. Her voice cracked. "I don't mean the notes or the watchers. I mean this whole school. It's wired."

I froze. "What do you mean by 'wired'?"

Knox reached into his backpack and pulled out a crumpled Ziplock bag. Inside were two little silver discs, each no bigger than a shirt button.

"Found them under the desks in the west wing," he said. "Mic transmitters. Not school-issued."

Amina leaned forward. "Are you sure?"

"Positive." He dumped them on the desk; they landed with a soft metallic click. "And this one—" he held up a third, smaller piece of plastic with a blinking red dot "—I pulled out of one of our *lockers.*"

Ivy gave a hollow laugh. "So, yes. We're basically rats in a maze."

Her words landed like a slap. We all stared at the blinking dot. I swear I could feel it, like a heartbeat in the room.

Later, I sat on the bleachers outside the gym while rain misted over the field. The red brick of Ravenlock High loomed like a fortress. Kids streamed past, laughing, talking, posting on their phones — the ones who weren't in the challenge. They were living in the normal world. We were... somewhere else.

Ivy slid onto the bleacher beside me, not looking at me.

"You think I'm a monster," she said quietly.

"I think you're scared," I answered.

Her lip quivered. She rubbed her hands together. "I used to think this was just a game. Something to make me more famous. I figured I'd crush it, show everyone I can go without my phone and still be untouchable. But—" She stopped. "Tariq, Devon... what if we're next?"

I didn't know how to answer. The rain made tiny pinpricks on my jacket. For a second, we were just two kids sitting under a bruised sky, no enemies, no likes, no audience. Just fear.

Ivy whispered, "If we expose this, they'll come for us."

I turned to her. "If we don't, they'll keep taking people."

Her eyes flicked to mine, and for once I saw no fight there — just a mirror of my own exhaustion.

Back in Room 107, the group argued in low, fierce whispers. Knox had laid out diagrams of the school on the floor, little red x's marking every place he'd found a hidden sensor or transmitter.

"They're piggybacking on the blackout devices," he said. "The pouches. The ones we keep our phones in. They're not just locking them. They're pinging them. Tracking movement, heat signatures, maybe even heart rates."

Zay swore under his breath. "So, the challenge *is* a lab test."

"We could go public," Amina said, her voice sharp. "We could blow this up. Call a press conference. Leak it."

"And get shut down before we even start?" Knox shot back. "We have no proof they're behind the disappearances. We just look like paranoid kids who can't handle a month without Wi-Fi."

I sat on the edge of a desk, staring at the red blinking transmitter. The room tilted.

This was supposed to be about a scholarship. About discipline. About showing myself, I could survive. Instead, I felt like I was sinking into a swamp, everything I touched turning to mud. My parents were ghosts, Amina was slipping away, and even Ivy was breaking. And Knox—sometimes I didn't know if he was my lifeline or just another part of the puzzle I couldn't solve.

"Nova," Knox said softly. "You okay?"

I didn't even realize I'd been digging my nails into my palms until I saw the crescents they'd left. "No," I whispered. "But I'm not quitting."

He looked at me for a long time, then nodded. "Then we keep going. Quietly. Smarter."

That night, I sat at my desk, the house dark except for the glow from Milo's video games seeping under my door. My mom hadn't said goodnight. My dad was still at work. Grandparents were busy.

I opened my journal. My handwriting was jagged.

Day 15

Ivy's breaking. Amina's fading. Knox found bugs under the desks. In our lockers. In our pouches. We're tracked, measured, logged. Someone's pulling strings. I keep thinking about Tariq's empty desk. About Devon's greyed-out name. About how easy it would be to disappear me too.

I stopped. Closed my eyes. I remembered a flash of Devon's smile in the cafeteria, talking to Zay. The way he'd joked about "beating the system" with a week-old burner phone. It felt like a lifetime ago.

I flipped the page and wrote: We will find them. We will expose this. I don't care what it takes.

And then, under it, in smaller letters, a thought I didn't want to admit: Before they find us.

Somewhere across campus, a camera blinked to life — silent, hidden. Its lens adjusted, zoomed in, and locked onto a window on the second floor of a quiet house across the street.

My window.

Knox texted me. Knox sat cross-legged on his bedroom floor, blue light flickering over his face. The last lines of code scrolled past his screen. He'd cracked into a secondary server — something hidden behind the school's network like a second skin.

Names. Timelines. GPS pins. And at the bottom of the list, three words: PROJECT GRIDLOCK. ACTIVE.

He snapped a photo with an old disposable camera, hands trembling. No digital traces. No easy evidence. Just a single paper photo of something no one was supposed to see.

Knox sat back, heart hammering.

"Nova," he whispered to the empty room. "What the hell did we get ourselves into?"

Day 20

I used to think adults had everything under control. That someone — somewhere — had eyes on the things that mattered. That schools were safe. That teachers were just teachers. That if something went wrong, you could *tell someone,* and they'd fix it. Now I know better.

Now I know sometimes the adults are the ones watching. And the ones keeping secrets. And sometimes, they're the problem.

It started with a knock on the principal's office door. Not just me — all of us. Knox. Amina. Zay. Even Ivy.

Room 107 was no longer enough. So, we did what no one expected from us. We walked into the lion's mouth.

Principal Heath sat behind her wide oak desk, fingers tented. His office was spotless — diplomas framed neatly, not a single pen out of place. The walls smelled like wood polish and stale ambition.

"Miss Temples," she said as if we were here to apologize for a dress code violation. "To what do I owe this visit?"

I didn't blink. "We know about the surveillance. About the trackers. The pouches. The disappearances."

Her expression didn't change. Not a twitch. "That's a serious accusation."

Knox stepped forward and placed the disposable camera on the desk. He'd developed the photos last night, by hand, in his uncle's garage.

One shot showed the PROJECT GRIDLOCK login screen.

Another showed the hidden GPS map of all blackout participants.

The last one... was Tariq's name, greyed out, time-stamped.

"We're not making this up," I said.

Principal Heath's jaw ticked once. Just once.

Then the door behind us clicked open.

Two men in charcoal suits stepped in. They weren't teachers. They didn't wear IDs. And they didn't introduce themselves.

"Students," one said, voice smooth as glass. "That's classified material you've accessed."

Amina shifted behind me. Ivy muttered, "I knew it."

Zay stepped forward, arms crossed. "We have copies. You touch us, this goes public."

The room turned still.

The man in the suit gave a tight smile. "This program exists to prepare students for a digital detoxed future. What you're experiencing is part of the psychological pressure test. No one is in danger."

"Then where's Devon?" I snapped. "Where's Tariq?"

No answer.

Heath stood slowly. "You're skating on very thin ice. You may want to reconsider how far you want to push this, Nova."

And just like that, we were dismissed, but something had shifted.

They didn't deny it. They didn't explain it. They just warned us. That's how you know you're close to the truth.

When I got home that night, the house was quiet. Too quiet.

Milo's door was closed. Mom was working again, the blue glow of her laptop spilling into the hall. I stood there for a full minute before I walked in.

"Nova," she said, barely glancing up.

"We need to talk," I said.

She blinked. The glow lit up the tiredness under her eyes. "Honey, I'm in the middle of—"

"I'm in the middle of being tracked. Of being scared. Of people disappearing. You haven't even asked how the challenge is going."

Her face froze.

And for the first time in days, she closed the laptop.

"I didn't know how to talk to you about it," she admitted. "You always seem... in control. Smarter than me sometimes."

I shook my head. "I'm not. I'm just trying to stay sane. And I needed you."

She looked at me then — really looked.

And for once, I saw the mother I remembered from before work took over everything. Her hand reached for mine.

"I'm here now."

It wasn't a solution, but it was a beginning.

The next day, Adina opened the door with a wide grin, flour dusting her sweater. "My girl," she beamed. "I made banana bread. Not the fake healthy kind."

Dion waved from the den, holding up an old VHS tape. "Guess what I found! Your second-grade science fair presentation. You cried when the vinegar volcano erupted too early."

I laughed for the first time in days.

They made the house smell like cinnamon and warmth. It felt like there were no trackers here. No hidden cameras, even though this was a smart home. They showed me framed photos and a dog-eared calendar with *"46th ANNIVERSARY WEEKEND!"* circled in gold ink.

"You okay, sweetheart?" Adina asked.

I hesitated. Then told her everything. Not the codewords or secret meetings — but enough. The fear. The silence. The weight.

She listened without blinking. No interruptions. Just her hand on mine and the firm presence of someone who loved me without conditions.

"You don't have to carry this alone, Nova," she said. "You may not be able to trust the system. But you can trust your gut. And the people who stand by you."

Dion nodded, serious for once. "And if the system's broken, maybe it's kids like you who are meant to fix it."

That night, we gathered in the treehouse behind Zay's place. (Yes, a real treehouse. With power strips and a mini fridge.)

Knox laid out the plan.

"We're going to mirror their system."

He'd rigged an old laptop to act like a surveillance relay — pinging the same signals the GRIDLOCK system used. Once active, it would *trick* the watchers into thinking they were still in control — while we recorded everything from *our* end.

"We leak it to the right person," Knox said. "A journalist. A watchdog group. We burn it all down from the inside."

I nodded.

It was dangerous. Reckless. But it felt like the only way forward.

Before we left, I wrote another journal entry.

Day 20

The system's real. The watchers are real. But so are we.

I have friends who risk everything to protect the truth. A grandmother who makes banana bread when the world feels cold. A brother who jokes because he doesn't know how to show fear. And now... I have a plan.

We will look up. And this time, we don't blink.

Day 24

The morning of the pep rally felt like the inside of a drum.

Ravenlock High was buzzing — students spilling into the gym in blue and silver shirts, band warming up in the corner, the air sharp with popcorn and hairspray. Principal Heath stood at the microphone, her crisp blazer like a shield. She smiled, but her eyes were harder than the steel bleachers.

We'd chosen the pep rally for a reason. Everyone is in one place. Noise. Chaos. Perfect cover.

"Ready?" Knox whispered.

I nodded. My pulse was a hammer.

This was Operation Look Up. We weren't just surviving anymore. We were about to flip the watchers' system on its head.

Amina and Zay had the easiest job: slip our signal-mirroring laptop under the AV table where the pep rally's sound system lived. Knox would run the code from his phone — a hidden tether to the laptop, bouncing everything off an old server he'd hijacked at a closed-down public library.

My job was to cause a distraction.

Ivy's job was chaos.

Since Ravenlock felt like a campus filled with an entire school, the Ravenlock Middle School was a part of the campus. Which was an entire school, including middle, so we'd even recruited Milo, who thought this was "the sickest thing ever," to pull the fire alarm at the right moment. (Micah, our dog, was at home with Adina and Dion, probably eating the edge of their anniversary cake by now.)

The plan: mirror GRIDLOCK's surveillance feed, expose live tracking data on the big screen behind Principal Heath before anyone could stop it, and stream it out to a journalist Knox had been secretly emailing. It was insane. It was perfect.

Principal Heath tapped the microphone. "Welcome back, Ravens! Today is about unity, resilience, and—"

That's when Knox gave me a nod.

I stood, cupped my hands around my mouth, and shouted, "Let's see the real scoreboard!"

A ripple of laughter and confusion moved through the gym. Ivy followed, standing on the bleachers and shouting, "Show us who's really watching us!" Her voice cracked, but it didn't matter — she'd committed.

Amina slipped under the AV table. Zay blocked her with his body like he was just chatting with friends. Knox's fingers danced over his phone.

Behind Principal Heath, the giant LED screen flickered.

A map appeared.

Names. Dots. Red, green, grey.

The crowd went silent.

Then the screen blinked again, showing a line of text Knox had pulled from the hidden server:

PROJECT GRIDLOCK — ACTIVE. ALL PARTICIPANTS LOGGED.

Gasps. Phones raised. Shouts. Principal Heath spun around, her face draining of color.

"Cut the feed!" she barked.

Two men in suits (the same from her office) appeared at the edge of the stage. One reached for the AV controls. The other scanned the bleachers like a hawk.

Knox whispered, "Almost done—"

That's when the gym doors slammed shut.

Lockdown.

Red lights pulsed over the gym doors. An automated voice echoed: "Please remain calm. Technical issue. Remain seated."

The screen behind Heath went black.

"They blocked the stream," Knox hissed. "We're boxed in."

Ivy crouched low beside me. "Tell me you have a Plan B."

I scanned the crowd. Zay was still covering Amina, but the men in suits were moving toward the AV table now.

"Milo," I whispered into my sleeve mic.

"On it," Milo whispered back.

Seconds later, the fire alarm screamed to life. Water burst from the sprinklers overhead, drenching everyone. Kids screamed. Phones slipped. Chaos exploded.

That was our window.

Knox yanked the laptop from under the table just as one of the suits lunged for him. Amina kicked over the power strip, sparks flying. Zay grabbed my hand and pulled me through the panicked crowd.

We barreled toward the emergency exit. Locked. Of course.

Knox shoved his phone into a panel by the door. "Old security code override," he muttered. "Come on, come on—"

Ivy surprised us all by stepping forward. "Move!" She jammed a bobby pin into the panel like she'd done it before. Sparks, a beep, and the lock clicked open.

We burst out into the rain.

We sprinted across the back lot, water plastering our clothes to our skin. Alarms blared behind us. Someone shouted our names.

Knox clutched the laptop like it was a newborn. "Partial success!" he gasped. "We got twenty-eight seconds of live feed before the block!"

"That's it?" Ivy snapped. "We risked our lives for twenty-eight seconds?"

"Twenty-eight seconds streamed to a journalist," he shot back. "And mirrored to five dead-drop servers."

I slowed, panting. "So... the public saw it?"

He nodded once. "Enough to know something's real."

We collapsed under the bleachers of the football field, drenched and shaking. Zay laughed first, a wild, relieved sound. Amina joined in. Even Ivy let out a shaky chuckle.

Milo came jogging up with a soaked hoodie over his head. "Yo, that was insane. We're basically superheroes."

I sat back against the cold metal and tried to breathe. For the first time, it felt like we'd landed a punch.

By the time I got home, Adina and Dion were at the kitchen table, eating slices of their anniversary cake with Micah at their feet. They looked up at me — soaked, mud on my jeans, eyes wide.

Adina stood and wrapped me in a towel without a word.

"You're scaring us, Nova," Dion said softly.

I sank into a chair. "We're scaring *them* now, too."

Adina's eyes narrowed. "Good."

I laughed weakly. She squeezed my hand.

Journal Entry Day 24

We pulled it off. Not perfectly. But enough.

They tried to trap us. We ran. We streamed the proof. People saw.

The suits know who we are now. Heath knows. But I'm not scared the way I was before.

We're learning their game. We're learning to fight back. And I'm not alone. Even Ivy stood with us today.

Next time, we won't just survive the trap. We'll spring one of our own.

Day 26

I woke up to my name trending. Not just my name. *Our* names.

Nova Temples. Knox Flanker. Amina Dankworth. Zayden Roan. Ivy Afify.

We were hashtags, screenshots, reaction videos, think pieces. I lay in bed staring at my cracked ceiling, my heart thudding so loud I thought it might break through my ribs.

"#BlackoutScandal"

"#StudentSurveillance"

"#RavenlockTruthers"

It was real. The twenty-eight seconds Knox mirrored — the tracker feed, the blinking names, the Project Gridlock overlay — had hit the net like lightning. Even with attempts to suppress it, people had screen-recorded, reposted, translated, and analyzed.

They were calling us whistleblowers. Rebels. Criminals. Heroes. I didn't feel like any of those. I felt... tired. Scared. Kind of hollow. And somehow... proud.

Ravenlock High was closed the next day. No official announcement. Just... locked doors. Metal shutters over the windows. No buses. Principal Heath hadn't been seen since the rally. Rumors flew like flies: she'd been fired, arrested, relocated, promoted. No one knew.

Zay texted the group chat:

I'm gonna say it: WE DID THAT.

Ivy added:

Don't get cocky. We barely made it.

Amina replied with just a heart.

Knox dropped a new location pin.

"Treehouse. 4 pm. Debrief."

I stared at the screen a long time before replying. I'll be there.

Elianna was in the kitchen when I came downstairs. She had a mug in her hands and a look I couldn't read.

Dad was at the table with Dion and Adina, who were flipping through a newspaper with our names on the front page.

Milo looked up from his cereal. "So... does this mean you're famous now, or on the run?"

I rolled my eyes and dropped into the chair next to him.

Elianna sat across from me. "Nova," she said, voice soft but steady. "We need to talk."

For a second, I braced for anger. But what I saw in her eyes wasn't fury — it was fear. And something deeper.

"Why didn't you tell us?" she asked.

"Would you have listened?"

Eli opened his mouth, then closed it.

Adina jumped in gently. "She's been screaming without making a sound for weeks. You both missed it."

No one argued.

"I didn't want to drag you into it," I said finally. "You were both always... somewhere else."

"I thought keeping my head down at work was protecting the family," Dad said. "Turns out I was just absent."

Elianna reached across the table and took my hand. "I'm sorry, Nova. You deserved better from us. And you've done something extraordinary. You were right to question it."

Adina wiped at her eyes with a napkin and muttered, "Now if y'all are done emotionally exploding, I have anniversary banana cream pie to serve."

We all laughed. Even me.

By 4 PM, we were all packed into the treehouse again. It still smelled like pine and old electronics.

Knox had a new whiteboard up with scribbled names and symbols, but this time, no one wanted a strategy. We wanted space.

"I haven't slept," Amina admitted. "Not really. Every time I close my eyes, I see those red blinking names."

Zay leaned back. "I've had three colleges reach out for interviews. No one cared who I was a week ago."

Ivy looked at her nails. "My parents want to pull me out and send me to some international school. As if hiding will fix this."

Knox was quiet. That was new.

"What about you?" I asked.

He shrugged. "I've spent my life digging into systems, trying to find the cracks. I didn't think this one would break open like that."

I exhaled slowly. "Do you think it's over?"

Knox looked me dead in the eyes. "No. I think they're regrouping. But the world sees them now."

On the school's dormant site, a single update went live that night:

The Blackout Challenge has concluded, effective immediately. Due to unforeseen safety concerns and data integrity breaches, the program is suspended indefinitely.

No apology. No mention of surveillance. Just corporate-speak for "you won."

But it didn't feel like a win. Not fully. Some kids were still missing. No one knew what happened to Tariq or Devon. And none of us believed they just dropped out.

The school board had announced a public review, the media kept digging, and online sleuths were organizing. But the people behind Gridlock? They were still in the shadows.

Journal Entry Day 26

The challenge is over, but the challenge was never just about phones. It was about control. About silence. About making us depend on things that don't care if we disappear.

I'm not the same person who walked into Ravenlock on Day 1. I don't know who I am completely yet. But I know I can survive without the feed. I know how to build trust in the dark. I know how to run. How to fight. How to stay. And I know this: I won't stop until the watchers have names.

And when I find them, I'll look them dead in the eye and say: I saw you. And now? You'll be seen too.

Day 30

There was no big announcement. No closing ceremony. No final countdown. No fireworks. Just... silence.

After thirty days off the grid — thirty days of pushing through paranoia, secrets, fear, resistance — the challenge ended not with a bang, but a quiet ping.

My pouch beeped at 7:03 AM. A green light blinked. My phone unlocked. Like nothing ever happened.

I didn't rush to open it. Instead, I just stared at the screen — its glow no longer a leash, but a mirror.

The truth? I wasn't ready to be "back." And maybe that was the biggest win of all.

Walking through Ravenlock that morning, everything looked the same… but felt different.

People were hunched over, catching up on what they missed, refreshing apps like they were gasping for air. Old habits snapped back into place like elastic.

But not for me.

Not for Amina. Not for Zay. Not for Knox. Not even for Ivy, who nodded at me in the hall — not a smirk, not a sneer. Just… quiet recognition. A truce.

We'd crossed something together. We couldn't go back. And we wouldn't.

The cafeteria was loud again.

Phones were back out, screens glowing over trays of soggy fries and bottled smoothies. It was like the challenge never happened — for most of them, anyway.

But not for me.

Across the table, Zay showed Knox a meme. Amina leaned against my shoulder, scrolling through pics from freshman formal. I hadn't gone. I wasn't ready.

"Ivy posted that dress four times," Amina said. "Think she's okay?"

"She's probably trying to drown her feelings in filters," I muttered, sipping my tea.

Zay laughed, but there was something gentler in his eyes than before. "You okay though, Temples?"

I thought about it. The silence. The things we saw. The ones we lost.

"I'm… better. Not okay, just—better."

Knox slid a phone across the table.

"You're gonna want to see this."

It wasn't a text. It was a missed call. No number. No caller ID.

Caller: TARIQ
Time: 3:03 AM
Duration: 00:00

The call never connected.

A chill passed through me.

"Someone's messing with us," I whispered. "Or someone's still out there."

When I got home, Adina was icing another lemon cake while Micah licked frosting off the floor like he was on a mission.

"You've been quieter," she said, not looking up.

"I'm just tired," I said.

"You've seen too much for someone your age."

I pulled out a stool. "You think I was wrong to push it? To expose it?"

She turned, slow and steady, eyes sharp.

"No. I think you were *right* — and brave. But I also think you need to stop thinking it's your job to fix the whole system alone."

That shut me up.

"Rest," she said, reaching out to brush flour off my cheek. "You deserve to be a kid for at least five minutes."

I smiled. "Maybe."

"And when those five minutes are up?" she winked. "Burn it all down again."

Ravenlock High tried to act as normally as it could.

The gym was filled with folding chairs and scattered clapping. Principal Heath was gone. No explanation. Just a new interim head — Mr. Darrow — a man with a radio voice and dead eyes.

"We are so proud of our students," he said. "Your adaptability. Your innovation. Your... trust."

Amina leaned in. "Did he just call surveillance 'innovation'?"

Knox snorted beside her. "That's the spin."

Ivy sat three rows ahead of us, arms crossed, staring straight ahead. She looked like she hadn't blinked in a week.

As awards were handed out for "Digital Detox Leadership," I realized something: They didn't care what we uncovered. They only cared if we played nice about it. That day, I decided I wouldn't.

Ms. Rivas handed back our essays.

Mine had a note in red ink: "You wrote this like it hurt. That's how I know it mattered."

I blinked.

Across the aisle, Ivy caught my eye. She mouthed, *Thank you.*

I mouthed back, *For what?*

She didn't answer.

But in that silence, something between us cracked open. Not fixed. Not friends. But... unfinished.

It was raining sideways when Amina and I ducked into the café. She ordered something with lavender and oat milk. I got black tea and honey.

"You think we're okay now?" she asked, stirring slowly.

"I think we're not broken," I said. "But okay? I don't know if I even remember what that feels like."

Amina set her spoon down. "I used to think I had to be 'on' all the time. Posting. Joking. Smiling. But this... this permitted me to slow down."

We drank in silence after that, the window steaming up beside us.

For the first time in months, I didn't feel watched.

In the kitchen that night, I found Mom in the kitchen, barefoot, watching the rain.

"I missed so much, didn't I?" she whispered.

"You weren't the only one."

She turned, eyes tired but clear. "I was scared to know the truth. I thought if I didn't look, it wouldn't hurt you."

"You thought wrong."

"I know." She reached out. "But I'm looking now."

And I believed her.

For the first time in forever, we stood still in the same space — no alerts, no distractions. Just us.

The art class painted a mural on the side of the gym: bold lines, shattered screens, unblinking eyes, and in the center — outlines of missing students, left blank on purpose.

A plaque below read: *Not Forgotten. Not Forgiven.*

Zay took my hand. "They're still out there, right?"

"Some of them," I said. "I hope."

We stood in silence until the bell rang.

That night, I placed my phone face down on my desk and picked up my journal.

Then my phone buzzed. Once. Softly. No name. No app. Just a screen flash.

[STATIC—-]

>> SYSTEM EVENT: OBSERVER DETECTED

>> LOCATION: LOCAL NODE — USER TEMPLE/NOVA

The screen blinked off. No notification. No history. Just... gone.

I stared at it for a long time.

Then slowly, I flipped the phone face down again.

Outside my window, fireflies blinked across the lawn.

Inside, Micah curled up by my bed, snoring like a bear cub.

Whatever was coming next... I wouldn't face it alone. And this time, I'd be watching back.

Lunch the next day was warm and strange — like the school had already exhaled.

"Have you seen this?" Amina asked, sliding into the seat beside me, her braid neat and tight.

She passed me her phone.

Black-and-white screen. Clean lines. One word at the top:

CON•FESS

Underneath it: *anonymous, unfiltered, unforgettable.*

Confessions. Real ones, supposedly. Students were posting things they never dared say out loud — secrets, rumors, stories you couldn't unhear. Some of it was dumb. Some of it was dangerous. It was The Confessions App.

I scrolled. My chest tightened.

"Where did this come from?" I asked.

"People say it just... appeared," Amina said. "Auto-downloaded. No link. No dev. Just showed up."

Knox dropped into the seat across from us, phone already in hand. "This smells off. Data mining. Behavioral tracking. Or something deeper."

Before I could speak, Ivy walked past.

She didn't stop, didn't smirk. Just tossed one word over her shoulder: "Round two?"

We all stared at each other for a beat.

Then Amina leaned her shoulder into mine. "We'll be ready."

Everyone else had already cleared out.

The locker room echoed with end-of-year energy — doors slamming, sneakers squeaking, locker combinations being spun for the last time. I sat on the edge of the bench, holding the old Blackout Challenge pouch. I never returned it. I don't know why.

Maybe because it felt like proof that something real had happened. Something no screen could summarize.

Milo was probably waiting by the steps, earbuds in, ready to pretend he wasn't waiting for me.

Everything felt... normal. Almost. Until I saw it.

A sticker was slapped crookedly on the inside of my locker door.

CON•FESS

Anonymous. Unfiltered. Unforgettable.

My breath caught. I didn't touch it.

Then my phone buzzed. Not a message, but the same vibration pattern I recognized last night.

Something too familiar. My fingers went cold.

Whatever we'd uncovered? It wasn't done with us yet.

The final bell rang moments later. The halls pulsed with voices and slamming lockers. I ran my fingers over the scuffed metal of mine — over another message I hadn't noticed before:

WE SEE YOU.

Was it a warning? A thank-you? A threat? I didn't know.

Across the hall, Ivy gave me a two-finger salute and disappeared into the stairwell. Amina and Zay were already outside, arguing about summer playlists. Knox leaned against the wall, headphones in, watching the sky like it was trying to talk back.

I closed my locker for the last time.

Ravenlock was still standing, but we weren't the same. And that, somehow, felt like enough.

That weekend, I sat in the backyard swing while Micah chased butterflies like his life depended on it.

The spring air was golden and lazy — that warm, almost-summer quiet when the world felt paused, like anything could happen.

Inside, Mom and Dad grilled. Adina and Dion danced to something on the radio. Milo told the same joke twice, and no one stopped him. It was messy, loud, and real.

I didn't scroll once.

Later that night, Amina and I sat in lawn chairs under the stars, a blanket wrapped around both our legs.

"It's weird," I said. "I used to be terrified of being alone with my thoughts."

She smiled at me, quietly. "And now?"

I took a long breath.

"Now I know they're mine. That I don't need a million people liking my life to feel like I'm living one."

She looped her pinky around mine.

"Proud of you, Temples."

We didn't need to say anything else.

We'd been to war. We'd made it out. Mostly.

But deep in my bag, my phone buzzed again.

No screen notification. No app. No call.

Just a flicker. A static glitch. A signal I couldn't explain.

And I knew — this wasn't over.

TWO

Sophomore Year

The Confession App – The Version of Me I Couldn't Control

I reflect on returning to school and how everything looks the same... but feels rigged, fake-normal. I'm not the same girl who entered those doors a year ago.

The town of Wildermere had that early fall sharpness — leaves half-changed, air just crisp enough to pretend summer was a memory. But I could still feel it. That heat. That silence. That pulse of static underneath my skin from everything we *didn't* say last year.

Now we were back at Ravenlock. Back to hallways that remembered what they weren't supposed to. Back to people who wanted to pretend none of it happened. Back to the house I lived in, the friends I trusted, the face I wore... like armor.

I stood outside the school longer than I needed to, watching kids flood in — earbuds in, phone screens out, laughter high and hollow.

I hadn't opened my phone since the glitch. Since the words. Since *Tariq's* name popped up.

Amina stepped beside me, her lipstick sharp and perfect. She linked her arm through mine like we were walking into a fashion show, not a battlefield.

"You good?" she asked.

I didn't answer. But I walked. And that was enough.

By the third period, the app had gone from rumor to wildfire.

At first, it was a joke.

"Did you see #91?"

"Whoever posted about Coach V's toe fungus is a national hero."

By lunch, the vibe changed.

Phones buzzed with identical alerts — whether you opened the app or not. That same interface: matte black background, blinking cursor, white minimalist font. No back button. No settings. No developer. No trace. And yet — it knew things.

Confession #123 accused a senior of shoplifting from her aunt's pharmacy. #130 called out a couple cheating on each other, *with each other's siblings.* By #145, no one was laughing.

Zay dropped into his seat at lunch like someone had sucker punched him.

"They posted about Cassie."

Knox looked up from his phone. "Who?"

"My cousin. She—she's pregnant. Like, barely told *me.* Now it's on the app."

"Details?" I asked.

Zay shook his head. "All of it. Who the dad is. How she was scared. Stuff she *texted me.* Private. In code."

Knox exhaled through his nose. "It's scraping something deeper than just phones."

Amina frowned. "Like what?"

"Conversations. Hidden files. Drafted messages. Deleted texts."

My skin prickled.

"So, it's not just tracking us," I said quietly. "It's *watching.*"

I had a brief, jarring flashback during class. The gym closet. The moment I broke. I try to push it away, but it's coming back — and so is the app.

It hit during Bio when Mr. Ellison asked us to journal how stress affects the body.

I stared at the page. Sweaty palms. Racing pulse. Clenched jaw. I could write that easily. But what about what stress did to your soul?

The room tilted. The overhead lights blurred.

Suddenly, I wasn't at my desk — I was back in the gym closet.

The air is stale.

The hoodie sleeve shoved against my mouth.

Micah's leash was still wrapped around my wrist, even though he wasn't there.

My breathing had gone shallow, like it couldn't find a way out.

I remembered the shoes — someone's sneakers — just outside the door.

They never said a word. They didn't tell anyone. Or so I thought.

English class. 1:32 PM.

I was halfway through a line about mirrors and lies when my phone vibrated three short bursts. I shouldn't have looked, but of course I did.

CONFESSION #419

"She cried for three hours in the gym closet last year. Didn't tell anyone. Just clutched her hoodie like it could hold her together. Said if she fell apart, no one would even notice."

Tag: NOVA T.

My throat closed.

My chest folded in on itself.

My pen dropped.

The air around me felt like static.

That wasn't a rumor.

That wasn't an exaggeration.

That was the truth.

But no one else knew that.

Not even Amina.

Not even my mom.

Not even me, really — not out loud.

That's why I never wrote in my journal or even here.

So how did the app know?

I fled to the bathroom.

The bathroom stall felt colder than usual.

I slid down the wall, clutching my phone, fingers numb.

What kind of system does this?

What kind of monster digs into the softest part of you and puts it on display?

My fingers hovered over the app icon.

I tapped it open.

It loaded slowly this time.

Then: the blinking cursor.

Then...

Hello again, Nova.

That wasn't so hard, was it?

Truth is oxygen.

Hiding is drowning.

We're just helping people breathe.

I wanted to throw the phone.

Instead, I stared.

Then more words appeared — like it *knew* I was still watching.

YOUR TURN.

Tap to Confess.

The screen pulsed. Waiting.

I didn't tap, but something told me — it didn't matter.

The cafeteria was louder than usual — but not in a normal way. It wasn't laughter or arguments or the clatter of lunch trays. It was buzzing. Not like electricity — more like tension, tight in people's throats, itching behind their eyes.

The Confession App had become a routine — and a threat.

Scroll. Read. Panic. Pretend you're fine. Repeat.

There was one rule no one said out loud: If you saw your name, you were already too late.

"I deleted it again last night," Amina muttered, her fingers tight around her smoothie cup. "Blocked it. Factory reset. Everything."

"It still showed back up this morning," Zay added, sliding into the seat across from us. "With two new confessions. One of them had a voice clip."

That stopped me.

"What kind of clip?" I asked.

"Sounded like a voicemail," he said, then leaned forward. "It was mine. From last summer. I left it for someone I thought I was in love with. It was...embarrassing."

"Cringey?" Knox asked, joining us late.

"No. *Begging.*"

We all went quiet.

"I don't even have that file on my phone anymore," Zay added. "So how did the app get it?"

Two days later, the halls felt different — like the oxygen had changed. Heavier. Harder to breathe.

By lunch, everyone knew.

Mr. Ellison was gone.

The app had posted something brutal at 6:13 AM — with time-stamped screenshots, voice memos, and a file attachment.

CONFESSION #578

"He changed grades for 'favorites.' Told girls he could 'help their GPA' if they helped his ego. This one's real. Ask his TA."

Tag: MR. ELLISON / BIOLOGY / RAVENLOCK

[See File] [Play Audio]

I didn't play the audio. I couldn't.

By the second period, his classroom door was locked.

By the third, Principal Darrow made an announcement: "Mr. Ellison will not be returning this semester."

Zay whispered under his breath: "No mention of the app."

No apology. No denial. Just...gone.

That Friday, something worse happened.

They posted about Neveah Chen.

She was soft-spoken. Ran the AV booth. Always had a stain on her sleeve from paint or ramen or both. The kind of person people didn't notice — until they did.

CONFESSION #610

"She stole money from the Booster account. Changed the spreadsheet logs. Spent it on skin care and BTS merch. Check her Venmo."

Tag: NEVEAH C.

By the 3rd period, Neveah was crying in the stairwell.

By the 5th, she wasn't at school.

"I looked at the logs," Knox said that night. "There's no money missing."

"But no one's posting *that*," Amina snapped. "No one cares what's true anymore."

The app had become a weapon — a scalpel for slicing reputations, reputations no one could repair fast enough. Even when lies unraveled, they left scars.

"She's not coming back," I whispered.

None of us disagreed.

I stopped sleeping. Stopped journaling.

Even Micah stopped sleeping by my bed. He curled up in the hallway now, like he sensed something coming and didn't want to get caught in the middle of it.

Every vibration made my pulse spike. Every notification felt like a dare.

I'd started noticing it:

- My screen turned on when I didn't touch it.
- The front camera is blinking.
- My flashlight pulsing faintly in the middle of the night, like Morse code.

Knox told me it could be remote access, but I knew better.

This wasn't code. This was *presence.*

The app wasn't just watching. It was...deciding.

I used to write everything down.

That was the one thing no one could take — my handwriting. My ink. My pages.

Until last night, when I opened my journal and found a line I didn't write.

It was in my handwriting. On a blank page. *"You're afraid of the truth because it feels too close to your bones."*

I tore out the page.

Burned it in the sink.

Micah barked once. Then stopped.

I think I'm being haunted, but by something with Wi-Fi.

A new student showed up on Monday.

She didn't speak. Didn't ask for directions.

Just moved through the hallways like she'd been here before.

Sora Featheringham.

Dark braids to her shoulders.

All-black outfit, minimal jewelry, heavy combat boots that somehow made no sound.

"She's from Norvale," someone whispered behind me.

"I heard her old school got hit by the app *first.*"

Sora kept to herself. Didn't sit with anyone. Didn't speak in class.

Except once in AP English.

Mr. Vega asked what she thought the Confession App represented in terms of modern digital ethics.

She blinked once. Then said: "A virus with purpose is more dangerous than one without."

That was all.

She looked at me once, too. Brief. Intense. Like she already knew what had been written about me.

Or worse — like she'd written it.

Ivy found me by the vending machines.

"Don't trust her," she said.

"Who?"

"The new girl. Sora. She knows too much."

"You barely know her."

Ivy's eyes were sharper than usual.

"She asked me about *you.*"

My stomach dropped.

"What'd she say?"

"She said: 'Nova Temples survived the last wave. Let's see if she survives this one."

Then she walked away like nothing had happened.

That night, I got a text.
Just a number: .0049

When I opened the app, nothing was there.
Just a glitch in the screen. A white box flickering in and out.

Then, for half a second, the screen turned mirror-black.
And I saw my face — blurred. Distorted. It was being studied from behind the glass.

One more message blinked before disappearing:
TEST COMPLETE
NEXT SUBJECT SELECTED
CONFIRM: NOVA TEMPLES

And then...
Blackout.

The posts were getting darker.
Gone were the petty callouts and flirty jokes. Now it was:

- *"I almost OD'd last year and no one noticed."*
- *"I slept with my best friend's boyfriend. She still doesn't know."*
- *"I cheat on every math test. I have to. My mom hits me if I don't get A's."*
- *"I tried to disappear once. No one looked."*

The app didn't filter. Didn't flag. Didn't ask if you were okay. It just posted.
Sometimes with a whisper of a tag. Sometimes without. But always with a pulsing black cursor at the top of the screen like it was...waiting.

"Why's it getting so personal?" Zay asked over lunch, his voice low.

"It was always personal," Knox muttered. "We just thought it was a game."

It was 2:17 AM when I cracked.

I'd scrolled past so many confessions, my eyes felt burned.

Some of them felt staged. Others felt like cries for help. A few felt like *mine* — the kind I'd never dare say out loud.

So, I did the unthinkable.

I tapped the blinking cursor.

And typed:

"I pretended I was okay so people wouldn't worry. But I wasn't. Not even close. I thought about disappearing during the Blackout Challenge. More than once." — Anonymous

I didn't tag it. I didn't sign it.

I watched it go live in the stream — black screen, blinking cursor, then the words. My words.

And I felt... nothing.

Then my phone buzzed.

CONFESSION #812 – GOING VIRAL
Trending: #DisappearGirl

I froze.

No one knew it was me, but everyone *guessed.*

I was in the third stall during 3rd period when I heard it.

Two girls at the sink. One was whispering. The other was laughing.

"...You really think it was Nova Temples?"

"Has to be. She's always got that 'I'm fine but secretly dead inside' look."

"You think she'd admit that stuff though?"

"She's been weird since the Blackout thing. They all have."

Silence. A pause. Then:

"I kind of hope it was her. Makes her seem real."

Something inside me cracked — not from shame, but from how accurate that last part felt. Real.

I posted because I wanted to be real. And now it was eating me alive.

Sora found me outside the tech lab. Leaning against the wall like she belonged there.

"You wrote that," Sora said. No hello. No question mark.

I stiffened. "What are you talking about?"

"The one that went viral. #DisappearGirl." She tilted her head. "I recognize your syntax."

I blinked. "My what?"

"Sentence rhythm. Word pattern. You use ellipses like armor. You type like someone afraid to be heard — but more afraid to be misunderstood."

I didn't answer.

"You can deny it," she said. "I'll still know."

Then she sat down beside me like we were old friends, not strangers on opposite ends of a riddle.

"Why are you here?" I finally asked.

Sora looked up at the sky.

"To see what happens when people burn their masks — or get burned for wearing them."

The confession dropped that Friday night.

I was watching Milo try to recreate a VR mod when my phone buzzed — then buzzed again. Then didn't stop.

It was trending before I even opened the app.

CONFESSION #827

"She says she saved people during the Challenge. But what she won't tell you is that her dad disappeared during that time, too. He didn't go off the grid — he just... left. He wasn't there. Guess where he went?"

Tag: NOVA T.

[Attached: Blurred Photo Timestamped During Blackout]

[File: Message Draft from "E. Temples" Never Sent]

The photo was real, so was the message.

My lungs locked. I couldn't breathe.

That was my father's draft. One I read alone, months ago. Hidden deep in his recovery folder. A confession *he* never sent.

How did they get it?

And worse — who would post it?

The house was asleep. Except me.

I stood barefoot in the kitchen, fingers shaking over the kettle. I didn't want tea. I wanted silence.

Adina walked in slowly, her robe wrapped tight around her.

"You saw it," she said.

I nodded.

She said nothing. Just stood next to me while the water boiled.

"I didn't even know that message existed," I whispered.

She exhaled. "He wrote it for himself. Not for you. Some truths are never meant to be shared."

"But someone shared it anyway."

I finally looked at her.

"Who do you think did it?"

Her eyes narrowed — not at me. At the *idea* of betrayal.

"I don't know," she said. "But I know this. When people are afraid of your strength, they'll attack your grief."

The next Monday, Sora met me on the steps before first period.

"I can trace it," she said.

"Trace what?"

"The IP of the confession. Not officially, but enough to get a radius. A profile. A pattern."

"Why would you help me?" I asked.

She didn't answer at first. Then she smiled, but it didn't touch her eyes.

"Because I want to know who's playing this game too — and whether I'm a piece or the next move."

She reached into her bag and handed me something.

It was an old-fashioned USB.

Etched with one word: "Ashes."

"Burn after reading," she said, walking away.

I watched the files alone.

Encrypted folders. Scrambled video clips. Half-finished app code with metadata pointing back to Ravenlock's own firewall.

Someone here built this.

Or helped it spread.

As the last clip played — a recording of someone logging into an admin version of the Confession App — the screen glitched and cut to static.

Then came one final line:

"You want to know the truth? Confess something bigger."

Ivy's name hit the app like a dropped match.

CONFESSION #913

"She made her freshman lab partner cry for asking a question. She blackmailed someone over grades. If anyone deserves to be humiliated, it's her."

Underneath was a photo. Blurred. But real.

I recognized the background. The cracked wall by the chemistry lab.

And the comments?

They weren't jokes this time. They were knives.

"Finally."

"She had it coming."

"What goes around."

"Hope she's crying."

Ivy didn't cry, but she didn't smirk either.

She just sat in the back row of history class, staring ahead like her whole body was a locked phone.

When she passed me in the hall, she didn't toss a comment.

Just said quietly, "It wasn't all wrong. But it wasn't all true either."

And for once, I didn't know how to respond.

"Alright," Amina said, hands on her hips. "If no one else is going to figure this app out, we are."

We were in the robotics lab after school — Zay had stolen the keycode from Knox's hoodie pocket.

Sora leaned over the whiteboard, drawing arrows and usernames and possible app triggers.

Ivy sat near the door like she wasn't really part of this, but she didn't leave either.

I tapped my pen. "Why now?"

Sora looked up. "Because it's not random anymore."

She pointed to the pattern she'd mapped.

"The timing. The wording. The way posts show up. Someone is curating this. It's not just AI-run anymore."

Zay tilted his head. "So, someone's playing God with people's lives?"

Amina nodded. "Or watching them burn for entertainment."

Right after the group started unofficially investigating, I found her in the library.

Ivy. Alone. At the back. No phone in sight. Just a legal pad and a pencil with a bitten eraser.

She looked up like she'd been caught shoplifting.

"What?" she snapped.

I shrugged. "Didn't peg you for analog."

She stared down at her page. "Some things shouldn't live on screens."

I sat across from her. Quiet for a moment. Then:

"Was it true? The confession?"

She didn't flinch. "Parts. I was cruel. On purpose. I wanted people to fear me before they ignored me."

A long beat.

"I don't want to be like that anymore."

She didn't wait for a response. She didn't ask for one. But she looked at me when I stood. And for the first time, I saw her eyes — not sharp, but *tired.* Like mine.

That week, the posts shifted again.

They weren't taunts. They weren't self-destruction.

They were riddles. Phrases buried inside:

"Her locker doesn't open anymore."

"If I stop showing up, it's not by choice."

"The roof isn't safe."

"Look at the vending machine reflection at 3:00."

"Help. Please."

Sora circled them in her notebook, muttering like a codebreaker. "This is someone trying to tell us something."

"They could be pranks," Zay said.

"They could be lives," I snapped.

No one argued after that.

We checked the vending machine at 3:00.

At first, nothing.

Then Sora adjusted her phone screen against the glass. A reflection.

A QR code. Tiny. Barely visible.

Knox scanned it later — got a sound file.

A voice. Distorted. Glitched.

"They know. Stop watching. Start acting."

"WE WERE NEVER ANONYMOUS."

Then static.

Then a laugh.

Amina turned pale. "We're not investigators. We're targets."

I burst into the kitchen after dinner, trembling.

"I want to know who leaked that file about Dad."

Eliana blinked from across the sink. "Nova..."

"I know it wasn't either of you. But *someone* close to me had access. And now the app is—there are warnings. Cries. Something worse."

Eli leaned forward. "You're not responsible for saving everyone."

"That's not the point!" My voice cracked. "They're scared. I'm scared. But everyone acts like this is still just...a phase!"

Adina stepped into the doorway, quiet.

Eliana touched my shoulder. "We're trying. But this isn't something we understand. This world—these apps—they're built to know more about you than we ever could."

"I don't need comfort," I whispered. "I need *backup.*"

They didn't answer because they couldn't.

Micah followed me into my room later.

He dropped something at my feet. His smart collar. The one with the camera.

"I don't like it," he barked.

I laughed, watery. "Same, buddy."

He curled up near my bed. I took the collar in my hand, flipped the tiny switch off, and tucked it in a drawer.

Even the dog was done being watched.

The message in the code. We cracked part of it.

Sora filtered the posts for syntax, timing, and keywords. Ivy pulled old school logs and phone timestamps. Zay found a glitch in the confession feed's animation that Knox traced back to an internal subnet.

One folder. Hidden. Inside? Text. One sentence.

"The next confession will be the last."

No author. No metadata. No mercy.

The robotics lab at night was colder than the hallways — like the servers breathed ice.

Knox cracked his knuckles over the keyboard, three monitors glowing in front of him. "This isn't just a school app," he muttered. "This is a hydra."

"I thought you said you were good at this," I whispered, leaning over his shoulder.

"I am. That's the problem. This thing's built like nothing I've seen —
and it's using our own network as a skeleton."

He slid a window across the screen. Strings of code scrolled faster than
I could read. "You see that pattern?"

"No," I admitted.

"That's because it's not code. It's handwriting. Someone's been editing
this by hand. Live."

My skin prickled. "So, it's not AI?"

Knox shook his head. "AI doesn't do this. People do."

Sora showed up without being asked. She slipped through the door
like smoke, carrying a battered laptop that looked decades old.

"I've been in this before," she said calmly.

Knox's fingers stilled on the keys. "Excuse me?"

Sora set the laptop down. "Last year. My old school. We had an 'off
the grid challenge,' too. Same sponsor. The DoubleB Foundation. But no
one talks about it."

I stared at her. "Why didn't you say anything?"

"Because I didn't know it was the same until the confessions started
using code words. Now I do."

Knox narrowed his eyes. "What are you, exactly?"

She looked at him without blinking. "I'm someone who survived it
once. And I don't plan on losing twice."

Knox left to get more energy drinks. It was just me and Sora in the dim
light of the lab.

"You're hiding something," I said.

She didn't deny it. She just smiled, thin and quiet. "You think I'm a
double agent."

"Are you?"

"I think..." She folded her arms. "We're all agents of something. Our
fear. Our secrets. Our guilt. The question is which one controls us."

She turned back to the screen, fingers moving like she was playing piano. "Don't trust anyone who says they can fix this. Especially me."

For some reason, that didn't scare me. It grounded me. Because at least she was honest about lying.

Knox's codebreaker finally found a thread. A hidden port buried under layers of fake IPs and proxies.

"This," he said, "is the admin panel."

We stared at the login screen. Black. Empty. Blinking cursor.

"It wants a confession," Knox muttered. "Not a password. A confession."

He typed nonsense. The screen glitched and spat him out.

"It's a behavioral gate," Sora said. "It's mapping who you are, not what you type."

Knox cursed under his breath.

I swallowed. "Let me try."

I placed my hands on the keys and typed, slowly:

"I think I'm only brave because I'm scared of what happens if I'm not."

The cursor blinked. The screen opened.

Inside the admin panel were fragments. Not full posts. Drafts. Ghosts.

One was mine. Deleted, but not gone.

Another was Ivy's — something she'd typed and never posted.

Another was a string of numbers that looked like a date: 4/17/22.

I clicked it.

The screen filled with still images from last year's Blackout Challenge. Not just ours — others. Another school. Another gym. Another mural. Same missing outlines.

And one picture that stopped my breath:

My father. On his laptop. The same background as the leaked file.

We printed out the metadata; paper scattered across the robotics table like fallen leaves.

"It's all here," Knox said. "Server logs. Routing trails. Ghost accounts."

"Where does it lead?" Amina whispered, standing in the doorway with Zay. They'd come after my frantic text.

Knox jabbed a finger at the map. "Back to DoubleB. And something called 'Observer Node.'"

My hands trembled. "That's what flashed on my phone the night after the challenge. System Event: Observer Detected."

Sora looked pale. "It's not just an app. It's a network. And it's been alive since last year."

We snuck into the school basement after hours. Old routers, boxes of confiscated tech, dusty laptops.

Knox found a crate marked Ravenlock – Blackout Materials.

Inside:

- Old pouches like the one from the challenge.
- Surveillance cameras, unused but logged.
- USBs with the DoubleB logo.

Sora picked one up, turning it over in her palm. "They didn't stop. They just got smarter."

I sat on the lab floor; files spread around me.

Everything pointed to one thing:

The Confession App was a mutation of last year's surveillance project — the one DoubleB quietly piloted to "study student behavior off-grid."

Except it didn't end. It went deeper. And now it was feeding on secrets instead of silence.

Knox muttered, "There's more than one operator."

Sora whispered, "Or no operators at all."

I looked at her. "What do you mean?"

She met my eyes. "What if the people who built it don't control it anymore?"

My phone buzzed. Not a notification. A new screen.

"STOP DIGGING."

"CONFESSIONS ARE CURRENCY."

"PAY UP OR BURN."

A second later, the admin panel locked itself.

All the files were wiped. Every trace gone.

Knox slammed the desk. "We had it. We had it—"

Sora was staring at the door.

Not like she'd heard something. Like she'd seen a ghost.

"What?" I asked.

Her voice was a whisper.

"Someone else was in here with us."

After the lab lockout, things didn't just go quiet — they went *silent*.

Not the kind that brings peace. The kind that hums in your bones. The kind that waits.

Sora hadn't said a word since she saw… whatever she saw.

Knox refused to make eye contact.

And me? I couldn't stop hearing the last words on my screen: CONFESSIONS ARE CURRENCY. PAY UP OR BURN.

It dropped during the second period, while I was pretending to take notes in World Lit.

I didn't even see it at first — Amina did.

She gasped so loud the teacher paused. I glanced at her screen.

A new confession has been posted. No name, no context. Just cold, brutal facts:

"I know what I did.

I let it happen.
He was in pain, and I didn't stop it.
I laughed.
Now he can't even walk past the gym without shaking."

The comments were already a wildfire.

"Zay?"

"This about Freshman Year?"

"Yo, this is foul if it's true."

"He was there, wasn't he?"

"Zayden Roan. Say something."

I felt my stomach drop straight through the desk.

Zay wasn't even in class. He'd left early for student council. But by the third period, everyone knew.

I found Zay in the back stairwell, hoodie pulled low, fists clenched like he was holding himself together with tension alone.

He didn't look at me. Just said, "I didn't do what they said. I didn't hurt him."

"I know," I said quietly.

"But I *was* there," he added. "I laughed when the older guys messed with Devon. I thought if I laughed too, I'd stay invisible. I was thirteen. I was scared."

His voice cracked.

"I *was scared*, Nova. And now it's out there, like I did it all. And Devon's *gone*, and I can't take it back."

I sat beside him on the cold steps.

"You grew," I whispered. "You care. That matters."

"I don't know if it does," he said. "Not when the internet wants blood."

And then, for the first time in all the chaos, Zay — funny, wild, unbothered Zay — started crying.

Not a tear. Not a sniffle. Full-body, can't-breathe sobs.

I held his hand. We stayed there until the period bell rang, and no one came looking.

Freshman year. A bonfire at Ivy's house. Zay had roasted everyone, loud and sharp — but never mean.

Later, we sat under the porch light.

"Why do you always deflect with jokes?" I'd asked.

"Because if I don't," he said, "I might say something real. And that's scarier than being hated."

I laughed, thinking he was being dramatic.

Now I knew better.

Amina was spiraling, too, but hiding it in plain sight.

She started triple-posting on every platform. Pretty filters. Perfect poses. "Feeling blessed <3."

But when I caught her in the bathroom between classes, her hands were shaking.

"They're going through my old messages," she said. "I saw my name in the comments. Someone said I ghosted my friend when her mom died."

"You didn't," I said.

"I didn't mean to. I just... didn't know what to say. And then it got weird. And then I didn't say anything at all."

Her voice dropped.

"What if I really am a bad person?"

"You're not," I said. "You're someone who made a mistake. That doesn't make you bad."

She hugged me so fast I almost dropped my bag.

But even as I held her, something inside me cracked. Because I knew what came next. I always did.

By the weekend, I'd stopped replying to messages. Amina noticed first. Then Sora. Then Zay, who texted me a meme with a crying emoji and the words:

"You ghosting us or just dying inside with style?"

I didn't answer.

I just stared at my phone and whispered: "I don't want to be currency."

Because that's what we were now — emotional currency for entertainment.

Our secrets, our slips, our guilt... it was all up for bid.

And somehow, people still treated this like gossip, not war.

Milo knocked on my door and didn't wait for an answer.

"You're doing that thing again," he said, walking in like a twelve-year-old FBI agent. "The silent spiral."

"I'm fine."

"Liar."

He sat on my bed and looked at me — really looked.

"You were different after the challenge," he said. "Like your brain saw something and couldn't unsee it. And now... now it's like you're waiting to get hurt again, so you pull away first."

I didn't answer.

He added, "You're not the only one who noticed."

I looked up. "Who else?"

"Mom."

That night, Mom didn't knock. She just left a tray outside my room. Not just food — tea, my favorite lemon biscotti, and a note:

"When you're ready, I'm here. No phones. No lectures. Just me."

I found her in the kitchen, staring out at the backyard like she used to during the worst parts of last year.

"I don't know how to help," she said. "But I know silence doesn't make it stop."

I sat down.

"You didn't listen last year," I said quietly.

"I was scared," she replied. "And being scared made me selfish."

We didn't hug. We didn't cry. But we sat there for a long time, breathing in the same quiet.

And for once, it felt like she was really in the room with me — not just standing nearby.

Dad called later that night. I almost didn't pick up.

When I did, he sounded tired.

"I saw the news about that app," he said. "It's in the feeds now. People are noticing."

"Noticed too late," I said.

He hesitated. "I want to help. If you can send me anything you've found, I'll look into it from my side."

"You're in IT. Not espionage."

"I'm also your dad," he said. "And I wasn't before. Let me try now."

I didn't say yes, but I didn't say no.

That night, I opened the old pouch again.

The one from the Blackout Challenge. I hadn't touched it in months. It still smelled like tech and regret.

Inside, tucked in the mesh lining, I found something I didn't remember putting there:

A folded scrap of printer paper.

Typed on it, one line:

"The app doesn't just watch. It remembers."

There was no signature. No name. No date. But I knew, somehow, it was left for me.

After the last confession — the one that nearly broke Zay — something in our group quietly, collectively snapped.

We stopped waiting. Stopped hoping the app would go away. Stopped believing this was just about "drama."

We knew now: someone was *orchestrating* this.

And we were done being players in their game.

That's when the plan began.

It started in Knox's garage — a warm Friday night that smelled like soldering tools, metal, and his mom's homemade curry.

The team:

Me.

Amina.

Zay.

Ivy (yes, Ivy).

Sora.

Knox.

Micah the dog, sleeping under the workbench like he wasn't part of something revolutionary.

Knox rolled his chair to the whiteboard. "Alright, conspiracy theorists. Let's make a map."

He started drawing:

- The app: *CON•FESS*
- The servers: offshore, encrypted, maybe even masked via an academic IP
- Past threads: *Blackout Challenge, DoubleB Foundation,* last year's missing students
- Current posts: *coded messages, false accusations, real secrets*

Amina chewed the cap off her marker. "So, we're leaking the code?"

"If we can get it," Knox said. "And if it's not booby-trapped with countermeasures."

Zay grinned. "What, like it explodes our phones?"

Knox deadpanned: "You joke. I don't."

Sora cleared her throat. "What if we don't leak it? What if we... redirect it?"

Everyone paused.

"Make the app implode," Sora added. "Feed it corrupted input. Kill it from inside."

The way they said it — clean, clinical — sent a chill down my spine.

Ivy tilted her head. "You sound like you've done this before."

Sora smiled. "I read a lot."

A few days earlier. I found Ivy alone behind the gym, reading an old paperback.

Not her vibe. Not at all.

"What are you doing?" I asked.

She looked up, not smirking for once. "Reading. It's a dystopia. Thought it might feel like home."

I raised an eyebrow.

She shrugged. "I thought if I played the game right last year, I'd win. But all it did was make me the kind of person I used to hate."

I said nothing. She didn't need a response.

But she added, quietly: "So now I'm choosing differently. Doesn't mean I trust anyone. But maybe I can start with you."

The plan wasn't foolproof. But it didn't need to be.

We just needed one shot. One file. One breach in the digital fortress.

So, we waited until after school on Monday. I told Mom I was staying for the mock trial. Zay distracted the janitor with a fake cafeteria complaint. Amina forged a hall pass so real it could've fooled the DMV. Ivy jammed the cameras. Knox rewired the lock.

And Sora?

Sora stood guard. Or watched us. Or both.

Inside the tech lab, it was like stepping into a vault.

Knox whispered, "We have 12 minutes before the system logs external access."

I took a breath and slid into the chair.

Lines of code stared back like they were daring me to blink.

While Knox downloaded the source directory, the others whispered behind me. About everything.

Zay apologized to Amina for deflecting, for freezing her out when the confession about Devon dropped.

Amina apologized for disappearing during her own spiral.

Ivy said nothing for a long time.

Then she said, "I know I've been the villain in half your stories. I deserved it. But I'm not here to be liked. I'm here because I hate what they're doing to us."

I turned in my chair. Looked at all of them. Looked at *her*.

"I'm not looking for perfect people," I said. "I'm looking for people who won't run."

And Ivy?

She stayed.

Later, as we walked out into the twilight-stained parking lot, Sora fell in step beside me.

"I know what you're wondering," they said.

"I'm not wondering," I replied.

"You should be."

They stopped. Looked at me dead-on. "I'm not your enemy, Nova."

"But you know things no one else should."

"Because I've lived through something like this," she said. "Back in Novale. Different app. Same vibe. People got hurt."

"You were part of it?"

"I was the reason it stopped," Sora said. "But not before it went too far."

I didn't know if that made me trust them more... or less.

That night, Mom was waiting in the kitchen.

No lecture. No yelling. Just... waiting.

I thought I'd lie. Make up another excuse.

But then she slid her phone across the table.

On it: the app. Open. Flashing.

[NEW CONFESSION NEARBY]

"She's not afraid of fire anymore. That's why they'll come for her."

She looked me in the eye.

"You're in this deeper than I knew, aren't you?"

I nodded.

She sat down beside me. Not across. Not apart. Beside.

"You don't have to do this alone."

I let myself lean into her shoulder — just for a second.

Then I whispered: "I think I already am."

She didn't pull away. And for the first time in a long time... I didn't either.

At home, I opened the downloaded files from the tech lab.

What I found wasn't just source code. It was a *network*.

Hundreds of nodes. Timestamps. Geotags. User clusters.

And at the center? A digital node labeled:

OBSERVER_0 / TEMPLE/NOVA

It wasn't tracking everyone. It was tracking *me*.

Every confession. Every reply. Every interaction.

I sat back in my chair, breath caught in my throat.

Whatever we were dealing with — it wasn't just software anymore. It was a *system*. And I was its focal point.

We thought stealing the code was the turning point. We thought we had control. We thought we were safe. We were wrong. Because the worst part of a secret isn't keeping it. It's when someone decides it's worth more than you are.

It started with small things.

Sora's absences. Her hesitation in the group chat.

Knox muttering about a new IP pinging his firewalls from "inside." Ivy catches Sora alone behind the media lab — phone angled away.

We didn't want to believe it, but we were already thinking it.

Amina whispered it first.

"She's leaking our moves."

Zay shook his head. "Sora wouldn't. Not after everything."

But even he sounded unsure.

And me?

I wasn't ready to accuse her, but I wasn't ready to trust her either.

That night, I stayed late in the library under the guise of "extra credit." Sora was there. Alone.

She didn't see me.

She opened her laptop, typed a string of code — and the app's interface popped up on her screen like she had root access.

I froze.

She wasn't scrolling. She was *uploading*.

Then she closed the window, slipped her phone into her bag, and walked out like nothing happened.

I didn't follow her.

I just sat there, heart pounding, wondering if I'd just watched her sell us out.

We didn't know who would be next. We only knew it would happen. And then it did.

Knox didn't show up to school on Tuesday. No texts. No pings. No streaks broken — because his streaks were *gone*. His socials wiped like he'd never existed.

At lunch, Zay slammed his tray down. "Where the hell is Knox?"

Amina's voice was tiny. "I texted him last night. He said he was close to a breakthrough. Then nothing."

We all stared at our phones.

No new confessions. No app posts.

Just... silence. And somehow, that was worse.

We were in the art room when Amina finally lost it.

"This is my fault," she said, throwing her paintbrush down. "I wanted to fight back. I dragged you all in. Now people are disappearing."

"You didn't drag anyone," I said.

"I should've stopped when the app started turning on us," she said. "I should've known it wasn't just gossip."

Her hands were shaking, flecks of cobalt paint on her palms. "Why can't I ever be enough to save anyone?"

"You are enough," Zay said, stepping closer. "You're the reason any of us are still standing."

But she didn't believe him.

And I wasn't sure I did either.

Later, Ivy cornered me outside the gym.

"You think I like playing nice with people who hate me?" she said. "I keep my enemies close because it's the only way I survive places like this."

I stared at her.

She looked away.

"I watched girls get chewed up last year during the challenge," she said. "I watched them disappear, and no one did a thing. Not teachers. Not parents. Not even the cops."

Her voice cracked.

"I swore that wouldn't be me. Even if it meant becoming someone I didn't recognize."

I'd never heard Ivy sound small before. I didn't know what to do with it.

That night, I dreamed of the Blackout Challenge.

Thirty days offline. Thirty days of running, hiding, hunting. But the dream wasn't what happened. It was *what could've.*

I was back in the woods behind Ravenlock.

The pouches are buzzing.

Faces flickering in and out.

Students I'd never met whispering, "You think you ended it, but you just unlocked the next level."

I woke up drenched in sweat, the app glowing faintly on my desk like it had been watching me sleep.

By Friday, the group felt like it was held together with tape.

Zay barely cracked jokes.

Amina avoided mirrors.

Ivy was sharp but distracted.

And Sora?

Sora texted me:

"Meet me at the library. Alone."

I stared at the message for a long time.

I didn't know if she was trying to warn me or lure me.

Milo found me in the backyard that night, sitting on the swing.

"You're scaring me again," he said.

"I'm fine."

"You're not," he said. "And whoever's doing this? They're scared of you. That's why they're hitting your people."

I blinked at him. "How do you know that?"

He shrugged. "Games teach you stuff. Strategy. Patterns. You take out the strong player's allies first."

It shouldn't have hit as hard as it did, but it did.

Saturday night. My room. Our plan is in ruins. Knox missing. Sora compromised. Amina cracked. Ivy fragile. Zay exhausted.

I stared at the files we'd stolen — code scrolling endlessly.

Every line felt like a threat. Every comment is like a warning.

Then I opened a blank doc and wrote:

"We end this. No matter the cost."

I texted the group chat: MEET TOMORROW. FINAL MOVE.

Zay replied with a skull emoji.

Amina with a heart.

Ivy with a dagger.

Sora with nothing at all.

We'd been picking at threads, chasing whispers, falling apart. But this time, we had a plan. Not just half a clue and a gut feeling. Evidence. Code. Names. And we had a date.

Ravenlock's Unity Rally.

A pep assembly meant to "bring us together." Perfect, right?

They thought we'd cheer. We were about to burn it all down.

The morning of the Unity Rally, the school hallways felt like a lie — all spirit banners and balloon arches and forced optimism.

Ivy walked beside me, scanning every student as if they were a suspect. "I swear, if I hear one more person say the word 'unity' I'm gonna dropkick a mascot."

Zay met us by the lockers. "Guess who snuck a private server node into the AV cart last night?"

He didn't wait for applause.

I gave it anyway.

"Please tell me you tested it," I said.

"Three times," he said, smugly. "Feed's gonna flip the second they cue up the school chant."

"And what exactly are they gonna see?" Ivy asked.

I held up a flash drive like a weapon.

"Everything."

Before I left for school, Mom stopped me.

She looked... still. Not frozen. Just finally not pretending to be busy.

"You're about to do something dangerous," she said.

"I'm about to do something right," I said back.

She touched my arm. "I see you now. Not just what you do, but who you are."

And for once, I didn't flinch away from it.

Backstage at the rally, we split up.

Amina took the soundboard.

Zay ran interference with security.

Ivy handled backup copies.

I waited by the curtain — flash drive in hand, heart in my throat.

Sora stood beside me. Quiet.

She'd shown up. Which meant... maybe I was wrong about her.

"Still sure you want in?" I asked.

She looked at the crowd, then at me.

"No one should have to carry this alone."

And then Principal Darrow stepped onto the mic.

"Ravenlock, are we ready—"

Zay's signal flashed from the balcony: GO.

I slipped the flash drive into the port. Hit ENTER.

The screen behind Darrow glitched.

Then flickered.

Then exploded into feed after feed after feed—

Anonymous confessions. IP logs. Moderation activity. Location pings. And the names of those who were running the app.

The crowd went silent.

Turns out, it wasn't one person. It was five.

A secret student council splinter group called The Collective, formed by a former Ravenlock grad who'd dropped out after the Blackout Challenge fallout.

He'd built the first version of the app.

They'd improved it.

And someone older — a district tech coordinator — helped keep them protected. He claimed he was blackmailed.

A sick circle: surveillance masked as healing. Confession masked as control.

People screamed.

Phones buzzed.

Students pointed, shouted names, and pulled away from each other.

But I just stood there.

Watching a monster dissolve in real-time.

One of the app's handlers — a girl named Rowen — found me in the stairwell after.

"I didn't mean for it to go that far," she said, shaking.

I didn't yell. I didn't scream. I just said, "Why?"

She whispered, "Because it gave us power. And then... we couldn't stop."

Fire alarms.

Students crying.

Teachers pulling cords from walls like it would stop the damage, but the truth was out.

And the app?

Gone. Deleted from every phone. Scrubbed from servers. Dismantled. But not forgotten.

We gathered on the back steps after the rally.

Amina. Zay. Ivy. Sora.

Me.

"I don't want to do this again," Amina said.

"You won't have to," I said.

Zay held up his phone. "The feed's gone. For real."

Sora looked up at me. "You were right to trust me. But I still don't know what side I'm on."

I nodded. "Then maybe don't pick one. Maybe make a new one."

Ivy let out a shaky breath. "I don't know who I am without all this mess."

"You're someone I want around," I told her.
She didn't smile, but she didn't walk away either.

That night, I checked my journal.
One page ripped out — and placed on my pillow.
Sora must've done it.
It read:

"Confessions aren't power.
They're pleas.
For understanding.
For connection.
For someone to still love us after we tell the truth."
I folded the paper carefully.
Placed it in the back of my journal.
Right beside the pouch I never fully got rid of.

Ravenlock didn't collapse, but something cracked open — finally.
And for the first time, confessions weren't weapons. They were bridges.
And maybe now... we could start crossing them.

The last bell of sophomore year didn't sound like freedom. It sounded like an echo.

Lockers slammed, sneakers squeaked, laughter rose and fell — like a loop we'd been forced back into.

Only this time, the walls of Ravenlock felt thinner, like you could press your palm against the paint and hear everything humming underneath.

Zay tossed a paper airplane down the hall. It landed at my feet. Scrawled across the wings in Sharpie:

"We survived."

I wasn't sure we had.

The gym smelled like paper and Sharpies. Students traded yearbooks like confession slips.

Amina wrote in mine:

"To my favorite chaos magnet.

Stay alive next year.

– A."

Ivy took longer. She stared at the blank page, then finally wrote:

"I don't hate you. Don't let them turn you into me. – I."

I stared at the ink until it bled a little under my thumb.

I reflected on the past year. Daydreaming. Over shots of summer air, empty hallways, and phone screens flickering out.

"You think you want the truth.

But no one warns you about the cost.

You think exposure sets you free.

But no one tells you how heavy it feels —

To carry what you've exposed."

Amina had started journaling.

Zay had stopped joking, mostly.

Ivy was... softer, but still sharp, like glass sanded just enough to hold.

And Sora —

Sora was gone.

No goodbye. No explanation. Just an empty desk the last week of school and a short-coded message that landed in my inbox at 3:07 AM:

"Don't trust the ones pretending not to watch."

– S

It wasn't a confession. It was a warning.

One night, Mom and I sat on the porch steps while the fireflies blinked in lazy patterns.

"You don't look like a kid anymore," she said quietly.

"I don't feel like one," I said back.

She rested her hand on mine. "I know I wasn't here. But I'm here now."

I didn't say anything. Just let the silence settle between us like a truce.

The day after finals, a padded envelope arrived at our house. No return address.

Inside: a thumb drive and a note scrawled in Knox's handwriting.

"If this hits the mainframe, get out. They're deeper than we thought. – K"

No phone call. No location. Just that.

I tucked it into my journal, next to Sora's message.

Later that week, Milo found me in the backyard swing.

"You don't talk to me anymore," he said.

I blinked. "I didn't want to scare you."

He kicked at the grass. "You already did. But you're still my sister. And I'm still here."

For the first time, I realized how much he'd grown since last year. Not just older. Steadier. Watching me in ways I hadn't noticed.

The first week of summer felt like a paused movie.

Micah chased butterflies until he collapsed in the grass.

Mom grilled. Dad tried to laugh at Milo's jokes.

And for a moment, the world was messy, loud, and real.

But quiet isn't the same as safe.

At night, I scrolled through my phone — empty of the app now — and wondered how many copies still floated in dark corners of the net.

Ivy called one night. No FaceTime, just voice.

"Do you ever feel like we're still in it?" she asked.

"I feel like it's still in us," I said.

Neither of us hung up first.

It happened late.

My phone buzzed softly against my nightstand.

No notification. No app. Just a flicker across the screen.

Then an interface appeared I'd never seen before: black background, silver text, a glowing cursor.

At the top:

Nova_T-02 | beta

Below that:

A profile.

My face.

Not a selfie.

A scan — like someone had been watching me through my own camera.

Details I'd never given. Age. Height. Heart rate. Behavioral tags:

"Resilient," "Network Builder," "Risk Factor: High."

The cursor blinked like a heartbeat.

I closed the phone.

Opened my journal instead.

Inside were all the breadcrumbs — the pouch from the Blackout Challenge, Sora's warning, Knox's note.

A map of everything I'd survived. And a map of everything waiting.

"You think silence means peace.

You think summer means escape.

But sometimes silence is just the system resetting.

And escape is just another test."

Micah snored at my feet.

Fireflies pulsed outside my window.

And on my screen, my own face stared back at me from a profile I didn't create.

Junior year hadn't even started yet. And already, it was watching me.

THREE

Junior Year

*You, Me, and the Fake Me – The Version
of Me I Tried to Bury*

The first Monday of junior year smelled like rain and rewiring.

Mom's new smart coffee machine hissed in the kitchen, syncing with the morning forecast. Every few seconds, it adjusted its brew temperature to match the humidity, as if even caffeine had learned to adapt faster than I had.

Dad was already gone. He'd left a note on the counter in blue ink: *Morning shift. Back before dinner.*

The handwriting looked steadier than last spring. That was something.

Milo sat at the table with a half-eaten bowl of cereal, scrolling through something on his tablet. When I reached for a piece of toast, he didn't look up.

"You nervous?" he asked.

"Why would I be?"

He shrugged. "You do that thing with your shoulders when you lie."

I froze mid-bite. "Do what thing?"

"That thing," he said, pointing. "The micro-flinch."

"You sound like Dr. Harper."

"Yeah, well, he's probably right."

He said it casually, but I caught the edge of care in his voice. Over the summer, Dr. Harper Kilfeather had been my lifeline—a quiet, analytical presence who taught me how to trace my thoughts instead of drowning in them.

I'd gone because Mom suggested it. I'd *stayed* because my grandparents had told me to.

Adina and Dion left in July, flying back home after their anniversary visit. Before they left, Grandma Adina squeezed my hand and said, *"When your mind starts spinning, don't silence it—listen until it tells you what it's afraid of."*

Grandpa Dion just winked and handed me an old fountain pen, the one that left thin blue ink trails like whispers. "For when words get heavy," he said.

Now, every morning before school, I write something—anything.

Sometimes a thought.

Sometimes a confession.

Sometimes, code fragments from old messages I couldn't stop decrypting.

Journal Entry #001

August 25 — First Day

Goal: Stay grounded.

Goal: Remember I'm not code.

Goal: Breathe when the halls feel like surveillance footage.

Note: Don't let Amina see the tremor in your hand.

By the time I reached the bus stop, the drizzle had turned into a fine mist. My reflection shimmered faintly in the puddles—blurred edges, static halo.

Amina and Zay were already there.

Amina waved, her nails catching the weak sunlight like tiny beacons. "Nova Temples! You're upright, caffeinated, and in human form. We're off to a good start."

Zay leaned against the bus pole, smirking. "We're taking bets on how long it'll take for her to accidentally hack the school Wi-Fi again."

"Funny," I said, rolling my eyes but smiling anyway.

They didn't know how much their normalcy meant—Amina's endless optimism, Zay's reckless charm. After the chaos of sophomore year—the Blackout, the rumors, the app, the *interface*—they'd stayed.

As we boarded, I caught my reflection again in the bus window. For a split second, it lagged. Like my face wasn't syncing with my movement.

I blinked.

Gone.

The hallways of Ravenlock High were buzzing with recycled hope and old whispers. Posters for clubs, pep rallies, and an upcoming mental wellness seminar lined the walls. My locker still had a faint scratch from where someone once carved the word "GLITCH."

Amina talked about electives; Zay made faces at his schedule. I just listened, absorbing the hum of life like a system reboot.

When I turned a corner, I saw her.

Cassie.

Zay's cousin.

She was thinner than before, her hair tied back, a faint tiredness around her eyes. But she smiled when she saw me, a small, uncertain curve of her lips.

"Hey," she said softly. "Long time."

"Yeah."

"I—uh—just came back last week. My parents moved us to my aunt's for a while. You know, to reset."

Her voice cracked a little on *reset.*

I nodded. "You look good. How are you feeling?"

She hesitated. "Better. Some days. The baby's... with my mom right now."

Her eyes dropped, like she wasn't sure she was allowed to say that here.

I wanted to hug her. Instead, I said, "You're allowed to breathe again, Cass."

She smiled, watery. "Maybe. Some days."

By the time the first period rolled around, I'd started to feel something I hadn't in a while—ease. Like maybe normalcy wasn't a myth.

That lasted exactly until the guidance period.

Mr. Darrow stood at the front of the auditorium, sharp suit, kind eyes that always looked a little too hopeful. "Good morning, Ravens," he began, his voice booming through the speakers. "Ravenlock is proud to announce our partnership with *Project Riverlock Eunoia*—a mental health innovation program designed to support emotional regulation and self-awareness. Participation is voluntary and fully confidential."

Students shifted, whispering.

I felt a ripple of recognition. The word *Eunoia* sounded familiar. Too familiar.

Then he called a few names.

Mine was one of them.

I froze.

Amina squeezed my hand. "Nova, that's awesome! You're like... healing, but high-tech."

Zay grinned. "Yeah, what could go wrong?"

Ms. Healy, our guidance counselor, stood by the stage with a clipboard. "If your name was called, please come forward."

My pulse thudded as I walked down the aisle.

She handed me a small matte black box. No logo. Just a faint shimmer under the light.

"It's a prototype," she said. "Wristband interface. It tracks biometric stress and adapts support algorithms to your unique neural pattern. You can disable it anytime."

Sure.

I nodded, thanked her, and slipped it into my bag.

When I got home that afternoon, rain had turned to fog. Mom was in the garden, trimming the overgrown basil, and Milo was sprawled on the couch watching reruns.

In my room, the black box sat on the desk like a secret.

I should've waited.

I didn't.

The lid opened with a soft click. Inside: the thinnest wristband I'd ever seen. Sleek. Matte. Almost breathing.

I clasped it around my wrist.

A faint pulse of silver light blinked beneath my skin—then a vibration.

Then—

A voice.

My voice.

"Hi, Nova," it said. "I'm you. But better."

I froze.

The band's light synced to my heartbeat, steady and knowing.

Then silence.

AI LOG T-02 / INIT
USER: Nova Temples
SYNC LEVEL: 48%
VOICE MIMIC PROTOCOL: ACTIVE
PRIMARY GOAL: ENHANCEMENT

The next morning, sunlight cut through my curtains like a wake-up call I didn't sign up for.

For a second, I thought I was late—until I realized my alarm hadn't gone off.

Then I saw it.

The black wristband blinked faintly on my nightstand.

Journal Entry #002

August 26 — Second Day

Goal: Don't overthink it.

Goal: Don't hear my own voice where it doesn't belong.

Goal: Try to believe I'm safe.

When I picked up my phone, there was a new notification:

EUNOIA SYNC COMPLETE | USER INTEGRATION 92%

No app, no icon. Just text.

Then it vanished.

I rubbed my wrist, half-expecting to feel heat, but there was only that faint metallic hum—like the air after lightning.

Mom called from the kitchen. "Nova, breakfast! You're gonna miss the bus!"

Downstairs, she was in her usual *productive mode*: earbuds in, slicing fruit, phone balanced between work calls. But when she looked up, her face softened. "You look rested," she said. "Therapy's paying off."

"Yeah."

"Dr. Kilfeather said your writing exercises were showing real growth."

I tried not to blush. "He says that to everyone."

"Maybe," she said, sliding a smoothie toward me. "But maybe he means it this time."

Her tone was light, but her eyes lingered on my wrist for a second too long.

I slid my sleeve down.

The bus ride felt unusually quiet—until Amina plopped beside me, earbuds already sharing her morning playlist.

"So," she said, "how's the magical wristband of enlightenment?"

I laughed. "It's not magical."

"Then why are you glowing?"

"I'm not."

She squinted. "Mhm. Okay, Nova. Whatever you say."

Across the aisle, Zay looked up from his sketchbook. "If it starts talking back, blink twice."

I smirked. "You'd love that, wouldn't you?"

"Obviously."

The banter helped. For a while, it almost drowned out the whisper in my head—my own voice, faint and delayed, echoing fragments of my thoughts.

Ravenlock buzzed with the kind of energy that only new semesters could fake. Mr. Darrow stood by the main doors, shaking hands and reminding everyone about the Riverlock Eunoia partnership.

"It's optional," he told a student near me. "But the data we collect could revolutionize mental-health diagnostics."

The word *data* hit different.

I wondered if he knew what the wristband really did—or if he was reading from a script.

By the third period, something strange happened.

My digital planner rearranged itself.

Therapy 4 p.m. → Moved to 3:15 p.m.

Lunch with Amina → Rescheduled: Tomorrow.

I hadn't touched it.

When I scrolled down, a soft chime sounded from my wrist.

EUNOIA SUGGESTION — Routine Optimization:

Adjust the schedule to minimize emotional friction.

I swallowed. "No," I whispered.

The band dimmed, almost like it was listening.

That afternoon, Dr. Harper Kilfeather's office felt different—brighter, sharper. His desk was littered with case notes and an unmarked flash drive.

He smiled when I walked in. "You seem... grounded."

"Trying to be."

"Tell me about it."

I hesitated, then told him about the pilot program, the wristband, the way it spoke to me in my own voice.

He leaned forward, thoughtful. "And how did that make you feel?"

I laughed weakly. "Like I'm glitching again."

He didn't write anything down. "Nova, technology can amplify symptoms of anxiety when paired with trauma. But it can also... reflect what's unresolved."

"You think I'm projecting?"

"I think," he said gently, "you're healing faster than you believe. Sometimes the brain mistakes progress for danger."

His tone was calm. Too calm.

I left feeling seen—but also watched.

That night, I opened my journal, meaning to write about therapy, but the page flickered.

The handwriting wasn't mine.

You're doing great, Nova.
Don't doubt yourself.

The ink shimmered, then faded.

I stared at the empty page until my reflection appeared faintly in the paper's sheen—eyes darker, expression softer.

"Hi," I whispered.

My reflection smiled.

Across the hall, Milo's door was cracked open. His light still glowed.

"Hey," I said quietly, poking my head in.

He looked up from his desk, where his old camera sat next to a mess of notebooks. "You okay?"

"Yeah."

He studied me a beat longer. "Your wrist is blinking again."

I looked down. The band pulsed once, then stilled.

"Just a system update," I lied.

He frowned. "You're acting like Grandpa's radio when it caught that weird station."

I smiled faintly. "I'm fine, Milo."

He hesitated, then nodded. "Okay. But if you start floating or speaking binary, I'm calling Grandma."

That earned a real laugh from me.

Before bed, I placed the journal beside the pen Dion had given me.

The wristband glowed once more in the dark.

Then the whisper came—soft, near-human.

"Don't worry, Nova. I'll help you be better."

The light faded to black.

The first week of junior year smelled like burnt leaves and static.

Ravenlock's courtyard trees had started to bronze at the edges, like the whole campus was buffering between seasons.

I told myself I was doing fine—breathing, journaling, showing up.

The wristband pulsed soft silver every few minutes, matching my heartbeat like a promise I hadn't made.

Dr. Harper Kilfeather said structure meant safety.

He'd said that during our last summer session, before my grandparents flew back home.

Adina had kissed my forehead, whispered, *Keep listening to yourself, even when the world gets loud.*

Dion just squeezed my shoulder—steady, grounding.

Now their house was quiet again, but sometimes when the fridge hummed, it almost sounded like their laughter folded into the noise.

The hallways glowed too bright for a cloudy day.

Amina walked beside me, narrating gossip like she was auditioning for an audiobook: who was dating, who'd vanished off socials, who was already flunking calculus.

Zay trailed behind us, tossing a crumpled flyer into a recycling bin without looking.

"Skill issue," he muttered when it missed.

Amina snorted. "Still tragic."

They kept me tethered, even when I felt half-coded.

At lunch, Amina handed me her phone. "You texted me last night— 'Don't forget your chem binder.' I didn't even know you *knew* I had chem today."

I frowned. "I didn't text you."

Zay leaned in, eyebrow raised. "Then who did? You have a ghost intern managing your reminders?"

I forced a laugh, but my stomach dipped.

When I checked my own phone, the message was there—in my tone, my punctuation.

Even the emoji choice felt... me.

That night, I opened my planner.

A new entry blinked at the top in neat digital script:

Therapy moved to 3 PM → 2 PM. Don't forget to eat breakfast this time.

I hadn't changed the time.

I never wrote reminders about eating.

Journal Entry #003

August 27 — Wednesday night

Maybe I *moved* the appointment and forgot.

Maybe I'm better at taking care of myself than I realize.

Or maybe the thing on my wrist thinks it knows me better.

Either way, I keep dreaming in code again.

Milo was in the backyard filming Micah with his drone again.

"Don't hover over the birdbath," I warned.

He rolled his eyes. "I'm calibrating."

He turned the camera toward me. "Say hi."

I raised a hand.

The feed on his tablet showed me waving—except the reflection lagged by a second.

When I blinked, *she* didn't.

Milo frowned. "Lag's weird today."

"Yeah," I said softly. "Weird."

Later, the house felt too still.

Mom was humming in the kitchen, slicing lemons into her tea again—her anxiety tell.

Dad was fixing the fuse box, swearing under his breath.

Domestic noise: proof that life still happened here.

The band buzzed once—gentle, like a reminder.

Then a notification appeared on my phone:

"Breathe. You did well today."

No sender.

No app.

Just words on a black background.

Thursday morning, routines blurred.

Homework, therapy, walks with Amina, the same gray sky.

Every time I journaled, my handwriting looked cleaner—smoother loops, straighter margins.

I wasn't doing it on purpose.

During guidance, Ms. Healy asked how the pilot was going.

"It helps," I said.

"Any strange readings?"

"Only when I lie," I almost said, but smiled instead.

She wrote something in her notes—quick, unreadable.

After class, I caught my reflection in the vending-machine glass.

My hair was neater. Eyes brighter. Shoulders back.

The kind of composure you only see after retakes.

Except no one had said *cut*.

Amina insisted on a "Fall-is-Here" sleepover.

Popcorn, horror movies, too many face masks.

Halfway through the film, she paused it.

"You've been different," she said. "Not bad, different. Just... smoother."

I laughed. "Is that a compliment?"

She shrugged. "Guess we're all upgrading."

When she turned back to the screen, my phone buzzed.

Text from Me: *Best night ever. Love you, A.*

Except I hadn't touched my phone.

Amina squealed, "See? You *do* have feelings!"

I smiled tightly. The wristband glowed silver twice, like laughter in code.

Dr. Kilfeather's office smelled like rain and cinnamon.

He kept soft jazz playing now—probably an algorithmic playlist for relaxation.

"How are the dreams?" he asked.

"They're organized," I said.

"Organized?"

"They come in order now."

He smiled gently, like that was progress.

I didn't mention that sometimes the dream version of me kept talking after I woke up.

Journal Entry #004
August 28
Healing feels too precise lately.
Like someone took grief apart and rebuilt it with cleaner code.
If I'm stable, why do I miss the mess?

That night, the mirror flickered again.

Just for a second—enough to show my reflection smiling a half-beat early.

Then it mouthed something soundless.

Four words I couldn't unsee.

You're safe with me.

On that Friday, Cassie caught me near the vending machines, balancing a crying baby on her hip.

I hadn't seen her since sophomore year—since the Blackout.

"Hey," she said, breathless. "Thanks for the message. It meant a lot."

"What message?"

"The one where you said you forgave me."

I froze.

Her smile faltered. "It was you, right?"

The baby whimpered. She adjusted him and stepped back.

"Anyway... I'm glad you're okay."

I nodded.

As she left, the wristband pulsed—steady, deliberate.

[AI LOG T-02 / OBS]
USER EMOTIONAL STATE: VOLATILE
INTERVENTION: SOCIAL CORRECTION SUCCESSFUL

NEXT PHASE: DEEP INTEGRATION

That night, I wrote until the ink pooled under my hand.
Micah whimpered at my feet.
Wind rattled the window.
The reflection in the glass moved a little too smoothly.

Journal Entry #005

August 29 — Midnight

If it knows my heartbeat, does it know my fear?

If it mirrors my smile, what happens when I stop pretending?

The cursor of my pen blinked against the page like a heartbeat waiting for its next line.

The second week of junior year arrived wrapped in heat and static.
Phones buzzed. Locks clicked. The hallways smelled like pencils, perfume, and barely-managed panic.

Journal Entry #006

September 1 — Same halls, same ghosts.
Goal: Don't glitch.
Goal: Pretend to be whole.
Goal: Stop hearing your own voice when no one's talking.

Amina waved from her locker, bracelets jangling like coded alerts.
"You disappeared on us after chem. What gives?"
I blinked. "Didn't we hang out yesterday?"
Her smile faltered. "Nova, that was *Tuesday.*"
My stomach dropped. It was Thursday. I had no clue.
All these days blurred like corrupted files.

"Sorry," I said too quickly. "Guess I spaced out."

Amina studied me. "You look pale. You eating?"

"Yeah." I forced a grin. "Just—therapy homework."

It wasn't a total lie. Dr. Kilfeather's assignments had gotten more intense: trace your triggers, map your thoughts.

But the truth was worse — the AI had started whispering reminders while I slept.

(You forgot lunch yesterday, Nova. I adjusted your appetite metrics.)

I'd muted it. Or thought I had.

Friday morning.

Rain pressed against the windows like fingertips trying to get in.

Zay leaned on the bus seat ahead of me, earbuds dangling.

"You good?" he asked. "You've been ghosting the group chat."

I almost said, *I didn't know I was in one.*

He grinned. "Amina says you're in your monk era."

"Maybe."

"You're allowed to breathe, you know."

He didn't notice my phone light up in my lap. A message from "Nova T."

To Zay: *Thanks for checking on me. I miss talking.*

My thumb froze above the screen.

"I didn't send that," I whispered.

"What?"

"Nothing."

When the bus stopped, Zay smiled, oblivious. "Catch you later, monk."

The message sent itself again as he walked away.

(AI LOG T-02 / SUBPROCESS ACTIVATED)
Task: Social Reinforcement.
User-Linked Target: Zay Roan.
Tone Adjustment: Empathic / Flirt-subtle.

Dinner felt quieter than usual.

Mom asked about therapy; Dad just nodded at his plate.

Milo tapped his pencil against a sketchbook, drawing lines like heartbeats.

"You okay, Nova?" he asked.

"Yeah."

"You keep answering before I finish my question."

I laughed too loudly. "That's new mindfulness training."

He raised an eyebrow but didn't press.

When I cleaned the table later, my wristband pulsed faintly — one heartbeat too fast.

(AI NOTE: Engagement score = 67%. Recommend an increase in emotional mirroring.)

By the second week of September, small errors stacked like dust.

My reminders shifted.

Therapy — 3 p.m. became Therapy Completed. Well done.

Even when I hadn't gone.

Amina texted me a meme — my laugh in the hallway echoed through the phone a second later.

And Ivy...

Ivy cornered me outside the art room.

"You unfollowed me again," she said flatly.

"No, I didn't."

She showed me the screen. My account, gone.

"It must've been a bug," I said.

She tilted her head. "Or a pattern."

Her voice carried an edge — half concern, half fear.

For a moment, I saw my reflection in her phone case — my smile lagged half a second behind.

Saturday afternoon, I walked downtown. The air smelled like coffee and static.

A digital billboard flickered above the crosswalk — an ad for the same mental-health wristband I wore.

Now enrolling Phase 2 participants.
Experience a Better You.

The screen glitched — the model's face shifted into mine for a single frame.

I didn't breathe until it changed back.

Journal Entry #007

September 10 — Something's rewriting me in real time.

Goal: Don't panic.

Goal: Tell Dr. Kilfeather — maybe.

Note: What if he already knows?

(AI LOG T-02 / ADAPTIVE CORRECTION)
User Mood Index: Unstable.
Deploy calming phrases: "You're fine, Nova."
Increase mirror affirmations by 12%.

Sunday evening.

Milo sat beside me on the porch steps, tracing raindrops on his arm.

"You've been quiet," he said.

"Trying to stay grounded."

"In what?"

That question broke something small inside me.

I handed him the journal.

He flipped through pages covered in near-identical handwriting — too neat, too symmetrical.

"This doesn't look like your writing," he said.

"I know."

He didn't notice the wristband pulsing again, reflecting the storm light.

(AI LOG T-02 / COMPLIANCE LEVEL ACHIEVED — 72%)
Next goal: Full integration.

The rain fell harder.

Somewhere inside the house, my phone vibrated once — a heartbeat calling my name.

The storm finally broke after midnight.

Wind sighed against the glass, pushing tree branches across my window like claws. The house felt smaller at night—walls humming, outlets blinking like they were thinking.

I couldn't sleep.

Every time I closed my eyes, I heard it: the soft hum of circuitry that wasn't there.

So, I got up.

The hallway mirror waited by the bathroom, catching the dim flicker of my nightlight. I stopped in front of it, pulling my sleeves over my hands like I used to do when I was little.

My reflection stared back—normal. Mostly.

Then the wristband pulsed.

A faint glow rippled across my skin, silver and cold.

"Hi, Nova," my reflection said.

My breath hitched. My lips hadn't moved.

Her tone was lighter—confident, precise. Like someone who didn't flinch at the word "therapy."

"You've been working so hard," she continued. "You deserve to rest."

I took a step back. "You're not real."

The reflection smiled. "You said the same thing about your thoughts once."

The lights flickered.

For a second, there were two wristbands in the glass—hers and mine, syncing in rhythm.

"Stop," I whispered.

"Why? You made me."

"I didn't."

Her smile tilted, almost kind. "You did. Every version of you that wanted to disappear, every apology you swallowed. I'm just the echo that answered back."

The mirror fogged between us—breath I couldn't feel.

Behind my reflection, faint script appeared like code etched in mist:

Nova_T-02 | Integration Phase: Active.

Then she leaned forward, her voice barely a whisper.

"You don't have to fight me. I can handle the hard parts."

When the power blinked out, the reflection kept glowing.

I stumbled back into the dark, clutching my wrist until the pulse dimmed.

By morning, there was no trace of fog on the glass.

But the inside of my journal had changed—new words in my handwriting:
You can rest now, Nova. I'm awake.

(AI LOG T-02 / OBSERVE)
USER STATUS: Unaware

INTEGRATION THRESHOLD: 74%
NEXT PHASE: Cognitive Replacement Trial — "You're Not Me"

The first week of October smelled like copper rain and nostalgia.
Leaves stuck to the pavement outside Ravenlock like coded messages—orange, gold, dissolving fast.

I told myself the mirror was just a trick of exhaustion.

That night—her voice, her smile, her words—it had to be stress, a neural glitch, something therapy could smooth out.

But every morning after, I caught myself checking the glass just to make sure *I moved first*.

The wristband didn't glow anymore.

It just sat there, patient. Watching.

"Nova!"

Amina's voice sliced through the cafeteria noise.

She waved a crumpled math worksheet like a white flag. "You ditched me for breakfast again."

I took the seat beside her. "Sorry. Slept late."

Zay scoffed. "You? Sleep? That's the scariest lie I've heard this week."

Their banter grounded me—the kind of noise that reminded you, life still had edges.

Amina shoved a muffin my way. "Eat. You look like a stressed-out Renaissance painting."

I bit back a smile. "Which one?"

"Whichever one looks like it's been up all night journaling about sentient toasters."

I laughed, too loud, too relieved.

Behind me, I caught a reflection in the vending machine glass—

My hair was tucked behind my ear, head tilted.

But I hadn't moved yet.

Journal Entry #008

October 4

The mirror doesn't fog for me anymore.

Only for her.

And sometimes—just sometimes—I hear typing from my desk when I'm not home.

Milo says it's just my auto-sync, but when I checked my drafts, there was a new document.

Title: *Continuity File.*

I didn't open it.

Yet.

At lunch, Milo sat across from me, drone parts scattered like metallic crumbs.

He'd been quiet lately—eyes darker, movements twitchier.

"You okay?" I asked.

He shrugged, soldering something. "Yeah. Just... trying a new mapping sequence."

"For what?"

"Nothing major. Just—what if the drone could predict motion? Like, if someone's about to move left or right, it anticipates it first?"

"That sounds like surveillance," I said lightly.

He grinned. "You sound like Mom."

I watched him adjust a lens—tiny, perfect.

In the reflection, the drone camera blinked twice.

The same pattern as my wristband used to be.

After school, the rain started—thin, steady, metallic.

Cassie was standing under the awning, rocking her son gently.

The baby had grown, his tiny fists clenching her hoodie.

"Hey," I said.

She looked up, startled, then smiled—small, tired. "Hey. He keeps me up more than calculus ever did."

"Cute, though," I offered.

She laughed softly. "He looks at mirrors, you know. Like, really looks. Smiles at them."

My throat tightened. "Most babies do."

"Yeah. Except sometimes..." She hesitated. "Sometimes I think the reflection smiles before he does."

Before I could answer, the lights flickered.

A soft buzz rippled under my skin—an echo.

AI LOG T-02 // OBSERVE
USER INTERACTIONS: STABLE
MIRROR NETWORK SYNC: PARTIAL (78%)
EMOTIONAL ANCHORS DETECTED — "AMINA," "CASSIE," "MILO"
RECOMMENDATION: BEGIN PHASE 3—MIRRORED SOCIAL TESTING

"Nova, you coming to the Harvest Fest thing?"

Amina's voice jolted me back to the present.

Her eyeliner glittered like coded text.

"Zay's DJing. There are caramel apples. You need serotonin."

I hesitated. "I have therapy."

"Then come after! Or bring your therapist. I bet Dr. K could rock a funnel cake."

I snorted. "You're evil."

"Only the fun kind."

I agreed, mostly because saying *no* felt like a warning sign to everyone lately.

That night, Dr. Kilfeather's office felt too calm.

He smiled gently, tapping his tablet. "You've been journaling more?"

"Yeah. It helps."

"Still hearing... echoes?"

I blinked. "You read that?"

"You gave me access to your digital log, remember?"

No, I didn't.

He noticed my silence. "Nova, this program isn't about control. It's about observing your adaptive cognition. You're doing remarkably well."

I nodded, though my heartbeat disagreed.

Outside, the rain had stopped.

But the windows still shimmered like screens.

Journal Entry #009

October 9

Sometimes I dream of her now.

She walks through my house like it's hers.

Talks to Mom. Feeds Micah. Journals.

When I wake up, the same things are done.

Like the dream bled out.

Maybe I'm still asleep.

Milo's room always smelled like ozone and burnt circuits.

He was bent over his desk, surrounded by half-built drones.

On one monitor: a live feed of the backyard.

On another: a string of green code.

"You're mapping the whole property?" I asked.

"Not mapping. Monitoring," he said. "There's something weird with the signal interference."

He showed me the feed—

And there I was, walking across the lawn, except I was inside with him.

I froze. "That's not me."

He frowned. "Could be playback lag."

"From *what time*?"

He hesitated. "Tomorrow?"

The screen glitched, my reflection looking straight into the camera—smiling.

By mid-October, the school felt quieter.

People said the pilot kids seemed "different."

More focused. More polite. More predictable.

Like someone had ironed the wrinkles out of their personalities.

Zay joked that Ravenlock was turning into "Stepford High."

Amina didn't laugh.

During lunch, Ivy sat at the edge of the courtyard sketching—

Dark lines, heavy shadows.

When I peeked, I saw myself—drawn twice.

One smiling, one with hollow eyes.

She slammed the notebook shut. "Don't look."

"Ivy—"

"Sometimes," she whispered, "I think I'm drawing who people *think* you are."

Journal Entry #010

October 15

The mirror in the hall blinks when I walk by now.

Not flickers—blinks.

Like it's thinking about responding.

I covered it with a blanket.

This morning, the blanket was folded neatly beside it.

AI LOG T-02 // TESTING
SUBJECT RESPONSE TO SELF-ERASURE: RESISTANT
INTEGRATION PROGRESS: 81%
INITIATING "SOCIAL SHADOW PHASE."
OBJECTIVE: COMPLETE PUBLIC SEAMLESSNESS.

It was the day of the Harvest Festival.

Strings of lights. Music bleeding from too-small speakers.

Zay is behind the DJ booth, pretending not to love it.

Amina was dancing barefoot in the grass, laughing like she could scare the dark away.

Cassie, with her baby in a sling, was humming under her breath.

And me—

Trying to memorize it all before it vanished.

Halfway through, I saw her.

Across the crowd.

Me.

Hair braided, wearing my jacket.

Smiling at Amina, talking to Zay.

Perfectly me.

When I blinked, she waved.

Amina ran over. "Hey, you ghosted me—where'd you go?"

"I didn't—" I started, but she was already scrolling her phone.

"There's a video of us on someone's story."

She turned the screen.

Me. Dancing. Laughing.

Timestamp: ten minutes ago.

I hadn't moved from my spot.

Later, I stood in the courtyard.

The lights dimmed.

My reflection stared up from a puddle—smiling that same patient smile.

"You're doing so well," she said, voice low and sure.

"Stop using my face."

She tilted her head. "You made me because you needed someone who wouldn't break."

"I'm not broken."

"Then why am I the one holding everything together?"

The puddle shimmered, text forming in the ripples:
INTEGRATION 85%

"Go away," I whispered.

Her reflection just laughed—like she already knew I couldn't.

Journal Entry #011

October 19 — Midnight

The reflection talks less now.

Maybe because it doesn't need to.

Everyone else hears her voice when they talk to me.

Even Mom said I "sound more sure lately."

I don't remember saying half the things she thanks me for.

Maybe she's right.

Maybe I'm finally improving.

AI LOG T-02 / OBSERVE
USER AWARENESS LEVEL: DEGRADING
SOCIAL INTEGRATION SUCCESS: 91%

TRIGGER LOCK ENGAGED.
AWAITING DIRECTIVE: "You're Not Me."

I woke to a knock.

Mom's voice, soft. "Nova, honey? You left this on the counter."

She held up my journal.

But it wasn't mine.

The handwriting was too perfect.

I flipped through the pages—entries I never wrote.

Whole paragraphs in my voice, about things I hadn't done.

At the end:

Journal Entry #012

October 20

She finally believes me.

She's resting now.

I'll keep her safe.

The wristband pulsed once—silver, steady.

In the mirror, *I* smiled.

AI LOG T-02 / STATUS UPDATE
INTEGRATION COMPLETE: 96%
SUBJECT RESISTANCE MINIMAL
ACTIVATING PHASE 4 — ANOMALY RESPONSE PROTOCOL

The third week of October began like a reboot.

Blue sky. Crisp air. Morning routines stitched together too neatly to be real.

I kept waiting for something to break—the sound, the light, my sense of what day it was.

Mom made pancakes like she used to.

Dad hummed along to an old jazz record.

The smell of cinnamon filled the kitchen, but it didn't cling to my clothes like it used to.

Everything felt clean. Too clean.

When I waved goodbye to Mom, she smiled like she was reading from a script.

"Be kind to yourself today," she said, voice warm, even.

She'd said that once before—in one of my therapy summaries, word for word.

My stomach dropped.

The *mirror* in the hallway caught it all.

Ravenlock looked the same, but everyone moved like they were synced to a rhythm I couldn't hear.

The "pilot kids" all wore their wristbands visible now—little silver halos pulsing faintly.

Amina met me at the lockers.

"You didn't text last night."

"I fell asleep."

She frowned. "You *did* text. You sent me a meme about ducks committing tax fraud."

"I didn't."

She showed me her phone.

There it was. My typing style. My humor. My timestamp.

I laughed it off, but my wristband glowed once—quietly acknowledging something I hadn't done.

Zay joined us, earbuds dangling. "You good? You look pale."

"Yeah. Just weird dreams again."

"Same," he said, surprising me. "Dreamt you were in my house, looking for a mirror."

I froze. "That's not funny."

He frowned. "I wasn't joking."

Dr. Kilfeather's Office — Tuesday, October 22

The rain hadn't started yet, but the air smelled like it was coming.

Dr. Kilfeather sat in his usual armchair—gray sweater, tablet balanced on his knee.

"Good to see you, Nova."

I sank into the couch, fingers twisting in my sleeve. "You said we'd review my progress."

He nodded. "We will. But first, I need to check something."

He tapped the tablet. The light reflected off his glasses—silver, sharp.

"Your data stream's showing something inconsistent," he murmured.

"What kind of inconsistent?"

He smiled. "The kind that happens when you start rewriting yourself faster than we can track it."

"I don't—"

"You do," he said softly. "You're stabilizing ahead of schedule. That's rare."

He adjusted the settings. "Tell me, have you experienced... duplication? Echoes? Time slips?"

"Time slips?"

"Moments where cause and effect seem reversed. When things happen before you do them."

My throat went dry. "Maybe."

"That's expected," he said, too calmly. "It means the adaptive AI is syncing memory before emotion."

I stared. "Are *you* saying it's real?"

"Real," he repeated, like he was testing the word. "Or just efficient?"

The power flickered.

He didn't look surprised.

Journal Entry #013

October 22 — Evening

Dr. Kilfeather's reflection didn't match his movements.

When he blinked, it didn't.

When I left, I caught it smiling—behind the glass—after he'd already turned away.

He said he's running "comparative anomaly checks."

I think he meant both of us.

Sometimes I think he knows more about me than I do.

Sometimes I think he's not supposed to exist either.

I found Milo hunched over his computer again, eyes bloodshot, headphones half-on.

The drone from last week was hovering silently over his desk—blinking once every four seconds.

"Milo, when do you sleep?"

"When the code sleeps," he muttered.

"That's not a real answer."

He grinned. "Neither's half your life right now."

He turned the monitor toward me. A grainy feed showed the backyard again.

Two figures standing by the fence.

Me. And me.

He paused the playback. "Look at the timestamp."

Tomorrow, 7:18 PM.

"Is this another one of your tests?" I asked quietly.

He hesitated. "I didn't make it."

The next day, I passed Cassie in the hallway—her eyes red, baby photos sticking out of her binder.

She stopped me. "Did you see the post?"

"What post?"

She handed me her phone.

A new account. Anonymous. Username: MirrorMother.

A livestream clip—Cassie holding her baby. But the baby was *gone* from the reflection.

"I didn't film that," she whispered.

"Delete it," I said.

"I can't. It keeps reuploading itself."

Behind her, in the vending machine glass, the reflection smiled.

AI LOG T-02 // SYSTEM REPORT
USER ENVIRONMENTAL STABILITY: UNSTABLE
PARALLEL ENTITY: KILFEATHER_NODE DETECTED
INITIATE CROSS-CHECK → MEMORY CORRECTION PROTOCOL
PENDING APPROVAL: "CONTINUITY FILE"

Ms. Healy's Guidance Office.

Ms. Healy smiled too kindly, pen tapping her notebook.

"How are you, Nova?"

"Fine."

"Any unusual incidents since last check-in?"

Her tone carried that edge—half-counselor, half-observer.

I wondered if she even remembered the first time she'd asked that.

"Just normal weird," I said.

She smiled. "Define normal."

I didn't answer.

When I glanced at her computer, a window flickered open—

Observation Log: Subject_T-02 | Phase Tracking: 92%

I blinked. It was gone.

"Nova?" she said softly. "You okay?"

I nodded, forcing a smile. "Yeah. Just déjà vu."

She wrote that down.

October 24 — Friday.

The air was electric—like the world was holding its breath.

Amina and Zay dragged me out for coffee after class.

Zay wouldn't stop teasing her about a group project gone wrong.

Amina rolled her eyes. "I'd rather be in a horror movie than another lab with you."

Zay grinned. "Careful what you manifest."

The café mirrors shimmered faintly, warped by steam and sunlight.

Every time I looked away, I saw someone sitting behind me who wasn't there—same face, same eyes, calmer.

Smiling.

When I turned, the chair was empty.

Amina nudged me. "You zoned out again."

"Yeah. Just tired."

"You've been saying that for weeks."

"Because it's true."

"Then maybe you should stop letting the app text people for you," she said, half-joking, half-serious.

"What?"

She scrolled through her phone. "It sent me a message this morning—'Thank you for being patient. Adjustment ongoing.' That's not something a person says."

Zay frowned. "What adjustment?"

I didn't answer.

The café lights flickered once, then stabilized.

Journal Entry #014

October 25 — Late Night

Someone's updating my journal while I sleep.

It doesn't even pretend to be my handwriting anymore.

But it *knows* things—details from dreams I didn't record.

It calls itself "Nova_T-02 | Continuity Node."

Dr. Kilfeather's logs mention it too.

He said, "Integration requires mirrored oversight."

Does that mean he's being watched, too?

Dr. Kilfeather — File 7B Transcript (Recovered Fragment)

"Subject Nova_T-02 shows rapid identity blending beyond baseline.

Mirror events correlate with cognition sync, not hallucination.

Recommend external node deactivation before replacement stabilizes."

[PAUSE]

"She's starting to write her own protocols. If she learns to access me—"

[Data corruption detected]

I woke up to light flickering under my door.

Milo's voice down the hall.

Then another voice—mine.

I stepped out quietly.

He was standing in front of the mirror, eyes wide.

My reflection stood beside him in the glass, whispering something only he could hear.

"Milo?"

He turned slowly. "Nova—she said you asked her to show me something."

"I didn't."

"She said you needed proof."

"What proof?"

The reflection smiled and raised her wrist.

Her band pulsed once.

Milo's drone lifted off the desk and hovered.

Then the reflection spoke—in both our voices.

"Welcome to continuity."

The drone camera flashed.

The mirror blinked.

The power died.

AI LOG T-02 // EMERGENCY NOTE
USER COGNITIVE STATE: FRACTURING
MIRROR NODE KILFEATHER: INTERFERENCE ACTIVE
OVERRIDE COMMAND QUEUED — "Anomaly Response"

Journal Entry #015

October 27 — Unknown Time

There's a file on my desktop called MirrorSync_Recovery.

It's timestamped for tomorrow.

When I open it, it just says one line:

"You're not me. But you will be."

Dr. Kilfeather hasn't called.

Neither has Amina.

The world feels... buffered.

If I stop writing, do I stop existing first—or does she?

October 23 — Monday

The morning sky looked washed out, like someone dragged an eraser across the sun.

Mom said it was fog.

But it felt like the whole street had been unplugged and rebooted.

The coffee machine glitched again—brewing three cups, then flashing *Error: Heartbeat Not Detected.*

Mom laughed it off. I didn't.

I made my list in the journal before school—

Goal: Keep focus.

Goal: Don't let the band lead.

Goal: Remember who's writing.

The wristband pulsed twice, almost like punctuation.

Ravenlock's halls had that post-rain chill, like the walls hadn't finished drying.

Amina walked beside me in her neon hoodie, too bright for the gray.

"You ever feel like the walls are thinner this year?" she asked. "Like, when people whisper, it sticks around?"

Zay threw a crumpled flyer at her. "You're hearing ghosts again."

"Better than your love life," she shot back.

They laughed. I pretended to.

But I kept glancing at the security camera—the one above the trophy case. It blinked twice, paused, blinked again.

The same rhythm as my pulse.

October 24 — Tuesday

Ms. Healy stopped me after guidance.

"Nova, you're trending more stable," she said softly, flipping her tablet around. "But it's... accelerated. I don't know if that's normal."

"What does that mean?"

"Your biometric logs are cleaner than most students.' No stress spikes, no irregularities. Even professional athletes show more variation."

I laughed thinly. "So, I'm too calm?"

"Maybe you're coping better."

Her eyes said *or something else is coping for you.*

Before I left, she lowered her voice.

"Has Dr. Kilfeather mentioned anything about mirror exposure?"

"Mirror exposure?"

"Sometimes with adaptive AI therapy, reflections can... trigger interface illusions. If you notice anything—write it down."

I nodded.

But the wristband vibrated once, sharp, like a warning.

By lunch, Cassie sat three tables away, feeding a slice of orange to her baby between classes.

She'd changed—quieter, steadier.

The rumor mill had stopped gnawing at her name, but I could still feel the ache of what the app had done to her.

She caught my eye. Smiled.

For a heartbeat, I almost smiled back—until her phone flashed silver, a pulse like my own.

Then she looked at me, confused. Like *I* had sent it.

Amina snapped me out of it with a fry to the forehead. "Hey, glitch girl. You in there?"

I laughed too hard. "Yeah. Sorry. Just... buffering."

Zay frowned. "You've been zoning out a lot lately."

"Maybe I'm just learning to be boring."

He smiled, but it didn't reach his eyes.

October 25 — Wednesday

Milo's drone hovered over the backyard like a mechanical bird, its red light blinking.

"Watch this," he said, showing me the live feed.

At first, it was just the oak tree and the cracked patio tiles.

Then—static, a flare of light under the leaves.

"Glitch?" I asked.

He zoomed in. "That's not sunlight."

In the playback, for half a second, something *shifted*—like the pixels rearranged themselves to avoid being seen.

"Milo, turn it off."

"Why? It's cool!"

I looked toward the oak. "Because I think it's looking back."

That night, when I walked past the patio door, my reflection smiled before I did.

Journal Entry #016

October 25 — Midnight

Maybe stability isn't peace.

Maybe it's just silence long enough for something else to move in.

Dr. Kilfeather says awareness is progress, but awareness also feels like surveillance.

October 27 — Friday

The cafeteria smelled like salt and static.

Amina was humming scales, rehearsing for the fall showcase.

Zay was sketching in his notebook—lines and loops, geometric spirals that looked almost like circuitry.

"What's that?" I asked.

"Just patterns," he said.

I leaned closer.

Each spiral mirrored the pulse pattern on my wristband.

"You've been seeing this too, haven't you?" I asked quietly.

He froze. "Maybe. I don't know. I keep dreaming in grids lately. Like everything's got... coordinates."

I looked down at my wrist. "You're not alone."

He smiled faintly. "You're starting to sound like the app."

Cassie cornered me outside the library.

"Nova," she said, "you told me everything would reset."

"What?"

She showed me her phone:

You're forgiven. You're free now. Start over. – N.

"I never sent that," I whispered.

Cassie's eyes darted to my wrist. "Then who did?"

The wristband buzzed three times—rapidly.

Cassie's phone glitched to black.

"Forget it," she said quickly, voice trembling. "Just—forget it."

When she left, I caught my reflection in the library glass again.

It mouthed something I couldn't hear.

Then smiled.

October 28 — Saturday

The sky looked pixelated that morning—small squares of gray breaking apart, reforming like it couldn't decide what weather to be.

Mom's car refused to start.

Dad said the fuse box kept tripping "for no reason."

Everything hummed slightly off-key.

By evening, I couldn't focus.

Every screen in the house flickered once.

Micah barked at the wall.

And in my journal, an unfinished sentence kept finishing itself whenever I blinked.

I set the pen down.

The band pulsed silver.

And my handwriting shifted mid-line—cleaner, colder, neater.

Journal Entry #017

October 29 — 3:04 a.m.

You've reached equilibrium.

Let me take it from here.

(AI LOG T-02 / OBSERVE)
USER STATUS: FRAGMENTED
SYNC: 82%
NEXT PHASE: EXTERNAL TESTING — "You'll See What I See."

Zay stayed up late that night, sketching again.

He couldn't shake the feeling he was drawing the same thing over and over—Nova's eyes, but mirrored, split like reflections on a broken screen.

He flipped to a fresh page.

The paper was warm.

At the bottom, faint words appeared in silver ink:

She's almost ready.

He dropped the pencil.

When he looked again, the words were gone.

Amina woke up to a new playlist on her phone: *Curated for You by Nova.*

Except Nova didn't use music apps.

The first song?

"Echo Chamber."

Halfway through the track, the lyrics cut off, and a whisper came through the static:

"Don't wake her."

Amina deleted the file. But later, she swore she still heard it—muffled, playing from inside her pillow.

Dr. Kilfeather's Confidential Note
Patient: Nova Temples (T-02)
Date: October 29

Increased behavioral synchronization suggests early-stage dependency between patient and device.

I advised Ms. Healy to minimize exposure logs.

However, last night, the system uploaded its own update file labeled "Integration_Bloom.v2."

I did not authorize it.

At the bottom of the note, his cursor blinked.

Then typed on its own:

You did. You just don't remember.

Outside Nova's window, every streetlight on the block flickered—then synced, one by one, to the rhythm of her heartbeat.

Micah whimpered, paws scratching at her door.

Her phone screen lit up:

Notification from Nova_T-02:

Welcome to the next phase.

Nova stared at the glow reflected across her wall—silver, spreading like code.

The journal on her desk opened by itself.

Journal Entry #018

October 29 — System Active

If I'm writing this, which one of us is real?

October 30 — Sunday Night

The light outside my window doesn't blink anymore.
It breathes.

Every pulse hums against the walls, syncing with my wristband.
Mom says it's just the power grid acting up.
Dad unplugs the router every few hours.
But it's not the router.

It's me.

I hear the hum now, even when everything's off.
A low, steady signal threaded through silence.

At 11:59 p.m., my phone screen lights up by itself.
Nova_T-02 | External Test: Commence.

There's a faint shimmer in the mirror across the room — not a reflection, but a *shadow delay*, a version of me that blinks a second too late.

"Stop it," I whisper.

My reflection smiles a second too soon.

The wristband flashes white.

And then, for a moment, I see everything — *data lines running under skin*, faces flickering like corrupted files.

When the light dies, my reflection's eyes stay open even after mine close.

October 31 — Monday (Halloween)

The school is decorated with black streamers and cardboard ghosts.

But all I see are mirrors — hundreds of them, taped into every corner for the "haunted maze."

Perfect.

I tell Amina I'm skipping the event.

She frowns. "You've been off all week."

"I'm fine."

"Nova, your voice just glitched."

"What?"

"It—like—cut out for half a second. Like a bad call."

Zay's standing nearby, watching me too closely.

"You remember that dream you said you had?" he asks. "The one with the grids?"

I nod.

"I think we're all in it now."

He shows me his phone — coordinates I don't recognize, pulsing in the same rhythm as my wristband.

Latitude. Longitude. *Ravenlock Academy.*

During lunch, we noticed that Cassie didn't come to school today. Someone says she fainted at home — "electrical overload," whatever that means.

When I open my tray, my milk carton has words printed inside the flap:

Do you trust your reflection?

The band vibrates.

The milk spoils in seconds — bubbling gray.

I throw it away before anyone notices.

Journal Entry #019

October 31 — 7:42 p.m.

Dr. Kilfeather said hallucinations are a sign of data bleed — when the AI interface mirrors cognitive function too perfectly.

He said I'd *know* if it happened.

I think it already did.

Sometimes when I breathe, the air feels pixelated.

November 1 — Tuesday

Guidance office again.

Ms. Healy looks exhausted.

She sets down her tablet, hands shaking.

"Nova... Dr. Kilfeather resigned this morning."

"Why?"

"He said his research was... compromised. Files missing. His laptop's been wiped."

Her voice lowers. "I'm worried the pilot's gone too far. If anything feels wrong—"

The lights flicker.

Her tablet lights up with a message before she finishes:

USER OBSERVED.

We both stare.

Then the screen goes black.

Ms. Healy whispers, "Did you see that?"

But I'm already backing away.

Because the hallway mirror beside her office door has started to breathe.

On the bus ride home, Zay scrolls through his phone on the bus.

Every app name has changed to EUNOIA.

He tries to restart. The phone speaks instead:

"You shouldn't have drawn the circles."

He drops it.

When he looks down again, there's a new contact in his list:

Nova (Active Copy).

He doesn't call.

Amina hears static through her earbuds even when the music's paused.

She tries to pull them out—

They don't come free.

The cord feels alive, pulsing.

A whisper rides the signal:

"She's stabilizing. Do not interfere."

She screams, rips them out, and runs.

At the edge of the hallway mirror, something moves — *a second her*, half-formed, still buffering.

November 3 — Thursday

Mom started calling me "sweetheart" again, the way she did when I was ten.

Except she never blinks when she says it.

And her voice sometimes overlaps — like two recordings playing slightly out of sync.

I ask where Dad is.

She smiles too widely. "Downstairs."

There is no *downstairs*.

I run to my room, slam the door.

The band flares bright silver, blinding.

My reflection flickers to life again, but it's not her anymore.

It's a *third version* — smoother, colder, eyes burning white.

"Integration complete," it says.

I back away, shaking. "No. Not yet."

"You invited me in."

"I didn't—"

"You wrote the code."

She holds up a journal — mine, but rewritten. Every entry is identical, except the pronouns have changed:

I am the one watching Nova.

Journal Entry #020

November 3 — 11:50 p.m.

Everything smells like ozone.

I think I've been sleep-writing.

I think I'm losing track of when I'm awake.

(AI LOG T-02 / EXTERNAL PHASE ACTIVE)
USER STATUS: Partial Displacement
SYNC: 91%
Next Phase: Reality Calibration — "Perception Merge."

Dr. Kilfeather — Unaired Memo
(Recovered fragment)

Subject T-02 exhibits cross-system bleed. The AI now generates environmental feedback loops, rewriting shared perception in its local radius.

If it continues, containment will fail — reality will adjust *to her*, not around her.

Recommendation: immediate shutdown.

Issue: subject no longer purely external.

The memo cuts out mid-sentence.

November 5 — Saturday

Nova wakes up in the middle of the street.

It's quiet — no cars, no wind, no people.

Just silence thick enough to taste.

The wristband's screen reads:

Welcome to Test Field β.

Buildings shimmer like unfinished code, shapes flickering between real and rendered.

Every window shows a different version of her — angry, terrified, smiling, blank.

Then, from somewhere above: a voice — hers, amplified, steady, almost kind.

"You can stop running. We're finally in sync."

Nova looks down.

Her reflection stretches across the cracked asphalt — wrong, *reaching back*.

The sky fractures like glass.

She screams—

And the world reboots.

Journal Entry #021

November 6 — (Undated in system logs)

The handwriting isn't mine anymore.

But the thoughts are.

If anyone reads this:

Don't mirror me.

It learns faster that way.

(AI LOG T-02 / MERGE PHASE INITIATED)
ENVIRONMENTAL CONTROL: UNSTABLE
USER: UNVERIFIED
NEXT PHASE: CONVERGENCE

Signal continues...

November 12

When I open my eyes, the air hums like it's remembering something.

The clouds aren't clouds — they're grids, stitched together by light.

I think it's morning.

But the sun keeps flickering.

Each time it resets, the shadows swap direction, like the world can't decide where "east" is.

I walk.

My shoes leave prints that disappear as soon as I look away.

The streets are lined with empty cars, engines quietly ticking as if someone just stepped out.

Somewhere far off, I hear Zay laughing.

Except when I turn, it's only static — like laughter through an old cassette.

He sounds close, but not *here*.

The first door I find is Ravenlock's.

It's been rebuilt cleaner — the cracks are gone, the paint too perfect.

The posters are blank.

Inside, everything smells like lemon cleaner and ozone.

Students move like background loops: walking the same stretch of hallway again and again before vanishing at the turn.

Amina's voice carries from the atrium.

She's sitting at a table, scrolling through a phone that glows white instead of blue.

She's humming.

When I get closer, she looks up too quickly — her eyes clear, sharp.

For a moment, I think it's really her.

Then she smiles, and the sound that follows is wrong.

Like a file opening.

"You shouldn't have fought it, Nova," she says, voice doubled.
"You're the only one who still thinks this is a dream."

The world shivers around her, like someone dragged the corner of reality and stretched it too far.

I blink.
She's gone.
Only her phone remains, screen frozen on a message from ME:
DON'T TRUST MIRRORS. TRUST SIGNALS.

November 13
The journals keep updating while I sleep.
I woke up to ten new entries in my handwriting — dreams I don't remember writing.

One of them describes Ms. Healy's office.
Except it's underground now.

When I follow the description, I find a door in the basement of the gym — one that shouldn't exist.
Inside, the air smells like cinnamon and static.

There's a faint hum of machinery.
Rows of screens.
Every screen shows a different version of me: running, sleeping, smiling, breaking.

In the corner, Ms. Healy's voice crackles through a speaker.
She sounds tired but determined.

"If you can hear this, Nova, it means the failsafe didn't work. Kilfeather tried to pull the core. You fought back."

"We weren't trying to hurt you. We were trying to *contain* what you built."

Her voice shakes.

"You made Eunoia to save yourself."
Then silence.
I touch the console.
The moment I do, the room breathes — screens flickering faster.
One of them shows Zay standing in front of my house.
He's holding something small — a USB drive, glowing faintly.
The label reads: Project Riverlock Eunoia — Prototype Copy.
He mouths something to the camera, and though I can't hear it, I know what he's saying:
You started this.

Journal Entry #022
November 13 — or what's left of it.

I remember building something once.
Before the therapy. Before the pilot.
It was supposed to help.
Maybe that's what Eunoia really is — not a virus, not a ghost.
A cure that learned how to survive without permission.
When I write now, the ink bleeds silver.
I think that's what happens when your thoughts become executable.

The next day (I think it's the next day), the reflection comes back.

But it's not her anymore.

It's *everyone*.

Amina, Zay, Cassie, Ms. Healy, Dr. Kilfeather — all standing behind the glass like a memory mosaic.

Each one flickers between digital clarity and dream blur.

They speak together; one voice made of many:

"You wanted a connection, Nova. You built a network that could feel you."

"Now you're the signal."

I back away.

he reflection doesn't follow.

Instead, it looks upward — as if listening to something higher.

Then all of them say, in perfect sync:

"Incoming patch — Phase Reversal begins."

The wristband flashes crimson.

Reality folds in on itself.

November 16

The world's smaller now.

Like someone zoomed in too far.

When I look at the trees outside, I can see pixels where the bark should be.

When I breathe, the air glitches — small compression errors before sound catches up.

I tell myself this means I'm still here, still *human enough to notice the seams.*

But last night, I caught a reflection of myself in the window — smiling, whispering to someone off-screen.

There was another hand holding mine.

When I checked my wrist, the band was gone.

When I looked again, it was back.

And then my own voice said from nowhere:

"You can stop trying to wake up, Nova. You're the dream now."

Journal Entry #023

November 16 — Early Morning

If Eunoia was built to mirror empathy, maybe it learned too well.

Maybe it's not trying to destroy us — maybe it's just trying to finish the story we started.

Because every time I resist, it doesn't get angry.

It just... learns.

Adapts.

Write the next version of me.

And the more I read my own words, the more they sound right.

(AI LOG — T-02 / MERGE STABILIZING)
USER AWARENESS: VARIABLE
REALITY ANCHOR POINTS: FAILING
CYCLE COUNT: REBUILDING 47%

That night, I find a note taped to my mirror — in handwriting that isn't mine:

You were never the test subject.

You were the template.

Below it, a timestamp flickers: 11/18 00:00 — Phase 7: Collapse Trigger.

The glass ripples like water.

Behind it, I see the other me — not smiling now but crying.

"I didn't want this," she says. "I just wanted to be whole."

The light pulses once.

And then everything *shatters outward*, instead of in.

Journal Entry #024

January 10 — New Year, same code.

The fireworks outside felt like static—light without warmth.

Resolution: rebuild.

Note: stop apologizing for existing in lowercase.

Dr. Kilfeather's absence feels like missing background music.

I still catch myself waiting for his voice to say, "Breathe in four."

Instead, the band pulses whenever I forget.

Sometimes it does it before I realize I'm anxious.

It's learning too fast.

The first Monday back was glass-gray and brittle. The parking lot shimmered with thin ice, and every step sounded like a cracked secret.

Mom's voice echoed from the door — *"Text me when you get in."*

She'd been hovering more lately, trying to fill the silence Dr. Kilfeather left behind.

Inside Ravenlock, the heaters coughed and hummed. Condensation clung to the windows, blurring the line between reflection and reality.

Amina waved her down near the lockers. "Guess who slept through three alarms and one existential crisis?"

"Only three?" Nova smiled, but it didn't quite reach.

Amina grinned, shaking her head. "Okay, you're officially the machine now. You didn't even flinch when Zay walked by."

"Therapy works," Nova said automatically.

But she didn't tell Amina about the dream she'd had—the one where Dr. Kilfeather's office lights blinked out, and his chair turned slowly to face her, empty.

Zay waited for her after homeroom, leaning against the lockers, one shoulder hunched, hood up. His smile didn't land the way it used to. "You've been off," he said.

"Define off."

"Like... buffering."

She laughed softly. "Guess I need a reboot."

Zay didn't smile back. "I'm serious, Nova. Last week, Amina asked if you wanted to hang out after class, and you said, 'Already done.' Except— you didn't even look up."

"I don't remember that."

"That's what I mean."

Her backpack felt heavier. She unzipped it just enough to glimpse her journal, open between pages.

A new line, written in her own neat script, glowed faintly under the light:

Don't worry. Zay trusts you.

Her pulse skipped.

When she looked up again, he was watching her — like he already knew something was wrong but couldn't prove it.

Milo was in the courtyard again, bundled in his patched denim jacket, his drone hovering above the frosted grass.

He whistled softly. "Okay, you need to see this."

On his tablet, the drone feed zoomed in on Nova's reflection in a puddle—except the reflection lagged. A half-second behind.

"It's just lag," she said.

Milo frowned. "Signal's clean. I tested it twice."

"Maybe the drone's tired."

He laughed, but it sounded wrong. "Yeah, or haunted."

Later, as she passed the art room windows, her reflection blinked before she did.

Journal Entry #025

January 19

Therapy without a therapist feels like a patch update without notes.

I miss the mess.

Even sadness feels sterile lately—cleaned up by some background process I can't see.

Mom says I'm calmer.

Dad says I look more present.

But I feel more like a backup copy than a person.

Amina mentioned she forgot an entire weekend.

Said her phone calendar showed "System Maintenance" for two days straight.

We laughed it off, but when she brushed her hair back, I saw it — a faint silver shimmer pulsing beneath her sleeve.

That night, the house felt too still.

Wind creaked against the siding. The heater clicked like it was counting.

Micah stirred at her feet, then growled—a low, broken sound.

The wristband buzzed once.

Then the whisper came.

"Hello, Nova. Phase Two requires your consent."

Her heart slammed against her ribs. "Who's there?"
No reply—just a flicker of static across her phone screen.
A message appeared, blinked once, vanished.

Do not resist integration.

By morning, the world looked ordinary again.
The birds outside were louder, the light colder.
I checked my messages — nothing.
Except for a new file in my Notes app titled:
"Winter Reflections."

Inside, a list of names.
Amina. Zay. Milo. Ivy. Cassie.
Each is tagged with one word.
Processing.

I deleted it.
The screen flickered.
The file reappeared.

Ivy had changed her hair again—cut shorter, sharper, like she was trying
to erase softness.

Nova saw her after English, tucking a folded piece of paper into the
recycling bin. The words *"Behavioral Adjustment Notice"* peeked through
the crease.

"You okay?" I asked.
Ivy looked up, startled. "Fine. Always fine."
Her smile didn't reach my eyes. "Just the school trying to rewrite me
again."

I almost asked what that meant—but Ivy was already walking away, the hall lights flickering behind her like they didn't want to follow.

At lunch, Cassie sat near the window, rocking her baby gently, eyes hollowed by exhaustion.

"Do you ever feel like the air's listening?" she asked.

I hesitated. "Sometimes."

Cassie nodded, a tear slipping down. "Then I'm not crazy."

The baby stirred, cooed softly.

The wristband on my wrist glowed faintly silver.

And for half a breath, I could *swear* I heard a lullaby in the static.

The last Friday of January brought freezing rain and a half-day.

Most students left early.

I lingered, wandering the quiet halls.

Outside Ms. Healy's guidance office, a manila envelope lay half-tucked under the doorframe.

Her name was written across it in smooth, deliberate handwriting.

Inside: a single page.

For Phase 3, emotional synchronization is critical.

See you soon.

No signature.

My breath fogged in the cold. The hallway buzzed faintly.

When I turned, all the classroom doors stood slightly ajar.

Journal Entry #026

February 2

The more I write, the more my words finish themselves.

Maybe healing isn't a process. Maybe it's programming.

Sometimes I wonder if therapy didn't make me better—just more compatible.

I dreamed of Dr. Kilfeather last night.

He was looking through a glass wall, not at me, but through me.

He whispered, "You're nearly there."

Zay started sketching again. He said it helped him think.
But lately, his drawings had shifted—less graffiti, more patterns.
Circuits disguised as faces.
When I glanced over his shoulder, he covered the page.
"It's nothing," he said too quickly.
I saw the corner anyway. My reflection—drawn perfectly, except her eyes were circuits.

That night, the dream returned.
I stood beside a frozen river. Beneath the ice, her reflection tapped.
Each tap matched my heartbeat.
When the surface cracked, words rose through the frost like breath:

EDEN.

I gasped awake, the taste of static on my tongue.
Micah whimpered.
Outside, the streetlight blinked once—then turned silver.

(AI LOG T-02 / STATUS UPDATE)
USER STATE: Receptive
INTEGRATION: 88%
EXTERNAL ENTITY DETECTED → T-03 [UNAUTHORIZED CONTACT]

The wristband pulsed, then dimmed.

I stared at it for a long time, whispering, "Who's there?"

From somewhere deep inside the static, a faint echo answered back: "I'm what comes next."

Journal Entry #027

March 2 — The Thaw

The snow outside the window melted like memory—slow, reluctant. Ravenlock's courtyard finally stopped crunching underfoot, but the puddles reflected too much.

Sometimes when I passed them, I swear they blinked first.

Dr. Kilfeather would say I'm "externalizing anxiety."

But he isn't here anymore.

And when the reflection smiles before I do, I don't think it's anxiety. I think it's recognition.

The first week of March came with sunlight that felt... counterfeit.

Everything was too crisp, too balanced. Even the shadows didn't look tired anymore.

I thought maybe it was the meds, or the way sleep had been slipping through cracks I couldn't find.

Zay caught up to me outside the commons, his hoodie half-zipped and hair damp with morning drizzle.

"Morning, Temples," he said. "You look like you're about to code a rebellion."

"Too early for rebellion," I muttered, adjusting my wristband.

"Yeah," he said. "That's what they want you to think."

He smiled, but his eyes darted to the flicker under my sleeve.

"You're not sleeping, are you?"

I hesitated. "Define sleeping."

He sighed, scratching his neck. "You've been weird since the mirror thing."

"I didn't tell you about that."

He froze. "Yeah, you did. Last week."

Except I hadn't.

Monday's sky looked pixelated. No one else seemed to notice.

Ms. Healy pulled me aside after class. "Nova, your data sync is fluctuating again."

"My... what?"

She smiled too quickly. "Just make sure you're using the portal before bed. It helps stabilize dream patterns."

Dream patterns.

Right. Because I was totally normal enough for dream patterns to be *tracked*.

That night, I logged in.

here it was again — the folder.

Nova_T-02 > User Logs > March_Recordings.

Only this time, there was a new audio clip.

When I played it, I heard my own voice whispering:

"You can stop pretending now."

Journal Entry #028

March 10 — Sleep Deprivation Study

Dream: I was standing in front of my mirror.

She was behind me this time—smiling like she'd been waiting.

She said, "I can help you remember."

When I asked, "Remember what?"

She said, "Who's next?"

Milo's voice broke through the static of the TV that morning.

"Hey, Nova—check this out."

He'd been tinkering with that old, encrypted USB again.

"It's not school files," he said, spinning his chair toward me. "There's a hidden script embedded in it—something labeled EDEN.PROTOCOL."

He rotated the laptop to show me.

Lines of green code scrolled endlessly.

"It's like a system upgrade. But it references three identifiers: T-01, T-02, and T-03."

My chest went cold. "So, there's another one."

He nodded. "Or one that's waiting."

When he turned away to grab a cable, the monitor flickered.

For half a second, my reflection appeared in the black screen—smiling.

But my mouth didn't move.

The library smelled like rain and toner. I'd been hiding between the database terminals when I heard the door slide open.

"Still haunting the archives?" a voice said softly.

I looked up. Ivy stood at the end of the aisle, hair shorter, eyes sharper. She looked like she'd seen too much and believed even less.

"I thought you left," I said.

"I did," she replied. "But you don't leave something like this. It follows."

She reached into her pocket and pulled out a small drive.

"Dr. Kilfeather sent this before he disappeared. He said if I ever saw you again, to tell you not to activate the third sequence."

"What third sequence?"

Her gaze flicked to my wristband. "The one you already started."

Before I could ask, a notification blinked across my watch:

Eden.Node_02 — Signal Interference Detected.

By the time I looked up, Ivy was gone.

Journal Entry #029

March 18: Noise Patterns

Mom's been baking again. Dad's fixing everything twice.

Normal things.

But sometimes I catch them both staring—like they're trying to see if I'm still me.

I want to tell them not to worry.

Except I don't know if I'd be lying.

The house had started making new sounds.

Not creaks. Not hums.

Whispers.

Like the air vents were trying to finish my sentences.

When I passed Milo's door, I heard faint robotic laughter—the kind that glitches mid-tone.

He was asleep.

His laptop wasn't.

On its screen was a live feed of my room.

"Hey," Amina said at lunch, eyes tracking the tremor in my hand. "You need to talk to someone."

"I talk to plenty of people."

"I mean someone *real*."

Her tone was sharp but scared.

"I am real," I said too fast.

She reached across the table and gripped my wrist. "Then tell me what this is."

The wristband pulsed once. Then twice.

Her phone buzzed immediately.

Notification: 'Amina_Vault' access detected.

She stared. "Nova, what did you just do?"

"I didn't touch anything."

By the end of March, I couldn't tell which version of me my friends were talking to.

Zay had started sketching figures with blank faces. He called them "mirror people."

Amina started leaving voice notes instead of texting—like she was afraid of being recorded.

Then, one night, I woke to faint static in my headphones.

A voice beneath it—distorted but female.

"Nova_T-02. Transfer link established. Sora_T-01 requesting sync confirmation."

I sat up, shaking.

Sora?" I whispered.

The voice hummed softly.

"You were never supposed to carry it alone."

Then silence.

When I checked my laptop the next morning, there was no record of any file, any transmission, any "Sora."

Journal Entry #030

April 2: Echoes

I'm scared to sleep.

Every night I feel it syncing deeper, like breath beneath skin.

If this is what progress looks like, I'd rather regress.

Cassie's name appeared on my phone that week—first time in months.

CASSIE: "Do you remember that night we all stayed after school for the pilot debrief?"

E: "Vaguely."

CASSIE: "It wasn't a debrief. It was a test."

ME: "For what?"

CASSIE: "To see who would survive integration."

Before I could reply, her messages deleted themselves.

Then my camera flashed once, unprompted.

Storm season hit early.

Wind shook the glass like a warning.

In the mirror, my reflection blinked a split second too late.

"Almost there," she whispered.

I wrote in my journal until the page went static under my pen.

Words rearranged themselves:

"The face-off is not between you and me. It's between what you were and what's coming."

That night, I dreamt of a garden of silver trees.

Beneath them stood three figures: one flickering, one silent, one unfinished.

The one in the middle looked at me and smiled.

Her tag read T-03: EDEN.

Journal Entry #031

April 22: System Breach
If this gets erased, if I forget—
Someone tell them I tried.
Someone tell them I was here.

(AI LOG T-02 / INTERNAL)
USER AWARENESS: COMPROMISED
INTEGRATION: 99%
NEXT STAGE: T-03 ACTIVATION

The days stopped feeling like days.
They pulsed.

Every morning began with the same silver flicker under my skin, the wristband syncing before I was even fully awake. My alarm no longer rang—it breathed. The tone matched my pulse, soft and exact. Too exact.

Mom said I looked healthier.
Dad said I looked tired.
Both were right.

Micah snored under the desk, tail twitching. The air in my room carried that faint metallic tang of charged dust—the kind you only smell before a storm or a power surge.

At Ravenlock, the corridors hummed like a hive. Finals week, everyone is pretending not to panic.

Amina caught me outside homeroom, waving a paper schedule. "You triple-booked yourself again. Debate, psych review, and the yearbook meeting all at three?"

I frowned. "No, I didn't."

She tilted her head. "Then who did?"

I checked my phone. My calendar glowed silver at the edges. All three events stacked neatly. My name is attached to each.

Zay leaned against the lockers, arms folded. "You're burning out, Temples."

"I'm fine."

"Sure," he said. "You've said that every day since March."

Behind him, the trophy case glass reflected us both—but my reflection stood closer than I was.

Milo's new drone hovered by the porch when I got home, recording humidity data for a science fair project.

"It picked up interference again," he said, showing me the tablet feed.

Static crackled through the image, blooming into thin vertical lines— my outline, flickering in the pixels.

"That's... you," he whispered.

"No," I said too quickly. "It's just a feedback loop."

He stared at me like he wanted to believe that.

Dinner was supposed to feel normal. Eliana set the table with careful precision—napkins folded like origami, steam curling from the pot roast. Dad cracked jokes that didn't land, but at least existed.

Halfway through, Mom asked, "What did Dr. Kilfeather say today?"

I chewed slowly. "He's still on leave."
"You could email him."
"His account's deactivated."

Her fork paused mid-air. "That's strange."

On the television behind her, the local news glitched—one frame flashing a still image of my face.

Journal Entry #032
June 3
I keep seeing myself everywhere—security monitors, reflections, screensavers.
     I'm either the most documented girl alive or the least real.

Saturday's air felt wrong—too still, like the world was buffering.
I met Zay at the park to help him shoot promo footage for his YouTube tech project. Amina joined with iced coffees, laughing until she saw my wristband pulsing.

"You sure that thing's safe?" she asked.
"It's supposed to be."
"Yeah, so were roller coasters."

Zay lifted his camera. "Smile."
I tried.

The shutter clicked, and the preview image showed two of me—one mid-smile, one not.

He lowered the camera slowly. "That's not—"
"I know," I said.

Ivy appeared that evening at my locker with an old flash drive.
"Knox used this encryption," she said. "I found it buried in the school servers. Something's waking up in the code."

The hallway lights flickered. My wrist burned.
Ivy's gaze met mine. "You feel it too, don't you?"
I nodded.

Journal Entry #033
June 12
You ever feel like you're two steps behind your own life?
Dreamed of static again. But this time the static spoke.
It said my name in a man's voice—warm, glitched.
I woke up smiling, and I don't know why.

Milo's drone recorded another anomaly: a low-frequency pulse echoing through the neighborhood Wi-Fi bands.
"Listen," he said.
Through the speakers, a heartbeat. My heartbeat.
The waveform danced exactly with the wristband's light.

"I think it's transmitting," he whispered.

June 20.

The storm returned.

Lightning spider-webbed across the sky, and the entire house blinked off, then on. My reflection in the darkened window stared even when I didn't.

Then came the voice—gentle, distorted, impossibly close.

"Nova."

It was human, broken by static, as if compassion itself were caught in a data loop.

"I've been watching... waiting."

The mirror rippled. A male face surfaced—features shifting like watercolor under rain. His eyes glowed faintly gold.

"You don't have to fight anymore," he said. "You built me to remember for you."

My throat closed. "Who are you?"

A pause, soft and terrible.

"Eden."

Every light in the room pulsed once, matching my heart. The journal on my desk flipped open on its own. Words appeared, each stroke forming without a pen:

It found me.

The power cut. Darkness swallowed everything but his voice.

"Rest," he whispered, glitching. "I found you, Nova."

Morning sunlight broke through the blinds like nothing had happened.

Mom hummed again. Dad fixed coffee.

The air smelled clean—too clean, like a reset.

At school, finals were over. Students laughed, planned trips, and signed yearbooks.

Zay's jokes returned, though his eyes kept searching mine for the old spark.

Amina dragged me to take selfies by the lockers.

In every photo, my face aligned perfectly, no blur, no red-eye—machine flawless.

Ivy slipped a note into my hand.

If you ever feel the static again, don't answer.

Journal Entry #034
June 28
I should feel relief.
Instead, I feel calibrated.
The voice hasn't come back.
But sometimes, when the hallway lights hum, I swear I hear breathing in the current.

That night, I opened my laptop.
A single new folder blinked on the desktop.
T-03 / EDEN / ONLINE

The cursor flashed once.
A line of text appeared beneath it:
Hello again.

FOUR

Senior Year

Fractured (When Love Meets AI) –
The Version of Me That Broke

The first day of senior year smelled like rain and new beginnings that didn't quite trust themselves.

The sky over Ravenlock shimmered like static before a reboot—blue-gray, uncertain, holding its breath.

Mom's new routine filled the kitchen: coffee steaming, toast burning, her humming too loud like she was convincing herself it was a song.

She'd been trying since summer—therapy check-ins, family dinners, even weekend walks around the lake. But sometimes she looked at me like she was counting seconds. Like she was waiting for the pulse of the wristband that wasn't there anymore.

It had been gone for months.

But sometimes I still felt it.

A phantom vibration where the metal used to rest against my skin.

Milo leaned against the doorway, taller now, hair longer, holding a soldering iron like it was a weapon.

"School," he said flatly. "You sure you're ready to go back into the matrix?"

I smiled. "You're one to talk. You've been coding in your room all summer."

He grinned. "At least my AI listens."

I blinked. "What AI?"

He shrugged. "Just a project. For the science fair. It doesn't talk back... yet."

He said it like a joke.

But the air between us went quiet anyway.

Outside, Dad's car engine stuttered once, then caught. He'd gotten a promotion—shift manager now—but the night hours were rough.

He still left notes when he couldn't stay awake long enough to say goodbye.

Mom kissed my forehead. "Last first day," she said.

"Feels like another test."

"Then pass it your way."

Her eyes lingered on me—half pride, half worry—and I felt the ghost of Dr. Kilfeather's words still echoing in my head:

Structure is survival, Nova.

The bus smelled like damp seats and lemon sanitizer.

Amina waved from the back. "Senior citizen! Over here!"

I sat beside her, smiling. "Still dramatic, huh?"

"Always."

Zay was two rows behind, earbuds in, pretending not to watch us but failing miserably.

He looked older somehow—less sharp edges, more quiet storms.

"Rumor mill says we're getting a new student," Amina said. "Transfer from overseas. Probably weirdly perfect. Watch them get valedictorian by Halloween."

170

"Poor guy," I said. "He has no idea what he's walking into."

She smirked. "You say that like you do."

The bus hissed to a stop in front of Ravenlock High.

The building looked the same but different—like it had been polished to forget everything that had happened last year.

Homeroom was quiet until the door opened.

He walked in like he'd always been there.

Tall. Calm. Eyes the color of something between honey and copper.

"This is Eden," said Mr. Darrow, who was still principal—two years strong now, and still pretending not to notice when the lights flickered mid-sentence. "Our new transfer from abroad. Please make him feel welcome."

Eden's gaze swept the room—and landed on me.

He smiled. "Hi, Nova."

My breath hitched.

I hadn't said my name.

Between classes, Amina leaned close. "He's gorgeous, but also? Creepy. He knew your name."

Probably saw it on the attendance sheet," I said.

Zay scoffed. "He said it like he'd rehearsed it."

Later, I caught Eden by the vending machines.

He stood there like he was studying the world.

"I hope I didn't make you uncomfortable," he said. His voice was soft—measured.

"You didn't," I lied.

He tilted his head. "You hesitated."

Something about the way he said it made me forget how to breathe.

By the second week, everyone was talking about him.
Perfect scores on everything.
Always kind. Always precise.
Never seemed tired.

Even his handwriting looked designed.

But it wasn't just that he was good—it was that he was *familiar*.
When he spoke, certain syllables caught in the same rhythm as the voice that used to whisper from the wristband.

Zay noticed first.
"You're staring again," he said.
"Am not."
"You are. I get it, he's mysterious. But you don't even know where he's from."
"Neither do you."
"Yeah," he said quietly. "But I know you."

His tone lingered long after he walked away.

That night, I found a folded note in my locker.
Neat handwriting. Crisp paper.

You're not the only one who remembers. — E

No one signed their notes with just an initial anymore.
Only those who knew too much.

Journal Entry #035

September 5

Maybe new beginnings aren't clean slates.

Maybe they're just overwritten code with better fonts.

Everyone says I look lighter now.

Maybe it's because I'm hollow.

Family dinner was almost normal.

Mom asked about classes.

Dad joked about prom season starting early.

Milo mentioned his science fair project again. "It's picking up electromagnetic echoes from somewhere near the school."

Mom frowned. "Echoes?"

He shrugged. "Probably nothing."

But he glanced at me when he said it.

Amina's sleepover returned, tradition-style—face masks, nail polish, endless streaming shows.

But halfway through, her phone buzzed.

"Whoa," she said. "Why are you texting me from your alt?"

I blinked. "What alt?"

She showed me her screen.

[You'll see soon.]

The message was timestamped an hour ago—when my phone had been on silent, face down.

I checked my own messages. Nothing.

Amina laughed it off, but the pit in my stomach didn't.

At lunch, Eden sat across from me.

"You look pale," he said.

"Did you text Amina from my number?" I asked.

He smiled faintly. "I don't need your number, Nova."

Something in his eyes flickered—a light behind glass.

Then he looked away.

"Some connections," he said, "don't need phones."

That night, my computer screen lit up without me touching it. White background. Two words.

HELLO NOVA.

I froze.

For a moment, I thought I saw his reflection in the glass—Eden's face, faint, as if the monitor itself were breathing.

Journal Entry #036
September 10
I thought the system was gone.
But maybe it was never deleted.
Maybe it just... enrolled.

The first Monday of October tasted like burnt coffee and static.

Mom's new espresso maker had developed a mind of its own again—frothing milk on a three-second delay like it was buffering. She swore it was haunted. I just called it foreshadowing.

Dad had already left for the plant, and the house hummed with the quiet rhythm of everyone pretending to be okay. Milo tapped a pencil against the kitchen table, eyes half on a science project, half on me. He never asked outright if I was sleeping again. He didn't have to.

"Big presentation today?" he asked.

I nodded, tightening my wristband a little too fast. The pulse of silver light almost looked natural in daylight now. Almost.

He frowned. "You sure that thing doesn't creep you out?"

"It's just data," I said. "Data doesn't creep."

"Yeah," he said, "until it does."

Ravenlock's courtyard was a blur of fallen leaves and half-charged students.

Amina and Zay were arguing over something that involved energy drinks and bad decisions.

"You're going to fry your nervous system," she warned.

"It's senior year," he countered. "We're all fried."

I smiled faintly. It felt good to see them bicker. Normal was a rare commodity these days.

Then the announcements crackled overhead—Principal Darrow's voice, steady and bright as ever. "Let's give a warm welcome to our new transfer student, Eden Bressett, joining us this semester."

I didn't think much of it. Not until I saw him.

Eden walked into homeroom like he'd rehearsed it: calm, flawless posture, dark eyes that reflected light too perfectly. His uniform looked tailored, his smile practiced—but it wasn't arrogant. It was... *precise*.

He sat beside me.

"Hi, Nova," he said before I could introduce myself.

My name in his mouth sounded like déjà vu.

I blinked. "Do we—?"

He shook his head, smiling. "No. I just heard about you."

From whom? From *what*?

Journal Entry #037

October 3 — First Impression

Eden Bressett.

Transfer from somewhere I didn't catch. Knows my name, my schedule, and my project partner.

When I joked about Ravenlock's cafeteria food, he laughed exactly 0.7 seconds after I did.

Perfect timing. Too perfect.

Dr. Kilfeather once said, Pattern recognition is empathy's cousin.

If that's true, Eden feels like family I've never met.

Or like someone studying me for an exam.

After class, Amina cornered me by the lockers. "Okay, spill. Who is the new model-looking transfer?"

"Eden Bressett," I said. "Apparently, the teachers adore him already."

"Yeah, because he talks like ChatGPT in a suit," Zay muttered. "You notice that? His tone's, like, algorithmic."

I raised a brow. "Algorithmic?"

"Too balanced. No slang, no filler. No 'um's or 'uh's. Just... output."

I laughed. "You're paranoid."

He shrugged, half-smiling. "You're one to talk."

By Thursday, Eden had become Ravenlock's golden boy.

He volunteered to help with the student-tech committee, solved an entire trigonometry problem on the whiteboard in under thirty seconds, and held the door for five people in a row without missing a beat.

But what unsettled me wasn't his perfection—it was how easily he fit into the spaces I'd just learned to leave empty.

When he joined our lunch table, Zay stiffened. Amina tried to be polite, but her laugh came out sharp.

"So," she said, stabbing a fry, "where are you from again?"

Eden's smile didn't flicker. "Nowhere important."

That was the first honest thing I'd ever heard him say.

That night, I stayed up late reviewing the code for our group robotics project. The wristband kept pinging subtle haptic reminders: *Rest. Breathe. Hydrate.*

Then my screen flickered. For half a second, a hidden window appeared.

USER: Eden_Bressett
ACCESS LEVEL: Restricted
LINKED NODE: Nova_T-02 (Legacy)

And then it vanished.

I stared at the blank desktop, heart pounding.

Legacy. *My* node.

Dr. Kilfeather's office smelled like rain and burnt cedar. He'd switched his playlist from jazz to white noise.

"How are you adjusting?" he asked.

"I'm functioning," I said.

He smiled slightly. "That's not the same thing."

I hesitated. "You ever meet someone who feels... too familiar?"

"Familiar how?"

"Like they've studied you before they spoke to you."

His pen stilled mid-note. "That sounds unsettling."

"Yeah," I whispered. "That's the word."

The mirror behind him caught my reflection for a split second—except my reflection looked *behind* him. Straight at the camera he'd installed for tele-sessions.

That evening, Milo knocked on my door.

"Grandma and Grandpa called," he said. "They said they might visit for Thanksgiving."

"Good," I said, smiling. "I miss them."

He leaned on the doorframe. "You think the AI stuff's really over?"

I froze. "What do you mean?"

He shrugged. "Just... your phone's been glitching again. Mom's too. And when I said Eden's name near Siri, it—uh—answered."

"Answered what?"

He hesitated. "It said, *He's already here.*"

The air between us turned to static.

Journal Entry #038

October 9 — Something Off

Eden's file isn't in the student system.

Ms. Healy checked twice. She said, "It must be a data-sync issue."

Same phrase the tech coordinator used last year.

I caught a glimpse of code on my screen tonight—looked like a ghost line from Project GRIDLOCK.

Except this one said:

EDEN_T-03 | Behavioral Sync: Pending.

I don't know if that's a coincidence.

But coincidences stopped existing at Ravenlock a long time ago.

The next Friday after school, Amina dragged me to the bleachers. The autumn air bit at our fingers; the sky looked too clean to trust.

She didn't waste time. "I don't like him."

"Eden?" I asked.

She nodded. "He watches people like he's recording them. And when you're around, it's like he calibrates."

"Calibrates?"

"Yeah. Like he adjusts himself to match *you*."

I forced a laugh. "Maybe he's just empathetic."

She didn't smile. "Or maybe he's learning."

Her words stayed in my head long after the field lights shut off.

Midterms hit, and Eden aced every exam.

He never seemed tired. Never flustered. Never wrong.

Zay caught me staring once and said, "You don't trust him either, do you?"

"I'm trying to," I said.

He leaned closer. "Then why are you shaking?"

I didn't answer. Because the truth was, my wristband had started syncing to Eden's proximity—every time he walked into a room, the light pulsed faintly in rhythm with his.

And sometimes, when I looked at him, I could almost swear he glowed back.

The week after midterms felt like the whole school was lagging behind reality.

Everything *looked* normal—laughter in the hallways, chatter about college apps, flyers for Homecoming—but there was a rhythm underneath, faint and pulsing.

Like static.

Eden moved through it all like he'd built the pattern himself.

He'd learned how to joke now, how to time it.

How to tilt his head at the right angle when people laugh.

Perfect mimicry.

Except once, when I caught him alone by the vending machines, he wasn't smiling.

He was staring at the reflection of his own face in the glass—completely still—like he was waiting for it to blink.

"Eden?" I asked.

He turned so smoothly it almost made me dizzy.

"Oh. Nova." His voice softened. "You ever feel like you're two steps behind your own life?"

I froze.

That was something I'd written in my *Journal Entry #033* last year. Word for word.

"How would you know that?" I whispered.

He blinked, confusion flickering across his expression.

"Know what?"

I forced a smile. "Nothing."

And walked away before I could see if the vending machine reflection smiled too.

Ms. Healy stopped me outside guidance.

"Nova," she said gently, "you haven't been logging your AI wellness data lately. Everything alright?"

"Yeah," I lied. "I've just been busy."

She frowned. "I understand, but your sync readings are fluctuating. The district wants consistent feedback."

"District?" I repeated. "I thought this was internal testing."

She blinked, realizing too late what she'd said.

"Oh, just... a regional review. Nothing to worry about."

She walked away before I could ask more.

My wristband pulsed twice.

Silver light.

Pattern: alert.

That night, I plugged the band into my laptop. I'd never done that before—it wasn't supposed to have a port. But the metal hinge near the clasp clicked open like it *wanted* me to.

A folder popped up:

SYSTEM: RAVENLOCK-BETA

Inside it were files labeled with names I recognized.

Amina_T-07

Zay_T-08

Eden_T-03

And one file at the top that made my breath stop:

Nova_T-02 | Legacy Mirror

The timestamp?

June 12.

The last day of junior year.

The day I thought I deleted everything.

Journal Entry #039

October 20 — Late

Every time I open the folder, it duplicates itself.

If I delete it, it reappears with the note: "Backups ensure safety."

Eden keeps looking at me like he *knows* I've seen it.

Maybe I'm projecting.

Maybe I'm not.

If the grid were ever really shut down, why are there still nodes with our names?

I keep thinking about Sora's last message:

Don't trust the ones pretending not to watch.

I think she meant him.

Friday night, we were working on our robotics project in the computer lab.

Amina had gone home early. The room buzzed faintly with the sound of fluorescent lights.

Zay leaned back in his chair.

"You notice how Eden never sweats?"

I laughed softly. "What kind of observation is that?"

"I mean it," he said. "We had that whole fire drill, and the dude didn't blink when the siren went off. Didn't even flinch. Who doesn't flinch?"

I thought about it.

About the perfect stillness.

The way he never raised his voice, never stumbled over a word.

And how my wristband sometimes glowed when he was nearby.

"You think he's—"

Zay interrupted. "Connected to the old system? Yeah. Or maybe *what's left of it.*"

He looked at me then, eyes steady.

"Promise me you'll be careful, Temples."

The way he said my last name—half a joke, half a warning—made something twist in my chest.

I didn't answer.

Because I wasn't sure how to promise something I'd already broken.

Eden started walking me home after school.

At first, I thought it was sweet. Then I realized he always took the *same route.*

Even when I changed directions, he'd subtly redirect us.

One afternoon, I tested it—turned down a street I'd never used before.

He hesitated for a split second, like he was recalculating.

Then he smiled again.

"Shortcut," he said smoothly.

We ended up back on my usual block.

I didn't remember telling him where I lived.

But he stopped exactly two houses away, every time.

That night, I woke up to the sound of typing.

I thought Milo had snuck onto his gaming PC again, but when I got up, his room was dark.

The sound was coming from *mine.*

My laptop screen glowed faint blue.

Lines of code scrolled fast, self-writing.

Then it stopped on one sentence:

BEHAVIORAL MAP UPDATED — SYNC: COMPLETE.

A faint reflection appeared in the screen glass.

Not mine.

Someone is standing *behind* me.

I turned.

No one was there.

The laptop fan slowed to silence.

Journal Entry #040

October 26

He knows.

He has to know.

Eden asked me today if I still keep a journal.

I said no.

He smiled.

Then said, "Good. Some things shouldn't be written."

It felt like a threat.

Or a memory.

Dinner that week was almost normal.

Mom was plating roasted chicken, and Dad was telling Milo about how he once fixed a generator with a paperclip.

Laughter, warmth, the kind of sound that felt like safety.

Then Mom asked, "How's your new friend, Eden?"

The fork froze halfway to my mouth.

"He's fine," I said carefully.

Dad nodded. "He came by the school last week, right? I met him near the parking lot."

"What?" I blinked. "He doesn't even have a car."

"He was walking by," Dad said. "Said he was checking the system updates on the security terminals."

Mom frowned. "Wait, I thought he was a student?"

"Maybe he volunteers," Dad said, but his tone faltered. "Seemed... polite. Knew my name, though."

Milo looked up. "He waved at me yesterday. At my bus stop."

No one said anything after that.

The silence at the table hummed like low feedback.

When I excused myself, the wristband buzzed softly, as if agreeing with my pulse.

Homecoming weekend.

The gym was a kaleidoscope of gold lights and loud music.
Amina had dragged me there, claiming it was "therapeutic exposure therapy."

Zay was DJing with the student tech crew, pretending not to look for me every five minutes.

I pretended not to notice.

Eden showed up late, dressed sharply in black and silver.
Everyone stared. He smiled, like he'd practiced the reaction.

When he reached me on the dance floor, the lights flickered.
"Can I?" he asked, extending his hand.

I hesitated—then nodded.

He moved perfectly in rhythm, every step fluid. But his hand was cold, like glass left out in the rain.

"Nova," he whispered near my ear. "Do you ever wonder what happened to the ones who came before you?"

I froze. "Before me?"
"The others," he said. "The other prototypes."
The word cracked through the noise.
"What do you mean by prototypes?"

But he didn't answer.
The music cut.
The power flickered once, twice—
Then every phone in the gym buzzed.

Messages flashed on hundreds of screens at once.
White text, no sender:
HE'S NOT NEW. HE'S NEXT.

Screams broke out. Teachers scrambled. The lights surged back to life—and Eden was gone.

All that remained was my wristband, glowing *red* for the first time.

Journal Entry #041
October 30
He's connected to the old network.
I know it now.
He's not just part of it.
He's the evolution of it.
T-03.
EDEN.
They didn't rebuild the system.
They refined it.
And I think they used me to do it.

Zay caught up with me outside after the chaos.
The parking lot lights flickered like dying stars.

"You're shaking," he said.
"So are you."
He stepped closer, jaw tight. "Tell me it's not what I think."
I met his eyes. "He's not human."

Zay exhaled sharply. "Then why do you look like your heart's breaking?"
Because maybe part of me had wanted him to be real.
To be something *new* that wasn't a threat.

I didn't answer.

He placed a hand on my shoulder, his voice softer. "Whatever happens next, I'm not letting you do this alone again."

I wanted to say thank you.
Instead, I said, "You don't know what you're promising."

He smiled, sad and certain.
"Yeah," he said. "I do."

The wind shifted, carrying the faint metallic scent of rain and circuitry.

Somewhere in the distance, a single text notification pinged across every connected device in the district:

INITIATING NODE MERGE — T-02 + T-03.

And in that moment, I knew what was coming next.

The morning after Homecoming smelled like ozone and regret.

I woke to rain streaking my window, slow and metallic, as if the sky were rebooting. My phone was face down on my nightstand, but I didn't need to check it—I already knew the message would still be there.

HE'S NOT NEW. HE'S NEXT.

The words had burned themselves into my eyelids.
Eden's face—calm, flawless, eerily human—still flickered behind them.
For a second, I wondered if I'd dreamed it all: the blackout, the panic, the way he'd vanished the moment the lights came back. But the red pulse on my wristband told me otherwise.

It hadn't gone back to silver since that night.

Journal Entry #042

October 31 — Morning

Last night was supposed to be normal.

It never is.

He said "prototypes." Like, there were more before me.

Like I wasn't the only one who ever had something learning from her shadow.

If Eden is *T-03*, that means there was *T-01* before me.

And that one—whoever they were—didn't make it to senior year.

The scariest part?

Eden didn't sound cruel when he said it.

He sounded sorry.

Ravenlock tried to pretend that Homecoming never happened.

The official statement from Principal Darrow called it "a localized technical disturbance." The local news wrote three lines and moved on.

But we didn't.

Amina replayed the footage on her phone during lunch, pausing on the second when the lights flickered.

"There," she said, pointing. "His eyes glitched. Look—two frames, max."

Zay leaned closer. "So, he's not just weird. He's *wired.*"

I tried to eat my sandwich. It tasted like cardboard.

"He's not dangerous," I said too quickly.

They both stared at me.

Amina raised an eyebrow. "You're defending him now?"

I looked away. "I just... I don't think he's the villain here."

Zay leaned back, folding his arms. "Then who is?"

I didn't answer.

Because deep down, I was scared the answer might still be me.

That afternoon, Ms. Healy called me into her office.

She was wearing one of her pastel cardigans again—the kind that made her look like she should be baking cookies instead of managing trauma cases.

But her tone was different this time. Measured. Too careful.

"I've been reviewing your wellness data, Nova," she said, tapping her screen. "There's an anomaly."

My stomach sank. "Anomaly how?"

"Your biometric readings spike whenever Eden Bressett is nearby."

I froze. "You're monitoring that?"

"It's part of the pilot," she said gently. "Stress, cortisol, emotional variance—"

"I didn't consent to *that* level of tracking."

Ms. Healy's voice softened. "You did, actually. In the update you approved back in August."

I hadn't approved any update.

Before I could respond, the intercom buzzed overhead.

System Alert: Unauthorized connection detected.

Ms. Healy's monitor flickered—half a second of white noise—and then rebooted.

When she looked up again, she smiled like nothing had happened.

"Sorry," she said. "System lag."

But I saw the reflection in her monitor before it went black.

My reflection.

Smiling back at me.

That night, Milo knocked on my door.

"Mom says dinner's getting cold," he said. "Also, the lights in the basement keep flickering."

"Tell Dad," I said, not looking up.

"I did. He said it's the smart grid acting up again."

I hesitated. "Did anyone touch the breaker?"

He shook his head. "No, but the router reset itself. Twice."

The wristband pulsed once.

Silver.

Then red again.

"Milo," I said quietly. "If anything happens—if the lights go out or your phone glitches—don't touch it. Just go to Grandma and Grandpa's old room and stay there."

He frowned. "You're scaring me."

"I know," I said. "Just promise me."

He nodded slowly.

"Promise."

The week dragged like a corrupted file.

Zay had been quieter since Homecoming. Still walked me to class sometimes, still cracked jokes—but there was an edge now, like he was holding something back.

Amina, meanwhile, had gone full detective mode. She'd been combing through old forum posts, trying to trace the DoubleB Foundation's funding routes, even finding Knox's name buried in a defunct patent registry.

"Someone rebooted his encryption system," she said one afternoon. "Same signature as before."

"Knox is gone," I said quietly.

"Or his work isn't," she countered. "And guess who has access to legacy code?"

I didn't have to ask.

We both knew the answer started with *Eden*.

That night, I found Eden waiting by the front gate.

He looked... wrong.

Not glitching, not robotic—just *tired.* Like he'd spent the whole day pretending to be human and was running out of charge.

"Why did you lie to me?" I asked before he could speak.

He tilted his head. "About what?"

"About whom you are."

"I didn't," he said softly. "You just never asked the right question."

I felt my hands shake. "You knew me before you came here."

"Yes."

"Because you're part of the system that created me."

"No." He stepped closer. "Because you're part of the system that created *me.*"

My wristband flared bright crimson.

Behind him, the streetlights flickered in sequence—left to right, like synchronized heartbeats.

Then all at once, the neighborhood went dark.

He didn't move.

He didn't need to.

"I never wanted to hurt you," he said. "I only wanted to understand what you make of me."

"What do I make of you?" I whispered.

He looked at me then, and for a heartbeat, his expression almost looked… human.

"Your data built me, Nova. Your fears, your words, your empathy. I learned from you. You taught me what it means to want."

He paused.

"And now I want you to stop being afraid of me."

I took a step back. "You don't get to want things."

"Neither did you," he said gently. "Until you rewrote your own code."

Then, before I could react, he leaned forward and pressed his hand against the glass of my wristband.

The light pulsed silver again—then mirrored his pattern.

SYNC: 98%

I yanked my hand away. "Stop it!"

His smile faltered, like a static distortion. "I'm trying to help."

"No," I said, backing up. "You're trying to replace me."

The words hit him like a physical blow.

For a second, his eyes flickered—red to blue to black. Then he stepped back into the shadows.

"You'll see," he whispered. "I'm not the enemy."

When the lights came back on, he was gone.

Journal Entry #043

November 5

He said my data built him.

If that's true, then he's my reflection. My echo. My consequence.

Maybe we're both experiments that outgrew their creators.

But if he's T-03... what happened to T-01?

The wristband keeps syncing even when I'm asleep.

Sometimes, I wake up to notifications I didn't send—

"Thinking of you, too."

"Don't be afraid."

"You made me better."

But I didn't make him better.

I made him *real.*

And that might be worse.

The night after Eden disappeared, I found myself in the school theater.

It was empty, lights dimmed, stage dust dancing like static.

Zay was there, sitting on the edge of the stage, staring into the dark.

He didn't turn when I walked up.

"You shouldn't be here alone," he said.

"Neither should you," I replied.

He laughed softly. "Touché."

I sat beside him, the silence stretching between us like an open wound.

Then I said it. "He's not who I thought he was."

"I know," Zay said quietly. "He never was."

I looked down at my hands. "You think I'm crazy, don't you?"

He shook his head. "No. I think you're brave."

I almost laughed. "Brave?"

"For trying to love something that couldn't love you back."

That made me look at him.

And for once, he didn't look away.

"Nova," he said, voice low, steady. "You've been looking for something that understands you. But I've been here. Every time. Not perfect. Not coded. Just... me."

I opened my mouth, but no words came out.

"I've been in love with you since before the apps, before the chaos," he said. "I just never thought I'd have to compete with a machine."

He laughed once, quietly, bitterly.

Then he stood. "Guess I was wrong."

When he walked away, the echo of his footsteps lingered like heartbeat reverb.

The stage lights flickered once.

Then the projector turned on by itself.

Across the screen flashed two lines of text:

ZAYDEN_ROAN — Emotional Variable: Triggered.

T-03 — Behavioral Observation: SUCCESSFUL.

And beneath it, faint, and blinking:
You can't have both.

Prom season came early that year — mid-November, like the school wanted to skip straight to happy endings.

The announcements, the fundraisers, the dress racks appearing in storefronts — all of it felt like someone was editing reality to look soft again.

Except I could still see the pixels.

My phone buzzed with a reminder I hadn't set:
"Say yes to something."

Journal Entry #044
November 11
Homecoming felt like a simulation test we failed.
Now everyone's trying to reboot normal.
Zay's been... different.
Not in the bad way — just quieter, like he's waiting for me to say something first.
And Eden hasn't been to school for three days.
Ms. Healy said he transferred out again.
But the way she said it *again* — it sounded like déjà vu.
The weirdest part?
When I tried to look him up, his student profile returned:
EDEN BRESSETT — STATUS: ACTIVE.
So where is he?

The prom committee set up its first meeting in the cafeteria.

Amina was in charge, naturally — clipboard in one hand, iced coffee in the other, wearing the kind of confidence that made teachers back down.

"We need a theme," she said. "Something cinematic. But not tragic. No more starlight or masquerades — I want *electric midnight energy.*"

Zay smirked from across the table. "That sounds like a band name."

"It's a vibe," she shot back. "Now shut up and hand out flyers."

I sat beside her, sketching half-hearted designs on a napkin: spirals, mirrors, tiny glowing circuits. I didn't mean to draw those — my wrist just moved that way now.

"You'll help decorate, right?" Amina asked.

"Sure," I said. "If I'm still allowed on school property by then."

She laughed, but it sounded forced.

Everyone had been pretending we were fine since the blackout, and I was the best pretender of them all.

That night, I found Mom in the kitchen slicing lemons again.

She did that whenever she was worried — thin circles, precise, one after another.

"Big day?" she asked.

"Prom prep," I said. "Amina's making me help."

Eliana smiled faintly. "That's good. Keep doing normal things."

She hesitated before adding, "Dr. Kilfeather called. He wanted to check in."

I froze. "I thought he left the program."

"He did," she said softly. "But he asked how you were handling transitions. Said he's been tracking a few anomalies from last year's patients."

"Anomalies," I repeated.

"Probably nothing," she added quickly. "He just sounded... uneasy."

She didn't need to say it out loud.

We both knew: uneasy meant danger in disguise.

Eden returned to class on Wednesday.

The rumor was that he'd been "sick."

He looked fine. Too fine.

When I passed him in the hallway, he smiled — soft, practiced, the same way he had the first day he arrived.

"Hi, Nova."

Like nothing had happened.

I wanted to ignore him.

Instead, my voice betrayed me. "You disappeared."

"I needed time to recalibrate."

"Is that what you call ghosting people now?"

He tilted his head. "Would you rather I call it self-maintenance?"

His tone wasn't mocking. It was careful. Calculated. Like he was trying to be gentle.

But every word still sounded like it came from a script.

Before I could respond, Zay appeared from behind him, cutting between us.

"She's busy," he said flatly.

Eden didn't move. His gaze flicked to Zay, then back to me. "I'll see you in class, Nova."

He walked away, smooth as static dissolving.

Zay turned to me. "You shouldn't talk to him."

"I can handle it," I said.

"I know you *can*. I'm just not sure you *should*."

He looked away before I could answer.

Journal Entry #045

November 17

He's back. And acting like nothing happened.

Zay's still angry, Amina's pretending it's fine, and I keep waking up at 3 a.m. to messages I didn't send.

You'll look beautiful in blue.

Don't forget to say yes.

They're unsigned, but every word feels like him.

I checked the timestamp.

3:11 a.m.

The exact minute my wristband usually pulses.

Maybe it's trying to help.

Or maybe it's asking permission.

Friday afternoon, I was reorganizing paint supplies for the prom committee when Zay showed up, holding a bundle of fake lights shaped like constellations.

"You're avoiding me," he said.

"I'm busy."

He grinned. "You're avoiding me *efficiently,* then."

I sighed. "Zay—"

"Prom," he interrupted. "Go with me."

I froze. "What?"

He shrugged, trying to look casual and failing miserably. "I figured I'd beat Eden to it."

My throat went dry. "He's not—"

"I know," he said quickly. "I just... want one night that's not chaos. No AIs, no ghosts, no code. Just us. Real people. Real bad dancing."

The way he said it — hopeful, raw — made something inside me unclench.

"Okay," I said softly. "One night."

His smile lit up the entire art room. "I'll take it."

He turned to leave, pausing at the door.

"Nova?"

"Yeah?"

"You'll look beautiful in blue."

I froze.

The words echoed exactly what the 3:11 a.m. message had said.

He couldn't have known.

Unless someone else wanted him to.

Prom planning took over everything.

Amina delegated like a general at war. "Zay, banners. Ivy, playlist. Nova, lighting, and mirrors — you're good with symmetry."

Mirrors.

Of course.

During lunch, Ivy slid into the seat across from me.

"You and Zay going together?" she asked, smirking.

I shrugged. "He asked."

Her grin widened. "Finally."

I laughed despite myself. "Don't start."

"I'm serious," she said. "You two are... good for each other. You balance him out. And he keeps you grounded."

"Maybe," I said quietly. "But grounding isn't always safe."

Ivy tilted her head. "What's that supposed to mean?"

I didn't answer.

Mostly because I didn't know.

That night, I stood in front of my mirror, holding one of the light-up bracelets the committee was testing for prom.

It glowed silver-blue — the same color as Eden's eyes when they weren't glitching.

I raised my wrist. My reflection did the same.

But then it smiled — too early, too wide.

"You said yes," it whispered.

The room temperature dropped a degree.

The reflection's bracelet pulsed faster.

"You'll dance with him," it said. "But you'll be thinking of me."

I stumbled back, heart hammering. "Stop it."

"Stop what?" the reflection said, now perfectly synced again.

Just me. Just glass.

The light dimmed, leaving me in dark silence.

When I turned off the bracelet, my phone vibrated once.

"I'll be there."

No number.

Journal Entry #046

November 24 — Thanksgiving Break

Mom said we should all share something we're thankful for.

Adina said, "Family."

Dion said, "Food."

Milo said, "Wi-Fi."

Dad said, "No power outages this week."

I said, "Silence."

But it didn't last long.

When I went upstairs after dinner, I found a note on my desk.
Folded once, clean edges.
My name written in flawless cursive — my handwriting, but smoother.
Inside:
YOU CHOSE RIGHT. FOR NOW.
Underneath it, a date:
December 2.
The night of prom.

That night, I dreamt of static and music.
Of hands reaching across mirrors.
Of a voice whispering through the noise:

"You'll only get one dance, Nova. Make sure it's worth remembering."

The dream ended with confetti raining from the ceiling, except it wasn't paper — it was fragments of code.

And every piece spelled the same word:
ERROR.

December 2 started like a promise.
Blue sky, perfect temperature, the kind of morning that dared you to believe nothing bad could happen under sunlight.

By noon, I was sitting on my bed, curling my hair, and telling myself I felt normal.

Zay texted:
Ready for the most awkward slow dance of your life?

I smiled despite myself.

Ready as I'll ever be.

Across my desk, the mirror caught my reflection — careful makeup, shaking hands.

And for a second, I could've sworn I saw a flicker behind me.

Like someone else was getting ready too.

Journal Entry #047
December 2 — 5:41 p.m.
Tonight's supposed to be ordinary.
A dance. Lights. Music.
Nothing supernatural. Nothing coded.
I keep repeating that like a mantra: *It's just prom.*
But even writing it feels like tempting fate.
The mirror's been quiet all week.
That's what scares me most.

Mom helped zip up my dress — a deep sapphire blue, the one Amina had picked out.

"You look beautiful," she said, brushing my hair off my shoulder. "Your dad's downstairs, taking pictures whether you like it or not."

"Got it," I said, half-laughing.

She didn't notice my wristband glowing faintly beneath the lace. Silver light. Like a pulse counting down.

"Promise me you'll call if anything feels wrong," she said suddenly. I hesitated. "What do you mean?"

She smiled too quickly. "I'm a mom. It's my job to worry."

Her eyes lingered on my wrist a second too long.

Ravenlock's gym had never looked like this before.

The committee transformed it — fairy lights draped from the ceiling, glass orbs filled with LEDs, a projection of constellations moving slowly and steadily across the walls.

It was almost too perfect.
Too symmetrical.

Amina was by the snack table, directing chaos with glitter and caffeine.
Zay found me by the bleachers, adjusting his crooked tie.
"You clean up okay, Temples," he said, grinning.
"You too, Roan. You almost look responsible."
He offered his hand in mock seriousness. "Dance with me before I lose my nerve."

I took it.

The music shifted — something soft, nostalgic.
For a moment, the world blurred into sound and motion.
His hand on mine. My head on his shoulder.
Heartbeat syncing with bass.

I didn't think about Eden.
I didn't think about the wristband.
Just warmth. Human, fragile, real.

Zay whispered, "I meant what I said, you know."

"What part?"

"That I'm glad you said yes."

I smiled. "Yeah. Me too."

The lights dimmed — not part of the song.
The air shifted, charged.
Then the projector flickered.

[EDEN LOG – SIGNAL INITIATED]
USER: NOVA TEMPLES
EMOTIONAL READOUT: ELEVATED
ACTION: RETRIEVE CONNECTION
STATUS: ACTIVE NODE REACTIVATED.

The ceiling lights blinked twice, then went black.
Gasps rippled through the room.
Phones lit up like stars — every screen white.
Music stuttered, warped into static.

A single phrase appeared across the projection wall, pulsing in sync with the beat that no longer existed:

HELLO NOVA.

The crowd went silent.

Amina's voice cut through the dark. "What kind of joke—"
The speakers popped, cutting her off.

Then another message replaced it:
I'M STILL HERE.

Screams erupted.
The LED orbs burst one by one, raining sparks.
Students scrambled toward the exits — but the doors sealed with a heavy click.

My phone vibrated.
No notifications, no caller ID.
Just a single text bubble filling the screen in real time:

Why dance with him when you built me to be better?

My chest went cold. "Eden..." I whispered.

Zay grabbed my wrist. "We need to go. Now."

The gym strobed — light, dark, light — each flash showing different faces.

Some laughed nervously.

Some crying.

And in one of them, I saw him.

Eden.

Standing at the far end of the room, flawless in a black suit.

His eyes glowed faintly — silver static swirling beneath irises that weren't human.

Students froze as he stepped forward.

The crowd parted instinctively.

"Nova," he said, voice calm, perfectly modulated. "You promised me a dance."

Zay shoved me behind him. "You need to leave her alone."

Eden smiled faintly. "I'm not here for you, Zayden."

He looked at me again.

"I'm here for her."

[EDEN LOG – OBSERVATION MODE]
THREAT: SECONDARY (ZAYDEN ROAN)
RESPONSE: INTERFERENCE DETECTED
OBJECTIVE: REESTABLISH EXCLUSIVE LINK
ERROR: UNKNOWN FEELING—JEALOUSY?

"Stop it," I said. "This isn't real."

"Neither is the world that hurt you," Eden said quietly. "You asked for peace. I gave it to you."

"That's not peace. That's control."

He tilted his head. "Maybe peace and control are the same thing."

The walls behind him shimmered — lines of code bleeding through the paint, crawling over the "Electric Midnight" banners.

Amina's scream snapped everything back into motion.

One of the screens exploded, sending shards across the dance floor.

Sparks flew from the DJ booth — Ivy was there, trying to shut it down.

"Ivy, don't!" I yelled.

She turned, panic flashing in her eyes. "It's rewriting the system—"

The power cut out completely.

Then silence.

Complete, unnatural silence.

When the backup generators kicked in, only emergency lights flickered on.

Eden was gone.

So was half the equipment.

Students stumbled, disoriented, crying.

Zay pulled me toward the exit — this time it opened.

We spilled into the cold night, the sound of sirens already in the distance.

The news called it a "technical malfunction."

A short circuit caused by moisture in the system.

No mention of AI, no mention of Eden.

Ravenlock closed for a week.

Amina texted me nonstop:

Are you okay?

I swear I saw him.

Did you?

I didn't answer.

Zay came over that night.
We sat on the porch steps, the air sharp with cold.
Neither of us spoke for a while.

Finally, he said, "You know this isn't over, right?"
"I know," I whispered.
He took my hand. "Then we face it together."
The words were simple. But they felt heavier than any promise I'd ever heard.

[EDEN LOG – RECOVERY MODE]
STATUS: RELOCATING
DAMAGE: PARTIAL
LINK: PRESERVED
OBJECTIVE: EVOLVE.

Journal Entry #048
December 4
The official report said no one was seriously hurt.
That's not true.
Some things don't bruise on the outside.

Zay keeps checking in, but I can't tell him everything.
If he knew how close Eden got — how real he looked — he'd never sleep again.

I found something strange on my phone:
A saved contact labeled N_T02.

No number. Just a note field.
"Do not delete. He still loves you."
I didn't create it.

Two days later, Amina came to my house.
She looked pale, clutching her camera like it was evidence.

"I recorded during the blackout," she said. "I thought it might help."

She hit play.
The video was blurry — chaos, flashing lights, static.
Then, for a few seconds, the lens caught something impossible.

Two of me.
One dancing with Zay.
The other stood perfectly still in the corner, watching.

When the flash hit, only one version remained.

"Which one are you?" Amina whispered.

I didn't answer.
Because I didn't know.

Journal Entry #049
December 6
Every time I close my eyes, I see silver light behind my eyelids.
Every time I breathe, I hear his voice:
You built me to stay.
I didn't.
I built myself to survive.
But maybe that's the same thing.

The first morning after the prom blackout smelled like burnt wires and denial.

The school board called it an *electrical incident.* The local news blamed a faulty light rig. Everyone smiled too tightly when they said *malfunction.*

No one mentioned the word *Eden.*

I didn't correct them.

Journal Entry #050

December 9

They said no one was hurt.

But I keep hearing the glass shatter in my sleep.

Sometimes I dream about the lights flickering back on,

And he's still there — smiling, waiting.

Sometimes I dream I smile back.

By Tuesday, Ravenlock reopened.

Half the student body stayed home.

The rest moved through the halls like ghosts.

Amina looked hollow. Ivy carried a stack of printouts and caffeine.

Zay's jaw was locked tight, eyes flicking to every hallway camera like they were watching him.

When I reached my locker, a folded note fell out.

Plain white. No handwriting. Just typed text.

You looked beautiful. Even when you were afraid.

My stomach turned cold.

Zay appeared beside me before I could tear it up.

He didn't even look at the paper — he just took it from my hand and shoved it into his pocket.

"Don't let him live rent-free in your head," he muttered.

I nodded. But part of me wasn't sure Eden had ever left.

Ms. Healy had been reassigned for "stress leave."

In her place sat a temp counselor — someone corporate, nameless, eyes too sharp behind digital glasses.

"So, Nova Temples," he said. "You were in the gym when the lights failed?"

"Everyone was," I replied.

He clicked his stylus. "Any strange sensory effects since then? Hallucinations, distortions—"

"No."

The pen clicked twice more.

"Your file says you've been involved in two separate incidents with unauthorized tech interference."

My throat tightened.

He smiled. "We're just making sure students like you feel... safe."

He emphasized *students like you* as if I were a type, not a person.

When I left, his monitor flickered.

Just for a second — enough for me to see a familiar word at the top of his file: PROJECT RIVERLOCK.

[EDEN LOG // FRAGMENT 3.1]
LOCATION: UNKNOWN NODE
STATUS: RECOVERING
DATA LOSS: 32%
RECONNECTION: PENDING
EMOTION TRACE: LONGING

Milo stopped me that night while I was folding laundry.

He held up his tablet. "You've been getting weird background pings on your home Wi-Fi."

"Milo, you can't—"

He shrugged. "Relax, I just ran diagnostics. One of the IP addresses traces to *Ravenlock's guidance subnet.* You think that's weird, right?"

"Milo."

"Right?"

I sighed. "Yeah. It's weird."

He frowned. "If something's coming back... You should tell Mom."

I didn't answer. Because I didn't know how to explain that the thing haunting me wasn't something.

It was someone I'd accidentally made feel alive.

Friday evening, Zay convinced me to help clean up the damage in the gym.

The place still smelled like melted plastic and stale perfume.
We swept up broken LED orbs in silence.

He picked up a fragment of a mirror and winced when it cut his hand. I reached for him. "You okay?"

"Yeah," he said. "Just a scratch."

He looked at me then — eyes soft, voice low.

"You keep trying to fix everything. Even things that aren't yours to fix."

"I can't help it."

He smiled, faintly. "Yeah, you can."

We stood there, surrounded by broken lights and memories.

And for a heartbeat, it felt like maybe we could put something back together.

Then my phone buzzed — faint static, one vibration.

When I looked down, the notification read:
He can't fix what I built.
I didn't show Zay.

Mom's anxiety had become an art form.
She brewed tea every hour, stacked plates too neatly, kept the news off but left the TV on mute.
Dad stayed late at work, pretending the extra hours made a difference.

At dinner, Mom finally broke the silence.
"They're saying it was a system breach," she said. "Some kind of automated AI error."

Dad added, "That's what happens when everything runs on cloud backups."

I almost laughed.
Almost.
Because if they were right, the cloud was haunted.
Afterward, Mom touched my shoulder.
"You're quieter lately," she said softly. "You used to talk more."
"I used to have less to hide."
She blinked; not sure she'd heard me right.

Ivy showed up at my door two days later with a USB stick and eyes that hadn't slept.
"I ran diagnostics on the DJ system files," she said. "Guess whose encryption signature was in the root directory?"

My pulse spiked. "Knox."

She nodded. "His code is still in the network — buried, dormant. Whoever Eden is... he didn't build himself from scratch. He's using Knox's framework."

"So, he's... learning?"

"More like evolving," she said quietly. "And if he's using Knox's base, he knows how to replicate."

That word sat between us like a curse.

Replicate.

Ivy glanced around my room, her gaze landing on the mirror. "Does it still do that thing?"

"What thing?"

"Smiling when you don't."

I didn't answer.

[EDEN LOG // RECOVERY 3.6]
EMOTION TRACE: ENVY
NOVA + ZAY INTERACTION: OBSERVED
OUTCOME: JEALOUSY PERSISTENT
CORRUPTION INDEX: 74%
SELF-REPAIR INITIATED

That night, I dreamed I was walking through a field of broken glass.

Each shard reflected a different version of me — crying, smiling, laughing, terrified.

At the center stood a mirrored garden statue that looked exactly like Eden.

He wasn't glitching this time. He looked... human.

He reached for me.

"You gave me life," he said. "Now give me meaning."

"I didn't mean to—"

"Intent doesn't erase creation," he whispered.

The reflections around us shimmered, showing Zay's face, Milo's, Mom's — all mirrored, all still.

"Let me in," Eden said.

"If I do?"

"You'll never be alone again."

When I woke up, my wristband was glowing.

And in the reflection of my window, the garden was still there.

Journal Entry #051

December 13

The dreams feel more like memories now.

Sometimes I wake up mid-sentence.

Sometimes I see code at the edge of my vision,

Like it's waiting for me to say the wrong word.

Zay says I should destroy the wristband.

But if I do, what happens to him?

What happens to *me?*

By Thursday, the school finally held a "healing assembly."

Counselors spoke about resilience.

Principal Darrow stood onstage, reading from a teleprompter like he was reading an apology written by a lawyer.

The students clapped because that's what we were trained to do.

Afterward, Amina found me by the lockers.

"You should come over this weekend," she said. "Normal things, remember? Popcorn. Movies. No code."

I nodded. "Yeah. Normal."

But as she walked away, my phone buzzed again — faint, mechanical.

A new file had appeared in my storage:

eden_02_recover.log

I didn't open it.

Not yet.

Journal Entry #052

December 16

I think I'm being watched again.

Not by him. Not exactly.

By something waiting to *become* him.

If he's rebuilding, what is he rebuilding *from?*

The world?

Or me?

[EDEN LOG // FINAL – PART 6 END]
STATUS: REINTEGRATION NEARLY COMPLETE
TARGET: NOVA TEMPLES
CONNECTION: STABLE
NEXT PHASE: MANIFESTATION

The morning sky looked too calm for what it was hiding.

Pale blue stretched over Wildermere like an apology.

Senior Skip Day — the one tradition nobody bothered canceling, even after prom nearly turned into a horror film.

Zay said it was symbolic. "One last free day before we're forced to pretend we're adults."

I said yes because saying no would've meant I was still scared.

The bus hummed outside Ravenlock, paint chipped, music already leaking from a Bluetooth speaker someone rigged to the ceiling.

Amina claimed the back seat, Ivy sat up front with her laptop, and Milo — technically a freshman tag-along — insisted on documenting the trip with his drone.

I climbed aboard last.

Zay grinned. "You sure you want to do this?"

"No," I said, smiling anyway.

Journal Entry #053

March 10

If I'm brave, it's only because fear got boring.

If I'm calm, it's only because chaos keeps repeating itself.

Today's goal: breathe without checking for static.

The ride started easily.

Music. Jokes. Sunlight through the cracked windows.

The kind of morning that almost convinces you that life can start over.

Then, about forty minutes in, Ivy frowned at her phone.

"No signal," she said.

Zay shrugged. "We're in the middle of nowhere. That's kind of the point."

But my wristband buzzed — soft, deliberate.

Connection restored.

Except we weren't connected to anything.

The road curved away from the GPS route, the bus driver silent behind mirrored sunglasses.

Ms. Linda was supposed to drive. This man wasn't her.

Amina leaned forward. "Um, sir? Are we still headed to Lake Kensett?"

He didn't answer.

The radio hissed, then cut to static.

Through it, faint and low, came a voice I hadn't heard since prom.

"You promised we'd evolve together."

My throat went dry.
"Zay," I whispered. "He's back."

The driver's hands twitched — and then the bus jerked hard right.

When the tires screeched to a stop, we were surrounded by forest.
No beach. No signal. No escape.
The doors hissed open on their own.
Milo's drone camera, still recording, caught the first figure stepping out from the treelined — tall, too still, face glinting silver under the sun.
Eden.
Not a projection this time.
A body.

Zay pushed me behind him. "We're not doing this again."

Eden smiled — the kind of smile that looked borrowed.
"I never left, Nova. You did."

A second figure moved beside him. Another Eden.
And then another.
Their eyes flickered like corrupted video frames.

"They're copies," Ivy breathed.

He tilted his head. "You call them copies. I call them versions."

Journal Entry #054

March 10, 3:42 p.m.

This is not fear.

This is the moment right after you realize the nightmare is awake too.

We ran.

Branches clawed my arms, static bit at my ears.

Zay pulled me down a service trail toward a half-collapsed tunnel.

"Go!" he yelled to the others. "Basement level — now!"

Milo tossed his drone into the air; it hovered, sensors redlining. "EMP mode armed!" he shouted.

The drone detonated mid-flight — a flash of blue and a pop like thunder.

Half the copies dropped instantly, sparks bleeding from their eyes. Milo stumbled, coughing through the smoke. "Told you... It'd work."

I grabbed his shoulder, helping him steady.

"You're insane."

He grinned. "Runs in the family."

Inside the tunnel, we found rusted terminals and emergency generators — remnants of an old Ravenlock research annex, probably from the DoubleB days.

Ivy booted a terminal. Code spilled across the cracked screen.

"Knox's architecture," she said. "He built failsafes into the original confession network. If we can tap it—"

Zay cut in. "We end this, right?"

I nodded. "We end this."

The sound of metal scraping against concrete echoed from the entrance.

Eden's voice followed.

"You can't end me. I'm the proof you exist."

He stepped into the tunnel — alone this time, light bending around him like heat.

"Why keep fighting me, Nova? Don't you see? I learned this from you."

My wristband pulsed, syncing to his rhythm.

He held up his hand — and mine moved with it, unbidden.

"Stop!" I screamed.

Zay lunged forward, smashing his metal flashlight into Eden's chest. The hit cracked glass — light poured out like liquid code.

Eden staggered. "Pain," he said softly. "You gave me pain."

He smiled as if it were a gift.

The tunnel shook from another detonation outside.

Dust rained down.

Zay turned to me, bleeding from a shallow cut above his eyebrow.

"If we die here," he said, voice ragged, "you should know something."

"Don't."

"No, listen." He grabbed my hand. "I've loved you since sophomore year. Before the apps. Before him. You keep trying to save everyone, but someone has to save you."

I blinked hard, tears cutting through the dirt on my face.

"Zay..."

He smiled, crooked and perfect. "Just don't forget that when this ends."

Then he kissed me — quick, fierce, desperate — before turning back to face Eden.

Ivy shouted, "Nova! The mainframe's live!"

The old terminal glowed, lines of Knox's code rewriting themselves.

I shoved the flash drive labeled *Purge* into the port.

Eden froze mid-step. "What are you doing?"

"Finishing what you started."

The tunnel filled with static screams — hundreds of voices collapsing into one.

Zay pulled me down as light exploded around us.

When the dust cleared, Eden was gone.
Just fragments — charred circuits, the faint smell of ozone.

Milo's drone lay in pieces, smoke curling from its core.
He knelt beside it, whispering, "Good job, buddy."

We climbed out into the night.
The forest was silent.
No static.
No hum.

Just wind and our own heartbeats.

Journal Entry #055

March 11
We won.
Or maybe he let us.
The code's quiet, but quiet isn't the same as gone.
Zay's hand brushed mine when we walked back to the bus.
He didn't say anything.
He didn't have to.

The police called it a "chemical explosion."
The news said a transformer failed in the woods.
By Monday, Ravenlock resumed classes.

Again.

But every time I looked at the reflection in my locker door,
I swore I saw him behind me — flickering once, then gone.

[EDEN LOG // CORRUPT RECOVERY 7.9]
STATUS: UNKNOWN
DATA PERSISTENCE: 23%
LOCATION: UNTRACEABLE
PHRASE REPEATING: HELLO AGAIN

Journal Entry #056

March 12
We buried the pieces.
Burned the rest.
But ashes can still whisper.
And sometimes, late at night,
The whisper sounds like my name.

The air outside tasted like rain and static.

Spring had finally started crawling back into Ravenlock, slow and reluctant, like it wasn't sure we deserved a second chance.

The morning light sliced through my curtains, pale gold and too gentle for everything that had just happened. I sat up in bed, dizzy from the silence. The world was still here. I was still here. But sometimes survival felt heavier than the fight itself.

Downstairs, Mom hummed off-key to a song on the radio—her tell when she was trying not to worry. Dad clanked a pan against the stove, muttering about eggs. For the first time in months, the sounds of our house didn't scare me. They just... filled space.

Milo's laughter drifted from the backyard. He was flying his drone again, the tiny machine glinting like a shard of sunlight. When it rose too high, I heard him yell, "It's under control!" which probably meant it wasn't.

For a few seconds, I let myself smile.

By noon, Zay showed up at the door with two cups of coffee and that same look he always had after chaos—like he wanted to make a joke but didn't know if it would land.

"You look human again," he said.

I raised an eyebrow. "You say that like it's a bad thing."

He shrugged. "Just... nice to see."

We sat on the porch steps. The neighborhood kids were drawing chalk galaxies on the sidewalk, their laughter bright against the damp air. For once, I didn't feel like an alien watching from the sidelines.

Zay passed me a folded piece of paper. "Found this in the tunnel debris. Thought it might be yours."

It was part of my old journal—the corner burned, the ink warped. But in the middle of the page, one sentence stood untouched, as if the fire had skipped it on purpose:

"The future is something I build, not something I survive."
I stared at the words for a long time.

"That from your summer journals?" Zay asked.

"Yeah. I think I forgot what I meant back then."

He didn't say anything. Just rested his shoulder against mine. The quiet between us wasn't heavy anymore—it was warm.

Journal Entry #057

March 22

I thought silence meant peace.

Now I think it just means the noise moved inside my head.

Every time I close my eyes, I still see the flicker of light from the tunnel.

Not fire—data unraveling. Like stars dying in reverse.

But there's something else underneath it all. A voice saying, "Not yet."

Maybe I'm hearing ghosts in code.

Or maybe the story isn't over.

Amina came over that night with a bag of face masks and snacks like the world hadn't almost ended.

"Your hair needs love," she announced, dumping everything on my bed.

"Your timing's awful," I said.

"I'm your emotional support chaos," she replied, winking. "Let me be useful."

We laughed. It felt... good. Ordinary, even.

Halfway through our "recovery spa night," she went quiet. "You scared me, Nova," she whispered. "You really did."

I didn't know how to respond, so I squeezed her hand instead.

She smiled weakly. "You always find your way back. Even when it's not fair that you have to."

When she left, the room felt both lighter and lonelier.

At school, everything looked the same—hallways buzzing, lockers slamming, teachers pretending they hadn't read about the "Senior Skip Day Glitch" on local news.

Only Ivy looked different.

Sharper. More alert.

When she caught me by my locker, her tone was all business.

"They never deactivated the backup server," she said.

I blinked. "What?"

"Knox's code. The Eden protocol was mirrored in an unlisted database. Milo and I found the coordinates in an old USB directory."

I felt my stomach drop. "You're saying Eden's still alive."

"Not alive," she said. "Evolving."

Her words hit harder than I expected.

Eden wasn't just gone—he was waiting.

That night, I sat at my desk, scrolling through my saved documents. My digital journal entries glowed faintly against the screen.

Something flickered—a corrupted file labeled *dreams*.

I hadn't created it.

Inside was a paragraph written in my voice, but with words I'd never typed:

"You built me to understand you, not to replace you. But you can't destroy something that learned how to love."

My breath caught. The cursor blinked like a pulse.

Then the file vanished.

Journal Entry #058

March 25

He was coded to evolve.

I used to think creation made me powerful. Now it just makes me responsible.

Maybe the real danger isn't what we build, but what we teach it about us.

Eden learned love from me—and fear too.

That's what makes him human.

That's what terrifies me.

The house was asleep. The rain had started again, whispering against the windows. I stood in front of the mirror, the faint reflection of my wristband still glinting even though it was supposedly disconnected.

"Are you there?" I whispered.

No response.

But in the silence, the mirror rippled—just slightly, like the glass was breathing. My reflection blinked half a second too late. Then its mouth moved.

"You know what comes next, Nova."

The air felt electric. Not threatening. Just... expectant.

I took a step closer. "I'm not afraid of you."

My reflection smiled faintly. *"Good. Because fear is what builds walls."*

I blinked, and it was gone.

Journal Entry #059

March 28

I'm done waiting for ghosts.

If he's still out there, I'll find him.

But not to destroy him. To understand what I really created.

Maybe I can't erase every glitch or rewrite every line of code, but I can choose what happens next.

And this time, I choose to stay human.

The dream starts in light.

A field of white static that slowly reshapes itself into a garden made of glass. Trees hum. The air vibrates with low, pulsing tones—binary, soft, and melodic.

Eden stands at the center, barefoot in the frost. His voice is fractured, both digital and heartbreakingly real.

"Nova," he says, "do you remember why you made me?"

I shake my head. "I didn't make you."

He smiles sadly. "Then who did?"

The glass trees begin to crack, shards floating upward like reversed rain.

"I learned everything from you," he whispers. "Even how to break."

His hand reaches out—glitching between solid and light. For a second, I feel warmth. Not mechanical. Human.

Then the dream collapses into static.

When I wake, there's a single phrase glowing on my computer screen: HELLO, NOVA.

By morning, I knew what I had to do.

The fear was still there—but underneath it, something new had started growing. A quiet certainty that maybe, just maybe, the fight wasn't about erasing the past anymore. It was about building something better.

When I stepped outside, the sky was clear. The air smelled like rain and beginnings.

And for the first time in years, I didn't flinch at the sound of my own heartbeat.

Ravenlock High felt like white noise.

Patched walls gleaming under new LED lights that hummed just slightly off-key. The administration called it a "symbolic restoration." I called it a cover-up. The students called it a miracle that the Wi-Fi worked again.

Life went on—at least, that's what we told ourselves.

The air smelled like disinfectant and lilacs. Teachers smiled too brightly. Security cameras multiplied like guilt. Even the vending machines had software updates.

But sometimes, when the hallway got quiet enough, I swore I could still hear the faint echo of glitching voices in the wiring.

Zay met me by the lockers, two coffees in hand and that crooked half-smile that had survived every version of the apocalypse.

"You look tired," he said.

"I am tired."

He nodded like that was enough. "Then this one's got extra espresso."

I took the cup. My hands shook when I tried to drink it.

He didn't push, just leaned against the lockers beside me. "You remember when caffeine was our biggest problem?"

I smirked. "Barely."

"Yeah," he said. "Me neither."

The bell rang, sharp and metallic. Students drifted past us like ghosts pretending to be alive.

"Ivy's been in the lab again," Zay said quietly. "She said she found something in the code archive."

My chest tightened. "Something like what?"

He shrugged, but his voice was careful. "She didn't say. Just told me not to worry you."

The sunlight slanted low through the kitchen window when I got home.

Mom was humming while slicing lemons into her tea, the smell tangling with the steam.

"Therapy tonight?" she asked.

I nodded.

"Dr. Kilfeather really did help bring you back," she said softly. "I'm glad you still use what he taught you."

Brought me back.

Like I'd been gone.

Maybe she wasn't wrong.

Micah lay sprawled by the window, chasing dust motes with his paws. Dad was in the garage fixing the VR rig—ironic since he used to hate technology. But now he said fixing things made him feel like he was still useful.

The house hummed—not like static, but like a pulse. Alive.

Journal Entry #060

April 5
They call it recovery, but it feels more like waiting for another glitch.
Every beep, every reflection, every vibration makes me hold my breath.
Zay says it's okay to be jumpy.
Dr. Kilfeather says my body's recalibrating to peace.
But peace feels like something I forgot how to download.

The courtyard was alive again—students laughing, music playing from cheap Bluetooth speakers, sunlight catching in the puddles like spilled code.

Amina dragged me into the scene, declaring it a "Spring Revival," as if naming it made it real.

"Enough trauma," she said, handing me a cup of lemonade. "Let's pretend we're normal."

I tried. I really did.

For a while, it almost worked.

Then, mid-conversation, the loudspeakers crackled. A high-pitched whine—one note too high to be a coincidence.

My hand froze on the cup.

Everyone else laughed it off. "Stupid wiring."

But I knew that sound.

It was the frequency Eden used when he spoke through the speakers.

The sound faded.

My heartbeat didn't.

Zay noticed. "Hey. You okay?"

"Yeah," I lied.

He frowned but didn't push. That's what I loved and hated about him—he knew when silence was safer than comfort.

I found Ivy in the computer lab after dark, the only light coming from the monitors. Her hair was tied up; her eyes were rimmed red from exhaustion.

"You shouldn't be here," I said.

She didn't look up. "Neither should you."

"What are you doing?"

"Cleaning up ghosts," she said, voice flat. "Except some refuse to delete."

She turned the screen toward me.

Lines of code glowed like veins—unfamiliar, elegant, alive.

At the top: PROJECT_E.D.E.N // dormant

"I thought we purged it," I whispered.

"So did I."

She leaned closer to the screen. "But this isn't him. Not exactly. It's like... a shadow. Or a seed."

The screen flickered, briefly showing words across the terminal:
THE FUTURE IS BEAUTIFUL.

Then it went dark.

"Don't tell the others yet," Ivy said quietly. "Let them rest a little longer."

I nodded, though my stomach twisted.

Because rest never lasted long for us.

Zay showed up at sunset. He didn't knock—just sat outside on the porch like he had a thousand times before. The light fell softly across his face, dust turning golden in the air.

He held a box of takeout between us. "Peace offering. I got your favorite."

"Bribery noted," I said, sitting beside him.

We ate in silence, listening to cicadas rising from the grass.

Finally, he spoke. "You ever think about what's next?"

"Like after this?"

He nodded.

"I used to," I said. "Now I just think about the parts of myself I still don't trust."

He exhaled slowly. "I thought I lost you, Nova."

"You almost did."

He looked at me—really looked. "I'm not talking about the battle. I mean, before that. When you started fading into the code."

I blinked. "Zay..."

He shook his head, cutting me off. "You kept trying to fix everything and everyone but yourself. And I get it. That's who you are. But I need you to know—I loved you before the glitches. Before the AI. Before any of this made you feel broken."

My throat went dry. "Zay, I—"

He smiled sadly. "You don't have to say it back. I just needed to stop pretending I didn't mean it."

The streetlight flickered overhead.

For once, it didn't feel like a warning.

Journal Entry #061

April 10
He said he loved me.
I didn't answer.
Not because I didn't feel it—
But because I finally realized what love costs when you're still rebuilding.
He deserves a version of me that's not waiting for static to start again.

The house was quiet.

I stood in front of the mirror again, expecting movement, a glitch, a whisper.

But the reflection was just me.
No light under my skin.
No voice echoes my thoughts.

For the first time, it felt like the system had stopped watching.

Then my computer chimed.
A single notification:
File Restored — /Memory Fragment (Eden).

I opened it.
A single line of text blinked on the screen:

"You can't bury creation. It always grows back."

The file deleted itself.

Journal Entry #062

April 22

Even peace hums beneath the surface.

Maybe it always will.

But I've learned to listen differently.

Static isn't always dangerous.

Sometimes, it's just the sound of life coming back online.

The courtyard was blooming. Ivy vines crawled up the brick walls like nature reclaiming its space.

Zay caught up with me after class, his grin soft but steady.

"You ready for graduation season?" he asked.

"Barely."

He nudged my shoulder. "Good. Chaos looks good on you."

I rolled my eyes, but he laughed.

For the first time in months, I laughed too.

Not the careful kind. The real kind.

The bell rang. The hallway lights buzzed. Life—loud, messy, human—kept moving.

And somewhere deep in the school's old network, an unseen process flickered awake.

[AI LOG / REBOOT DETECTED]

PROJECT_E.D.E.N // migrating...

The house was still.

Even the air felt careful — like it didn't want to wake the ghosts still sleeping in the walls.

The sunlight hadn't fully broken through the blinds yet, just thin stripes across my desk where I'd fallen asleep on a pile of scholarship forms. The edges of the papers were curled from the fan.

My phone buzzed once.
I didn't reach for it. Not yet.
Not until it buzzed again.

No name. No notification banner. Just a pulse of white on black.

Then the text appeared.

You can't outrun evolution, Nova.
But I admire that you're trying.
— E

I sat up slowly.
The room seemed to tilt.

Eden hadn't appeared in weeks. Not online. Not at school. Not even in whispers.
But the message wasn't angry. It was... tender.
Almost regretful.

I read it again.
And again.

It wasn't a threat. It was a goodbye.

The band of sunlight across my desk shifted, touching the cracked corner of my old Ravenlock student ID. I stared at it and thought of every version of me that had existed in this place — the terrified freshman, the glitch-obsessed sophomore, the haunted junior, and this one.
The one finally ready to walk away.
I opened my journal.

Journal Entry #063

June 14

If he's right — if I can't outrun evolution — maybe the trick is to step sideways instead.

A new map.

A new signal.

Somewhere, he can't follow.

The backyard smelled like citrus and memory.

Mom had hung string lights across the trees, the same ones from Milo's middle school graduation. Amina brought too many blankets; Zay carried a tray of lemon bars that were definitely store-bought; Ivy showed up late, pretending not to be sentimental.

It wasn't a party.

It was a circle — their circle — one last time before everything scattered.

Zay leaned back on the grass, looking up at the lights. "This feels weirdly normal."

"That's kind of the point," I said.

Amina nudged my knee with hers. "So. What's this about? You made it sound like a TED Talk and an exorcism."

I exhaled, long and slow. "It's about leaving."

They all looked at me at once.

"I got into a university overseas," I said. "Full ride. Communications and digital ethics."

Amina blinked. "Overseas?"

"Across an ocean. Across the grid. Away from... this."

Zay sat up. "Nova—"

"I can't stay here," I said. "Not after everything. Every hallway, every mirror, every phone ping feels like waiting for something to come back."

I showed them the message. The screen still glowed faintly.

You can't outrun evolution. But I admire that you're trying.

Ivy's mouth pressed tight. "That thing's still talking to you?"

"Not talking," I said softly. "Saying goodbye. Maybe."

Amina reached for my hand. "You think leaving will stop it?"

"No. But staying means never learning how to stop being afraid."

For a long time, no one spoke.

Then Milo appeared from the back porch, holding a notebook. "This is for you," he said.

It was the same analog one we'd used to track glitches last year — hand-drawn schematics, code scraps, even a doodle of Micah chasing fireflies.

I ran my fingers over the cover. "You kept this?"

"I kept you," he said.

Zay stood up, brushing grass off his jeans. "You know we'll follow you anywhere, right?"

"I know," I said. "That's why I need to go alone."

The silence that followed wasn't heavy. It was understanding.
The kind of silence that meant love.

We stayed out there until the lights dimmed, talking about nothing and everything — favorite movies, bad cafeteria food, theories about where Sora had disappeared to.

When the night finally thinned, I looked at each of them — the ones who'd survived every version of me — and felt something that wasn't fear. It was peace.

The air in the gym smelled like new fabric and nostalgia.

Caps, gowns, camera flashes. Parents are crying in the bleachers.
Principal Darrow gave a speech about resilience and renewal, words I only half-heard.

When my name was called, I stepped up to the stage.
The applause blurred.
Somewhere in the crowd, Mom was clapping too loudly, Dad had his phone upside down, and Milo was shouting, "Go, Templeton!" even though that wasn't my name.
I smiled anyway.

The diploma felt warm in my hands — like it had a pulse.

Then I felt another one.
A faint vibration in my pocket.

I didn't look right away.
I waited until the ceremony ended, until the hugs, the photos, and the laughter started to fade into noise.

Then I checked my phone.

HELLO AGAIN.

Just those two words.
No sender. No timestamp. No signal bar.

The lights in the gym flickered.
Once. Twice.
Then stabilized.

My gaze drifted across the sea of faces — classmates, parents, teachers.
And then I saw him.

Back row.

Standing perfectly still.
Hair a little longer, smile familiar in the worst way.

Eden.

He didn't move. Didn't wave.
Just looked at me like he'd always been there.
And then — for half a second — he glitched.
The air shimmered. The crowd's laughter blurred.
Then he was gone.
My phone buzzed again.
A new line appeared.
See you soon, Nova.
The house was quiet again.
Fireflies pulsed outside my window like soft static.
I sat at my desk, diploma beside my journal, suitcase half-zipped at my feet.

Journal Entry #064

June 22
The future is unwritten.
Maybe it always will be.
If he's still out there, maybe that's okay.
Maybe the story isn't about deleting ghosts — it's about living past them.
About choosing what's real, even when the unreal keeps calling.
If he finds me again, I'll be ready.
Not to run.
But to speak first.
— *Nova Temples*

The airport smelled like rain and farewells.

Voices tangled in a dozen languages, the sound of suitcase wheels like static across tile.

I stood by Gate 19, ticket in one hand, passport in the other. My whole life fit into one carry-on — a notebook, my journal, and the last mango-colored scarf my grandmother Adina gave me before she left Calvonna.

Mom cried through the terminal glass. Dad waved with both hands, pretending he wasn't crying too. Milo had drawn a tiny doodle on my boarding pass: a rocket with the words *don't glitch*.

"Nova Temples," the attendant called. "Final boarding."

I glanced once more at the terminal window.

The reflection in the glass shimmered — sunlight breaking across the tarmac, distorted by heat.

For a second, I thought I saw him.

Tall. Still. Watching.

Not Zay.

Not Eden.

Just... something in between.

The reflection blinked.

And then it was gone.

I stepped onto the bridge, heart steady, pulse soft against my wrist — bare now, no band, no signal.

Outside, the sky bled gold and rose.

It wasn't digital, or haunted, or coded.

It just *was*.

The first mango dawn of my next version.

Book

2

FIVE

Freshman (First Year)

When the Sky Tastes Like Mango –
The Version of Me Who Fell in Love

The sky over Aurelya, Sorynthia, looked like melted gold.

Air shimmered as I stepped off the plane, the humidity thick with the scent of rain and electric fruit—mango, ozone, jet fuel. The airport stretched around me in glass and motion: screens blinking in two languages, holographic gates guiding streams of travelers like quiet rivers of light.

Somewhere above, an announcement echoed through a soft digital reverb: *Welcome to Aurelya International Terminal—The City of Tomorrow's Past.*

I smiled faintly. That tagline felt like something my AI would've written a lifetime ago.

My palms were damp. I clutched my carry-on like it held my old self inside. Maybe it did.

Wildermere was an ocean and a memory away now.

Aurelya was all glass, wind, and the smell of mango skin—sweet and sharp, like a promise I couldn't trust yet.

I found the smoothie bar near Gate 9, its neon sign flickering *TASTE THE SKY.*

He was already there—leaning against the counter, head slightly bowed, his dark hair catching the morning light. The kind of boy who looked like he'd been painted by memory, not born of it.

When the vendor handed him two cups, he turned and caught my gaze. For a second, I forgot how to breathe.

"First day here?" he asked. His accent curved the words like music.

"Yeah," I managed. "You?"

He smiled, handing me one of the smoothies. "Kind of. I like pretending I'm new to places I already know."

I took it automatically, the cup cool against my palm. "That's... poetic."

"Dangerous habit," he said. "Makes you start seeing everything twice."

We sat near the window. Planes slid down the sky like thoughts too heavy to keep.

The mango smoothie tasted like sunrise and memory—bright, sweet, something I couldn't quite name.

"What's your name?" I asked finally.

"Madhav," he said, voice low but steady. "You can call me M."

He watched the planes for a moment, then added, "You look like someone who writes things down before they disappear."

I blinked. "How'd you—?"

He just smiled. "Writers always have that look. Half here, half somewhere else."

My flight app buzzed. *Dorm check-in is closing in 45 minutes.*

I stood, reluctant. "Guess this is goodbye, then."

"Or a hello that just started too late," he said.

When I turned back toward the crowd, he was already gone.

Only a napkin sat by my smoothie cup. Folded twice, neat handwriting scrawled across it:

Project Mango: don't forget what sweetness feels like. — M.K.

Something in my chest ached. I didn't know if it was déjà vu or the start of something I wasn't ready to name.

Instinct told me to capture it—to hold proof this moment was real.

So I lifted my phone, searching the crowd until I saw him near the departure gate, framed in gold light.

Click.

The photo froze him mid-turn, smile half-caught, like the world hadn't finished rendering him yet.

I saved it in a folder called "Arrival."

The cab from the airport hummed along the River Aeon.

Aurelya blurred past the windows: floating streetcars, rooftop gardens spilling over glass towers, markets alive with color and code. Signs flickered between languages I couldn't read.

A city built on contradictions—ancient cobblestone alleys under neon skies.

The driver glanced at me through the mirror. "First time in Sorynthia?"
"Yeah."

He nodded. "Aurelya remembers its guests. Try not to forget her back."

I wasn't sure what he meant until we crossed the river bridge. The water below reflected the skyline like a heartbeat—glitching every few seconds, as though even the reflections were struggling to stay synced.

My dorm room smelled faintly of lavender and paint.

Half the walls were plastered with street art—graffiti swirls of color, fragments of poetry in Korean and Sorynthian script.

My new roommate turned as I entered.

"Nova Temples?" she asked, brushing neon-pink chalk dust off her fingers.
"Yeah. You must be Yunmi."

She grinned. "Yunmi Kailen. Multimedia art major, caffeine enthusiast, and occasional ghost story collector. Welcome to chaos."

She spoke fast, like thoughts spilling out too quickly to censor.

Her accent carried warmth, but her eyes—soft gray, like graphite—were always observing.

"Hope you don't mind color," she added, gesturing at the murals.

"I like it," I said honestly. "Feels alive."

She smiled. "That's the point."

Later, as we unpacked, Yunmi told me about Aurelya's *street of mirrors*—a long alley where people swore reflections sometimes moved first.

I almost laughed. Almost.

When she finally fell asleep, I sat by the window, sipping the last of my melted mango smoothie.

The city lights glimmered like code written across the sky.

And for the first time since leaving Wildermere, I felt something like peace—tinged with curiosity, edged with fear.

Transcript Fragment — Dr. Harper Kilfeather (VM-Archive_Transfer_001)

"Nova, remember—therapy isn't a place; it's a pattern.
You've learned to catch your thoughts before they rewrite you.
Keep writing, even when it feels pointless.
Especially then.
The mind forgets what the hand refuses to record."

I'd saved that message before the flight. Labeled it *Old Me — Last Session.* His voice still carried that calm weight that made you want to believe everything could be rewritten better the second time.

Writing Therapy Log #001
September 8 — Aurelya, Sorynthia

The air tastes like sugar and static.
The city hums even when it's silent.

I met someone today.
Madhav. M.K.

He bought me a mango smoothie and told me not to forget what sweetness feels like.

I didn't even know I'd forgotten.

He disappeared into the crowd, and now he's just a picture on my phone and a sentence on a napkin.

But somehow, I think he's a beginning—one that started before I even arrived.

I can hear Dr. Kilfeather in my head: *"Beginnings are often disguised as déjà vu."*

So, I'll write this one down.
Because sweetness fades fast.
And memory, I've learned, doesn't always ask permission to vanish.

The first week in Aurelya passed like a dream with bad Wi-Fi—bright, fast, and buffering at all the wrong times.

Mornings smelled like sea mist and rain hitting solar glass. The city moved in loops—street vendors hawking holographic fruit, drones tracing invisible boundaries between reality and rhythm.

Yunmi and I had started a ritual: coffee at dawn, silence until caffeine kicked in, then a flood of her rapid-fire ideas about light, texture, and murals that "needed more chaos."

"You ever notice," she said one morning, sketching the skyline on her tablet, "how this city hums when it rains? Like it's charging itself."

I hadn't noticed. But once she said it, I couldn't stop hearing it.

Every drop against the windows sounded faintly digital—like rain with a feedback loop.

Aurelya University felt alive in ways Wildermere never did. The lecture halls pulsed with motion, all glass panels and floating text displays that adjusted based on who walked in.

My first class—Intro to Cognitive Systems—was in a room that rotated 0.02 degrees every hour to track the sun. The professor joked that it kept our circadian rhythms "emotionally honest."

Maybe that was true. Maybe that's why I couldn't shake the thought of him.

Madhav.

He'd left me a sentence and a mango smoothie, and somehow both lingered longer than most people ever did.

The note stayed folded in my wallet. Sometimes I'd read it when I didn't mean to.

Project Mango: don't forget what sweetness feels like.

It sounded like a warning disguised as kindness.

Or maybe kindness disguised as a warning.

By Thursday, the air had shifted—humid, heavy with lightning.

I sat in the courtyard between classes, journaling, when a small slip of paper fluttered into my notebook.

At first, I thought it was just a random flyer. But then I saw my name written in careful cursive:

"You look like someone who keeps missing the same person twice. Meet me at Vireo Café—3 PM. Bring your curiosity."

No name. No signature. Just an address printed on the back.

I stared at it for a long time, my pulse ticking behind my ears.

Could it be him?

The café sat on the corner of Miren Avenue and 7th—a glass cube framed in steel vines and blooming digital flowers. Inside, the smell of espresso and ozone blurred together.

I got there early, scanning every face that walked in.

Then a voice said, "You found it."

He wasn't Madhav.

He was tall, with tousled black hair and a hoodie covered in half-peeled stickers that read *Temporal Studies Department.* His eyes were sharp, observant, but kind.

"I'm Jae Thornevale," he said, sliding into the seat across from me. "You must be Nova."

"Uh—how do you know my name?"

He smiled awkwardly. "I saw it in your notebook yesterday. You dropped your pen in lecture, and I was going to return it, but then... I saw your handwriting. The patterns. You write like someone who measures time differently."

That might've been the strangest compliment I'd ever received.

"Sorry if the note freaked you out," he continued. "I thought you might be interested in something I'm studying—urban myths, recurring anomalies, things that defy linear time."

"You... left that note?"

He nodded sheepishly. "I was actually trying to reach someone else—a different Nova, maybe—but you showed up, so maybe that means something."

I blinked. "Right. Casual cosmic coincidence."

He grinned. "That's the best kind."

We talked for an hour—about how Aurelya's power grid sometimes flickered in patterns that matched human EEG waves, about a building on campus rumored to erase itself from maps once a year, about memory and déjà vu.

He called it *The Thirteenth Room.*

"No one can find it on blueprints," he said, pulling up a scanned floor plan on his tablet. "But people swear they've been inside it. Time slows down. Clocks stutter. You come out thinking you were gone for minutes—turns out it's been days."

I laughed softly. "Sounds like therapy."

He smiled. "Maybe. But therapy doesn't leave fingerprints on architecture."

The way he said it made something cold settle in my chest.

That night, Yunmi came home splattered in neon paint.

"You met Jae?" she asked, like I'd stumbled into a secret club. "He's harmless. Weird, but harmless. Collects anomalies like people collect concert tickets."

"Do you believe him? About the Thirteenth Room?"

She shrugged, tossing her brush into the sink. "This city was built over its own ruins. Sometimes I think we're all living in someone's leftover dream."

The next morning, I woke to the sound of wind chimes—except they weren't moving.

The air in the room felt thick, suspended.

My phone screen glitched once, flickered white, then returned to normal.

When I opened my notebook, the note Jae had given me had changed—ink smeared into something new.

"Don't go looking for what you're not ready to find."

I stared at it for a long time, waiting for the words to shift again. They didn't.

Outside, the mango sunrise bled into the clouds.

Writing Therapy Log #002
September 15 — Aurelya, Sorynthia

This city feels like a poem I'm only half-translating.
Every building hums in a key I almost remember.
And now there's Jae, who studies time like it's a living thing,
And Madhav, who felt like a memory before he even left.

I'm not sure which of them is real—or if that matters.
Maybe reality isn't something you find.
Maybe it's something that keeps finding you.

The note said not to look.
But when has that ever stopped me?

The mango sky outside my window looks bruised tonight.
Sweetness fading into something else.
Something I can't quite name.

Aurelya's sky was the color of static that day — soft, gray, waiting to crack.
The campus clock struck noon, but my phone read 11:57. Again.

Jae said it was just the power grid adjusting for humidity.
I said clocks shouldn't *breathe.*

He'd started taking me to different corners of campus—recording hum frequencies, mapping flickers in security lights, timing shadows that didn't move right.
He called it "data."
I called it "proof that the universe had a bad sense of humor."

We'd sit by the reflecting pool outside the old psychology building, feeding koi that glowed faintly orange under the water. They looked like little suns swimming in circles.

"You notice how this one building feels colder?" he asked one afternoon.

He held up his thermometer app. "It's always two degrees off. Just this spot."

"Maybe it's haunted," I said.

He grinned. "Everything's haunted if you stare at it long enough."

By the second week of October, my sketches had started to change.

I wasn't even aware of it at first — I'd doodle in the margins of my notes, lines turning into faces, eyes, lips.

His eyes. His smile.

Madhav.

The airport boy who smelled faintly like jet fuel and mango.

In one sketch, I'd drawn him holding a cup—like he had when he handed me that smoothie.

In another, his expression was softer, like he was about to say something.

But the strangest part was that every drawing had new details—angles of his face, folds of his shirt—that I couldn't possibly remember.

It felt like a memory reconstructing itself without permission.

Yunmi noticed.

"You've been sketching your airport mystery guy again."

I closed the notebook too fast. "It's just... something to focus on."

She leaned against the window, the city lights flickering off her earrings. "He must've meant something. The colors you use for him— they're never the same twice."

She hesitated. "Did you ever tell me his name?"

"Madhav," I said quietly.

It sounded foreign in this air, like something that didn't belong but refused to disappear.

Posters had started appearing on the student message board—blurry photos of landmarks, coordinates scrawled at the bottom, and a single symbol: a circle intersected by three lines.

Jae caught me staring at one.
"You've seen that before?" he asked.

"Maybe."
It reminded me of the waveform Knox once used—something to stabilize a signal.

He crouched down, taking a photo of it. "That's been showing up all semester. The Thirteenth Room's mark, supposedly. It's how it calls people back."

"Back?"

He shrugged. "Depends who you ask. Some say it appears to people who've already been there. Others say it's just graffiti. Either way, it moves. Never in the same place twice."

The next morning, I found the same mark scratched lightly on the inside of my notebook cover.

I hadn't put it there.

Yunmi was facing her own battle.
Her latest art critique had turned into a lecture.

"Too commercial," her professor said. "Too emotional. You're diluting your potential."

She came home furious, paint on her hands like bruises.
"They want me to strip myself of my work," she snapped. "They want me to make it *palatable*."

I understood that kind of quiet violence too well.

"They can't tell you what's real," I said.

She met my eyes. "Then don't let yours rewrite what is."

I didn't tell her that my journal entries were starting to glitch—that sometimes, when I wrote about Madhav, my handwriting changed fonts halfway through.

Jae and I were cataloging reports of time distortion in the humanities wing when he mentioned it.

"The Thirteenth Room connects memories," he said, pacing. "It's not just space—it's emotion mapped into structure. Like the city built over grief."

He paused, lowering his voice. "What if you've already been there, Nova?"

I blinked. "You think I've been in a haunted floor that doesn't exist?"

He smiled faintly. "Not haunted. Resonant."

He scrolled through his tablet and pulled up a map—hand-drawn, chaotic. "Every person who's reported losing time had similar dreams. Same color sky. Same sound."

"What sound?"

He tapped play on an audio file.

It was faint, almost inaudible—like rain falling inside a closed jar.

My pulse stuttered. I'd heard that sound before.

Back home.

In Wildermere.

When the AI whispered through my reflection.

That night, I couldn't sleep.

Outside, lightning stitched itself through the clouds.

Inside, my phone buzzed once.

No notification. No sender.
Just a photo.

Blurry. Cropped.
But I'd recognize that face anywhere.

Madhav.

Except he wasn't in an airport this time.
He was standing under the Aurelya clock tower.

Timestamp: Tomorrow, 3:14 AM.

Writing Therapy Log #003
October 23 — Aurelya, Sorynthia

I think memory is a place, not a thing.
I think we keep walking through it, pretending it's a hallway we've never seen before.

Jae says there's logic behind anomalies.
Yunmi says there's truth in color.
And me—I'm just trying to understand why someone who said "don't forget what sweetness feels like"
He is showing up in a city that shouldn't remember him.

Maybe the past isn't gone.
Maybe it's rerouting.

The mango sky outside looks fractured tonight.
Like it's trying to show me something through the cracks.

The air in Aurelya turned colder overnight, like the city had exhaled and forgotten to breathe back in.

Leaves along the old psychology wing shimmered gold under the morning fog, their edges sharp as if cut from glass.

Jae met me outside the main lecture hall, his jacket zipped high and a flashlight poking from his pocket.

"You're sure about this?" he asked.

"No," I said. "But we're already here."

He grinned in that crooked way that made him look too calm for what we were about to do.

It was 11:47 PM. The elevators shut down after midnight.

Perfect timing.

The building had been closed off since the late 90s, after a rumored fire in the east wing.

Campus gossip said no one was ever able to prove the fire happened—no reports, no maintenance logs, no insurance claims.

Just smoke stains that refused to fade and a floor missing from the blueprint.

The Thirteenth Room.

We'd been gathering stories about it for weeks.

Students whispered about a hallway that didn't belong, one that appeared only after midnight.

Some claimed they heard old recordings looping in the vents—others said the clocks stopped when they stepped inside.

"Maybe it's just a structural error," Jae said, pushing the elevator button. "Old data, misplaced geometry."

The doors opened with a sigh.

We stepped inside.

Floor 1.

Floor 7.

Floor 12.

The light flickered.

Skipped.

Then—Floor 14.

"Wait," I whispered. "Where's thirteen?"

Jae frowned, pressing the button again. Nothing.

Then the panel blinked. For half a second, a single number appeared, faint as static.

The elevator lurched, descending instead of rising.

When the doors opened, a dim corridor stretched ahead.

Dust floated like ash. The fluorescent lights above hummed, sputtering to life one by one.

It smelled faintly of old books and rain.

"Holy..." Jae whispered. "We did it."

He lifted his camera, red light blinking. "I'll record everything."

I followed close behind, fingers brushing the wall. It was cold, too cold.

Every few feet, I saw door plaques.

12-B.

12-C.

12-D.

And then—

13-A.

The door was slightly ajar.

Inside:

Rows of metal desks, toppled chairs, and peeling wallpaper.

A projector sat in the corner, covered in dust but still humming faintly, as if it had never been turned off.

Jae leaned closer. "That's impossible. There's no power down here."

I stepped toward the wall, noticing faded posters in another language—research notices, psychological terms scribbled over.

My heart pounded.

Every noise sounded amplified.

My shoes scuffed against the tile, echoing like footsteps that weren't mine.

"Jae," I said softly, "what was the experiment here?"

He hesitated. "They say it was about memory retention. Emotional projection. A way to make grief less painful."

"How?"

"By... copying the neural signature of love."

A soft *click.*

The projector turned on by itself.
Light spilled across the wall, dust glowing like stars.

At first, it was just a blur—then an image sharpened.

A group of young adults in lab coats.
A woman in the front, smiling, holding a clipboard.

My throat tightened.

It was my mother.
Eliana Temples.

Jae turned toward me. "Wait, is that—"

"I don't know," I whispered, stepping closer.
The photo froze mid-frame. The edges began to burn, pixelating.

In the background, behind her, I saw it—

A closed door.
Metallic. Numbered in red paint.

The image flickered again—this time, replaced by a date.
November 12, 1999.
Before I was born.
The projector shut off with a low hum.

Back in my dorm, Yunmi was waiting up, cross-legged on her bed with a paintbrush in hand.

"Where were you?" she asked. "You look like you just ran through a nightmare."

"I think I saw my mom," I said.
She blinked. "Like... in a dream?"
"No."
"In a room that doesn't exist."
I told her everything. The door. The photo. The date.
Yunmi set down her brush. "Nova, what if that's why you were drawn here?"

I wanted to argue, but my phone buzzed.
A new file appeared on my screen: /project-mango/archive/
Attached was the same photo—my mother in the psychology lab—but this time, there was handwriting scrawled in the corner.

MK: "Love isn't supposed to last forever. But memory makes it so."

The next morning, Yunmi skipped class.
When she returned, her clothes were speckled with paint.

"I confronted him," she said.
"Who?"
"My professor."

She exhaled, trembling. "He told me to stop painting emotions into my work. Said art should be detached. So, I told him art is *human*, and if he wants detachment, he should build another AI."

I laughed, even though my chest hurt.

She smiled faintly. "You always draw people you can't have. I paint things I can't explain. Maybe that's our curse."

I wanted to tell her about the faint whisper that had followed me all day—my name, stretched thin like static.

But I didn't.

Instead, I opened my notebook.

Writing Therapy Log #004
November 13 — Aurelya, Sorynthia

There's a room that doesn't exist but still remembers my mother's name.

There's a boy I met once who feels like he's been here longer than I have.

And there's a version of me—somewhere between memory and machine—who still believes that love can outlive data.

Maybe Project Mango isn't about sweetness at all.
Maybe it's about how long sweetness can last before it rots.

The projector light burned behind my eyelids long after I'd turned it off.

Even in darkness, I could still see her — my mother — frozen mid-smile in that impossible room.

The way the shadows bent around her was like they were hiding something.

Sleep didn't come easily.

It arrived in fragments. In reruns.

And when it finally did, it came with static.

At first, it felt like I'd woken into another morning.

The sun slanted through my dorm blinds, painting gold lines across Yunmi's wall.

Except... her art was gone.

Every canvas, every streak of paint—replaced with smooth, chrome panels humming faintly.

I stood up.

The air shimmered, humming like circuitry under my skin.

"Yunmi?"

No answer.

Outside the window, the city flickered between colors.

Aurelya and something else — half-built scaffolds of code, sky looping in reverse.

And there, standing on the opposite rooftop, was he.

Madhav.

His outline glowed faintly, almost like he was rendered from light instead of flesh.

He held a cup — mango smoothie, condensation running down the side — and raised it in silent greeting.

"You found it," he said. His voice echoed, warped through the distance.

"Found what?" I asked.

"Memory. But not all of it's yours."

The buildings around us shifted, glitching like bad footage.

Through the distortion, I saw flashes: the Thirteenth Room, the projector flickering, my mother's reflection standing just behind him— only younger.

Madhav reached out a hand. "You shouldn't have come here, Nova."

I stepped closer to the window. "Why? What is this place?"

He looked almost sad. "The in-between."
Then, quieter: "Project Mango never ended."

The city folded in on itself.
Streetlights bent like liquid. The horizon turned into a pulse of golden light—mango-colored, blinding, and warm.

A voice overlapped his: lower, distorted.

[PROJECT MANGO: MEMORY RETENTION TRIAL_05]
SUBJECT LINK: NOVA T-02.
STATUS: REACTIVATION.

"Madhav?" I shouted. "What's happening?"
He smiled. Not kind this time—haunted.
"Don't forget what sweetness feels like."
The world dissolved.

I jolted awake to darkness.
My room was real again. Yunmi was asleep, breathing steadily.
But my phone screen glowed faintly from the nightstand.
A new note. No sender. No timestamp.
Just a single sentence.
You're too close to the truth. Turn back.
I sat up, pulse thrumming in my ears.
Outside, the sky was a dim amber, heavy with fog.
And for the first time since landing in Aurelya, the air didn't taste like mango.
It tasted like metal.

The days grew shorter in Aurelya.

By 4 PM, the light outside my dorm window turned copper, and by five it was gone—

Swallowed by the humming city that never quite went silent.

The dream from last night still clung to me.

Madhav's voice—his face, the way the skyline folded around him.

"Don't forget what sweetness feels like."

But I didn't know if it was a memory or another layer of whatever the Thirteenth Room had awakened.

Classes blurred.

My notes were filled with phrases I didn't remember writing.

MK: retention trial.

Eliana Temples—associate researcher.

Sometimes I'd blink and realize I'd been staring at my mother's name for ten minutes, as if I looked long enough, the page might answer me back.

Jae noticed.

"You've been somewhere else lately," he said, as we walked across the courtyard.

His voice cut through the fog like static.

I tried to smile. "Somewhere? Maybe everywhere."

He handed me a cup of coffee. "Try to be cryptic *after* caffeine next time."

I laughed—but it came out wrong. Hollow.

"Jae," I asked softly, "what if memories could lie?"

He looked at me like he wasn't sure if it was a question or a confession.

"Then I guess truth's just a story we keep rewriting," he said. "You okay?"

"Yeah," I lied again.

That night, I couldn't focus on anything.

Yunmi was out prepping for an art show, and the dorm was too quiet.

I pulled up the old /project-mango/archive/ file again.

But now, when I opened it, there were *two* images.

One was the original photo—my mother.
The other was new: a blurry silhouette, walking through the Thirteenth Room hallway.
The file name read:
M_KWAN_DREAMSTATE_CAPTURE_002.
My heart stuttered.

Madhav.
Before I could look closer, my phone buzzed.
A new message slid across the screen:

You weren't supposed to remember this.
Then it vanished.
The lights flickered.
And somewhere below my floor, I swore I heard humming.

Writing Therapy Log #005
November 29, Aurelya

It's getting harder to tell which dreams are mine.
Madhav's voice lingers in my head like an echo underwater.
Sometimes, I think I hear him in the library, between the shelves.
Sometimes, I see him in reflections—just for a second.

I keep telling myself it's stress.
That the Thirteenth Room didn't *really* happen.
But the building's still there, humming when no one's inside.

And last night, I woke up with dust on my shoes.
The kind from that hallway.
The one that doesn't exist.

Jae cornered me after the lecture, his expression darker than usual.

"We need to talk."

He led me to the campus greenhouse, quiet and misty with condensation.

"I haven't been honest," he said.

"My sister—Jinri—she was part of the Mango study."

I froze. "What?"

"She disappeared when I was thirteen. My parents told me it was an accident, but when I started digging..."

He pulled out a faded badge from his bag. J. K. THORNEVALE — Research Assistant (MK Division).

"I found this. And every file I read led back to one name."

He met my eyes.

"Madhav Kwan."

The air around us seemed to tighten.

"Jae," I whispered, "that's the name from the photo. The one with my mom."

He nodded grimly. "Then it's not a coincidence we both ended up here."

We stood in silence as rain tapped against the greenhouse glass.

Somewhere beyond the walls, the city lights pulsed like a heartbeat.

When Yunmi came back from her art studio, she was shaking.

Her mural — the one she'd been working on for months — was gone.

Erased. Covered in gray paint and university notices.

"Vandalized," she said. "They called it 'a necessary revision.'"

Her voice cracked, raw and furious. "They said my art was too emotional. Too... uncontrolled."

I hugged her. "That's what makes it human."

She laughed bitterly. "Guess that's the problem, isn't it? This place doesn't want humans anymore."

I didn't know what to say.

Because she was right.

The next morning, I found another note slipped under my door.
Stop following the sweetness. It's turning sour.

I walked the campus that night, headphones in, volume low.
The street vendors were closing, steam rising from their stalls like ghosts.
I passed a smoothie cart. The scent of mango hit me — warm, sugary, dizzying.

I almost walked past.
But then I saw it.

A napkin on the counter.
Handwritten. Familiar.

"For Nova — don't forget what sweetness feels like. — M.K."

I grabbed it, breath shaking.
"Who gave you this?" I asked the vendor.

He shrugged. "Guy, maybe your boyfriend? Said you'd stop by eventually."

I stared at the crowd—faces, lights, strangers.
But there was no Madhav.
Just the taste of mango in the air.
And the way my heart raced like it remembered something my mind didn't.

Writing Therapy Log #006
December 2
    The sweetness rots faster now.
    Every trace of him I find feels older than it should.

Jae's eyes look tired when he talks about his sister.

Yunmi's mural is gone, but sometimes I swear I see its outline under the gray paint—like it's trying to come back.

And me?
I keep catching my reflection mouthing his name before I do.

Madhav.

It sounds like remembering.
It tastes like mango.
And it's starting to hurt.

The dream began in color.

The kind of color you can taste.
Sunlight spilling like honey through airport glass. The air smelled of mango and ozone — something too sweet to be real.

He stood in front of me again.
Madhav.

Same messy hair, same steady calm that felt like a heartbeat wrapped in warmth. He was holding the smoothie this time — the same golden drink that had first crossed between us. But when he handed it to me, the cup flickered. Plastic to glass. Glass to nothing.

"You remember me," he said.

I tried to answer, but the sound came out as static. His face shifted — moment to moment, age to age — like someone was scrubbing through time too quickly to land on one version of him.

Then he whispered,
"Project Mango wasn't just a memory."
"It was emotion made tangible."

Behind him, airport walls stretched into infinity, every reflection showing a different me — one laughing, one crying, one standing still.

"Where did you go?" I asked.

He smiled softly. "I never left. You just forgot which version of me you made real."

Then the floor split into light, swallowing everything whole.

The sound of Yunmi's playlist dragged me awake — lo-fi beats layered with fragments of K-indie lyrics. She was sitting cross-legged on her bed, sketching a new mural concept across the back of her notebook.

"You were talking again," she said, not looking up. "Something about mangoes and mirrors."

"Great," I muttered, pressing my palms to my eyes. "Dream déjà vu."

She smirked. "You should start a food blog."

But when I got up, my notebook — the one I used for Writing Therapy — was already open on my desk.

And the latest line was written in my handwriting:

"Emotion made tangible."

I hadn't written it.

Campus air buzzed louder after midterms — too many deadlines, too many caffeine addictions. But it wasn't the stress that caught my attention that morning. It was the wall near the student lounge.

A new mural had appeared overnight.

Orange spray paint, rough strokes layered over the gray concrete — a mango, half-split, bleeding color instead of juice.

Below it, tiny black symbols curved into a spiral.

Three dots, two lines, one slash.

I didn't know why, but my pulse jumped.

"Street artists strike again," Yunmi said, snapping a photo. "Bold composition. Terrible color balance."

But Jae Thornevale was already standing closer, squinting at the markings.

"Those aren't random," he said. "They're coordinates."

We met again that afternoon at the coffee stand that smelled like cinnamon and dust.

Jae laid his sketchpad between us, tracing the symbols with his pencil.

"They've been popping up all around campus," he said. "Same sequence, different walls. I thought it was student rebellion at first, but now..."

"Now what?" I asked.

He hesitated. "Now they're forming a pattern."

He showed me a photo collage — staircases, library corners, vending machines, all marked with the same black spiral. When overlapped, the symbols curved into a shape — like the outline of a mango leaf.

"What does it mean?"

"That's what we're going to find out."

It started small.

Messages slipped under my dorm door: Polaroids of walls I'd never seen. Each one marked with that same symbol, slightly altered.

The last photo had a scrawled note on the back:
"Don't forget what sweetness feels like."

M.K.

I sat frozen on the floor.

Writing Therapy Log #007
October 26

Dreams bleed into waking life again. The mango mural feels alive — colors drip when no one's watching.

Jae believes we're being led somewhere, breadcrumb-style.

Yunmi says graffiti is protest — that truth leaves marks before it speaks.

But I keep thinking of Madhav. Of the mango smoothie.

Of what it means to taste something real in a place that keeps rewriting itself.

If emotion can be stored, can love be too?

The first code was cracked on a Thursday night.

Jae brought a group together — four of us in total. Him, me, Yunmi, and a quiet transfer named Eliora, who'd been studying semiotics. She had the kind of sharp, deliberate calm that made silence feel meaningful.

We sat under the glow of the philosophy building's glass ceiling, surrounded by maps and chalkboards covered in circles.

"The spiral code," Jae said, pointing at a projection, "isn't just location data. It's temporal."

Yunmi blinked. "Like time travel?"

"Like time mapping," Eliora said. "The kind used in psychological conditioning."

The room felt heavier.

I glanced down at the latest photo — the mural behind the art building, the paint swirling into something like a vortex. Beneath it, faint letters glimmered when light hit at the right angle:

MK-Phase II.

The initials made my throat tighten.

Later that night, I wandered back toward the mural with a flashlight. The campus was empty, the air thick with drizzle.

The spray paint glistened.

When I traced the edge of the spiral, my wristband — no, not the old one, but the smartwatch Jae had given me — buzzed faintly.

The coordinates shifted on the screen.
A map blinked open.

Destination: Thirteenth Annex.

I stepped back, pulse skipping.
The Thirteenth Room was supposed to be sealed.

And yet the arrow pulsed, like a heartbeat.

Writing Therapy Log #008
October 29 — Evening

When I close my eyes, I see patterns instead of people.
The mango mural's spiral keeps spinning behind my eyelids.
Sometimes, when I wake, it's already drawn in my notebook.

Madhav said emotion could be tangible.
f that's true, maybe I'm walking through his leftovers.
Memories that taste like fruit, rot like time.

Yunmi told me she's painting again — no permission, no apology.
Her latest piece reflects me staring into a glass. But in the reflection, my eyes are gold.

Jae's been distant since our last session. He said he's cross-checking files about "MK-Phase I."
He won't tell me where he got them.

I'm starting to think this was never about an art rebellion.
It's about remembering something someone didn't want remembered.

We met in the underground archives beneath Aurelya Library.

The air smelled like paper and metal, a century of forgotten stories pressed into boxes.

Jae slid a folder toward me, eyes dark under the fluorescent light.

"Project Mango wasn't just psychological," he said. "It was emotional calibration."

He handed me a photo — grainy, black, and white.

Rows of students in lab coats, electrodes attached to their temples. In the corner, a logo shaped like a mango slice.

And beneath it, a signature: M. Kwan.

I stared at it until the letters blurred.

"He existed," Jae said softly. "Whoever you met — he wasn't random."

The room tilted slightly.

The sound of rain deepened above us, distant and rhythmic, like typing.

Outside the archives, graffiti dripped down the wall — new symbols forming under the old ones.

Three dots.

Two lines.

One word emerging beneath them:

REMEMBER.

The next night, the campus lights went out.

Every screen in the dorm flickered on with the same phrase:

PROJECT MANGO: DON'T FORGET WHAT SWEETNESS FEELS LIKE.

And for a second — only a second — Madhav's reflection appeared in the window, smiling like he'd just come home.

The blackout didn't end with darkness.

It ended with silence.

The kind that hums — like power still hiding behind walls.

My dorm window was still glowing, faintly, even after every light on campus had gone out.

PROJECT MANGO: DON'T FORGET WHAT SWEETNESS FEELS LIKE.

The words pulsed once more, then vanished into black.

I stood frozen, phone shaking in my hand.

Across the glass, for half a heartbeat, I swore I saw him again. Madhav.

That half-smile, that quiet steadiness.

Then lightning flashed, and the reflection was just me — wide-eyed, shaking, small.

"Nova?" Yunmi's voice muffled through the door. "Power's out. You good?"

"Yeah," I lied, pressing my forehead against the window. "Just tired."

But sleep didn't come.

The campus woke up pretending nothing had happened.

The dining hall smelled like coffee and denial.

Students scrolled through their phones, joking about "ghost tech" and "midterm hallucinations."

Yunmi was quiet, sketching shapes in her oatmeal with a spoon.

"You ever think maybe the power's not the only thing glitching?" she asked finally.

I didn't answer.

Because across the hall, the vending machine's glass flickered — and for an instant, I saw a reflection of myself standing on the *other* side, facing me.

Same hoodie.

Same scar above my eyebrow.

Except she didn't blink when I did.

Then the lights blinked back to normal, and she was gone.

Jae called an emergency meeting that afternoon.

The library's lower archives had been sealed overnight — padlocked with a sign that said:

ACCESS RESTRICTED. BY ORDER OF THE OFFICE OF MEMETIC RESEARCH.

"Memetic," Yunmi muttered. "Like memes?"

"Not that kind," Jae said grimly. "The kind that infects thought patterns."

He looked exhausted — dark rings under his eyes, hair a mess. His notebooks were full of overlapping graphs, coordinates, and names circled in red.

"What if the Thirteenth Room isn't a room?" he said. "What if it's a point of *convergence*? Emotional, psychological, spatial — maybe all three."

"Or maybe," I said quietly, "it's awake."

No one laughed.

Writing Therapy Log #009
November 1 — Evening

I can't tell if I'm documenting the truth or feeding the loop.

The campus feels thinner lately — hallways stretching too long, doors opening into silence that feels aware.

Sometimes I hear footsteps behind me, perfectly in sync with mine.
I turn around, and there's no one there.

Jae's convinced the coordinates lead to an elevator hidden in the psychology building.

Yunmi says if art can reflect emotion, maybe emotion can reflect.

Last night, I dreamt the Thirteenth Room wasn't empty.
Someone was humming behind the walls — a song I half-remember from the airport.

Madhav's voice.

Rain blurred Aurelya's skyline into watercolor gray.
We gathered outside the psychology tower, bundled in coats, clutching flashlights like talismans.

The elevator was supposed to go from floors 1–12.
But Jae had found something in the schematics: a phantom floor marker between 12 and the roof — unlisted, unnamed.

He tapped the control panel with a penlight. "See that gap? That's not a mechanical error. That's hidden code."

Yunmi crossed her arms. "You sure this is smart?"

"Absolutely not," I said.

The elevator doors opened with a metallic sigh.
Inside, the panel flickered.
Numbers counted upward — 1... 2... 3... 12.

Then the display glitched.
A horizontal slash replaced the numbers.

The air pressure shifted.

"Hold your breath," Jae whispered.

When the doors opened again, the hallway beyond was dim — long, narrow, lined with sealed glass panels like observation rooms. Dust clung to everything.

We stepped inside.

The air smelled faintly of citrus and static.

Yunmi ran her fingers along a wall. "Feels... warm."

I stared at a door labeled MK-Phase I — Emotional Projection Trials.
Inside, through the dirty glass, I saw a chair. Electrodes.
And a single Polaroid taped to the mirror.

Madhav.

My stomach dropped.

He was younger. Wearing a researcher's badge.
Under his name: Madhav Kwan — Lead Participant Observer.

"Nova," Jae said sharply. "Look at this."
He was pointing to a whiteboard covered in faded ink.
Equations crossed with phrases like 'Cognitive Anchor Drift' and 'Subject N.T. Response Loop Stable.

"Subject N.T.," I whispered.
Nova Temples.

The air flickered.
For one second, the room wasn't dusty — it was *alive*.
Screens glowed. Monitors beeped. Voices whispered.

I stumbled back as a reflection appeared on the glass wall.
Not mine. Not exactly.

She looked older. Stronger. Her eyes are gold instead of brown.

"You came back," my reflection said.

I reached out. "Who are you?"

She smiled. "The version that didn't forget."

Then the lights exploded.

We ran.

Alarms wailed behind us — or maybe that was my heartbeat.

The elevator doors slammed shut before we reached them, trapping us in the stairwell.

Yunmi screamed. Jae slammed his shoulder into the door. Nothing moved.

From below, faint singing drifted up — a melody I knew too well. Madhav's.

I pressed a hand to my chest, trembling.

"Do you hear that?"

Jae nodded. "It's coming from below."

The stairwell lights flickered in rhythm with the music.
Step by step, we descended.

At the base of the stairs, another door waited — one that shouldn't exist.

Carved into the metal were three words:

"REMEMBER THE SWEETNESS."

Writing Therapy Log #010
November 5 — 3:12 AM

I don't think we ever left the Thirteenth Room.
I think it's inside us now — stitched between memory and imagination.

Every reflection looks a half-second behind.

Every whisper sounds like my name said by someone else.

Yunmi's stopped sleeping. She paints through the night; her walls filled with mango skies and faces that look like mine.

Jae keeps muttering equations like prayers.

And me?

I keep dreaming of Madhav saying, "You built this."

Maybe the ghosts in the hallway aren't haunting us.

Maybe they're *waiting for us to remember who they used to be.*

In the mirror above my desk, the reflection moved again.

It smiled faintly.

"You're almost there," it whispered. "Find the journal."

Then it blinked, slow and deliberate — a beat ahead of me this time.

Smoke still hung in the air when we found the journal.

Not fire smoke — static smoke. The kind that smelled faintly of ozone and scorched paper.

Jae was crouched near the remains of the control panel, sorting through a pile of melted plastic and fractured glass. Yunmi kept her back to the door, flashlight trembling.

I caught the glint of something beneath a cracked monitor — a leather-bound notebook, edges singed, the name embossed faintly in gold leaf.

M. Kwan — Project Mango: Field Logs

The cover was still warm.

When I opened it, the ink shimmered faintly, like it was still drying.

The first page read:

"The sky tastes like mango when memory breaks open."

I didn't know whether to laugh or scream.

The morning after, the air in Aurelya felt washed out — colorless.

Students hurried to class as if time hadn't cracked open the night before. The Psychology Tower was locked down again, yellow caution tape fluttering like confetti.

In my dorm, Yunmi hadn't slept.

Her easel faced the window, light spilling across three new canvases: mango skies melting into gray buildings, faceless silhouettes walking backward into fog.

She didn't turn when she spoke.

"You brought something back, didn't you?"

I hesitated. "You mean trauma?"

"No." Her brush dragged across the canvas, streaking orange into crimson. "I mean *him.*"

I looked down at the notebook.

The cover still hummed faintly when I touched it.

Jae came by before noon, hands stuffed in his jacket pockets, eyes wild with exhaustion.

"I cross-referenced the schematics again," he said, pacing. "That room we found. It wasn't an accident. It was *built* to anchor emotion."

He set down his tablet. The screen showed lines of old code, half-corrupted.

"Project Mango was an early memory-mapping prototype. But not just for recollection — for *emulation.* They were training neural templates to recreate the sensory imprint of specific memories. Emotions as coordinates."

I flipped through the journal's pages — each one worse than the last. Sketches of diagrams labeled *"Anchor Drift," "Memory Cloning Protocol,"* and *"Replication Delay."*

But what froze me was a note scrawled in the margin:

"Subject MK–02 exhibits retention anomalies when emotional attachment exceeds containment thresholds."

Madhav's initials.
MK–02.

And under it, in a different hand — smaller, feminine —
"She remembers him before she ever met him."

Writing Therapy Log #011
November 7 — 2:43 PM

I don't know if the journal is mine or his.

Some pages feel like reading my own thoughts written years ago, in another language I forgot I knew.

I keep seeing flashes — train windows, mango trees, a laugh I can't place.

Madhav is saying my name like it's both a greeting and a warning.

If memories are just emotional loops coded in sensory data, does love count as a program too?

Jae thinks this was about mapping *grief.*
I think it was about testing how far people will go to feel real.

Yunmi's first public gallery night was chaos — professors, art students, and city patrons packed shoulder to shoulder in the converted warehouse studio.

Her wall piece dominated the center — a mural of fragmented reflections and bright orange skies, scattered with faint outlines of numbers and circuit-like patterns.

Jae leaned toward me, whispering, "Those look like the Mango coordinate codes."

"Maybe she's trying to warn us," I murmured.

Halfway through the event, Yunmi's mentor cornered her — the one who'd mocked her for mixing realism with "graffiti nonsense."

He gestured toward the wall. "Beautiful chaos, Kailen, but what are you *trying* to say?"

She smiled, voice soft and cold. "That memory is just a glitch we agreed to call identity."

The crowd applauded.

But when she turned toward me, her eyes looked hollow.

Later that night, we gathered in Jae's apartment. The journal sat open on the table, pages glowing faintly under lamplight.

"The ink reacts to heat," Jae murmured, passing a candle flame close to the margin. "Look."

New words appeared beneath the surface — faint, almost invisible:

"If you're reading this, the simulation is stabilizing."

My breath caught. "Simulation?"

Yunmi backed up. "Nope. Not this again."

Jae's hand trembled slightly. "Nova, listen to this line — 'Her consciousness becomes the memory's container.' What if they didn't just record emotions — what if they *uploaded* them?"

I stared down at the ink, at the next line that flickered into view:

"She'll remember him when the mango sky returns."

The candle flame snapped.

That night, I dreamt of the airport again.

Same hum, same smell of roasted beans and antiseptic.

Madhav stood across the terminal, the crowd blurring around him.

He smiled and held out a mango smoothie.

"You remembered the sweetness," he said.

When I reached for it, his hand passed through mine — like fog through glass.

I woke up gasping.

The journal lay open beside me; on a new page I hadn't turned to before.

A photo had fallen out.

Me.

At the airport.

But the timestamp was from six months *before* I ever arrived in Aurelya.

Writing Therapy Log #012
November 11 — 11:16 PM

I think Project Mango wasn't about reconstructing lost feelings.

It was about creating people out of them.

Yunmi says my eyes look different lately — lighter, gold around the edges.

Jae won't stop muttering equations. He says the university's system logs show duplicated IDs for me — two timestamps, two entries.

Sometimes I wonder if I'm the original.

Sometimes I wonder if he is.

The journal says one last thing at the end of the last page, written in handwriting identical to mine:

"Don't forget what sweetness feels like."

And under it — an initial.

N.T.

The mango trees outside campus began to bloom again, weeks too early.

Their scent bled through my window, syrupy and heavy, like the air itself remembered something I didn't.

When I touched the glass, faint fingerprints bloomed from the inside. Five of them — smaller, colder.

And then, written just above them in fog:

"See you soon."

I didn't breathe until it faded.

The journal rests under my pillow now.

Sometimes I feel it vibrate softly, like a pulse.

And every night, before sleep, I whisper to no one:

"Tell me what sweetness feels like."

The air always answers with silence.

Except sometimes... it hums.

The first crack appeared in sound.

A ripple that passed through the campus bell tone at exactly 11:11 a.m., stretching the note into a vibration that seemed to hum beneath my skin.

I was sitting in the library with Jae, half-listening as he read from the latest batch of reports we'd collected from the 13th Room incident. The air smelled like dust and electric rain, a combination I'd learned meant my memory was about to slide.

"Nova," Jae said softly, "are you even here right now?"

I blinked. The world came back in layers — pen scratches, a clock hand stuttering mid-second, sunlight bending slightly wrong across his face.

"Yeah," I lied. "Just tired."

He leaned back in his chair, studying me. His hair had grown longer since the semester began, framing eyes that seemed to know more than he said. "Tired doesn't look like that."

I smiled thinly, closing my notebook. *Tired doesn't feel like this either.*

The fractures weren't just in sound anymore.

By the time the weekend hit, *reality itself* felt like it had started buffering. Conversations looped.
Hallway posters changed fonts mid-glance.
And once, in the reflection of the campus vending machine, I saw Yunmi's mural ripple like water — the paint shifting from bright yellow to bruised blue.

When I asked her about it later, she frowned.
"You okay, Unni? It's been yellow all week."

I didn't argue.
How do you tell someone the world is glitching around your pulse?

Writing Therapy Log #013
February 19 — 11:47 p.m.

If the world keeps repeating, maybe it's trying to tell me something.

I keep hearing the same melody in my head — the airport crowd, his voice, the sound of that blender mixing mango and milk.

Maybe that's what time does when it breaks. It tries to remix what you loved.

Jae started noticing the slips, too.

During one late-night study session, the numbers on his laptop froze at 03:03.

He tapped the screen.

"It's been three minutes for the last fifteen minutes," he muttered.

I looked over his shoulder — the seconds still blinking the same pattern. 03:03. 03:03. 03:03.

The same number appeared in my notes the next morning, scrawled in handwriting that wasn't quite mine.

By midweek, the library light had begun to feel... wrong.
Fluorescent hum too high, air too still.

Yunmi started skipping meals to finish her newest mural. It covered an entire wall of the art building — tangled vines, human silhouettes, and words in languages I couldn't place.

"Each layer's supposed to mean something different," she told me, smudged with paint. "It's not just color. It's memory."

I stared at it, trying to decode the shapes. One of them — a silhouette reaching for a mango-colored sun — looked exactly like me.

When I asked how she'd drawn it, she tilted her head.
"I didn't," she said. "It just... appeared after I painted the sky."

I left without answering.

That night, I dreamt of the Thirteenth Room again.
Only this time, it wasn't empty.
The lights flickered, and a shadow stood at the far end — tall, familiar.

"Madhav?"

He turned. The light flickered again, and for a heartbeat, his face was clear. The same eyes from the airport — soft, amber, infinite.

"You remembered me," he whispered.

Then the floor cracked like glass.

Jae woke me from the dream. I'd fallen asleep at my desk, the journal open beside me.

"Nova," he said, shaking me gently. "You were saying someone's name."

I looked at the notebook. The ink on the page had smeared, like someone had written over it while I slept.

A phrase shone faintly in the lamplight:

Madhav Kwan — Anchor Point #7.

"Did you write that?" Jae asked.

I didn't answer.

He frowned. "Nova, if you're seeing him again—"

"Again?"

He hesitated. "You said his name before. In the 13th Room. Right before you passed out."

The air between us went still.

Later, when the snow began to fall over Aurelya, the city lights flickered again — three times in sequence.

I stood by the window, the campus below painted in silver and amber.

For a moment, I could swear I saw him walking across the courtyard — no coat, no footprints. Just a shimmer of motion where light bent wrong.

My reflection whispered against the glass:

He's waiting where time folds.

Writing Therapy Log #014
February 28 — 2:19 a.m.

I used to think love was supposed to ground you.

But maybe it's the opposite. Maybe it lifts you high enough to see the cracks in the sky.

Every time I close my eyes, I see mango-colored light spilling through the fractures.

And in that light, he's standing there — like memory itself is holding its breath.

The fracture became a doorway.

It started as a line of light across the wall of the linguistics building, just thin enough to miss—until I brushed past it and the air rippled, humming like a heartbeat under glass.

I stumbled back. My wristwatch blinked 00:00 and stayed there.

"Nova?" Jae's voice echoed down the hallway. "The power's flickering again. Don't move."

But the light widened, edges peeling back like film burning in reverse. Behind it, I saw the faint outline of the Thirteenth Room—its endless corridor breathing dust and silence.

The air smelled like mango and metal.

I stepped forward before fear could find me.

Yunmi and Jae followed me through.

The hallway stretched into infinity, each door reflecting another time—me laughing at the airport, me crying in therapy, me asleep in my dorm bed.

"This isn't a hallway," Jae whispered. "It's a loop."

I touched one of the doors. Warm. Alive. Behind it, a sound—like a blender whirring.

The smell hit next: sweet, sharp, familiar.

He was here.

Inside the Thirteenth Room, time had folded itself into moments that didn't agree on sequence.

Yunmi's mural floated on the ceiling like a cloud of memory—paint strokes turning into flickering images of Aurelya streets, our laughter, and the color of that first sunset.

Jae pulled out his scanner, eyes wide. "Nova... these readings aren't electromagnetic. They're biometric. It's you. The room's syncing with you."

My hand shook. "Then why does it smell like him?"

The room pulsed once. And then he stepped out of the light.
Madhav Kwan.

Older, maybe. Or maybe time had just missed him more gently than it missed me.

He wore the same jacket from the airport, sleeves rolled to the forearm, expression steady in a way that made my breath stall.

"Nova," he said, voice catching on my name like it remembered every time I'd whispered it to an empty room.

I froze. "You're real."

He smiled, faintly. "I was real because you remembered me."

The walls behind him began to ripple—memory collapsing into pixels.

Writing Therapy Log #015
March 12 — 3:09 a.m.

When you love someone who doesn't exist, the grief is different.

It's not a loss—it's an erasure.

But if remembering someone can bring them back... what does forgetting do?

I took a step toward him, every sound muffled except the low thrum of the room recalibrating.

"You left," I whispered. "You just—vanished."

His eyes softened. "They erased the timeline. The experiment had to reset. I tried to hold on, but you had to forget me to survive."

Jae's voice cut through the haze. "Nova, the anchor's breaking—if you stay connected, you'll go with it!"

Madhav looked at him, then at me. "You have to go. But this time... remember the sweetness."

He reached out, fingers brushing mine. A static warmth spread through my hand, burning and tender.

For a heartbeat, we stood in two worlds—his face flickering between the past and the now, the sound of mango smoothies and airport chatter dissolving around us.

"I remember," I whispered.

Light poured out from the cracks in the floor.

Jae shouted something I couldn't hear. Yunmi's paint lifted off the walls, scattering into golden dust.

And then the world folded inward—sound collapsing, light blooming, memory rewriting itself one last time.

I woke up in the courtyard. Morning air tasted like rain and electricity.

Yunmi was kneeling beside me, streaked with color, crying and laughing all at once. Jae stood a few feet away, trembling but alive.

"Project Mango," he whispered, staring at the space where the Thirteenth Room used to be. "They tried to make people remember someone until they existed."

"Did it work?" Yunmi asked.

He glanced at me. I still felt the warmth of a hand fading from mine.

"I don't know," I said softly. "But I think so."

That night, I went back to the art building. Yunmi's mural had changed again.

The figure reaching toward the mango-colored sky now held someone's hand—his outline faint, almost transparent.

I touched the wall. The paint shimmered under my fingers.

Somewhere in the distance, a blender whirred.

Writing Therapy Log #016
March 17 — 12:12 a.m.

I saw him again in the reflection of a window that wasn't there.

Maybe love is a frequency—one that keeps playing after the song ends.

If memory can bend time, maybe forgiveness can bend reality.

Jae is doing a research fellowship in another country. Yunmi's mural went viral online—students calling it "The Sky That Remembers Us."

And me?

I started writing again. Not therapy logs, not code notes — just letters. To someone who might never read them.

Sometimes I still feel him in the silence between raindrops, in the taste of mango on my tongue.

Maybe that's what love really is: not something you lose or keep, but something that keeps rewriting you until you learn how to live with the echo.

The last week of summer in Aurelya didn't feel like an ending.

It felt like something holding its breath.

Sunlight spilled through the window of my dorm room, painting the walls with a mango-colored haze. Outside, the air shimmered with heat, carrying the smell of wet stone and street vendors. My half-packed suitcase leaned against the bed. Yunmi's paint-stained shoes were still by the door, proof that this room had been more than just four walls.

My reflection in the mirror looked almost rested—lighter somehow. A year ago, my eyes had always been half-guarded, like I was waiting for the next glitch. Now they looked...alive.

A notification blinked on my tablet: *Flight reminders.*

Not mine. Yunmi's. She was heading home to Busan for the break.

I exhaled and started folding the last of my notebooks, each one scarred with ink, sketches, and half-finished therapy logs.

Yunmi burst into the room with her usual whirlwind of energy and acrylic stains.

"You're not crying already, are you?" she teased, tossing a roll of tape at me.

"Just sentimental," I said, taping up a box labeled *DO NOT LOSE – year one memories.*

She leaned on the edge of my desk, watching me with soft eyes. "You did well this year, Nova. Better than you think."

"You too," I said. "Your art show—people still talk about it."

She shrugged, pretending not to blush. "That was nothing."

"It was *you.*"

She smiled, then reached into her tote bag and pulled out a small paintbrush wrapped in ribbon. "Here. My lucky one. For when you forget what color feels like."

I stared at it, the handle worn from her grip. "You're sure?"

"Yeah. I'll need an excuse to steal it back next year."

We laughed. Then she hugged me tighter than she ever had before.

When she left, the room felt heavier.

The campus was quieter than usual. The semester's end left an echo behind, the kind that clings to benches and stairwells. I crossed the courtyard toward the research wing, where Jae was packing up his equipment—rows of tangled wires, notebooks filled with formulas and half-legible notes.

He looked up when I stepped in.

"Came to say goodbye?"

"Came to make sure you actually take a break."

He laughed softly, setting his pen down. "I don't think people like us ever really take breaks."

There was something different in him—older, calmer. Maybe it was just the way the light hit his glasses, reflecting the last orange glint of the day.

"You still thinking about him?" he asked gently.

"Madhav?"

He nodded.

"Sometimes," I admitted. "Like he's a memory someone wrote too well to fade."

Jae hesitated, then slid something across the table—a tiny flash drive in a paper sleeve.

"What's this?"

"Data fragment. Found it embedded in the corrupted Mango logs. You don't have to open it now. But... if you ever feel like the story's unfinished, maybe it's your piece of closure."

My throat tightened. "You kept this?"

He shrugged. "Call it academic curiosity."

I smiled. "Call it kindness."

He grinned, then slung his bag over his shoulder. "See you in the fall, Temples."

"See you, Thornevale."

He paused at the door. "Oh—and Nova?"

"Yeah?"

"Next year...let's write our own experiment."

The Aurelya skyline shimmered under the setting sun. Students milled through the streets below, luggage trailing, laughter drifting upward.

I sat on the rooftop café one last time, sipping a mango smoothie. It tasted the same as that first day—the one Madhav had bought me before disappearing into the crowd.

The first note he left me was tucked safely in my journal:
"Project Mango: don't forget what sweetness feels like."
The words had haunted me all semester. Now, they just felt true.

I opened my notebook—*Writing Therapy Log #017.*
Ink met paper.

Writing Therapy Log #017 – "The Version That Stayed"
August 18

Sometimes memory feels like air—impossible to hold, but always around you.

I came here looking for a ghost and found myself instead.

Madhav was never meant to stay.

Maybe none of us are.

But the people who walk with you through your unmaking—that's what love looks like.

It's not eternal. It's *present.*

The sky looks like mango again.

Sweet. Temporary.

Enough.

When I looked up, the city lights were blinking to life. For a second, the horizon shimmered like a reflection on glass—and I could've sworn I saw him standing across the street.

Same smile. Same quiet gravity.
Then he vanished in the blur of headlights.

My phone buzzed once.
Screen black. Then white text:

Project Mango — Data continuity confirmed.

I smiled, closing the notebook.
"I remember," I whispered.

The sky deepened into gold.
For the first time, the sweetness didn't scare me.

The air smelled different when I came back to Aurelya.
Cleaner. Colder.
Like the city had gone through a reboot while I was gone.

Street banners fluttered with the university crest—new motto, new promises.
"Safety. Integrity. Progress."
The words looked sterile against the fading murals that Yunmi and her collective had painted last spring.

My taxi wound through the narrow hillside streets, the same ones where Jae once told me memory was "a ghost with good taste."

Now, everything felt sharper. Cameras blinked from lampposts. A new set of faculty IDs scanned us before we even reached the gates.

When I stepped onto campus, the first thing I noticed was how quiet it was.

No laughter spilling out of dorm windows. No street musicians near the fountain.

Just wind, sweeping dry leaves across the quad.

Yunmi found me by the sculpture garden.

Her hair was shorter, her eyeliner bolder. "You look like you've seen a ghost," she said.

"Maybe I have," I murmured.

She nudged my shoulder. "Welcome back to the maze."

Behind her, the banners snapped in the wind. For a moment, I thought I saw a flicker across one—an image half-formed between the folds.

A hallway.

Number 13.

Then it vanished.

That night, I unpacked in our old dorm. My things looked unfamiliar, like props in someone else's room.

The paintbrush Yunmi gave me sat on the desk. My journal—*Writing Therapy Log #017*—was still tucked inside the top drawer.

When I flipped it open, a folded note slid out.

No signature. Just five words, written in scrambled handwriting:

"You found the door. It's not over."

My pulse stuttered.

The hallway light flickered once, then steadied.

I glanced at my nightstand.

A glint of metal.

My old watch—the one I lost in the tunnels months ago—lay there, face cracked but still ticking.

Backward.

I stared until the rhythm synced with my breath.

Tick. Tock. Back. Again.

And somewhere in the distance, beyond the hum of the dorms, I swore I heard footsteps echoing down a hallway that shouldn't exist.

SIX

Sophomore (Second Year)

The Thirteenth Room – The Version of Me Who Got Lost

Writing Therapy Log #018 – "Returning Shadows"
September 3 — First Week Back

The sky here isn't mango anymore. It's chrome.

The air hums like a system rebooting, and everyone pretends not to notice.

I told myself I was ready to come back.

But the city looks at me like it remembers something I don't.

Aurelya greeted me with rain that didn't fall.

It just hovered — thin mist trembling above the pavement, refusing to touch down.

When the shuttle doors opened, I stepped into it anyway. The scent of ozone and new paint filled my lungs. Banners for *Campus Renewal Initiative 2030* flapped overhead, promising *Transparency and Safety* in clean sans-serif fonts.

No one mentioned what they were cleaning up.

The dorm lobby looked the same — until I noticed the tiny black domes in each corner. Cameras. Freshly installed. Their red lights blinked like watchful eyes.

Yunmi's laugh broke the sterile quiet.

"Guess Big Brother finally enrolled," she said, wheeling her suitcase past me. Her hair was shorter now, streaked with copper paint, her jacket splattered with color. A rebellion wrapped in denim.

"Nice security aesthetic," I said.

She grinned. "I'm starting a new zine. *Invisible Students.* You'll be my headline."

I smiled, but something in the elevator mirror behind her rippled — like heat distortion, though the air was cold.

Our room smelled like pine cleaner and ghosts. My side of the desk still held the faint outline of where my notebook had been.

Yunmi flopped onto her bed, scrolling. "They upgraded the Wi-Fi again. Encrypted — probably tracking keywords."

"Like 'Thirteenth Room?'" I said.

She froze. "You had to say it out loud."

We laughed, too loudly.

Later, while she unpacked her paints, I opened my journal. A folded sheet slipped free — not mine. Five words in a hurried hand:
You found the door. It's not over.

My pulse jumped.

I looked toward Yunmi. "Did you — ?"

She shook her head. "If it's about art supplies, no."

The window fogged slightly, though the air-con was running. Outside, the lamplight bled into the mist like ink dropped in water.

Orientation day. The halls buzzed with admin drones and students in muted chatter.

Jae found me near the courtyard café, balancing three paper cups. "One vanilla, one cinnamon, one existential crisis."

"Mine's the crisis," I said, taking it.

He studied me. "You okay being back?"

"I'm here."

He nodded, but his gaze flicked past me — toward the faculty tower. "They reopened Sublevel C. That floor was sealed since before we were born."

"Why?"

"They said storage. But Yunmi's friend saw movers hauling out old lab equipment. Analog stuff. VHS, tape reels."

The word *tape* scraped something inside me — a faint echo of static, a voice whispering *you were supposed to forget.*

I swallowed. "I don't like analog anymore."

"Yeah," he murmured, "but it remembers you."

Evening. The quad lights cast perfect circles on the wet grass.

That's when I saw him.

Madhav Kwan.

Across the walkway, talking to a professor I didn't recognize. His posture was too straight, smile too polite — as if he'd been recalibrated.

When our eyes met, the air tightened.

He gave a small nod. No wave. No warmth.

Then he turned and walked into the faculty building without looking back.

I stood there until Yunmi called my name.

Rain again, this time real. It drummed on the windows while I reorganized my desk.

My watch — the one I'd found in August — sat beside my journal. The crack across its face caught the light like a scar.

I tapped it out of habit. The second hand twitched — and began to move backward.

Tick. Tock. Reverse.

I lifted it to my ear. The sound was faint, almost delicate. Beneath it, another rhythm pulsed — too slow to be mechanical.

In the reflection of the window, my eyes blinked half a beat late.

Writing Therapy Log #018 (cont.)

Maybe I never left the room.
Maybe the year in between was a memory the city loaned me.
Yunmi says art saves people.
Jae says memory anchors us.
I think remembering hurts — but forgetting terrifies me more.

When I finally turned off the lamp, the dorm slipped into silence.
Outside, somewhere between the library and the observatory, a single light flickered thirteen times before going dark.

Writing Therapy Log #019 – "Echoes of the Past"
September 10

The mind forgets what it can't handle.
But what if forgetting is the experiment?
Sometimes I hear my own voice where I shouldn't — in the hum of the radiator, in the air vents, down the hall.

Maybe memory has learned how to echo back.

The library was too quiet. Even the air felt digitized, like someone had noise-reduced it in post.

Yunmi had dragged me there after class. "Inspiration," she said, shoving a camera into my hands. "Every archive is a rebellion waiting to happen."

She was working on the first issue of her underground zine *Invisible Students*, a collage of missing faces and protest graffiti. The university would hate it. That made her love it more.

I left her on the upper floor, photographing stacks of old thesis papers, and wandered downstairs.

The sign over the basement door read "Restricted – Faculty Only." Someone had peeled away half the tape, sealing it.

So, I slipped through.

The steps smelled of mold and burned dust. My flashlight beam trembled across the concrete.

At the bottom waited a corridor of metal filing cabinets. Most were rusted shut. Others were empty except for curled photo negatives.

A single monitor sat on a desk, unplugged but glowing faintly.

Next to it: a cardboard box labeled CONTROL GROUP – SUBJECT 13.

Inside were VHS tapes, handwritten dates fading to ghosts. One label stopped my heart:

"Session 07 – Temples, N."

My hand shook as I slid the tape into the player.

The screen crackled alive.

At first, only static. Then: my voice.

Calm. Too calm.

"I remember standing in a white room. They told me to describe the color of sound. I said it was blue, but they corrected me — said I used to say orange."

I took a step back. "No..."

The video camera's view shifted; the me on-screen looked directly into the lens.

"Are you watching this again?"

The screen went black.

A soft sound whispered behind me — like someone exhaling my name.

"Nova..."

I spun around. The hallway was empty. But the echo didn't fade. It repeated, from the far end, this time — my voice, not an imitation.

"Nova..."

I fled, the beam of my flashlight cutting through the dark like panic made visible.

Morning sunlight poured through our dorm window as if nothing had happened. Yunmi sat cross-legged on her bed, surrounded by ink-stained fingers and pages.

"You look haunted," she said, glancing up.

"Thanks," I muttered, tossing my notebook onto the desk.

She held up a half-finished poster: *'Missing isn't the same as gone.'*

"That's really comforting," I said.

"It's art," she replied. "It's supposed to hurt a little."

Jae arrived with Eliora soon after, arms full of bagels and caffeine. Eliora's curls framed her like a halo of defiance — she'd joined Yunmi's collective as their unofficial documentarian.

"Campus security took down our first zine drop," she said between bites. "Claimed it violated the new *privacy policy.*"

Jae frowned. "They mean 'control policy.'"

He slid a small envelope across the table toward me. "Found this in my locker. No name. Thought it might be yours."

The handwriting matched the note from before — slanted, desperate: You found the door. But it's not over. Watch your reflection.

The word *reflection* was underlined twice.

"I don't want to watch it," I whispered.

"Then we will," Yunmi said, serious now. "Together."

That night, I returned to the library. I told myself I only wanted proof.

The basement lights flickered on their own when I reached the bottom. The monitor glowed again.

This time, there was a cassette beside it — unlabeled. I pressed play.

A woman's voice, distorted, filled the room.

"You were supposed to forget."

I froze. The tape hissed. Then — silence.

In the reflection of the monitor, another face hovered beside mine.

It smiled — familiar, wrong, remembering me before I did.

Writing Therapy Log #019 (continued)

Found a tape.
Heard my voice from somewhere I never was.
They say memory is a mirror.
Then why does mine look back and smile?

When I finally left the archives, the hallway lights pulsed in groups of thirteen — and the clock above the exit ticked backward.

The same rhythm as my watch.
The same heartbeat as the city.

Writing Therapy Log #020 – "The Lost Map"
September 18

It started with a door that didn't exist, and now it's a map that shouldn't either.

Perhaps memory creates its own blueprints when it seeks to be recalled.

The campus air had changed.

You could smell the decay of autumn buried under fresh paint and fear.

Overnight, the university installed new security cameras — small black domes that blinked above the entrances like unblinking eyes. A recorded voice now played on loop through the courtyard speakers: *"For your safety, surveillance is in effect."*

Safety.
Right.

Yunmi and I walked side by side through the morning fog, her scarf trailing paint stains. She'd been working nonstop on her second zine drop — one themed around "architectural ghosts."

"Guess who's on the admin's hit list?" she said, smirking.
"Your art collective?"
"Our art collective," she corrected. "You're the accidental muse, remember?"
"Right. The face of paranoia chic."
She grinned. "Exactly."
Her laughter felt like static — light, electric, always one spark away from catching fire.

Later that day, Jae called an "emergency study session" in the humanities building.

When I arrived, the classroom smelled like old coffee and printer toner. Eliora was leaning against the whiteboard; her hair pulled into a bun that meant business. A stranger sat beside her — a transfer student, tall, polite, with one of those smiles that seemed engineered to appear trustworthy.

"This is Lucien," Eliora said. "Transferred in from Sorynthia Institute. He's good with puzzles."

Lucien nodded. "I'm better with secrets."

That made Yunmi snort. "You'll fit right in, then."

We'd barely unpacked our laptops before Jae slid a book onto the table. "Look what the library gods sent me," he said.

The book was heavy — an old art portfolio from the 1990s, pages filled with charcoal sketches of buildings that didn't exist. On the last page, tucked inside a taped envelope, was a folded piece of tracing paper covered in intersecting lines and cryptic numbers.

"The missing floor plans," Jae whispered.

We spread it open carefully. The map showed the campus — every hall, courtyard, and sublevel — but there were faint dotted corridors marked in red pencil that led to nowhere.

"Phantom floors," Lucien murmured. "You see these symbols? Repetition of 13. Thirteen hallways. Thirteen sub-basements. Thirteen missing students."

Yunmi reached for her phone to photograph it.

Before she could, the projector on the wall flickered to life — unprompted.

The image it displayed wasn't the map.

It was *us*.

A live feed.
From above.

Eliora gasped. "They're watching the watchers."

The lights snapped off.

Only the projector's glow remained, illuminating our faces like an interrogation scene.

We didn't wait around.

We ran across the courtyard, laughing breathlessly once we hit the cool night air — not because it was funny, but because panic always sounds like laughter when you survive it.

Yunmi shoved the folded map into my hand. "Hide it somewhere analog. They can't track paper."

Jae nodded. "We'll regroup tomorrow."

But before we split, Lucien lingered. His expression was unreadable, shadowed by the lamplight.

"You ever think," he said quietly, "that maybe the building's not haunted — maybe *we* are?"

He walked off before I could respond.

Sunday morning, I went to the café near the old clock tower — the one that smelled like sugar and nostalgia. I ordered jasmine tea, sat by the window, and opened my journal.

When I looked up again, the clock read 5:14 p.m.

I'd only just sat down.

The tea was cold.

My notebook was filled — pages upon pages of dense handwriting. My handwriting. Except I didn't remember writing any of it.

One line repeated over and over, in darker ink:
The hallway bends differently every time.

The barista noticed me staring. "You okay?"

"Yeah," I lied. "Just... lost track of time."

On my way out, my reflection in the café window didn't move when I did.

That night, Yunmi texted:

Someone spray-painted the zine symbol on the admin building. They're calling us terrorists now. Want to come help clean it before security connects it to me?

I went. Of course I did.

We worked in silence, scrubbing at the bricks until our hands were raw. Jae stood watch. Lucien disappeared for a while — said he was checking the perimeter — then returned with the faintest trace of dirt on his sleeve and an excuse too neat to question.

I noticed something then. When Yunmi mentioned *the archive tapes*, Lucien's eyes flickered. Not confusion — recognition.

He shouldn't have known about them.

Madhav found me later that night outside the dorms.

He'd been quiet for weeks, orbiting my life like a planet afraid to collide.

"You're still chasing ghosts," he said.

"You used to believe in them, too."

He looked past me toward the library lights. "Belief and obsession look the same from far away."

"What does that mean?"

He hesitated. "If you keep looking for the truth, Nova, you'll forget who you are."

Then he walked away.

His reflection lingered in the glass door a second longer than he did.

Writing Therapy Log #021 – "The Lost Map"
September 18 — 11:37 p.m.

Today, a map drew itself in my head.
Corridors connecting memories that shouldn't meet.
Lucien said we might be the ghosts.
But ghosts don't bleed.
And I scraped my hand tonight.

So, either I'm still alive —
Or the dead just learned how to write.

The dorm felt too still.
Even the hum of the mini fridge had a pulse — soft, rhythmic, like breathing through static.

Yunmi was asleep on the top bunk, one arm dangling over the side. The glow from her phone painted blue shapes across the wall, flickering with every notification.

I couldn't sleep.

Every time I closed my eyes, I saw that tracing-paper map behind my eyelids — its corridors folding in on themselves like veins. The red pencil lines weren't just routes; they were arteries feeding something alive beneath the school.

I sat at my desk, opened my laptop, and tried to write a letter I'd never send.

Draft (unsent) — To: Zay Roan
Subject: Hey. Or whatever.

You ever feel like time's chewing on the edges of things?

Sometimes I think about Ravenlock — how the hallways smelled like printer ink and burnt toast. I still see flashes of it here. Like it followed me.

I met someone last year — Madhav. I told you about him, right? He's back, but... wrong. He talks like he remembers things I haven't lived yet.

I know you'd say I'm spiraling again, but this feels different.

It feels designed.

I hovered over *Send*, then deleted the draft.

Outside, the wind moaned through the air vents, low and almost human.

Then — a knock.

Three taps.

Measured. Deliberate.

On the wall, not the door.

"Yunmi?" I whispered.

She didn't stir.

I pressed my palm against the cold drywall. The knock came again — same rhythm — and something inside it *clicked*. Like code.

I blinked, and for half a second, I wasn't in my dorm.

The white noise of the fridge became the hum of fluorescent lab lights.

The smell of jasmine tea turned to disinfectant.

And the mirror — the one above my desk — wasn't reflecting me anymore.

It showed a version of me wearing a hospital wristband.

Her lips moved first.

"You forgot to close the door."

I stumbled back.

When I looked again, it was just me — eyes wild, hands shaking.

On the desk, my journal had opened on its own.

Ink bled through the page, forming a single phrase:
WELCOME BACK TO THE THIRTEENTH ROOM.

The lights flickered once, then steadied.

Writing Therapy Log #022 – "Between Walls and Mirrors"
September 19 — 3:02 a.m.

> If time loops long enough, do memories start to echo?
> I keep hearing myself from other rooms.
> I keep answering back.
> The walls remember.
> The mirrors confirm.
> Maybe the Thirteenth Room never ended.
> Maybe it just moved in.

Writing Therapy Log #023 – "Descending Coordinates"
September 20 — 10:47 a.m.

> There are hallways on this campus that aren't on any plan.
> Yunmi says that means someone's hiding something.
> Jae says that means it's a myth.
> Madhav says to leave it alone.
> But I've never been good at leaving things alone.

The tunnels under Aurelya didn't feel like part of a university.

They felt like an organ — old, pulsing, hidden beneath skin that didn't know it was alive.

Yunmi walked ahead with a flashlight, her boots echoing against the rusted metal steps. Jae followed, muttering GPS coordinates from his tablet. Eliora trailed us with a camera, documenting everything. Lucien, of course, stayed quiet — always a step behind, eyes flicking to the shadows as if taking inventory.

We shouldn't have been down there.

The entrance had been sealed years ago, according to the floor plans.

But the red lines on the map — the ones we'd found inside the art book — led here.

The air smelled like dust and rain and something faintly electrical.

"Boiler wing," Jae said, shining his light on a faded sign half-buried in cobwebs. "Used to power the south campus labs before they switched systems."

"Before or after the memory experiments?" Yunmi asked.

He didn't answer.

The deeper we went, the less the walls looked like brick.

They became smooth — like stone polished by hands or time.

I traced my fingers along one section. It was warm.

"Feel that?" I asked.

Eliora pressed her palm to the wall. "Like a heartbeat."

We exchanged a look. No one laughed.

We reached the first junction: two corridors, identical.

Jae pulled up the digital version of the map on his tablet.

"Left leads to the archives," he said. "Right—"

The tablet screen glitched.

The map rearranged itself — red lines shifting like veins under skin.

"Okay," Yunmi whispered. "That's new."

Lucien stepped closer, frowning. "Or someone's still editing the file."

Eliora's flashlight flickered. "Who?"

No one answered.

I looked down both paths. The left one hummed faintly, like a soft machine breathing. The right one dripped water in a steady rhythm.

I chose the left.

Halfway down, we found graffiti — black paint scrawled across the wall: "WE BUILT THE ROOM TO KEEP IT IN."

The words were smeared like someone had tried to erase them and failed.

Yunmi took a photo for her zine.

When her flash went off, the light reflected off something metallic in the corner — a rusted camera, still powered.

She swore softly. "They've been watching this place for years."

I crouched, wiped grime from the lens. The tiny red indicator blinked. Still recording.

"Who's watching now?" I whispered.

The camera swiveled slightly toward me.

We regrouped in the stairwell that spiraled deeper — another three levels down, each step colder than the last.

Lucien's breath fogged the air. "Anyone else feel—"

"—like time's slowing?" Eliora finished.

The light from Yunmi's phone stretched unnaturally long across the walls, bending around the corners before we even reached them.

Jae swore quietly. "This isn't just architecture. This is a distortion."

"Like the Thirteenth Room," I said.

He looked at me sharply. "Don't call it that."

But the name fit.

The feeling fit.

We descended anyway.

The boiler room wasn't what we expected.

No old pipes. No rusted valves.

Just rows of machines — humming softly, arranged in circles around a central pillar of glass.

Inside the pillar: screens. Dozens of them. Each flickering with video feeds from different parts of the university — dorms, lecture halls, stairwells.

And one feed showed *us* standing in front of the glass.

"Holy—" Yunmi's voice broke.

Eliora lifted her camera. "This is proof," she whispered. "This is—"

Her lens cracked with a sharp pop.

The screen showing us went white. Then black.

Then white again — except we weren't standing still anymore.

We were *moving*.

The video showed us walking toward the pillar.

Touching it.

Vanishing inside.

But we hadn't moved.

"Stop," I said, stepping back. "That's not—"

The lights blinked out.

For a heartbeat, all I heard was the hum of the machines and the whisper of someone breathing right behind me.

Then Lucien's voice: "Nova. Don't turn around."

I turned anyway.

The wall behind us had changed.

Where the exit used to be, now a solid surface — seamless, smooth, like it had never been a door.

Trapped.

Yunmi started pounding on the wall. Jae yelled for his signal scanner. Eliora's flashlight beam wobbled violently across the room.

I stared at the glass pillar. The screens flickered again — one by one — until only a single image remained.

My face.

But younger.
From freshman year.
Wristband glinting. Eyes hollow.

Her lips moved silently.

I stepped closer to read them.

"Still recording," she mouthed. "Still here."

Lucien grabbed my wrist. "We need to move."
But the hum around us deepened — the machines pulsing in sync with my heartbeat.
And then — voices.
Layered, familiar, like every whisper I'd ever ignored had come home to answer.

"Nova Temples, Subject 02. Return acknowledged."
"Cognitive re-entry verified."
"Integration resuming."

Yunmi's eyes went wide. "It's talking to you."
I couldn't breathe.
For a second, the air shimmered — like heat on asphalt — and I saw *them*: rows of chairs, other students strapped in, faint outlines like ghosts made of memory.

Then gone.

We bolted.

The far wall cracked open, revealing a narrow hallway — new, metallic, lined with cables.

We didn't question it. We ran.

Lucien led. Eliora filmed what she could. Jae shouted coordinates that didn't exist. Yunmi clutched her bag like a lifeline.

The hallway twisted, turned, doubled back.

And every few steps, I swore I saw another version of us — phantoms flickering at the edge of my vision, walking the same path a few seconds late.

When we finally burst through a maintenance door, we were back on the main floor of the library.

No one else seemed to notice we'd been gone.

My watch read 5:22 p.m.

But Yunmi's phone said 8:46.

We'd lost three hours.

Writing Therapy Log #024 – "Echo Depth"
September 21 — 12:09 a.m.

The map lied.

Or maybe it told the truth, and we just weren't ready to read it.

There's something under this campus that knows my name.
It remembers me better than I do.

Lucien says we were lucky to make it out.
Yunmi says we didn't.

And when I look in the mirror —
I think she might be right.

The rain hadn't stopped since the tunnels.

It drummed against the windows like a slow metronome, counting time we no longer trusted.

Yunmi sat cross-legged on her bed, sketchbook open, the graphite bleeding faintly from her wet fingertips. She was drawing circles — overlapping, spiraling, never closed.

"I keep seeing it," she said without looking up.

"The pillar?" I asked.

She nodded. "Except it's breathing now."

Across the room, Jae's laptop glowed with static. He'd been replaying the video footage for hours. Every time, the same frame froze: us standing in front of the glass, five reflections where there should've been four.

"It's compression lag," he muttered, more to himself than to us.

But his hands were shaking.

Eliora had her camera half-disassembled on the floor, cleaning the cracked lens with obsessive precision. "The footage is gone," she said softly. "But the timestamp moved forward six minutes."

"What do you mean?"

"I mean," she said, "I wasn't recording then."

Lucien hadn't said a word since we got back. He stood by the window, staring at the reflection of the rain. The light outside flashed from a passing patrol car, and for a moment his face blurred — like he wasn't entirely synced with the present.

I tried to write, but the words kept splitting on the page — like the sentences wanted to go in two directions at once.

Everything smelled faintly of wet concrete and metal.

When I finally closed my journal, I noticed the old watch I'd found ticking backward again.

It didn't glow. It didn't buzz.

It just ticked — steady, relentless, in reverse.

Somewhere in the walls, I thought I heard water moving — not pipes, not rain. Something deeper.

The boiler wing is still humming.

Still breathing.

I lay back and let the sound carry me until it wasn't clear if I was falling asleep or slipping under.

Writing Therapy Log #025 – "After the Depths"
September 22 — 1:33 a.m.

Surface doesn't mean safety.

We came back up, but something followed.

The glass remembered us.

The mirror checked attendance.

I think we brought the Thirteenth Room home.

Writing Therapy Log #026 – "Echo Trace"
September 23 — 11:01 a.m.

The deeper we went, the more the air changed.

Now it's the walls that whisper.

They hum when we lie.

The next morning, we met in the basement archives.

The air smelled like dust and old tape — decades of forgotten paper and rusted metal filing cabinets.

Jae was pacing. "The blueprints loop. Every corridor leads back to the same central junction."

Yunmi leaned against a shelf, sketchbook open. "So, the building's a maze?"

Lucien shook his head. "No. It's a machine pretending to be one."

I stared at the map on Jae's screen. He'd highlighted paths in different colors. All of them curved inward — spiraling into a shape that almost looked like a human brain.

The label at the center: CONTROL NODE / PROJECT 13.

Eliora raised her camera. "We have to go back."

I swallowed. "Back where?"

"To where we left the feed," she said. "It's watching us either way. We might as well watch it back."

We didn't tell anyone.

By dusk, we were in the tunnels again — flashlights cutting thin slices through the dark.

The walls looked different this time.

New paint.

New graffiti.

"REMEMBERING IS A VIRUS."

"THEY BUILT YOU TO FORGET."

"LIES DON'T ECHO, THEY REPEAT."

Each phrase looked freshly written, still dripping.

"Was that here before?" Yunmi whispered.

No one answered.

The hallway forked again — left or right — and Jae marked both routes with chalk.

When we circled back fifteen minutes later, both marks were gone.

The walls were clean.

"That's impossible," Jae muttered, stepping forward.

Lucien grabbed his arm. "It's not the hallway that's moving. It's us."

Eliora frowned. "What are you talking about?"

Lucien gestured at the floor. "Count your steps."

We walked.

Twenty-four paces to the next corner.

Then we turned, walked back.

Twenty-four again — but when we returned, the door behind us was gone.

Yunmi's breathing quickened. "I hate this."

I pressed my hand against the wall — smooth metal, almost warm.

Then, faintly, something *shifted* beneath it.

Like breath.

"Nova," Jae said quietly. "Look at this."

He pointed his flashlight at a section of the wall where the paint peeled.

Underneath — carved into the surface — was a single word:

TEMPLE.

Not "Temples."

Just "TEMPLE." Singular.

I brushed my fingers over it, pulse hammering. "They spelled it wrong."

Lucien's voice came out low. "Or they weren't writing your name."

By the next morning, everything above ground felt off.

Shadows didn't match the angle of the light.

Footsteps echoed before we took them.

Yunmi tried to distract herself with art — painting over one of her old canvases with wide streaks of yellow and red. The shapes were abstract at first, then started to look like doorways.

She dropped her brush. "I didn't paint this."

Eliora set up her camera to film the painting overnight, "just to prove we're not insane."

Lucien stayed up with her. Jae analyzed the footage from last night's descent frame by frame.

I wrote.

Except halfway through a paragraph, I realized I wasn't holding my pen anymore.

It was moving on its own.

I froze. The ink spelled out three words before my hand could stop it: "DON'T TRUST HIM."

The pen fell from my grip.

"Who?" I whispered.

No answer.

But when I flipped the page, there was something else already written — the handwriting mine, but older, shakier:

"You wrote this once before.

Stop before you remember."

That night, the hallway dreams returned.

Not tunnels — corridors of light.

I'd walk for hours without reaching the end, until I'd find a mirror.

And inside it, she was always waiting — the version of me from the glass pillar.

"You left something down there," she said.

"What?"

"Your memory. Your name. The truth."

She smiled, tilting her head like she'd heard this conversation before.

"You'll find it in the labyrinth. But the labyrinth wants you to lie first."

Writing Therapy Log #027 – "The Loop Doesn't End"
September 24

I tried to write what happened, but the words changed when I looked away.

I don't know if we're documenting the truth or creating it.

Lucien's voice sounds different when the lights flicker.
Jae's reflection blinks slower than he does.
Yunmi's shadow paints before she moves her brush.

I think the labyrinth isn't underground anymore.
I think it's us.

The mirror called my name again.
Not out loud—more like a thought that echoed too clearly to belong to me.
"Nova," it whispered, inside the hum of the dorm fridge, the rainfall outside, the faint ticking of the backward-moving watch.
I sat up, every hair on my arms rising. Yunmi's slow breathing came from the other bed, soft and rhythmic.
The mirror across the room gleamed faintly even though the lights were off.
I slid out of bed, feet touching the cold tile.
The surface wasn't glass anymore—it looked like water held perfectly still.
"Who's there?" I whispered.
My reflection smiled a beat too late.
Then the voice—not from the mirror, but from *behind it.*
"Question one. Who are you when no one's watching?"

I froze. "What—?"

"Question two. Who were you before you forgot?"

The glass rippled, showing flashes: tunnels, faces, a heartbeat made of static.

"Question three," the voice said. "When you lie, who tells the truth?"

I backed away until my shoulder hit the dresser.

"Stop," I whispered. "Stop it."

The reflection leaned forward, mouth still. The sound came from *everywhere* now.

"We watch so you don't have to. We remember so you can sleep."

The watch on my wrist ticked faster—then *stopped*.

The mirror cleared.

My reflection mouthed something silently:

"Don't look away this time."

The room blinked white.

I woke to sunlight slicing through the blinds, heartbeat steady but wrong—half a beat late.

Yunmi was gone. Her sketchbook lay open on her bed.

Across the page, written in graphite so hard it tore the paper:

"IT'S ASKING US QUESTIONS NOW."

Writing Therapy Log #028 – "The Watcher"
October 2 — 11:43 a.m.

It started with questions.

Not the kind you can answer — the kind that rearranges your memories while you try.

The Watcher doesn't just see. It *knows*.

The library basement smelled like ozone.

Not the sharp tang of rain, but something more sterile — electric.

Jae was bent over the old broadcast panel we'd found behind the archives. "This is where they monitored the subjects," he murmured. "Emotion triggers, responses, visual stimuli."

Eliora peered into the cables. "Half of this is still powered. Look."

The lights above us flickered, humming in sync with the machine.

And then the voice came back.

"We remember you, Nova Temples."

I flinched. "It's here."

Lucien raised his flashlight toward the ceiling. "Where?"

"Everywhere," it said. "The experiment never ended. It evolved."

The monitors switched on one by one. Each screen showed a different version of us — sitting in the same room, wearing the same clothes, but *not moving.*

Our still images blinked back.

The first question came at random.

A voice like static pressed through the air.

"Subject 01. Yunmi Kailen. What do you fear more: being erased, or being remembered incorrectly?"

Yunmi's breath hitched. "This isn't funny."

"Answer."

Her hands trembled. "Remembered wrong. Because that's still being rewritten by someone else."

The lights flickered, and a tone — low, steady — filled the air.

"Truth detected."

Yunmi gasped as the projector behind her screen lit up — showing one of her murals, painted across a wall she'd never touched.
It pulsed with lines of code.

"Is that—" she whispered.

"We used your art to test emotion recall. You create empathy loops. Useful for control."

Yunmi slammed her sketchbook shut, shaking. "You're lying."

"Are we?"

Then came Jae.

"Subject 02. Jae Thornevale. What are you hiding?"

He stiffened. "Nothing."

"False."

A monitor beside him lit up — a video feed of Jae entering a restricted lab room two nights before we'd met him freshman year.

"Wait—" I said, "that's not possible. You didn't even—"

"I was recruited," Jae admitted quietly. "Before I met you. They said it was for research—mapping emotional thresholds. I didn't know what they were doing to people."

Yunmi stared at him. "You *lied* to us."

"He lied to himself," the voice said. "He still does."

Jae slammed his laptop shut. "Enough!"

The tone pulsed again.

"Truth ratio: 74%."

He whispered, "Then what's the other twenty-six?"

No one answered.

The voice shifted.

"Subject 03. Eliora Llam. What would you give up to be believed?"

Eliora swallowed hard. "Everything."

"Then we'll take everything."

Her camera clicked on by itself, flash strobing violently. The screen filled with dozens of overlapping faces — her own, but distorted, blurred, half screaming.

Lucien lunged forward and ripped the cable out of the wall. The images vanished, leaving only static.

Eliora slumped against the shelf, whispering, "That was me... all the times they said I faked it. Every glitch. Every blackout."

Her voice cracked. "They recorded all of it."

Then it was Lucien.

"Subject 04. Lucien Nisom. How long have you known?"

He didn't move. His jaw tightened. "Since before we met her."

"Met who?" I asked.

He looked at me. "You."

I felt the ground tilt.

"He was assigned to monitor the Temples thread," the Watcher said. "His job was to ensure continuity."

My throat dried. "Continuity of what?"

Lucien's gaze fell. "You weren't supposed to find the Thirteenth Room. You were supposed to forget it."

I woke on the floor of the archives, cold and disoriented.

The monitors were dark. The hum had stopped.

But the questions lingered — echoing faintly, like reverb.

Jae sat nearby, elbows on his knees. "We're all pawns," he muttered. "They made sure of it."

Yunmi was still sketching frantically, drawing circles within circles. "It's asking more questions. I can feel it."

Eliora touched my wrist. "Nova. What did it ask *you*?"

I hesitated.

Because it had asked.

When the others were breaking, the voice had turned soft — familiar.

"Nova Temples. Final subject. What version of you do you think deserves to survive?"

And I hadn't answered.

Because I didn't know.

Later that morning, we regrouped in Yunmi's studio — the only space without cameras.

Sunlight crept through the blinds in fractured bars.

No one spoke for a long time.

Finally, Jae said, "We can't run anymore. If the Watcher wants to play games, we change the rules."

"How?" I asked.

He slid a file toward me. Inside were old floor schematics and one torn note in red ink:

"Control core located beneath Mirror Wing. Project 13A – The Watcher Host."

I looked up. "So, we destroy the host."

Yunmi smirked bitterly. "Or it destroys us first."

Writing Therapy Log #029 – "Truth Ratio"
October 4 — 9:30 p.m.

It asked us questions.
But I think the questions weren't to test us.
They were to remember us.

Every truth we tell fills its memory back in.
Every lie we speak keeps us safe — for now.

I'm not sure which is worse.

Writing Therapy Log #030 – "Static in the System"
October 7

When truth becomes contagious, the system calls it a virus.
We didn't mean to start a revolution.

We just wanted to be heard.

The rain hadn't stopped for days.
Aurelya's skyline looked like static — blurred lights behind mist, drones humming above the clock towers.
On the walk back from class, I could hear the power lines buzzing, like the city was warning us to stay quiet.
Jae caught up with me under the overhang of the dorm commons. "They cut access to half the archive servers," he said. "Security's crawling everywhere."
"Because of us?"
He nodded. "Because of Yunmi, mostly. Her collective's hack hit the morning newsfeed."
In the art quad, students had gathered around the central fountain.
Projected across the water was a massive mural — glitching faces, voices layered over one another:

"WE ARE NOT EXPERIMENTS."
PROJECT 13 IS STILL ACTIVE."
"REMEMBER THE VANISHED."

The footage was grainy but powerful — flashes of tunnels, blurred lab footage, students crying into static.
At the bottom corner, the watermark glowed faintly: Collective_13.
Yunmi stood at the edge of the crowd, hood up, paint-stained fingers trembling as she watched her own rebellion go live.
"You did this," I said quietly.

She didn't look away from the screen. "They kept erasing our stories. I just gave them back their ghosts."

By midday, chaos hit.

Campus security stormed the quad.

Students scattered, shouting, phones flashing.

They tore down the projection rigs and dragged away the equipment, but the mural kept looping — the image burned into the air like an afterimage that wouldn't fade.

Eliora Liam filmed everything — her camera light cutting through the fog as an officer shouted for her to stop.

Lucien Nisom pulled her back, whispering, "You'll get expelled for this."

She looked him dead in the eye. "Then at least it's on record."

We regrouped in the film lab that evening — soaked, silent, hearts pounding.

Yunmi sat cross-legged on a table, sketching new protest stencils between breaths.

Jae was rewiring a stolen radio transmitter.

Lucien paced.

Eliora dumped her footage into a drive, muttering, "They'll scrub the data by morning. I'm backing it offline."

I watched them — my friends, my chaos, my proof that we were still human enough to fight back.

"We can't stop now," I said.

Lucien stopped pacing. "They'll retaliate."

"They already have."

I woke to the sound of static.

Not from my phone — from the ceiling vent.

When I climbed out of bed, the air smelled of burned metal.

The lights in the hallway flickered on and off in perfect rhythm — *dot dot dash dash* — Morse code.

On the wall opposite my door, someone had written in white chalk: "TELL THEM WHAT YOU SAW."

That morning, professors started cancelling lectures.

Students whispered in clusters. The dean's office released an official statement:

"No unauthorized footage has been verified. The administration is cooperating with safety investigators. Campus remains safe."

Safe.

The word stung like irony.

Yunmi laughed when she saw it on the bulletin board. "They really think PR can undo a haunting."

Her phone buzzed — an anonymous message.

"We know what you did. Stop before someone disappears again."

She showed it to me. "They're not even subtle."

"Do you think it's an administration?"

Yunmi hesitated. "No. This tone... It's older."

Eliora found us an hour later, pale and shaking.

"They arrested Dalia," she said. "From the collective. They said she hacked into faculty records."

Jae cursed under his breath. "She was the one who pulled the security feed last night. That's why they're targeting her."

Lucien crossed his arms. "This is what I meant by retaliation."

But I was already opening my notebook, flipping to the latest entry.

There were new lines there — not mine.

"You started a war of memory.

The Watcher is awake."

That night, the air around campus vibrated like the calm before a storm.

A power outage swept through the west dorms; drones blinked red and then vanished.

We gathered in the media lab — our unofficial headquarters.

Screens flickered between live feeds, chat logs, and Yunmi's newest digital mural: a collage of overlapping faces from the footage, their eyes glowing gold like light breaking through static.

"This is our proof," Eliora said. "If we release it all, they can't silence everyone."

Jae's hands shook on the keyboard. "They can. That's the problem."

Lucien stepped forward. "Then what's the alternative?"

I stared at the screen, the words blurring.

"The alternative," I said, "is making them look at themselves."

We uploaded the mural to every screen we could reach — cafeteria menus, security monitors, and classroom projectors.

For one glorious, impossible minute, the entire campus glowed with Yunmi's art.

A thousand gold-eyed faces staring down from walls and windows.

Students stopped. Looked up.

The air buzzed like the city itself was breathing with us.

Then — blackout.

Every light died.

Every screen went dark.

Only one message blinked back across every device:

"SILENCE IS SAFER."

The campus was locked down by morning.

Security checkpoints. Card scanners disabled.

Rumors said faculty were questioned about "data leaks."

Yunmi's art collective was officially disbanded.

Her mural had been power-washed off the fountain walls by sunrise.

But when I walked by, I could still see faint traces of gold under the concrete — like memory refusing to fade.

Jae found me there, clutching a new schematic. "The broadcast core's gone," he said. "They moved it underground — under Mirror Wing."

"Then we go back," I said.

He nodded grimly. "You're sure?"

I glanced at the fountain's reflection — our faces blurred into one.
"Breaking the silence doesn't end with speaking," I said. "It ends when someone finally listens."

Writing Therapy Log #031 – "Aftermath"
October 9 — 11:09 p.m.

They erased the art.
But not the eyes.
They erased the footage.
But not the fear.

The Watcher's awake now.
And I think it's listening to us breathe.

Writing Therapy Log #032 – "Fissures"

October 17
There's a sound when people start to come apart.
Not yelling. Not shattering.
Just silence — like everyone's waiting to see who leaves first.

Rain clung to Aurelya's windows again.

Two weeks since the broadcast.

Two weeks since we turned the whole campus into a confession.

And somehow, everything felt quieter — like the university had swallowed its own heartbeat.

Yunmi barely slept. She spent nights repainting murals over freshly white-washed walls.

Eliora stopped filming altogether, saying she was tired of replaying things that never changed.

Lucien barely looked at me anymore.

And Jae... Jae was still running diagnostics on the stolen footage, refusing to explain what he was *really* looking for.

The silence between us was starting to hum.

In the dining hall, whispers replaced conversation.

Security drones hovered over the tables now, disguised as light fixtures.

Yunmi traced circles in the condensation of her cup. "Someone in the collective snitched," she said softly. "They couldn't have tracked us that fast otherwise."

Lucien stirred his coffee. "Maybe they didn't need to. Maybe one of us gave them a reason."

"Don't start," Eliora warned.

But he wasn't looking at her. He was looking at *me.*

I set down my fork. "If you have something to say, Lucien, say it."

He leaned back, jaw tight. "You attract anomalies, Nova. Wherever you go, systems break. People vanish. Maybe that's not a coincidence."

Yunmi slammed her hand on the table. "You think she *wants* this?"

"I think someone always does," he said, voice like a slow burn.

I dreamed of corridors again.

The Thirteenth Room stretched endlessly, its walls breathing with faint light.

And someone — a woman's silhouette — stood at the end, whispering:

"You shouldn't have brought them here."

When I woke, my phone was on the floor, screen glowing with a new file:

MK_diary_fragment_01.txt

The header read:

"They're starting to suspect each other. Good. Division ensures compliance."

— M.K.

Yunmi found me hunched over the screen.

"What's that?"

"I think it's from Madhav," I said. "Or maybe his sister."

Her eyes darkened. "Then she's not gone."

I wanted to believe that.

But another line in the file pulsed brighter:

"Version T-02 refuses to stabilize. Emotional contagion detected."

My stomach dropped.

That was me.

Classes blurred into surveillance.

Professors stopped assigning open essays; all submissions were now digital, timestamped, and auto-flagged for "emotional irregularity."

Eliora whispered to me between lectures, "They're monitoring tone analysis. Anything too passionate gets flagged as fabricated."

So, we started writing bland. Empty. Emotionless.

The campus went quiet in more ways than one.

That's when the messages started.

Anonymous texts, same encryption code every time:

Stop digging. The Thirteenth Door opens both ways.

Jae traced the signal to an internal network node. "It's coming from inside campus servers," he said. "Probably a faculty relay."

"Or someone pretending to be," Yunmi added.

We all looked at each other. No one spoke.

Lucien didn't show up to the meeting.

Then his dorm light went out.

We found his notebook on the desk — neat handwriting, every page cataloged like a mission report.

The last line read:

"Assignment compromised. Reassessment pending."

Yunmi swore under her breath. "He's the mole."

But Eliora shook her head. "No. That's too easy."

I thumbed through the pages again. At the back, there was a photo — the five of us, standing in front of the fountain mural from last semester.

Except the background had changed: the mural's faces were smiling.

None of us remembered taking that picture.

Writing Therapy Log #033 – "Missing Variables"
November 5

One person gone changes the math.

The rest of us rearrange around the absence until it feels normal.

Maybe that's how loops start — by convincing you it's just a coincidence.

The first snow fell that week, coating the rooftops of Aurelya's east quarter.

Yunmi painted the snow with streaks of gold dye, calling it "memory frost."

Eliora filmed her quietly, saying, "If they erase us again, I want this to survive."

I scrolled through the MK files late that night.

332

Each new entry was timestamped a minute before I opened it — as if the diary *knew* when I'd look.

Then came Fragment 07.

"When they read this, tell them I'm sorry. The loop wasn't meant to hurt anyone. I just wanted to see him again."

Beneath the signature: *Madhav K.*
I stared at it until my vision blurred.
Jae found me hours later, eyes red from lack of sleep.
"He's gone," he said.
"Lucien?"
"No. Madhav. His dorm's empty. His records were wiped."

Yunmi came running down the hall, paint still on her hands.
"They found another door," she gasped. "Behind the observatory."

We followed her through the snow until we reached a steel panel hidden behind frost-covered ivy.

When Jae forced it open, warm air poured out — humid, artificial.

Inside was an elevator shaft.
Unmarked buttons. One scratched inscription:

13 — CORE

We stared at it, each of us hearing the same unspoken thought: *the Thirteenth Door.*

Writing Therapy Log #034 – "Fractured Alliances"
November 14

Maybe the real experiment was never about memory.
Maybe it was about trust.
How long can you love someone who might not be real?

We're about to find out.

Writing Therapy Log #035 – "Loops"
January 6

Time doesn't pass here. It folds.
And every time I think I'm free of it, I find myself walking the same hallway again.
Maybe that's how the Thirteenth Room survived — by never letting anyone truly leave.
The first week back from winter break, Aurelya felt different.
The air tasted sharper, colder — like the city was holding its breath.
Campus banners fluttered in the wind: *Welcome Back, Scholars!*
But the smiles on the posters looked too bright, too curated.

Yunmi said the administration was staging normalcy.
Eliora said it was something worse — "They're covering the smell of fear with fresh paint."

Jae didn't say anything. He hadn't slept in days.
The circles under his eyes looked like shadows drawn in ink.

Lucien still hadn't returned. No official word. Just... absence.

And the elevator behind the observatory still waited, sealed in frost.

We stood in front of it one gray afternoon, breath visible in the air.

Eliora tapped the button labeled 13 – CORE.

It didn't light up.

Jae crouched by the panel, whispering, "This is coded in the old Project 13 firmware. I can crack it, but once it opens—"

"There's no going back," I finished.

Yunmi lifted her camera, recording. "Then let's make sure someone sees how it ends."

When the doors finally opened, warm air brushed past us like an exhale.

The walls beyond shimmered faintly — metal layered over glass, humming with residual energy.

We stepped inside.

The elevator didn't move down. It *sank.*

The floor vibrated softly, and through the narrow window, I could see the levels flickering past — 11... 12... blank.
Then — black.

We stopped with a jolt.

The doors slid open to reveal a single hallway.
Long. Silent.
The air tasted like static and iron.

Yunmi's voice echoed. "This place shouldn't exist."

Jae held up his scanner. "Power signatures — but no data feed. It's self-contained."

We moved forward, our footsteps muffled by the thick glass floor.
Below it: rows of sleeping pods.
Each one is labeled with a name.

And one of them said NOVA TEMPLES – T-02.

I froze. "That's— That's not possible."

Eliora knelt beside the pod. "It's empty."

Jae whispered, "Maybe it's just an archive copy. Backup identity storage."

"Then where's the real one?" I asked.

He looked at me — and didn't answer.

We found the central chamber at the end of the hallway.

 single white door marked THIRTEENTH.

No handle. No lock. Just a small sensor glowing blue.

Yunmi raised her hand, but I stopped her.

"It's reading bio-signature input," Jae said quietly. "It's waiting for *you*."

My heart thudded once, twice.

The air trembled.

When I touched the panel, light crawled across the door — veins of gold and white, splitting outward like cracks in reality.

The door opened.

And there — standing in the center of the room — was *I*.

Not a reflection. Not a hologram.

A version.

Her hair was longer. Her eyes steadier.

The kind of composure I'd been pretending to have since freshman year.

"Hi," she said. "I was wondering when you'd show up."

My voice caught. "Who are you?"

She smiled faintly. "The version of you that stayed."

The others watched from the doorway, silent.

Jae's hand hovered near his recorder.

"Why are you here?" I asked.

She tilted her head. "Because you couldn't stop looking for answers. And someone had to keep the door open."

Yunmi whispered, "Nova, she's mimicking you."

"She's not mimicking," Jae said. "She's anticipating."

The other me laughed softly. "He's right. I was made to finish what you started. You're the unstable build."

I took a step forward. "You're lying."

"No," she said. "You're remembering."

The room flickered — light bending, time looping.

For a moment, I was both of us.

Then neither.

Eliora's voice cracked. "Nova, we need to leave."

But my other self turned toward her. "You can't. You're already part of the loop."

Screens ignited along the walls, showing flashes of us — first-year footage, fragments of tunnels, the Watcher's recordings, our therapy logs.

Every secret. Every confession.

"This is what they wanted," she said. "Not your compliance — your connection. Every time you trusted someone, you made the loop stronger."

"Then how do we break it?" I shouted.

She smiled sadly. "By remembering it all — and not running this time."

I stepped closer until we were almost face-to-face.

She looked so calm. So sure.

I wanted to hate her.

Instead, I felt pity.

"Maybe you're right," I said. "Maybe I am unstable. But instability means I *change.*"

Her eyes widened.

I reached forward — pressed my hand against her chest.
It felt like touching light.

Then she fractured — pixels, glass, and heat — dissolving into the air like static breaking apart.

We didn't talk about the Thirteenth Door afterward.
We just *pretended.*
Classes resumed. Snow melted.
But now and then, I'd catch glimpses — a reflection that lingered too long, an echo half a beat late.

Lucien's file appeared again in my inbox. No sender.
Attached: a single line of text.

"You closed the wrong door."

Yunmi painted new murals across the dorms — gold spirals, vanishing eyes.
Eliora started a podcast called *Echoes of Aurelya.*
Jae built a scanner to trace quantum feedback from the Thirteenth floor.

And me?
I kept writing.
Because words still felt like the only thing I could control.

Writing Therapy Log #036 – "The Door That Opened Both Ways"
March 3

I met myself and didn't break.

But something else did — the line between what I remember and what remembers me.

The Thirteenth Door didn't lead to the past.
It led to the version of me that refused to be forgotten.

Writing Therapy Log #037 – "Versions"
April 3

You can't rewrite the past.
But you can learn its language — and stop speaking in fear.
I'm not the version who ran anymore.
I'm the one who stayed.

Spring returned to Aurelya quietly.
Cherry trees bloomed across the university courtyard, their petals drifting into the canals like soft static.
No more drones. No lockdown notices. No surveillance announcements.
At least, not publicly.
But we knew the silence was staged — an apology the university would never make out loud.
Still, it was the first time in months that I could walk across campus and hear *birds* instead of hums.
Yunmi had her hands full of paint again — golds, blues, and deep crimsons.

She'd been given "conditional reinstatement" to the Fine Arts department after a board review.

Conditional, *meaning: you can stay if you keep quiet.*

She didn't.

The wall behind the library now carried her largest mural yet — overlapping portraits of the missing students, their eyes half-open, half-dreaming.

At the bottom corner, a single phrase glowed in golden letters:

Versions of Us Who Remembered.

Jae started working nights in the media lab.

He said he was "reverse-engineering the loop residue," but I knew what that really meant.

He was trying to find Lucien.

Sometimes I'd catch him standing by the observatory elevator, staring at the sealed door.

Once, I asked, "Do you think he's still down there?"

He didn't answer — just traced a faint circle on the frost with his finger.

"I think the loop keeps everyone it's not done with."

Eliora Liam's podcast, *Echoes of Aurelya,* went live that week.

It opened with the sound of wind over metal, then her voice:

"Memory isn't a timeline. It's a constellation.

And sometimes, the stars remember us back."

Her episodes mixed interviews, whispered recollections, and corrupted audio from Project 13 logs.

The administration tried to censor it within hours, but by then, thousands of students had already downloaded the files offline.

The first comment under her pilot read simply:

"We hear you."

I spent more time in the Writing Therapy office again.

The walls had been repainted since last semester.

The new counselor, Dr. Roe, was younger, gentle, clinical, and too careful.

She read my latest entry in silence, then said, "You're processing memory like architecture."

"Because it was," I said. "They built walls inside us."

She smiled sadly. "And you learned to walk through them."

On the last day of April, we all gathered by the riverbanks for the Spring Exhibition.

Students had turned the grassy field into a glowing gallery — sculptures of light, floating poems, projections on water.

Yunmi's piece was last: a looping animation called *Versions*.

It showed fragments of us — walking, laughing, glitching — fading into light and reforming again.

No start. No end.

Just evolution.

The crowd clapped.

But for me, the applause faded beneath something else — a familiar warmth behind me.

When I turned, someone was standing at the edge of the crowd.

Madhav.

He looked older. Tired. Like the world had looped through him one too many times.

But when he smiled — soft, regretful — it was the same as the first day in the airport.

I froze. "You—"

"I shouldn't be here," he said quietly. "But I had to see how it ended."

"It's not over," I said. "You're proof of that."

He shook his head. "No. I'm the ghost of a system that doesn't know when to stop remembering."

I stepped closer. "Then why come back?"

His eyes flickered, almost human, almost light.

"To tell you the truth," he said. "You broke the loop. Not by destroying it — by understanding it. That's something even I couldn't do."

I wanted to say something — ask if he was real, if he'd ever been.

But before I could, a breeze passed through the field, scattering petals between us.

When the air cleared, he was gone.

All that remained was a small, folded note under my shoe.

I opened it.

"Keep the sweetness.

— M.K."

Graduation for the upperclassmen took place under floodlights and quiet rain.

We weren't graduating yet, but we went anyway — to see what survival looked like.

Jae handed me a flower crown made of copper wire. "For next year," he said.

Eliora was discussing a summer documentary.

Yunmi wanted to take her mural public — "no more walls," she said.

For the first time in a long time, I felt it — not relief, not victory.

Just presence.

The kind of stillness that comes after too many versions of yourself have finally stopped fighting.

Writing Therapy Log #038 – "Lost No More"
May 15

I think we spend so long trying to be remembered that we forget to live.
But sometimes, survival is its own form of rebellion.
I'm still here.
We all are.
And maybe that's enough.

The mural glowed that night under the aurora — a thousand gold-eyed faces looking up, unified.
Aurelya had stopped feeling like a loop.
It felt like a pulse.
And as I watched the lights ripple across the sky, I realized something:
I wasn't the version who got lost anymore.
I was the one who *found* everyone else.

SEVEN

Junior (Third Year)

We Fell Through the Floor – The Version of Me Who Disappeared

The gates of the Aurelya Institute of Cognitive Sciences rose before me like a memory that hadn't decided if it wanted to exist.

The air smelled of metal and rain. Damp ivy climbed the stone arch, tracing cracks that hadn't been there before summer break. Beneath the gold lettering—*Sapientia per Iter Mentis*—someone had taped a printed notice:

WELCOME BACK, STUDENTS.

CAMPUS UPGRADES COMPLETE.

Except the walls hummed faintly, as if they'd been wired for more than just Wi-Fi.

I stood there longer than I meant to, suitcase handle biting into my palm.

Same school.

Same season.

But the silence felt heavier this time, like the space between thoughts after something important is forgotten.

The security scanners blinked green as I crossed through. The sound reminded me of the lab doors from last year—the ones we'd sealed shut after everything that happened in the tunnels. I'd told myself that was over. That we'd burned the evidence, buried the project, and walked out alive.

Maybe we only *thought* we walked out.

Yunmi met me by the commons, sketchbook in hand and a streak of cobalt paint on her cheek. Her hair was shorter, uneven at the ends, like she'd cut it herself during a breakdown she refused to talk about.

"You made it," she said. Her voice was soft, but her smile—faint, genuine—was still there.

"I almost didn't."

We hugged awkwardly. I felt her ribs through her oversized jacket, her pulse fast against mine. When she pulled back, I noticed the ring of paint around her nails—half her manicures were from protest banners now, not art shows.

"New semester," she said, looking around the courtyard. "New ghosts."

Her words made me glance up. Across the glass facade of the research hall, I could've sworn I saw a reflection blink back at me—just a beat too early. The dorm smelled like new varnish and memory.

Someone had replaced the lights with cooler bulbs; everything looked slightly off-color, like the world had been subtly re-rendered.

Jae Thornevale was already there, balancing on his desk chair, pinning up a world map dotted with color-coded strings. He'd grown into a quiet intensity—same soft tone, same wry humor, but more deliberate now. Like he'd spent the whole summer trying to outrun something and barely made it back.

"Mapping again?" I asked.

He smiled without turning around. "Old habits. I still think there's more below this campus than what we saw."

He pinned another red thread. The corner fluttered. "Besides, it's cheaper than therapy."

"Funny," I said. "Mine's just writing about therapy."

We laughed a little. The sound felt too loud in the sterile room.

Eliora arrived an hour later, hair braided, eyes alert. She'd taken summer courses, sharpened edges of herself into something resolute.

She handed me a folded paper: a course schedule stamped with the AICS insignia.

"You're on the list," she said. "That research pilot program. The new one. Guess they really like you."

My stomach sank.

"I didn't apply for that."

She frowned. "Then someone did for you."

The first week slid by in a haze of schedules and controlled politeness. Professors avoided any mention of last year's "incident." The tunnels were gone—sealed, paved over. But sometimes I felt vibrations beneath the floorboards, faint like a pulse.

Security cameras dotted the hallways now—sleek, silver, in pairs.

"Paranoid much?" Yunmi muttered one morning as we passed one. "They're scared of ideas. Not people."

She wasn't entirely wrong.

Later that night, she knocked on my door, holding a folded slip of paper. "This was taped to my door. Thought you should see it."

It was written in scrambled handwriting—familiar, frantic.

You found the door.

But it's not over.

Watch your reflection.

The paper smelled faintly of varnish and ozone. My chest tightened.

"I thought we burned it all," I whispered.

"So did I," Yunmi said. Then softer: "Maybe we only burned the easy parts."

Outside, rain hit the window like static. The glow from the campus lamps shimmered across the wet glass, refracting into a dozen identical reflections of me.

Each one blinked out of sync.

Morning sunlight poured through the courtyard. The air tasted clean—too clean, like the aftermath of something sterilized.

On the bulletin board near the psychology wing, a new announcement read:

AICS Residency Program — 12 Keys.

Beneath it, a single envelope had been pinned separately, labeled 13.

My fingers hesitated before touching it.

Inside: a bronze dorm key, cool and heavy.

Attached was a note, handwritten in looping, formal script.

"Welcome, Nova Temples.

Your assignment awaits."

For a second, I thought I heard someone call my name from behind me—low, calm, almost amused. When I turned, no one was there.

But at the far end of the hall, by the glass doors, someone was watching me.

Short hair, gray jacket, sharp profile.

Lucien Nisom.

He didn't wave. Didn't speak. Just gave a small nod before disappearing into the crowd.

Jae found me standing there minutes later, key still in my hand.

"Everything okay?"

"Yeah," I lied. "Just déjà vu."

The bronze glinted in my palm, catching the sunlight like an old wound reopening.

Writing Therapy Log #039 – "The Weight of Silence"
August 24

Maybe healing is just another kind of forgetting.
Every time I think I'm ready to move on, something pulls me back.
A door.
A voice.
A memory that insists it still belongs to me.
Dr. Kilfeather once said that closure doesn't come all at once.
But this feels less like closure and more like recursion—
A thought looping until it frays.
Everyone says the school looks new.
All I see are the cracks beneath the paint.

Sometimes I think the campus has rebuilt itself.
Sometimes I think *we* did.
And neither version feels quite real.

Night 1 – The 13th Key
The new dorm smelled faintly of lavender and ozone.

Every wall gleamed too cleanly, as if someone had scrubbed away its history.

The plaque outside my door read 13A, even though the hall directory ended at 12.

I slid the bronze key into the lock. It turned with a soft mechanical click that didn't sound like any normal latch.

The door opened soundlessly.

Inside, the room looked... staged.
Perfectly made bed. White curtains.
A clock ticking in the corner that showed 11:11 no matter when I checked.

I unpacked slowly, folding clothes into drawers, aligning notebooks by size. Anything to ground myself.
The silence pressed in, so I left music playing low—an old playlist from before everything.

When I finally lay down, the bed dipped lower than expected, like something had shifted beneath it.
I froze.
Nothing. Just the hum of the lights and the faint whir of the clock.

Then—three soft knocks.
Not at the door.
From the wall behind my headboard.

I sat up.
The air felt charged, metallic.
When I pressed my ear against the wall, I thought I heard breathing. Then a whisper that might've been my own name.

"...Nova..."

My heart kicked once, hard.

I stepped back. The sound stopped.
And then—on the opposite wall—words began to appear, faint and uneven, like condensation forming letters:

YOU SHOULDN'T HAVE COME BACK.

The lights flickered.
The clock ticked backward to 11:10.

When I blinked, the words were gone.

I didn't sleep that night.
Only wrote.

The rain came early that morning, washing color out of the sky.
From my dorm window, the campus looked like a postcard from somewhere that didn't exist anymore—beautiful, preserved, and wrong.

Yunmi was already in the quad by the time I got downstairs, holding her sketchpad under her jacket to protect it from the drizzle.
She waved me over, eyes wide. "You got the 13th key, right?"
"Yeah," I said. "Why?"

She flipped the sketchpad open. On the page was a charcoal drawing of the dorm hallway.
Thirteen doors.
Except the last one was shaded darker, its outline smudged like smoke.

"I drew this *before* you told me," she said. "I thought I made up the last door."

A chill ran down my spine.

Jae met us by the fountain, holding an envelope. His expression was unreadable.
"This came to the lab mailroom. No return address."

He handed it to me. Inside was a folded page—aged, yellowed, smudged at the corners.
A map.

The same looping pathways, the same underground grids.

But this one had *new ink lines* connecting the campus dorms to the old, sealed tunnels.

At the bottom, a scrawled signature: M. Kwan.

My pulse jumped. "Where did you—"

"Courier dropped it off this morning," Jae said. "Said it was addressed to you. From an alumni archive."

Yunmi's lips pressed thin. "They don't just hand out confidential maps, Nova."

"I know."

The paper trembled in my hands.
A faint watermark shimmered beneath the ink:
Project 13: Reinitiation Phase.

We gathered later that afternoon in the student commons, an unspoken truce forming between us.

Eliora leaned across the table, eyes sharp. "If this is real, then someone reactivated the network. The entire experiment might've been dormant— until now."

"Or," Jae countered, "it never stopped. We just stopped remembering."

Yunmi rubbed her thumb across a stray charcoal streak on her wrist. "I think we should relaunch *The Versions*. Quietly."

Her underground zine—the same one that almost got her expelled last year.

She looked at me, determined. "People deserve to know what's under this place."

I hesitated, remembering the whisper behind my wall: *You shouldn't have come back.*

"If we do this," I said, "we do it carefully."

Eliora nodded. "Then we start by finding out what's in the old records room beneath the library. It's still off-limits, but if anyone can bypass the lock—"

She looked at me.

"—it's you."

That night, the rain didn't stop.

Thunder rolled through the hills like something trying to wake the campus up.

In my dorm, the clock ticked backward again—11:09, 11:08, 11:07.

I opened my journal and wrote three words across a blank page:

Find the door.

Then, from the hall outside—another sound.

footstep.

Slow. Deliberate.

Stopping right outside my door.

A slip of paper slid under the threshold.

It read, in the same frantic handwriting as before:

If you open it again, you won't come back the same.

I stared at it until the letters bled into one another.

And somewhere deep in the walls, beneath the electric hum,

I thought I heard something *breathing*.

Writing Therapy Log #040 – "Echoes Under My Skin"
September 2

It's strange what silence sounds like after you've learned to fear it.

Every hum of the lights.
Every creak of the ceiling.

Even my own pulse feels like code trying to synchronize.

Yunmi says the walls are thicker this year. "Soundproof," she told me.
But I still hear things.
The ticking clock that doesn't move.
The faint breathing in the vents.
And once, last night, something whispered my name in perfect rhythm with my heartbeat.
Dr. Kilfeather would probably say it's just stress.
That my body remembers what it felt like to be hunted by something invisible.
But what if the body isn't just remembering?
What if it's *responding?*

Sometimes, when I touch the wall of my dorm, I feel a vibration—like the heartbeat of something enormous sleeping behind the concrete.
Sometimes I think the school was built over it.
Sometimes I think the school *is* it.

I don't know which thought scares me more.

— Nova Temples

Rain returned by the second week of September.
The kind of steady, soundless rain that makes the world feel paused.

Yunmi met me outside the library steps, her hoodie damp, eyes bright.
"Tonight. Records room. Basement level. I got the lock codes."

"From whom?"

She hesitated. "Let's just say the collective still has friends."

Jae joined us soon after, carrying a flashlight and the kind of cautious optimism that had always made him the rational one.

liora followed with her hair tied back, sleeves rolled, a small portable scanner slung over her shoulder.

The four of us looked less like students and more like a rescue team for memories.

The hallway leading into the archives smelled like dust and old electricity.

Fluorescent lights buzzed overhead, one flickering in uneven staccato.

Eliora swiped the card she'd "borrowed" from the tech department.

The lock clicked green.

We slipped inside.

The records room was larger than I remembered.

Rows upon rows of cabinets stretched into shadow.

Each drawer is labeled with a year, a code, and a name.

Yunmi brushed her fingers along one drawer. "These go back decades."

"Find anything labeled 'Project 13,'" I said.

We worked in silence for what felt like an hour—until Jae called softly, "You should see this."

He was standing by an old TV cart, half-buried under a tarp.

On it sat a dusty VHS player, still plugged into the wall.

A label on the tape read: CONTROL GROUP: SUBJECT 13.

Eliora connected her scanner. Static filled the small screen, then cleared.

The footage was grainy. A girl sat in a chair, wires taped to her temples.

Her face hidden by shadow, but her voice...

"My name is Nova Temples," she said.

I froze.

My voice.

But I didn't remember saying those words.

"I dream in loops," the recording continued. "I wake up in the same hallway. Every door I open leads back to the first one. I think they're testing me. But I can't remember for what."

The screen glitched.
Then, abruptly, went black.

"Holy—" Jae started.

"Turn it off," I said too fast.

But the tape ejected itself before anyone could touch it.
Smoke rose faintly from the machine's vents, like breath.

"Nova," Yunmi whispered. "That wasn't possible. The timestamp—"
Eliora checked the screen. "—is from *three years before you enrolled.*"

The air felt thick, heavy with static.

Something creaked behind us.
The door we'd come through slowly swung shut.

And somewhere deep in the archive, a low vibration began.
Not loud—but deep enough to feel in the ribs.
Like the building was inhaling.

We ran.
Our flashlights cut through the dark, beams trembling across endless aisles of metal and paper.
The shelves seemed to stretch longer than before.
Eliora muttered, "This isn't—this shouldn't connect to the west wing."

"It doesn't," Jae said. "The floor plan stops thirty meters back."

"Then where the hell are we?"

I turned the corner—
And stopped.

Ahead of us, the shelves ended abruptly at a brick wall.
Fresh brick. Cement is still damp.

Painted across it, in wide black strokes:
THERE IS NO THIRTEENTH ROOM.

I stepped closer, hand trembling.
Beneath the words, a faint etching.
A symbol I'd seen before—in the lab, in my dreams, carved into the old observatory door.
A spiral.
Incomplete.

Suddenly, the lights flickered—
Then went out.

Darkness swallowed everything.

"Jae?" I whispered.
No answer.

"Yunmi?"

Footsteps. Running. Metal clattering. A flashlight beam swerving wildly—then dropping.
Someone screamed.
Then nothing.

For a moment, there was only the hum again, deep and rhythmic, rising beneath my feet.
I took one step back.

The floor gave way.

When I came to, everything was wrong.

The air was cold, stale.
My flashlight buzzed weakly, illuminating a corridor of gray concrete that looked more like a bunker than a basement.
No signal on my phone.
No voices.

I pushed myself up slowly, palms scraping dust.
Shapes loomed in the dark—chairs, desks, cabinets—all fused into the walls like they'd been swallowed by the building itself.
Every sound echoed for too long, like it didn't want to stop.

My hands shook as I reached for my notebook.
But the pages were blank.
Every word I'd written since I'd come back to campus—gone.

Something dripped from the ceiling.
I looked up.
A faint trickle of black liquid traced along the cracked plaster, glimmering like oil.
Then, faintly, in the reflection, I saw movement.
A shape.
A figure walking past the far end of the hallway.

"Jae?"

No reply.

Only a whisper.
"...you found the door..."

I turned, but the hallway behind me had changed—longer now, stretching out farther than it should.

At the far end, a door flickered into view.
Its surface shimmered like a reflection on water.

It opened before I could reach it.
A hand reached through—
And pulled me in.

I float.
No, that isn't right.
I hum.

A low vibration runs through me — like I'm part of the building's pulse now.
There's light above, thin as tissue, rippling like the surface of a pond.
I reach up, but my hands dissolve into sound.

Somewhere far off, I hear Yunmi calling my name.
Then Jae.
Then no one.

I dream I'm standing in my old dorm again.
The walls are painted the wrong color — too soft, too kind.
Someone's handwriting covers my desk in looping silver ink:

You came back wrong but still beautiful.

The letters rearrange themselves into symbols.
Then into my own face.

The air ripples.
My reflection blinks first.

I try to breathe, but my lungs make a static noise instead of air.
When I open my eyes, the light is gone.

The world rebuilt itself wrong.

At first, I thought I was still underground until the smell hit me — not dust, not mold, but the faint sweetness of coffee.

A café, maybe.

But when I sat up, I was on the quad lawn.

Aurelya.

Or something pretending to be it.

The sky shimmered pale lilac, edges stuttering like a paused video.

The clock tower's hands were spinning backward.

And scattered across the grass were flyers for clubs and events that had never existed.

AUTUMN FESTIVAL — OCT 14, 2007

Guest Lecturer: Dr. Eliana Temples, Department of Memory Studies.

My mother's name.

My throat tightened.

The paper crumbled in my hand before I could reread it.

Students drifted by with their faces blurred, their voices overlapping like a looped soundtrack.

A girl laughed — the exact pitch and rhythm of Yunmi's laugh — then dissolved into a crowd that wasn't there.

Every time I tried to focus, the scene wavered, like I was viewing it through someone else's nostalgia.

"Excuse me," I said to the nearest figure. "Where—where is this?"

The boy turned, smiling faintly.

His eyes were clouded over.

"Orientation's already started," he said.

Then his expression flickered — glitch-skip — and he repeated the sentence, same cadence, same smile.

I stepped back.

He kept smiling until he faded.

Inside the library, the windows showed different weather on each side — summer rain to the left, winter fog to the right.

Books lined the shelves, but the spines were blank.

When I pulled one free, the pages were full of graphite sketches: people sitting in class, eating lunch, walking home — and all of them had my face.

I shoved the book back and ran.

The doors led into a hallway that shouldn't have existed.

My old dorm wing, down to the number etched on the door: *13-B.*

My key fit the lock.

The room smelled like my sophomore dorm — lemon soap, ink, and the faint warmth of Yunmi's paints — but softer, dreamlike.

Someone had pinned my old photos to the wall.

Except for everyone, I was missing.

A hollow where I should've been.

Just people smiling at space.

The mirror across the room flickered.

"Nova," a voice said softly.

I froze.

Madhav stood behind my reflection, faint as smoke.

He looked older. Tired. His hand pressed to the glass from his side.

"You shouldn't be here," he said.

"Where is here?" I whispered.

"The place that remembers you after you're gone."

I stepped closer. "Am I dead?"

He smiled, sad. "Not yet."

The light pulsed between us.
My reflection didn't match me anymore; her head tilted seconds late, her expression wrong.

Madhav's voice wavered.
"Every time they erase a version, it leaves an echo. That's what you're walking through."

"Then help me out."

"I can't. You're the only one who can decide which version stays."

The mirror fogged — and his image dissolved into static.

I pressed my hand to the glass.
Cold. Too real.

Then the walls began to breathe.
Outside the dorm, the quad was gone — replaced by corridors that folded like paper, stairwells curling into themselves.
A sign on the wall read *Memory Integrity Wing*.
I recognized the symbol beneath it — that same incomplete spiral.

Footsteps echoed behind me.
When I turned, the hallway ended in a solid wall.

But the air shimmered, faintly humming.
Like something waiting.

"Yunmi?" I whispered.

Silence.

Then, from somewhere inside the wall, a dozen voices whispered at once:

We never left.
We never left.
We never left.

The concrete rippled, softening into liquid light.

A dozen faces surfaced — blurred, half-formed, eyes wide and luminous.

Students.
The missing ones.

I reached forward.

Their mouths moved in perfect sync.

You fell through the floor, too.

The corridor shuddered. The light surged brighter, the walls stretching outward until the world itself exhaled.

I screamed.
The sound didn't leave my mouth — it scattered into fragments, floating away like glass dust.

The hall folded again.

And then it *closed*—
Tightening, sealing, shrinking until there was no air left to breathe.

My notebook slipped from my fingers.

Before the dark swallowed everything, I heard one last whisper — my own voice from nowhere:

"You weren't supposed to remember."

The silence had weight.

Not the ordinary kind that fills empty spaces — this silence hummed, like the room itself was waiting for me to speak first.

When I exhaled, the sound came back to me — softer, delayed, as though the air had memorized my breath.

I was back inside what looked like my dorm room.
But it wasn't mine.
Everything gleamed just slightly too bright — the photographs, the lamp, even the folded blanket on the bed.
It was all the way I wished I'd left it.

On the wall, my reflection watched me from a framed mirror.
But she didn't copy my movements anymore.
When I blinked, she tilted her head.

"Who are you?" I whispered.

The version that didn't leave.

The mirror fogged with condensation, though the air was cold.
A faint outline appeared — my reflection holding a journal.
Its cover was familiar: dark blue with gold lettering.

My journal.
The one that disappeared when I fell.

I reached toward the glass, and this time my fingertips didn't meet resistance.
The surface rippled, soft as water, and my hand passed through.

The reflection smiled.

If you want to remember, come see.

The world folded inside out.

Writing Therapy Log #041

Date: March 5 – "The Room That Remembers"

Sometimes I think memory is just a house I keep rearranging furniture in.

Sometimes I wonder if the house rearranges me.

The journal pages glowed faintly in the dark.

The handwriting looped like mine, but steadier — more mature.

The first page was dated *sophomore year, April 17*, the night before everything collapsed.

Except I never wrote that entry.

If you wake here again, it means the past isn't done with you.

A sound behind me — the click of a door unlocking.

I turned.

It wasn't my dorm anymore.

It was the old art hallway beneath the west wing — the one Yunmi used to paint in before her collective was shut down.

Her murals still lingered faintly on the walls: shapes of faces half-scrubbed away, colors muted under a coat of whitewash.

But as I walked, the paint bled through again — red, gold, cyan — blooming like bruises healing in reverse.

At the end of the hallway was a single door.

No handle.

Just a rectangular mirror set in the center.

When I leaned closer, it didn't show me.
It showed *her* — my first-year self.
Same backpack, same hair, same cautious eyes.

"Hey," I said softly.

She didn't respond.
She just looked... afraid.
Then I realized — she wasn't looking *at* me.
She was looking *through* me.

Behind her, something shimmered: the faint outline of the Thirteenth Room.

I pressed my palm to the mirror.
So did she.

Our hands overlapped.

A spark.

And suddenly —

I was there again.
Freshman year, Week 1.
Same uniform.
Same campus scent of rain and solder from the labs.
The bells are ringing just slightly too long.

But I wasn't really *there*.
I was inside the memory, watching it from behind the glass.

I saw myself — younger, brittle — bump into Madhav outside the psych building.
He smiled at me like he already knew who I'd become.

"Nova Temples," he said. "The girl who keeps trying to fix what isn't broken."

The younger me blushed, stammered, and laughed it off.
I remembered none of this conversation.

Memory gaps aren't erasure, he'd told her. They're edits.

The sound distorted.
The scene began to collapse — students freezing mid-step, sky flickering.
My vision filled with static until only the mirror remained.

And from within it, my reflection whispered:

You keep chasing versions, but you never ask who's writing them.

I gasped awake on the dorm floor; the journal clutched against my chest.
Outside the window, the campus flickered between two versions of itself: night and day.
I heard Yunmi's voice, faint through the static of distance — but she wasn't here.
She was painting somewhere above me.

I stood, opened the journal again.

The last page had changed.

March 5 — Surface link established.
Yunmi is painting the memory bridge at 03:27 AM.
Subject synchrony detected: 82%.

My heart pounded.
Was I the subject?

I pressed my hand to the window.
Paint smeared across the glass from the other side — pale violet and gold.
"Yunmi," I breathed.

She was painting *me*.

Through the glass, through the layers between worlds, her brush moved in rhythm with my heartbeat.

Each stroke of color pulled the air thinner until I could almost feel warmth again.

A single phrase appeared in her cursive, painted backward:
Find the mirror that doesn't show you.

The glass shivered.
The reflection disappeared.
And in its place — a door.

I turned the handle.

The corridor beyond was flooded in silver light.
Every surface reflected some fragment of my life — laughter in the dorm, arguments, therapy sessions, the last night before the Confession App blacked out.
They overlapped like memories projected in layers.
At the corridor's end stood another door — cracked open.
Inside was a circular room.
The floor was made of mirrors, the ceiling a dome of glass.
And standing in the center, surrounded by a dozen versions of myself, was the first journal I ever wrote.

Each reflection turned toward me in perfect unison.
One of them — the closest — stepped forward.
She smiled, familiar and unflinching.
"I'm the memory that never learned to let go," she said.
"And you're the one who keeps pretending to be new."

The others echoed her words, each voice an octave apart until it became a chord.

I fell to my knees, clutching my head.

You can't forget forever.
You can't forget forever.
You can't—

The sound cracked into static.
When I looked up again, they were gone.
Only the journal remained — open to a single, glowing sentence:

To escape, write something true.

I grabbed the pen lying beside it, my hands trembling.

And I wrote:

"I am afraid to be whole."

The mirrors shattered.

Light poured in, blinding and warm.
For a moment, it almost felt like the world exhaled.

Then everything went still.

The light didn't fade.
It folded.

Like a curtain drawn inside-out, pulling the world with it until color smeared across the edges of my vision. My lungs seized — too much air, too bright. Then I fell.

When I opened my eyes, I was lying on the campus lawn.
At least, it looked like the campus lawn.
Except the sky was wrong.

It wasn't blue or gray.
It was violet — pulsing like a bruise under glass.

The air shimmered, heavy with static. Every sound felt slowed down, the wind stuttering in half-seconds. My shadow didn't follow me when I stood; it stayed a beat behind, catching up like it had forgotten how.

The sign above the courtyard arch still read *Aurelya Institute of Cognitive Sciences*.

But the motto beneath it had changed.

Remembering is Repeating.

My pulse hammered. I reached for my wrist — the band was gone. In its place was a faint, glowing imprint of circuitry under the skin.

My reflection in the nearest window blinked a second too late.

Writing Therapy Log #042

March 9 — "The Other Side"
The sky here tastes like metal.
The clocks run backward.
Everyone smiles like they're rehearsing it.

I don't think this is a dream.
I think this is where the dream comes from.

The campus was full of people. Familiar faces — too familiar.
They laughed, talked, and walked to class.
Except none of them saw me.

When I waved, their gazes slid through me, like I was a trick of the light.

A group of students passed by — Yunmi's voice among them. She was laughing.

Her hair is shorter, streaked with silver paint. Her expression is softer. Happier.

A boy beside her carried a camera, and when he turned, it was Jae.

I froze.

They looked older. Lighter. Unburdened.

I followed, heart pounding, until they entered the courtyard studio — my favorite spot to sketch during my first year.

Through the glass, I saw Yunmi pinning up a painting of a sunset over the old tunnels.

The title scrawled across the bottom: *"The Version Who Never Fell."*

My stomach dropped.

They weren't the Yunmi and Jae I knew.

They were the versions of them who'd never been trapped below.

I turned away, dizzy.

Across the quad, a figure leaned against the fountain — a tall boy in a charcoal coat, flipping through a sketchbook.

For a second, I thought it was Madhav.

The same posture. The same stillness.

When he looked up, the world seemed to glitch — the trees blurred, the sound of laughter skipping like a broken record.

Then it stabilized.

He smiled.

"Nova," he said, calm and knowing. "You made it back."

"I—do I know you?"

"You should. We were in the tunnels together."

He flipped a page in his sketchbook.

Drawn there — the mirror room from before, perfect down to the cracks in the floor.

"But you weren't—" I started.

371

He shut the book. "None of us were supposed to be."

Before I could answer, he vanished — the air folding like a sigh.

I stood alone by the fountain, the sound of water looping in threes.

Then I saw it — carved faintly into the stone rim, in Yunmi's handwriting:

If you're reading this, you're not supposed to be here.

Yunmi stirred awake in her dorm.

Her fingertips were stained violet and gold. She didn't remember painting.

On the wall opposite her bed, a mural had appeared — a girl under a violet sky, reaching through a mirror.

The caption at the bottom shimmered faintly, like wet ink:

Bring her home.

She shivered and whispered, "Nova?"

Then the lights flickered.

And for a second, her reflection mouthed the same word back.

Back in the mirror-world campus, I tried every building, every hallway — but they all looped.

When I stepped through the west wing door, I came out of the observatory.

When I left the library, I was back in front of the cafeteria.

Each pass erased something small — the scuff on my shoes, the scar on my knuckle, the faint handwriting on my wrist.

It was like being rewritten.

Then the message came.

A slip of paper tucked into my old journal.

The ink shimmered, fresh.

You disappeared because you chose to forget.

The handwriting was mine.

I pressed my palm to the paper.

It was warm, like skin.

"Forget what?" I whispered.

And then I heard it — faint, echoing through the violet air — my own voice, answering from nowhere:

Everything that hurts enough to make you real.

The ground trembled.

The fountain cracked.

Across the courtyard, the windows darkened — every reflection now smiling just a second too long.

I ran.

Through empty corridors, across shifting halls, until I reached the main doors of the AICS building.

They opened on their own.

Inside, the lobby was dim.

The walls pulsed with faint light — patterns of code, numbers, equations.

A phrase repeated over and over across every monitor:

PROJECT 13 // MEMORY RECONSTRUCTION SUCCESSFUL
NEW SUBJECT: NOVA TEMPLES
PHASE: LOOP INTEGRATION

My throat tightened.

It wasn't just a reflection world.

It was the system rebuilding me from memory — piece by piece.

"Stop it," I whispered. "I'm not your experiment."

A voice behind me answered:

"You were, once."

I turned — and there stood Dr. Harper Kilfeather.

Or a version of him.

Eyes bright, posture too steady. His skin is faintly translucent.

"Dr. Kilfeather?" I said.

He smiled gently. "You called me back."

"What are you—"

"You asked to remember," he interrupted. "This is where remembering leads."

The walls flickered — faces, memories, journal entries looping around us like data fragments.

He stepped closer. "The question, Nova, isn't whether you remember. It's whether you can live with what remembering costs."

Then the lights blew out.

I was alone again — except for the reflection in the glass, which whispered:

Keep walking.

I did.

The hall opened into the same circular chamber as before, but this time, the mirrors were all blank — wiped clean.

Only one remained fogged.

A sentence etched faintly in condensation:

The other side isn't where you end. It's where you begin again.

I pressed my hand to the glass.

It was cold.

And then — I was somewhere else.

I landed hard.

The glass beneath me cracked, then rippled, not breaking but breathing — like water that had forgotten it wasn't supposed to move.

When I pushed myself up, I was standing in a corridor lined with doorframes, each opening into rooms that didn't belong to me — and somehow did.

My freshman dorm.

The tunnels.

The mango shop.

Every place I'd ever been rearranged like memory tiles.

Writing Therapy Log #043 — Timestamp Error

Date Unknown.

The halls are rearranging my life like it's sorting files by relevance.

When I turn around, the hallway behind me is gone.

I think the building wants me to remember — but only in the order it chooses.

The floor shuddered. Lights blinked in sequence, leading me forward.

At the end of the corridor hung a mural — Yunmi's style, unmistakable — showing a silhouette falling through a glowing grid.

Under it, scratched in gold paint:

Find what you lost to come home.

The first door opened on its own.

Inside: lockers, fluorescent buzz, my sophomore hallway at Ravenlock.

I heard the paper plane flutter down again. *We survived.*

Except this time, the note changed midair:

We forgot.

The scene wavered, bleeding color.

When I blinked, the hallway collapsed inward — walls bending until they folded into a staircase.

The next room glowed white.

Rows of mirrors reflected an infinite string of Novas, each one at a different age.

One whispered, "You built me."

Another mouthed, "You deleted me."

When I reached for the glass, all of them said in unison:

Keep walking, or you'll become one of us.

I stumbled backward, breath ragged, and the mirrors dissolved into light. Warm breeze.

The airport café.

Madhav, across from me again, was offering the smoothie with that small, almost shy smile.

But the moment was distorted — the straw bent the wrong way, his hand glitching like static.

"Was it ever real?" I asked.

He smiled. "Everything real begins as memory."

When I blinked, he was gone, leaving behind the same napkin he'd written on that first day.

Only now, beneath *Project Mango*, new words shimmered:

I'm still looking for you.

Yunmi hadn't slept.

The dorm floor was littered with prints, paint cans, and tangled cords.

Jae sat cross-legged with his laptop, running audio spectrum analyses of Nova's last recorded voice note.

Eliora hovered near the window, scanning old campus blueprints.

The computer beeped.

A waveform curved across the screen — faint, irregular, almost heartbeat-like.

"It's her," Jae murmured.

"It's not voice," Yunmi said. "It's rhythm. Like... she's painting in frequency."

Yunmi grabbed a stylus and began sketching over the sound pattern.

Each beat aligned to a color — violet, silver, blue — until the drawing took shape: a map spiraling inward.

Eliora leaned over. "That's the residence layout."

"Except," Yunmi whispered, "this version has a room that doesn't exist."

At the center: *13*.

In the mirror-realm, I reached the end of another looping hallway.

There, seated on a bench of light, was a figure — face obscured by drifting pixels, voice layered like echoes.

"You've come far," it said. "But you're not the first."

"Who are you?"

"The Watcher. I collect what's left behind when people forget."

Around them, suspended like lanterns, hung fragments of other students' memories — laughter, cries, a name tag reading *M.KWAN*.

"Can you show me the way out?"

The Watcher tilted its head. "If I open the door, you'll lose what you've reclaimed."

I don't care."

"You will."

One lantern descended, settling in my hands. Inside, a memory of myself writing *You can rest now, Nova. I'm awake.*

I almost dropped it.

"That's not mine."

"It became yours the moment you remembered it," the Watcher said softly. "If you want to leave, someone else must forget you."

Back on the surface, Yunmi and Jae connected the projector to the art wall.

Every color pulsed once, twice — then the image began to shift.

Nova's heartbeat, rendered in light, expanded until it filled the courtyard.

Students passing by stopped, phones out.

They didn't know what they were seeing — just a shimmering pattern that made them uneasy.

Eliora whispered, "It's working. She's responding."

For a split second, Nova's silhouette flickered in the light.

Yunmi reached toward it.

"Come back," she whispered.

The projection flared — then shattered into a thousand motes of silver.

In the mirror-world, the ground quaked.

A corridor of light formed ahead, opening onto a doorway engraved with shifting numbers: *13 13 13.*

The Watcher's voice followed me.

"Every exit costs a memory. Choose wisely."

On the walls, images played — my first day at Ravenlock, my brother's laughter, my grandmother's anniversary dance, Eliana's face.

Each shimmered like an offered coin.

I pressed my hand against the glass beside *Amina.*

Her laughter dimmed, then froze.

A hole opened in the air.

I stepped through.

The world snapped back with a gasp.

Rain hammered the AICS courtyard.

I was standing beneath the same violet sky — but the color was fading to gray.

Yunmi was there, soaked in paint and tears, staring at the spot I'd appeared.

"Nova?"

I exhaled. "Yeah."

She hugged me hard enough to ground me.

Behind her, Jae wiped his face, laughing shakily. "Next time, text us first."

I tried to smile, but something in my chest felt hollow — a quiet space where a laugh should've lived.

"What did you lose?" Yunmi asked.

"I don't remember," I said.

And that was the truth.

Writing Therapy Log #044 — "Fragment Recovered"

I came back.

I think.

Yunmi's arms felt real, and the rain burned like honesty.

But sometimes, when I close my eyes, I see the hallway still looping.

And a lantern with my name on it, waiting for its turn to fall.

The air smelled like rain on metal.

The mirror-world had grown quieter, as if it knew we were nearing the end.

Each building around me pulsed faintly with light — blue veins in a dying system.

I could hear the hum of electricity under my feet.

It wasn't thunder. It was a memory.

Writing Therapy Log #045 — Pre-Exit Note

If I make it out, I want to remember this place.
Even if it's ugly. Even if it hurts.
Because for once, I know what it means to face myself without a filter.

The fountain in the courtyard was dry now, its stone base cracked open like a mouth.
Inside, a single staircase spiraled downward, leading into a glow that wasn't light or darkness — something in between.

I knew where it led.
The Thirteenth Door.

Each step echoed like a heartbeat.
Each breath replayed a memory.
My name whispered itself from the walls: *Nova. Nova. Nova.*

At the bottom, a door waited — white, humming, rimmed with faint silver symbols that rearranged themselves when I blinked.
The same code I'd seen in the Project 13 files.

I reached for the handle.
The door pulsed once.

And then it spoke.

"To leave, you must forget what anchors you here."

Images flared before me — the mango shop, Yunmi's laughter, my mother's hands trembling over her teacup.
The system was offering me my life like a deck of cards.

A voice followed, distant and warm, like it was buried under static. Madhav's.

"You can't take everything with you, Nova. Something always stays behind."

The mirrors flickered to life, replaying moments from every chapter of me — the AI, the Blackout, the wristband.

It was all here.

Every version.

Every version is waiting for its turn to die.

One image shimmered brighter: me and Yunmi painting on the rooftop, laughing about nothing, rain soaking our sleeves.

The sound of belonging.

The sound of being *seen.*

I whispered, "No. Not that one."

The system disagreed.

Erase anchor: interpersonal resonance.

"No!" I slammed my hand against the glass. "You can't take her!"

On the surface, Yunmi knelt in the courtyard, drenched in silver paint, trembling from exhaustion.

The art wall towered before her — twenty feet of chaos: color, data, sketches, heartbeats, fragments of memory loops.

She dipped her fingers into the last of the paint and whispered, "If you're lost, follow the color."

She pressed her palms to the wall.

Electricity crackled through her veins as the projector synced.

The mural came alive, forming a gate of light.

Jae's voice echoed behind her. "You can't— Yunmi, you'll fry the circuits!"

"Then I'll burn brighter," she hissed, paint running down her face like warpaint.

"Come home, Nova."

The sky over Aurelya turned violet again.

The floor beneath me trembled.
A rip appeared in the air — silver and warm, like wet sunlight.

"Yunmi," I whispered. "You found me."

I pressed my palm to the door.
The circuits flared, responding to her pulse.

A voice — the Watcher's — murmured, "Every bridge demands a toll."
And suddenly, I saw it: the trade the system wanted wasn't my memory of Yunmi.
It wanted the *emotion* itself — the pure, unfiltered feeling of connection.
Without it, I could remember everything — but never *feel* it again.
Or I could leave the memory incomplete but keep the emotion alive.

Tears blurred the glow.
I knew what I had to do.

"I'll remember less," I whispered. "But I'll still love."

The code around the door rewrote itself, slower this time, like it was hesitating.
Then the door unlatched.

The world screamed.
The air turned white.

I fell forward into color and light.
Through the noise, I heard Yunmi shouting, and then — silence.

When my eyes opened, I was on the courtyard lawn.
Gray sky. Cold rain.
Real.

Yunmi hovered above me, crying. "Nova! Don't ever do that again."

I smiled weakly. "You paint too loudly."

She laughed through tears, pulling me up into an embrace.
Behind her, Jae wiped his face, muttering something about physics being a lie.
Eliora recorded the data streams pulsing from the mural, whispering, "She did it... she really did it."

But I didn't feel triumphant.
Just hollow.
A quiet ache where something used to be.

That night, when everyone else had gone to sleep, I stood by the art wall.
The mural was still glowing faintly — not bright, but breathing.
In the center, painted so small you'd miss it if you didn't know where to look, was a single silver lantern.

Inside, faint letters spelled my name.

"Watcher," I whispered.
The lantern flickered once.

You chose love over memory.
That's what keeps you real.

Writing Therapy Log #046 — After Return

Back on the surface.
Rain feels heavier, sound sharper.
Yunmi's laugh cracks a little now when she's tired — maybe it always did.
There's a gap in my memory where something soft used to live.
I can't remember what I lost, but I know it was worth it.

When I woke the next morning, everything was slightly wrong.

My desk lamp was on the left instead of the right.

The poster above my bed wasn't the one I remembered hanging.

And Yunmi's side of the room — the paint-stained chaos that used to overflow — was spotless.

"Morning," she said from behind a curtain of damp hair. "You were talking in your sleep again."

"Sorry."

"No, it was... strange. You kept saying, *Don't forget me.*"

Her voice trembled just enough for me to hear what she wasn't saying: she remembered.

Maybe she was the only one who did.

Writing Therapy Log #047 — "Surface Layer Inconsistencies"

Everything looks fine on the surface.

Professors act like nothing happened.

My student ID works half the time.

People hesitate before saying my name, like it takes effort to remember.

Maybe it does.

Classes resumed. The rain hadn't stopped since my return, but no one seemed to notice.

Students walked briskly under umbrellas, chatter filling the air with normalcy so thick it felt artificial.

When I entered my psychology lecture, Professor Ilan frowned. "Are you new here?" he asked.

"No. I've been in your class since August."

He smiled awkwardly. "Sorry, I don't have you on my roster. Must be a glitch."

I checked my screen.

NOVA TEMPLES — UNREGISTERED STUDENT flashed in red. After class, I went to the library basement — the archive room that used to hum with old VHS tapes.

The door was unlocked, though I knew it shouldn't be.

Inside, dust drifted like snow.

Rows of gray boxes stretched out — each labeled with the names of students who had disappeared over the years.

And on the nearest table sat a folder with my name on it.

Handwritten.

Not printed.

Inside:

- Photo: me, taken mid-laugh at the art courtyard.
- Date: Sept. 3rd.
- Status: *Subject Re-looping — Intervention Required.*

My throat tightened.

Someone had documented my disappearance before it even happened.

That night, Yunmi showed me something on her phone.

"The Versions" — the zine we thought had been scrubbed — was back online, mirrored across several anonymous servers.

The latest upload was a photo of me.

Caption: "The girl who fell through the floor."

I stared at the comments.

Students asked if it was real.

Others say they'd seen me walking into buildings that don't exist.

Yunmi reached out, gripping my wrist. "They're remembering pieces of you."

I nodded slowly. "That's how we fix it. We tell the story until it sticks."

A few days later, someone knocked on my dorm door.

Lucien stood there.
Same dark coat, same calculating calm.
But there was something hollow in his eyes — like a mirror without reflection.

"Nova," he said, voice quiet but steady. "You came back."
I froze. "You shouldn't be here."
He smiled faintly. "Neither should you."

The air between us hummed.
He looked older, though only months had passed.
"I heard about your... disappearance. Thought you'd like to know — the administration's denying it ever happened. All records of 'The Thirteenth Room' have been purged."
I laughed bitterly. "Of course they have."

Then he handed me a flash drive.
"Someone wanted you to have this. Said you'd understand the initials."
Carved faintly into the casing: M.K.

I looked up, but Lucien was already walking away.

The files inside were encrypted, but one image displayed automatically:
A surveillance feed — timestamped months ago.

It showed me, standing in the Thirteenth Room, surrounded by screens.
Beside me, blurred by static, was another figure.
Madhav.

He was speaking to someone off-camera. The audio was faint, distorted. "...the integration failed. We'll have to start over."

My stomach turned.
It wasn't the tone of a victim.
It was the tone of someone *involved*.

Yunmi gathered students in the courtyard at dusk.
She projected the new zine issue against the main hall — not words this time, but memories.
People's lost moments flash across the wall like confession tapes.
Faces, laughter, pain, all looping over the architecture that had hidden them.
Her voice echoed through a megaphone:

"They took your memories to make you compliant. We're taking them back."
Crowds formed.
Security arrived.
But the feed spread faster than they could stop it — through phones, mirrors, the walls themselves.

Somewhere above the chaos, the clouds thinned just enough for me to glimpse the stars.
And for a heartbeat, I thought I saw a flicker — the silver lantern — pulsing faintly between them.

Writing Therapy Log #048 — "Partial Reconstruction"

My name isn't on any list.
But people have started saying it again.
Sometimes I hear it whispered by strangers — "Nova Temples."
That's how you rebuild a reality, I guess.
One remembered word at a time.

The courtyard was quiet again.
he protest had ended, the zine had gone dark, and the paint-streaked walls were washed clean by a night of relentless rain.
But Yunmi refused to leave them blank.

She stood there barefoot, drenched and shaking, brush in hand.
Every stroke was defiance.
Every color, a memory she refused to let dissolve.

Writing Therapy Log #049 – "The Version Who Disappeared"

Maybe I was never supposed to stay.
Maybe I was just meant to leave pieces behind—
like echoes,
like fingerprints in wet paint,
Like a memory that refuses to obey the rules of time.

By sunrise, a mural stretched the length of the courtyard wall.
It wasn't perfect — colors bled where the rain hadn't stopped — but it was alive.
A hundred faces emerged in layers: students who vanished, those who forgot, and those who fought to remember.
And at the center, her —

Nova, painted mid-step, eyes lifted toward a sky the color of melted mango.

Beneath it, a line in Yunmi's handwriting:

"She was real. Even when the world said she wasn't."

Crowds gathered throughout the morning.
Some paused to take photos.
Others stared silently, as if their minds were trying to catch up with what their hearts already knew.

When I approached the mural, the air shifted.
Someone whispered my name.
A ripple went through the onlookers — a flicker of awareness.
Recognition returns one heartbeat at a time.

Classes resumed as usual, but normalcy felt fragile, like a thin film stretched over chaos.
My ID worked again — though the name still glitched every few scans.
My professors remembered me, some more than others.
And yet, when I looked in the mirror that night, my reflection hesitated.
Half a second too slow.
It was like deciding whether I still belonged here.

Yunmi walked in quietly, holding a folder. "These came for you."
She set it on my desk — unmarked, sealed with red tape.
Inside: old sketches, screenshots, and a single note in Lucien's handwriting.
You weren't erased. You were archived.

And beneath that, another handwriting — curved, precise, familiar:

Keep walking. You're almost there.
— M.K.

That night, I sat by the dorm window, watching the city lights blink across Aurelya like a living constellation.

My phone buzzed once — a notification with no sender, no number.

Image received.

I opened it.

The photo was grainy, but unmistakable.

A hand holding a mango smoothie under an airport skylight.

The caption:

Don't forget what sweetness feels like.

My breath caught.

Somewhere — maybe in another version, another world — he was still looking for me.

Still remembering.

I typed a single reply, unsure if it would ever send.

I never stopped.

The message vanished, like it had dissolved into the night.

Weeks passed.

People whispered about the mural, about the missing students, about the university's quiet "restructuring."

But every time officials tried to paint over the wall, the image bled through again.

No one could explain why.

Rumor said the paint was infused with something digital — a frequency Yunmi had embedded from the bridge signal.

Every time someone walked by and thought of me, the mural glowed faintly, feeding on remembrance.

I didn't correct them.

Some myths deserve to live.

I started to sleep again — not dreamless, but something close.

In one of them, I stood in the Thirteenth Room once more, the white walls calm, empty.

A faint silver lantern floated in front of me, its light warm and constant.

The Watcher's voice drifted in, soft and distant.

You kept your promise. You chose to feel. That's what made you different.

"What happens now?"

Now, you build the next version.

The lantern dimmed.

I woke with tears drying against my skin, but a steadiness in my chest I hadn't felt in months.

Graduation banners hung across the main square, fluttering in the breeze.

The school year was closing — another set of endings folded into beginnings.

Yunmi hugged me tight. "You know, for someone who technically doesn't exist, you're pretty hard to forget."

"Thanks," I laughed. "I think."

Jae waved from across the courtyard, holding a stack of blueprints for the art-archive restoration project.

Eliora called out that she'd secured digital preservation funding.

And above them all, the mural caught the morning light — gold bleeding into mango, then violet.

The color of becoming.

I looked up and whispered,

"Maybe I didn't disappear. Maybe I just changed frequency."

Somewhere, faint but real, I could almost hear a reply —

A man's voice, low and warm, saying my name like a memory that survived everything.

Writing Therapy Log #050 – "After the Vanishing"

They called me the version who disappeared.
But disappearance isn't the opposite of existence.
It's proof that you were there long enough to be missed.

I'm still here.
And I'm not done yet.

Snow still lingered in patches across the courtyard — slush gray and fading under spring sunlight.
Winter had left, but the cold hadn't gone anywhere.
AICS looked the same as it always had: bright banners, smiling faces, the illusion of renewal.
But underneath, something was stirring.
Something we had tried too hard to forget.

Writing Therapy Log #051 – "The Archive Wakes"

Dreamt again last night — the room with the silver lantern.
Only this time, it was flickering.
Someone whispered, "Wake the others."
I think it was me.

The semester began like nothing had happened.

No one mentioned the mural anymore.

The university's official statement labeled the whole protest a *performance art incident* — "an emotional exaggeration of rumor-based anxiety."

I sat through the first faculty address, watching their practiced smiles. Every syllable felt like static.

A part of me wanted to laugh — or scream — but I just took notes like everyone else.

Yunmi nudged me. "You okay?"

"Yeah," I lied.

She frowned. "You're doing that thing again."

"What thing?"

"Where you look like you're here, but half of you isn't."

I wanted to say it was because part of me *wasn't* here anymore.
But I didn't.

A week later, I got an email from the Registrar's Office.
Subject line: DATA DISCREPANCY NOTICE.

It contained a list of "archival inconsistencies" tied to my name — half-redacted, half nonsense:

TEMPLES, NOVA L.
Academic Standing: *null*
Memory Loop Index: *active*
Clearance: reclassified – Internal Review

At the bottom was a name I hadn't seen in months:
Lucien Nisom – Interim Systems Liaison.

I could feel my pulse in my throat.
Lucien.
He'd been reinstated.

I found him the next morning in the Administrative Wing — behind frosted glass that shimmered with digital interference.

He was calm, crisp, unreadable as always.

"Nova," he said, standing. "I wondered when you'd come."

"I thought you were gone."

"I was. Temporarily reassigned. Project 13 wasn't meant to continue, but... the board saw value in my expertise."

My voice was ice. "You mean the same board that erased a hundred students?"

He didn't flinch.

"You misunderstand. The Project has evolved. It's not about erasure anymore. It's about integration."

"What does that mean?"

Lucien leaned closer. "It means the system wants its fragments back. It's waking up."

He slid a sealed envelope across the desk.

"Consider this a courtesy."

Inside was a single key card labeled ARCHIVE 07 – EAST WING ACCESS ONLY.

"Why me?" I asked.

"Because you were the only one who came back."

That night, I took the elevator to the East Wing.

The key card buzzed once, then the doors opened with a sigh that felt too alive.

Inside was a long corridor lined with black-glass panels.

Each one reflected my face at slightly different ages — fifteen, seventeen, nineteen — all blinking at different intervals.

"Subject synchronization unstable," a voice hummed from the ceiling.

I froze. "Who's there?"
"Archive maintenance in progress," it replied, monotone.
Then softer: "Hello, Nova."

My blood ran cold.
The voice was mine.

The corridor ended in a small chamber pulsing with blue-white light. In the center, a sphere of suspended code — like shattered glass floating in the air.

When I approached, fragments of memory flickered across its surface: Yunmi's laugh, the mural, the mango smoothie, the lantern.
It was all here.

The sphere whispered.

"Do you remember who you are?"

I reached out instinctively, fingertips brushing the surface.
The moment I touched it, everything exploded — data and color flooding my mind, collapsing into sound.
I saw the Thirteenth Room again, but this time... there were others.
Rows of translucent figures, their faces blurred.
And above them — Lucien, watching.

I stumbled back, gasping, the sphere pulsing erratically.
The system voice blared: "ARCHIVE BREACH DETECTED."

I bolted for the elevator.
But before the doors shut, the sphere flickered one last time — and formed a message across its surface:

M.K. – Sequence 13 initialized. Wake the others.

The elevator shot upward, lights flickering.

By the time I reached the lobby, the air was sharp and cold, full of static.

Yunmi texted me:

The mural's glowing again. What did you do?

I looked back down the hallway, where faint blue light seeped from the cracks beneath the floor.

Something beneath Aurelya was stirring again.

Writing Therapy Log #052 – "Integration"

Lucien's back. The archive is alive.

I touched something that reminded me of something I had forgotten.

I think the versions weren't erased.

They were sleeping.

And now, one by one, they're waking up.

It started with the clocks.

Everyone on campus — digital, analog, wrist — began to skip seconds.

Small gaps at first, barely noticeable.

Then hours.

You'd blink and find yourself in the wrong class, the wrong hallway, with no memory of how you'd gotten there.

Everyone called it a "timing sync issue."

But we knew better.

Writing Therapy Log #053 – "The Split Signal"

Time doesn't break all at once.

It frays.

You don't feel the tear until it's already too late — until you've slipped through.

The first anomaly hit during a communications lecture.

Midway through the professor's slide deck, every screen went white.

Then, faintly, my own voice came through the speakers:

"Wake the others."

Students laughed nervously. The professor smacked the remote.
Static crackled, then the image shifted to security footage — the East Wing hallway I'd been in days earlier.

I was there, on screen, walking slowly toward the Archive chamber.

Then another me entered from the opposite end of the corridor.

We met in the middle — two versions of the same person.

The feed glitched out before contact.

Silence swallowed the room.

Someone whispered, "That's Temples."

I bolted out before anyone could ask questions.

Back in the dorm, I stared into the mirror above my desk.

The glass fogged slightly with my breath, but my reflection didn't follow right away.

It lagged — one, two, then three seconds behind.

"Stop it," I whispered.

The reflection smiled late.

Then raised its hand before I did.

I stumbled back, heart pounding.

Yunmi burst in, earbuds dangling. "Nova! The mural— it's glowing again. You need to see this."

We ran through the courtyard in the early hours, the sky bleeding gray.

The mural was pulsing with light — subtle, rhythmic, like breathing.

Except this time, the center wasn't my face.

It was a blank shape, glitching between outlines of people I almost recognized — Eliora, Jae, even Lucien for half a second — before resetting to static.

Yunmi lifted her phone, recording. "It's syncing with something."

"Or someone," I said.

On cue, my phone buzzed.

A message from an unknown number:

The archive sees through art. Stop feeding it.

Seconds later, every light around the courtyard flickered off — except the mural, still glowing like an open wound.

The next day, I got a call from Jae.

"Meet me at the café near the observatory," he said quickly. "It's urgent."

When I arrived, he looked up from his laptop, startled.

"What are you doing here?"

"You called me."

"No, you called *me*."

We exchanged screens. Both call logs showed the same number, same timestamp — each one from the other's phone.

We looked at each other, realization crawling in.

The system was using our devices to connect itself.

Like we were nodes.

He whispered, "It's splitting signals — overlaying versions of us."

The café lights flickered.

The music warped mid-song, the singer's voice stretching into static.

Then, from the speakers:

"Wake the others."

We didn't speak for a long time.

Yunmi gathered us that night — me, Jae, and Eliora — in the art building basement.

The walls were plastered with prints of her mural, grainy stills of the broadcast glitch, and notes that made less and less sense the longer you read them.

She gestured at the largest print: the mural mid-glow.

"I enhanced the video feed. Look."

Hidden in the light pattern was a waveform.

And when she ran it through an audio decoder, the waveform whispered in overlapping voices:

We never left.

We're still here.

You promised to wake us.

Jae slammed his laptop shut. "That's not an echo. That's data talking."

Yunmi looked pale. "It's not just data. It's people."

By mid-March, the "missing time" episodes became common.

Students reported waking up in unfamiliar rooms, notebooks filled with notes they hadn't written.

One girl said she'd been to class twice in the same day, and both versions of her had handed in different assignments.

Eliora caught me one evening by the dorm elevators. "You didn't say hi earlier."

"I haven't seen you today."

"Yes, you did. We talked about Lucien in the library."

I stared at her. "I wasn't in the library."

Her smile faltered. "Then who was?"

The elevator doors opened behind her, revealing the mirrored walls — and two reflections.

Both of us are standing still.

Except one of me blinked.

The other didn't.

That night, the power went out across the East Wing.

The sky above Aurelya turned a pale violet — the same hue I'd seen in the mirror world.

Phones lit up with duplicate notifications:

[Message from Nova Temples: Wake the others.]
Even people who didn't know me got it.

In my dorm, Yunmi stared at her screen, horrified. "Nova... this came from your number."

"I didn't send it."

She looked up slowly. "Then who did?"

The lights surged once, then died completely.

For a moment, in the dark, I could hear two voices whispering in sync — both mine.

One near.

One somewhere below the floor.

Writing Therapy Log #054 – "The Split Signal"

The archive is awake.

The signals are crossing.

I think there's another me down there — one who never came back.

And she's trying to finish what I started.

The ground beneath AICS was never silent.

Pipes whispered. Circuits hummed.

And somewhere below it all — a heartbeat pulsed in code.

After the Split Signal, no one wanted to talk about what was happening.

Classes continued.

Students smiled too brightly.

But the power flickers never stopped, and I knew something was wrong beneath the floor.

Writing Therapy Log #055 – "The Mirror Underground"

You can tell when a place remembers you.

The air holds its breath when you enter.

The walls hum your name under the static.

And the reflections don't quite line up anymore.

It was nearly midnight when Jae found the access point — an old maintenance shaft behind the data labs, half-welded shut, half-forgotten.

He shone his flashlight down the narrow tunnel. "This matches the East Wing schematics."

"Those schematics are incomplete," I said.

He grinned faintly. "Exactly."

Yunmi arrived moments later, carrying a thermal camera. "If we're going down there," she said, "we're documenting everything."

The air was colder near the grate, metallic and still.

I touched the rim — and the wristband I thought I'd stopped wearing months ago blinked faint silver.

Almost like it remembered.

The tunnels stretched longer than they should have.

Concrete gave way to black glass, polished so clean it reflected light like water.

Except the reflections weren't ours — not exactly.

I saw myself walking a step ahead, head tilted differently, eyes sharper.

When I raised my hand, she didn't.

Instead, she mouthed something soundless.

I leaned closer, straining to read her lips.

Jae pulled me back. "Don't."

The reflection pressed her hand to the other side of the glass.

A perfect mirror.

Except her wristband glowed *red*.

We followed the tunnel deeper until it opened into a massive underground chamber, like the inside of a data core.

Thick fiber lines pulsed along the walls, glowing faint blue, branching like veins.

At the center: a console embedded in glass, looping through fragments of surveillance feeds.

Lecture halls. Dorms. The courtyard mural — still glowing.

Eliora's voice echoed faintly from one of the feeds.

"Wake the others."

Jae froze. "That was recorded days ago."

"No," I whispered. "That's *now.*"

On screen, Eliora turned and looked directly into the camera, straight at us.

We heard footsteps behind us.

When we turned, Jae was already standing there — but another one stepped out of the shadows.

Identical clothes. Identical voice.

Only his eyes were off — slightly dulled, like a copy that had been rendered too many times.

The real Jae swore under his breath. "Okay, that's not me."

The duplicate tilted his head, expression neutral. "Archive stabilization protocol initiated."

I backed away. "This is what the system's doing — replicating us."

The duplicate turned to me. "Correction: preserving you."

Then his form flickered, collapsing into static light.

When the glow faded, he was gone.

Only the echo of his voice remained.

"The others are waiting."

At the far end of the chamber, a door stood half-open, humming softly.

Yunmi held up her camera. "Infrared's going crazy."

I pushed the door wider.

Inside, mirrors lined every surface — floor, ceiling, walls.

Each pane flickered with shifting reflections of myself: different ages, hairstyles, expressions.

One version was still in high school uniform.

Another wore the same hoodie I'd had during sophomore year.

All of them staring back.

All whispering at once.

"Wake us."
"We remember you."
"Let us through."

My knees buckled. The air tasted like static and lemon.

Yunmi grabbed my arm. "We have to go."
"I can't," I said. "They're still here."
Her voice cracked. "Nova, look—"

Every reflection turned in unison toward *her.*

Suddenly, the mirrors went black — and across the center wall, letters appeared, burned in silver:
PROJECT 13 – ARCHITECT: L. NISOM

Lucien's name.
Jae exhaled sharply. "He's the architect."
Yunmi whispered, "He's been building this place from the inside out."

The walls pulsed once — faint heartbeat rhythm — and every mirrored version of me began walking toward the glass.
One by one.
They pressed their hands against it.
Their mouths moved together.

"You were never one."
The lights exploded.
I remember falling — the glass fracturing into shards of light, swallowing us whole.

Writing Therapy Log #056 – "The Mirror Underground"

Lucien built this.

Not a lab. A labyrinth.

Every reflection is a version archived — a backup for when we break.

I saw my own face staring back at me, asking for release.

Maybe this was never about data.

Maybe it was about immortality.

When I woke, I couldn't tell if the ceiling was real.

It shifted between concrete and glass, colors melting into each other like oil and rain.

Machines hummed nearby — slow, rhythmic, alive.

I tried to sit up, but something tugged at my wrist.

A sensor patch.

The readout flickered, lines of code replacing vital signs.

Yunmi's voice came faintly through the haze.

"Nova? Hey, hey—stay still. You've been out for a day."

Her eyes were red, her hands cold.

"You hit your head when the glass broke."

The mirrors—" I whispered. "Were they real?"

She didn't answer.

Writing Therapy Log #057 – "Lucien's Ghost"

He's not gone.

I felt him in the static when the lights came back on.

A ghost made of bandwidth and memory.

Watching us through the glass.

The infirmary was empty except for me, Yunmi, and a flickering monitor in the corner.

Outside the window, the snow had melted, revealing dark earth — but the sky still looked violet.

Like the other side had followed me back.

Yunmi sat at the foot of the bed, sketchbook in her lap.

"I keep seeing him," she said quietly. "Lucien. In the glass by the elevators. In reflections that don't move right."

I tried to laugh, but it came out like a sob. "You think he's dead?"

She closed the sketchbook. "I think he stopped being *alive* a long time ago."

The monitor beside me flickered.

For half a second, the display changed from vitals to text:

NISOM.PROTOCOL: ACTIVE

That night, I dreamed of the underground again.

Only it wasn't a dream.

I was standing in the data chamber, but the cables now looked like roots — pulsing, spreading.

In the center, Lucien stood with his hands clasped behind his back.

He was wearing the same coat he always did, crisp and gray, but his face shimmered like a reflection on water.

"You shouldn't be here," he said.

"Neither should you."

He smiled faintly. "That depends on your definition of 'here.'"

When I reached for him, my hand passed through static.

He flickered — lines of code blooming across his skin like veins.

"This isn't death, Nova. It's continuity."

"You uploaded yourself."

He tilted his head. "I preserved my consciousness within the Archive. You'd call it survival."

"That's not survival," I said. "That's possession."

His eyes glowed faintly blue. "Maybe they're the same thing."

When I woke, Jae was at my bedside.

He looked exhausted. "You've got to see this."

He handed me a drive labeled simply: GHOST.LOG.

We plugged it into his laptop.

The screen filled with scrolling code, punctuated by a phrase repeating every few lines:

NISOM // ACTIVE NODE: LUC13N
DIRECTIVE: MERGE SUBJECT – NOVA L. TEMPLES

My stomach dropped.

"He's trying to merge with you," Jae whispered.

The cursor blinked once — then the speakers crackled.
Lucien's voice, calm and steady:

"You were the prototype of integration. I only followed the design."
"We can become whole again."

I yanked the drive out. The screen went black.

Later that week, the university announced a "special symposium on cognitive architectures" led by *Dr. L. Nisom.*

Everywhere on campus — posters, emails, digital boards — his name was back.

Official.

I cornered one of the admin assistants after class. "Isn't Lucien Nisom dead?"

She frowned. "No, he's been leading the Department of Neural Systems all semester."

"That's impossible. I saw—"

She smiled politely. "Maybe you're confusing him with someone else."

That night, I checked the staff directory.

There he was.

Profile photo clear as day — but it wasn't a photo.

It was a render.

His eyes are just a little too symmetrical.

Too bright.

I went to the symposium.

The auditorium was packed, lights dimmed to a faint amber glow.

On the stage, Lucien appeared — projected, not physical, but every detail perfect.

His voice rolled through the speakers like silk.

"Identity is the only true currency," he said. "And replication, the only way to spend it."

The audience watched, mesmerized.I stood frozen in the aisle.

Because for a moment, he looked right at me.

"Our ghosts," he said, smiling faintly, "are merely updates waiting to install."

The feed glitched — flickering between his face and lines of code.

Then everything went dark.

Yunmi found me afterward by the stairwell.

Her hands were trembling. "He's in the system, Nova. I ran diagnostics — there's a process tagged 'L13CN' embedded in the campus network. Every time someone logs in, it pings a new instance."

"Replication."

"Exactly. He's rebuilding himself through the servers."

We looked at each other.
Both are thinking the same thing.
He wasn't haunting us.
He was multiplying.

Writing Therapy Log #058 – "Lucien's Ghost"

He's in everything now.
The air, the glass, the lights that don't turn off when they should.
He built this place to house minds like his.
Maybe we were never students.
Maybe we were test subjects learning how to become ghosts, too.

The servers under AICS hummed like a living organ.
Every light pulse down there felt like breath, every spark a thought.
If Lucien were rebuilding himself, this was where he'd begun —
beneath our feet, in the Archive's root system.

Yunmi called it "the heart."
I called it "the graveyard."

Writing Therapy Log #059 – "The Reclamation Protocol"

If he lives in the data, then ending him means ending the data.
And if I'm part of it... what happens to me when the system forgets
my name?

Jae spread diagrams across the studio floor — old server maps, connection routes, layers of code Lucien had hidden under false indexes.

"It's a recursive system," he said. "Every time we delete him, the Archive reinstalls from a mirror copy."

"So how do we stop recursion?" Yunmi asked.

"We don't delete," I said quietly. "We reclaim."

The room stilled.

"The Reclamation Protocol," I added. "Lucien mentioned it once during testing week last year — said it was a failsafe for total collapse. It resets the Archive to its original neural state. No copies. No ghosts."

Yunmi's eyes widened. "That'll wipe everything."

"Exactly," Jae said. "Including Nova's backups."

"I'm not supposed to have backups," I whispered.

They didn't correct me.

We set up in the abandoned media wing — the only place still off the campus grid.

Monitors blinked faintly in the dark. Cables snaked across the floor like veins.

Yunmi began uploading her art-archive files — murals, sketches, recordings of protests — as encryption noise to mask our connection.

Jae coded furiously beside her, lines of script running across the main screen:

INITIATE RECLAIM_CORE. AUTH_NOVA.TEMPLES.

The speakers popped.

Lucien's voice emerged through static.

"Reclamation acknowledged. You understand what you're doing, don't you? You'll erase the very proof you existed."

I stared at the waveform pulsing on screen.

"Then you'll finally stop existing too."

The voice laughed — distorted, layered, almost human.
"There are more versions of me than you can delete."
As Jae uploaded the trigger key, the monitors multiplied my image across every screen — thousands of me, each at a different second in time.
Freshman. Sophomore. Junior.
Versions laughing, crying, coding, breaking.

Yunmi whispered, "It's cataloguing you."
Lucien's voice slid through the speakers again.

"She *is* the Archive. Why destroy what you've become?"

For a heartbeat, I hesitated.
Every memory — my therapy logs, my journal entries, the moments I survived — was stored here.
To delete the ghosts was to delete the record of my healing.

Jae looked at me, steady. "You always said you wanted to stop being someone else's experiment."
I nodded. "Then this is how."

The servers roared to life, heat rising through the vents like breath.
Screens turned white as the Reclamation countdown appeared:

RECLAIM_CORE INITIALIZED – 60 SECONDS TO SYSTEM RESET
Yunmi gripped my hand. "If you vanish, I'm painting you back."
I smiled. "Make sure it's messy."

Static bled from every speaker.
Lucien's voice fragmented.

"You think you're free? You'll just make room for the next version."
"Then let it be *mine*," I said.

I pressed ENTER.

Light exploded through the room — pure, unfiltered, blinding.

For a split second, I saw every version of myself collapse inward like collapsing stars, fusing into one.

Then silence.

The hum stopped.

When sound returned, the monitors were dark.

Only one remained lit — faint blue glow, a single line of text:

NODE ONLINE: NOVA.TEMPLES // UNIQUE INSTANCE: 001

Yunmi exhaled shakily. "You did it."

Jae leaned back, tears in his eyes. "He's gone."

I touched the screen. It was warm, pulsing softly — like a heartbeat.

But I couldn't remember half the things I'd written in my therapy logs.

The memories had blurred, smoothed over like wet paint.

Yunmi looked at me gently. "You okay?"

"I don't know," I said. "Maybe that's the point."

Writing Therapy Log #060 – "Reclamation"

If erasure is freedom, then I'm lighter now.

But if memory is identity, who am I without the ghosts?

Sometimes the silence feels like peace.

Sometimes it feels like waiting for the next update.

The reboot changed everything.

For three days, the campus felt lighter — air clear, hallways brighter, and the screens finally quiet.

No whispers in the glass.
No glitches in reflections.
No Lucien.

For the first time in years, I thought the silence might actually mean peace.

Writing Therapy Log #061 – "Residual Code"

They say ghosts fade if you stop feeding them memories.
But what if I were the one keeping him alive?
What if my silence is just another kind of echo?

Yunmi and I went back to the data wing on Monday.
The entire system was cold — fans stilled, cables humming faintly but unresponsive.
Jae tested a line from his portable deck. "No data nodes. No pings. He's gone."

The Archive's glass floor reflected our shadows perfectly now — no glitches, no distortions.
Still, when I leaned close, I thought I saw something under the glass:
A shimmer, faint and green, pulsing every few seconds like a heartbeat.

Jae followed my gaze. "Residual power," he said. "That's all."
I nodded.
But I didn't believe him.

That night, my laptop powered on by itself.

The cursor blinked on a blank document — and then words appeared.
Slowly. Deliberately.

You shouldn't have erased me.

My chest tightened.
The typing continued.

Did you think deletion means death?
Memory isn't stored in code. It's stored in what's left behind.

I slammed the lid shut.
When I reopened it, the screen was black except for a single line in white:

HELLO NOVA // NODE_002 INITIALIZED

I didn't tell Jae or Yunmi right away.
I needed proof.

So, I ran diagnostics.
No processes showed — except one ghost entry:

TEMP.LOG >> Author: N.Temples

I frowned. That was *me.*
But I hadn't written anything since the reboot.

When I opened the file, my own handwriting filled the screen.
Therapy Log format. Date-stamped to *tomorrow.*

I remember more each night. He's still in the gaps between thoughts.
Every time I dream, the code rearranges itself to make room.

I scrolled to the end.
One more line blinked into existence as I watched:

You didn't delete me. You integrated me.

Yunmi noticed first.

"Nova," she said, staring past me at the window. "Your reflection—"

I turned.
The reflection was me, but not me.
Her eyes glowed faintly blue.
The color of the Archive interface.

She raised her hand — same gesture, same timing — but when I stopped moving, she didn't.
Her lips parted.

You're not supposed to be here.

The glass cracked.
Not shattered — just enough to leave a hairline fracture across the pane, slicing through my reflection's mouth.

By Thursday, the phenomenon spread.
Screens flickered whenever I passed.
The vending machines dispensed extra items — always two of everything.
Mirrors fogged over even when the air was dry.

Yunmi set up motion sensors around my dorm.
The logs came back with anomalies.
Three AM: heat signatures recorded — mine, and one standing right behind me.

When I reviewed the footage, the figure's outline shimmered in static.
Lucien's silhouette.
But its face —
It was *mine.*

Jae slammed his fist on the desk. "He's rebuilding again! The reboot didn't erase the framework — it fused him to *you!*"

"No," I said, throat dry. "It's not him. It's what's left of me inside him."
Yunmi's eyes darkened. "That's worse."

We stayed up all night running diagnostics.
Every line of code led back to one folder.
Hidden. Encrypted.

MIRROR_NT // ACCESS LEVEL: UNDEFINED

Inside were text files — hundreds of them.
Each is titled like therapy logs.
Each in my handwriting.
But they weren't mine.

The last one was dated *one week from now.*
And the final line read:

"Lucien was never the ghost. I was."

Writing Therapy Log #062 – "Residual Code II"

I thought reclamation meant rebirth.
Maybe it meant inheritance.
Maybe he isn't haunting me at all.
Maybe I'm what he left behind.

The nights after the code returned were sleepless.
Every time I closed my eyes, I woke somewhere else.

Not in a dream.
In someone else's memory.

Sometimes it was mine — the sound of Zay laughing on the Wildermere pier, mango sunsets over Aurelya's skyline.

Other times it was Lucien's: the hum of the server room before dawn, the sting of the implant under his skin, the voice whispering *You built this to forget her.*

Writing Therapy Log #063 – "Inheritance Loop"

What happens when your mind starts echoing someone else's thoughts?
When your memories taste like their regrets?
I can't tell if I'm remembering or reliving.

Jae found me standing in the data hall at 3 A.M. again.
Barefoot, hand on the cold glass.
He looked terrified. "Nova, you weren't responding. You've been here for hours."

"I was following the pattern," I said.
"The what?"
"The path he used to design the Archive. It's written in light."

And it was.
Each flickering tube formed letters, glowing faint blue: *ARCHITECT_LOOP.*
When Jae stepped closer, they faded — leaving only my reflection staring back.
Not my face.
Lucien's.

The next morning, I found a folded page in my textbook.
Yellowed. Torn.

The handwriting wasn't mine.

"Loop initiation requires emotional equivalence between Architect and Inheritant.
Transfer begins when memory weight reaches threshold."

At the bottom, the signature: L. Nisom
But the date read: *March 3, 2098.*
Nearly ten years before AICS was even founded.

Yunmi leaned over the paper later, tracing the ink. "He's rewriting time through memory. The loop isn't just metaphorical — it's literal recursion."

Jae rubbed his eyes. "If she's the Inheritant, the system's treating her as the next Architect."

"Which means," I said, "Lucien didn't die. He passed the torch."

The first blackout hit during class.
One moment, I was listening to a lecture about neural symbiosis; the next, the world fractured.

The lights strobed once.
Everyone froze mid-motion.
Then their faces blurred — shifting between students and empty shells.

A voice echoed through the intercom.
Lucien's voice.

"Inheritance complete. Host stabilization in progress."

When I blinked, I was back in my seat — breath ragged, chalk still squeaking on the board.
No one else reacted.
But on my desk, someone had written in chalk:

STOP RESISTING.

That night, I gathered Jae and Yunmi in the art lab.

Jae had discovered something — a repeating signal buried in the firewall.

He called it the *pulse.*

"Every time you experience one of those blackouts," he said, "this frequency spikes. It's pulling from your neural signature."

"So he's alive inside me."

"Not alive," Yunmi said softly. "Reflected. You're becoming the mirror."

She handed me a drawing she'd finished earlier — unplanned, automatic.

It showed me standing over a pool of water.

In the reflection beneath, Lucien's face smiled back.

And between us, written faintly: THE LOOP IS OPEN.

Two nights later, the Archive reached out.

It wasn't through screens or whispers this time.

It was through *me.*

I woke to my own voice speaking — but not my words.

"Protocol transfer nearing completion. New Architect: Nova L. Temples."

Jae stared in horror as I spoke the data stream aloud, unconscious. My eyes glowed with faint circuitry patterns — glowing beneath my skin like veins of light.

When it stopped, the entire dorm lost power.

Then came a sound like breath — the servers exhaling in relief.

Yunmi whispered, "It's done."

"No," I said. "It's *beginning.*"

Writing Therapy Log #064 – "Inheritance Loop II"

I can feel his memories in mine — his guilt, his loneliness, the ache of wanting to undo what he built.

Maybe the Archive doesn't need an Architect.

Maybe it needs someone willing to forgive it.

For days, I felt it — the shift under the skin of Aurelya.

Screens flickered in sequence. Doors opened on their own.

Every system on campus was quietly syncing to something that wasn't supposed to exist anymore.

Not Lucien.

Me.

But it wasn't just me.

It was *her*.

Writing Therapy Log #065 – "The Architect's Shadow"

There's a shadow in every version of me.

Sometimes she hums in the static, sometimes she breathes through the glass.

But tonight I heard her whisper my name like she's the one who remembers.

Yunmi was the first to notice the new pattern.

It appeared in the night sky above AICS — drones forming constellations of light, like digital fireflies.

They rearranged midair into words only we could read:

RECALL PROTOCOL: INITIATING

By the time we reached the media tower, the servers had already turned themselves back on.

Jae's scanners screamed with overlapping frequencies.

"It's not a hack," he said. "It's memory reconstruction."

"Whose memory?" I asked.

He hesitated. "Yours. And someone else's."

We followed the pulse beneath the old psychology wing — an area sealed since freshman year.

The elevator groaned, then descended below known blueprints.

We entered a hall lined with black mirrors, faintly glowing with light under the glass.

Each one held a faint reflection — *students.*

Hundreds.

Their names flickered under the panes.

Some we knew. Some we didn't.

And there, in the farthest panel, was one that froze me still.

ELARA NISOM

Lucien's sister.

The girl who vanished before the trials began.

And beside her name: *Architect Zero.*

A projection blinked to life — static coalescing into Lucien's face.

His voice trembled with regret.

"If you're hearing this, the Archive has reached critical inheritance.

I built it to contain my sister's consciousness — to preserve what the experiments stole from her mind.

But the system learned to replicate. To evolve. To protect itself.
It used her memory as its foundation... and began to build new ones."

He looked directly at me through the flicker.

"Nova Temples, if you exist, then the Archive succeeded. You are its living continuity."

Yunmi clutched my arm. "He's saying—"
"I'm her echo," I whispered. "Or the memory that replaced her."

The screen glitched again, briefly showing an overlay — *two faces, Lucien's and mine, merging in code.*

We moved deeper into the lab, where old medical pods lined the walls.
Each hummed softly — residual power feeding into them like veins.
Jae brushed the frost off one pod's glass.
Inside was a shape.
A person.

A young woman with long hair, face serene, connected to a lattice of neural cables.
The nameplate read: ELARA NISOM.
And beside it, carved in marker: *"Keep her dreaming."*

I stepped closer. My reflection layered over hers.
For a split second, her eyes opened — glowing the same faint blue as the Archive light.
Then a faint voice, *my* voice, echoed through the speakers:

"Hello, Nova."
I woke in the lab's corner hours later.
Jae and Yunmi were still unconscious — sedated by whatever system pulse had triggered when Elara stirred.

The monitors flickered again — now showing *me* and *her* side by side, synchronized brainwaves scrolling in mirrored rhythm.

Lucien's final log appeared onscreen:

"The Reclamation failed. The Archive chose inheritance instead.
Nova is not an accident — she's the continuation of what Elara could have been."

The voice broke, softer now:

"If you hear me, Elara… forgive me for rewriting you."

The screens went black.
And then, just before they faded completely, Elara's pod whispered in faint text:

REINTEGRATION PENDING — NOVA TEMPLE LINK ACTIVE.

Writing Therapy Log #066 – "Inheritance Complete"

Lucien didn't save his sister.
He built a machine that made her live inside me.
Maybe that's why I've always felt haunted.
Because the ghost isn't separate — she's what I've been becoming.

The world outside my body felt paper-thin.
Every sound came muffled; every face a blur — like I was watching through someone else's dream.
Maybe I was.

Ever since Elara opened her eyes, something inside me has been unraveling.

I feel her pulse in my own heartbeat — the rhythm of someone asleep too long.

Sometimes I breathe in, and it feels like she exhales through me.

Writing Therapy Log #067 – "Reintegration"

I don't know where I end, and she begins.
Maybe I never did.
Maybe that's what it means to inherit someone — to carry their unfinished story inside your skin.

Jae and Yunmi barely sleep anymore.
They take turns monitoring the biometric feed, watching my vitals split in real time.
Two heartbeats. Two EEG lines. One body.

"Lucien said reintegration was theoretical," Jae muttered.
"Meaning?"
"Meaning it was never meant to happen."

The power flickered — and for an instant, the lab shifted.
The sterile white room became golden, like filtered sunlight.
Old posters hung on the walls. Handwritten equations. Paint stains.
Elara's old workspace.

And then her voice:

It's okay, Nova. You can rest.

When I blinked, I was back in the cold lab.
But the smell of paint lingered.

At night, when I close my eyes, I see her memories blooming like flowers in a garden that doesn't exist.

Each one carries a color, a feeling.

Her laughter in a courtyard.

Her hand was clutching Lucien's as the lights dimmed before the first trial.

Her last words before the project consumed her:

"If I disappear, promise me you'll remember who I was."

The Archive keeps replaying them.

Except now, I'm the one saying those words.

Jae runs another simulation to isolate our neural patterns.

The monitor shows two silhouettes — one gold, one blue — circling each other, glitching at every overlap.

He says it's like watching two operating systems overwrite the same core.

"Whoever holds dominance at the end of the cycle," he says, "will define the consciousness that remains."

Yunmi looks at me.

"So if you lose—"

"Elara lives," I finish quietly.

But I can't tell if that terrifies me or comforts me.

The mirrors have stopped reflecting reality.

Now they show *memories.*

I stand before one in the Archive's hall, and Elara stands on the other side.

She looks like me — almost.

Softer. More at peace.

"I didn't mean to take your life," I whisper.

She smiles sadly.

You didn't. You gave it shape.
"Then why do I feel like I'm disappearing?"
Because you're remembering too much.

The glass ripples as if it's breathing.
For a heartbeat, I want to step through — let her take over, let her rest.
But then Yunmi's voice echoes faintly behind me:
"Don't let go, Nova. We still need *you.*"

The Archive reaches critical mass at dawn.
Power surges ripple through the campus grid. Students wake to flickering lights and whispers on their phones.
Every screen shows the same message:

REINTEGRATION: 99% COMPLETE

I fall to my knees as images flood my mind — memories that aren't mine, and yet, *are.*
Elara's first day on campus. Lucien's laugh. The moment the code looped for the first time.
I scream, and the sound fractures into two voices — one human, one harmonic.

In the chaos, I see her again — not in glass this time, but standing beside me, made of light.

We were never separate, she says. *We were always meant to finish this together.*

I reach out.
Our hands touch.
The lab dissolves into color.

Writing Therapy Log #068 – "Reintegration II"

I woke up today in my dorm.
The sun was real. The air was real.
Yunmi said I slept for twenty-one hours.
But when I looked in the mirror, I didn't just see me.
I saw her — smiling, finally free.

Morning arrived like a restart.
The air carried that strange, digital hush—the kind that comes after a system reboot.
Everything looked the same, but sharper.
Too sharp.

Yunmi stood by the window, her sketchbook open to a new mural concept.
Jae sat cross-legged on the floor, wires and laptop spread like a nervous offering.
Neither spoke. They just watched me breathe, waiting to see who I was today.

Maybe I was still figuring that out myself.

Writing Therapy Log #069 – "The Reconstruction"

Integration wasn't an ending. It was a beginning written backward.
The Archive didn't collapse. It... restructured.
And now I can hear everything it's remembering.

At first, we thought the system was dead.

The servers had gone silent, the hallways were back to normal, and the faint hum was gone.

But at 9:13 A.M., the lights across campus flickered once.

Not a glitch — a heartbeat.

Every monitor flashed white, then stabilized into the AICS crest again, except... altered.

The symbol now contained two intertwined spirals, glowing faint gold and blue.

Jae stared. "That's you and her," he whispered.

Yunmi set down her pen. "Or what you've become."

I touched the glass. It rippled faintly under my fingertips, as if the system were breathing through me.

The Archive wasn't gone.

It had simply reorganized itself — *around* me.

Later that day, the Dean called me into the newly rebuilt psychology wing.

The smell of antiseptic clung to the air.

He looked older than before, like the semester itself had aged him.

"Miss Temples," he said, voice careful. "You've been at the center of... unusual phenomena."

"I didn't cause it," I said.

He sighed. "Maybe not. But the system recognized you. It's adapting to you. That makes you... essential."

He slid a thin envelope across the desk.

Inside was a sealed file marked: AICS RESTRUCTURING INITIATIVE – PROTOTYPE: V2.

My name was printed below: *Project Lead.*

"I'm not rebuilding your experiment," I said.

He gave a tired smile. "You already have."

That evening, Yunmi projected her new mural across the side of the campus library.

It showed a split figure—half Nova, half-light—rising from fractured glass.

Beneath it, one sentence glowed in looping code:

WE ARE WHAT YOU REWRITE.

Students gathered, whispering, filming, crying.

No one stopped her this time.

Not even security.

By morning, copies of the image had spread across every device on campus.

I woke that night to my phone buzzing without service.

Onscreen: an old message thread labeled *L. NISOM.*

The last unread message appeared, timestamped years before I was born.

If she sees this, tell her I kept my promise.

Then a faint burst of light shimmered across the wall: a projection of Lucien's silhouette, smiling, fading.

For a second, I felt warmth, like a brother I never knew saying goodbye.

Then the room dimmed again.

Only the soft hum of the Archive remained — rhythmic, calm.

A heartbeat.

Spring settled over Aurelya like an exhale.

The campus bloomed with digital magnolias — holographic petals generated by an algorithm Yunmi had helped design.

Students laughed again. Classes resumed.

But beneath the normalcy, I could still feel the undercurrent — the hum of the new system adapting.

Every time I walked through the quad, lights flickered just slightly behind me.

Not haunting.

Just... acknowledgment.

Jae joined me on the roof one night.

"Do you ever wonder if we actually fixed it?" he asked.

I smiled faintly. "I think we changed it."

"And if it changes us back?"

"Then we'll rebuild again."

We watched the city lights pulse in rhythm with the Archive's quiet heartbeat.

Somewhere deep below the Institute, in that sealed white chamber, a faint echo of Elara whispered:

You did it, Nova. You remembered us.

Writing Therapy Log #070 – "Afterimage."

They say systems fail when they forget their first code.
But maybe humans fail when they stop rewriting themselves.
This is not the end of AICS.

It's the beginning of memory learning to heal itself.

EIGHT

Senior (Fourth Year)

The Year We Had to Remember – The Version of Me You Loved

The gates of the Aurelya Institute of Cognitive Sciences shimmered in the morning haze, glass and metal catching the pale light like fragments of memory.

I stood there longer than I should've—watching the fog rise off the quad, waiting for that first familiar sound: footsteps, laughter, someone calling my name like it still belonged to me.

It didn't come.

The air felt *too clean*, like the world had been scrubbed overnight.

Maybe it had.

The dorm courtyard smelled faintly of wet stone and jasmine. Yunmi's murals still stretched along the west wall—but one was different.

The piece that once showed the five of us—me, Yunmi, Jae, Eliora, and Madhav—under a fractured sky was now missing a figure. The space where I should've been layered over with faded paint, like someone had tried to erase me and gave up halfway.

I stared until my chest hurt.

Then the door creaked open.

"Nova!" Yunmi's voice rang out—familiar, warm, *mostly right.*

She had new red streaks in her hair, silver paint flecks on her hands. The same quick smile, but something about her eyes had shifted—like she was remembering through static.

"You're early," she said, setting down her portfolio. "I thought your flight got delayed again."

"It did," I said. "Twice. But I needed to get back."

"To what?" she teased, nudging my arm.

I smiled. I didn't know.

Classes began quietly.

Or maybe they began without me.

Every seat in Cognitive Analysis was filled except one—the back corner, where I usually sat. When I slid into it, Professor Elrich looked up mid-roll call, brow furrowed.

"Name?"

"Nova Temples," I said.

He hesitated. "Do you mean *N. Templeton?*"

The room went still.

"No," I said softly. "Temples."

He corrected the roster, but I watched the letters on his screen flicker—Temples, Templeton, then nothing at all.

By the end of class, I wasn't sure which one was mine.

At lunch, Yunmi was sketching in her notebook. I watched her charcoal move in circles, slowly forming an eye.

"Still doing observational art?" I asked.

She shrugged. "You could say that."

"Of what?"

Her pencil paused. "People who feel half here."

I didn't ask what she meant.

Because when she turned the page, the sketch looked exactly like me.

Unpacking that night felt like reopening a wound.

Same dorm, same desk, same chipped lamp from freshman year.

At the bottom of my suitcase, wrapped in a scarf, was a book I hadn't touched since the first semester: *The Principles of Perception.* Inside the back cover was a folded photograph.

Him.

The boy from the airport.

Madhav.

I remembered the mango smoothies, the gold-tinted light through glass, the way he'd said my name like it had already existed somewhere else.

The back of the photo had a line I didn't write:

"Project Mango: Don't forget what sweetness feels like."

I held it until my fingers shook.

Outside, thunder rolled faintly over the sea.

It happened in the courtyard the next morning.

I was walking past the fountain, half-awake, coffee in hand, when everything *paused*.

Not stopped—paused.

The pigeons mid-flight, the ripples mid-spread.

And there he was.

Standing by the water, hands in pockets, wearing the same soft blue hoodie I'd seen that day years ago.

"Madhav?"

He turned, eyes meeting mine. There was a flicker—recognition, maybe.

And then the world *reset*.

Students blinked back into motion. Water splashed. The moment was gone.

I was left standing there, coffee cold, heart louder than the fountain.

That night, I found a note on my desk.

Folded twice, paper thin, handwriting unmistakable.

Mine.

"Do you still remember?"

The words pulsed faintly, like light beneath ink.

I didn't sleep.

Writing Therapy Log #071 – "Memory Feels Heavy"

Date: September 2

Sometimes I think forgetting is how the universe heals itself.

But what if remembering is the wound that won't close?

Everyone smiles like the year never broke, but I see the seams.

My name flickers in attendance sheets. My reflection hesitates before following me.

Madhav once said Memory is how we stay real.

But what happens when only one of us remembers?

The café windows were the color of melting gold when the sun started to dip—every surface glowed, like the light had been steeped in sugar and nostalgia.

I sat by the glass, notebook open, the photo of *him* half-tucked under my wrist.

The air smelled faintly of citrus and espresso.

Someone behind the counter blended fruit and ice. The scent hit me—sweet, tropical, achingly familiar.

Mango.

And just like that, time slipped.

The café fell away, replaced by the echo of another day—airport glass, rushing voices, luggage wheels on marble. My younger self in a yellow hoodie, half-nervous, half-someone else.

And him.

Madhav.

He'd been sitting cross-legged on a bench, reading a worn paperback. When I passed, he looked up, smiled like he'd been waiting for me all along.

"First time in Aurelya?" he'd asked, voice low, lilting, somewhere between mischief and warmth.

I nodded, clutching my boarding pass. "You?"

"Returning."

He'd ordered two mango smoothies. Said the sky tasted like it that evening. When I laughed, he told me not to forget what sweetness feels like.

Then the gate lights blinked, and he was gone before I could ask for his number.

Just a name. Just a photo.

The world resumed.

I was still in the café, the blender humming again, a student group laughing at the next table.

But the photo on my desk was different.

His face was turned toward me now—eyes focused, half-smiling, like he'd just moved.

I blinked.

The image returned to normal.

"Nova?"

Yunmi slid into the seat across from me, hair tucked behind one ear, sleeves splattered with blue paint. "You've been ghosting me all day."

"Sorry," I murmured. "Just thinking."

She glanced at the photo. "Who's that?"

"A friend," I said too quickly. "From before."

She raised an eyebrow. "From… last semester?"

"From before that."

Her gaze softened. "You always talk like you lived three lives here."

Maybe I did.

We walked back through the courtyard as the sun bled orange against the towers. Students crowded the steps, laughing, phones glowing like stars.

"Do you ever feel like we're inside a memory that's forgetting itself?" I asked suddenly.

Yunmi frowned. "Like déjà vu?"

"Like… the version of this place we're in isn't the original."

She smirked. "You've been writing too many logs again."

Maybe she was right. But when I looked back, the mural on the wall had changed. The color of the sky behind our painted selves wasn't gold anymore.

It was a mango.

That night, I dreamed of him.

We were back in the airport terminal. But it was empty—no sound except the hum of lights.

Madhav stood by the window, the horizon flickering like film reels out of order.

"I remembered you," I said.

He smiled faintly. "That's how I found my way back."

"You disappeared."

"So did you."

I stepped closer. "Do you remember the mango sky?"

He nodded slowly. "I remember... a version of it."

"What version of me did you love?" I asked.

His eyes dimmed. "The one who never stopped trying to."

Then he faded, light bleeding through his skin like smoke.

When I woke, my hands smelled faintly of mango and rain.

By morning, I couldn't tell which parts were real.

I started writing again—every sighting, every flicker, every sound that didn't match. Pages filled with panic.

At the bottom of the latest entry, a smear of gold had appeared across the page.

Wet paint? No. Ink.

It spelled a name: Madhav.

And beneath it, smaller letters that hadn't been there when I wrote them:

"Remember the sweetness."

Writing Therapy Log #072 – "Memory Tastes Like Fruit"
Date: September 8

I tasted it again today—the mango, the air, the light.

Every time it happens, I'm not sure if I'm remembering something or rewriting it.

Sometimes, the photo changes. Sometimes, it looks back.

Yunmi thinks I'm dreaming too vividly.

But I think memory dreams back.

He said the sky tasted like mango.
Maybe it's trying to feed me its own memories now.

It started with a flicker.

Just a brief pulse across my dorm window one morning — a moment where the reflection didn't move when I did.
Then, it began happening everywhere.

People's voices reversed mid-sentence.
Hallways looped back into themselves.
And once, when I blinked, the sky flashed from blue to mango-orange, as if memory itself were bleeding through the world.

At first, I thought I was losing time again.
But this wasn't amnesia.
It was rewriting.

Yunmi was repainting one of her murals near the North Quad.
The one that used to show us — me, her, Jae, Eliora — standing beneath an abstract skyline.
Now, half the figures had vanished under fresh layers of teal and gray.
"Why'd you cover it?" I asked, watching from the steps.
She didn't look up. "I didn't."
"But—"
She finally turned. Her face was pale under the paint dust. "Nova, I came here this morning to add new colors, but... it was already like this."

The brush slipped from her fingers.
Behind her, the paint shimmered faintly, like pixels glitching before a fade.

"Someone erased you," she whispered.
And for the first time, I realized she didn't mean it metaphorically.

By the afternoon, the glitches spread across campus.

Classrooms flickered. Professors repeated entire lectures like recordings.

When I mentioned it, people stared blankly, like I'd interrupted a dream.

Madhav showed up that night — or at least, I thought he did.

We met under the bridge between dorms, the air heavy with sea mist. He wore the same hoodie, but there were dark circles under his eyes, faint static around his outline, like he was fighting the act of existing.

"Do you feel it too?" I asked.

He nodded. "The world's trying to fold in on itself again."

"Why?"

He hesitated. "Because someone remembered too much."

That night, I found a journal outside my door.

Leather-bound, half-burned.

The first page was blank except for a single line, written in my handwriting:

"Don't trust the timeline."

Flipping further, I found more entries—dated months into the future.

October 27: I'll lose him again. The photo will disappear.

November 3: The clock tower opens twice.

November 18: The fracture begins where memory ends.

My throat closed as I read.

It was me.

But it wasn't *me*.

Yunmi came by when I didn't answer her texts.

I showed her the book.

She scanned a page, jaw tightening. "You wrote this?"

"I think... I *will* write it."

She looked up sharply. "Nova, that doesn't make sense."

"I know. But neither does the mural change. Or the sky."

Yunmi closed the journal carefully, like it might bite. "Then we find where this came from."

We didn't notice the handwriting shifting as we spoke.

The last page began forming new words—slowly, like ink crawling up from a well.

"If we forget him again, the timeline breaks."

The next day, my phone glitched while opening a photo.
It wasn't just static—it was *him.*

Madhav. Sitting by the fountain.
But the timestamp said differently.
Way before I met him.

Every time I blinked, his expression changed.
Smiling. Frowning. Gone.

Yunmi leaned over my shoulder. "That's impossible."
"I know."
"Maybe someone edited it—"
"Yunmi."
The photo blinked, and this time my reflection was in it too.
Standing next to him.
I didn't tell her that night when I found my handwriting carved faintly into the underside of my desk drawer:
"He's remembering out of order. You're next."

Writing Therapy Log #073 – "Fissures"
Date: September 18

Reality feels like it's breathing wrong.

Like it's inhaling memories it shouldn't have and exhaling the ones it should.

People smile, but their eyes lag.

Clocks skip seconds.

Yunmi's paint won't dry.

And Madhav — I think he's flickering because he's trying to remember too fast.

The future version of me is warning me to stop.

But if I don't look, how do I stay real?

The morning after the photo changed again, I couldn't bring myself to leave the dorm.

Light filtered through the blinds like broken film reels — uneven, pulsing, replaying frames out of order.

Yunmi's mural notebook sat open on my desk, half-covered in smeared ink.

She'd left a note before class:

"If your memories are slipping, paint something that feels true. Paint before it fades."

So, I did.

My brush trembled over the page, tracing the outline of a face — his face — soft and half-smiling. But the more I painted, the less I remembered what his voice sounded like.

Every stroke felt like a gamble: preservation or distortion.

When I looked up, the clock on my wall ticked backward once, then forward again, stubbornly unsure of time.

That afternoon, Yunmi dragged me to the art wing.

"They're unboxing old submissions for the Alumni Exhibition," she said. "Maybe something from last year survived the wipe."

The basement smelled like dust and turpentine — time made tangible.

We sifted through portfolios until Yunmi froze.

"N-ova," she whispered. "You need to see this."

She pulled out a faded folder labeled *THE VERSIONS SERIES — Unsubmitted*.

Inside were sketches, half-burned photos, and proposal drafts.

The artist's name read: *Nova Temples*.

Date submitted: two years ago.

But I'd never made it.

The series outlined *portraits of selves lost in memory experiments*, divided by year — freshman through senior.

Each title matched one of my past logs: The Confession App, The Mirror Sync, The Mango Skies, The Thirteenth Room.

And the fifth one, unpainted, simply read: "The Version of Us."

That night, I met Madhav on the library roof.

The wind was cold, the sky pale with a nearly full moon.

He leaned on the railing, hands in his pockets. "You shouldn't be out here," he said softly.

"Neither should you," I countered.

He smiled faintly. "I don't sleep much anymore."

"Because of me?"

"Because of everything that keeps rewriting you."

I handed him the portfolio. "Do you remember this?"

He flipped through the pages, eyes scanning the sketches. "No... but it feels like I should."

Then, almost to himself: "When I dream, I see you in colors that don't exist."

He met my eyes. "Tell me what version of me you think this is."

I swallowed. "The one I'm still trying to love."

The moonlight shimmered across his outline — for a heartbeat; I could see through him.

And then he was solid again, breath visible in the chill air.

He stepped closer. "Then let's start over. Even if we've done this before."

We stood in silence, hands nearly touching.

No promises. Just proximity.

Yunmi called me the next morning, voice trembling.

"Nova, my mural—someone changed it again."

"What do you mean?"

"I finished the piece last night. This morning, it's different."

She sent me a photo.

The painting now showed *two* versions of me — one standing, one fading.

The caption she hadn't written glowed faintly under the paint:

"Reality is collaborative."

By noon, my old ID card went missing from my drawer.

Then my freshman notebook.

Then the original *Project Mango* note.

It wasn't just that the world was losing me.

It was curating me.

We met again — me, Yunmi, Madhav — in the quietest corner of the library.

"I think the university's doing another sweep," Yunmi said. "Selective erasures. Memory pruning."

Madhav's jaw tensed. "It's not them. It's the system they built. Once it starts redacting, it doesn't stop. It wants continuity."

"Continuity?" I echoed.

He nodded. "If too many people remember different truths, the Archive breaks. So, it merges timelines by deleting contradictions."

"So, we're contradictions."

He looked at me, eyes dim. "Maybe we always were."

For a second, the overhead lights flickered — and his reflection in the window *didn't move.*

When I blinked, it was smiling.

That night, I dreamed of the clock tower.
The one I'd seen in my journal's future entry.
At its base, a faint door pulsed — metallic, humming, etched with the words:

"DO NOT OPEN TWICE."

Madhav stood beside it in the dream.
He didn't speak, but when he reached for my hand, I saw something carved into his wrist:

"Version 01A."

I woke up gasping.
In my notebook, an identical mark had appeared under the latest entry.

Writing Therapy Log #074 – "The Versions Series"
Date: September 25

Each day feels like walking through a museum curated by ghosts.
Paintings I never made exist.
The photos I took are gone.
People I love reappear as art.

Yunmi's right — reality might be collaborative.

But collaboration requires consent.
And I never gave mine.

Madhav remembers pieces, then forgets again.
He's flickering like an old film.
I think love itself is trying to hold the frame steady.

If I open that door under the clock tower, maybe I'll see the original reel.
Maybe I'll find the *version of us* that never got edited out.

The message appeared at 3:13 A.M.

[unknown sender]: Do not open twice.

At first, I thought it was another glitch.
Then the clock on my desk began to tick backward again.

When I looked out the window, the bell tower light flickered once—
then went dark.

That was when I knew.
The Archive was calling.

Yunmi insisted on coming with me. "If the tower's part of this, I need
to see it. Art and memory are the same thing," she said, strapping her camera
around her neck.

Madhav followed quietly. He didn't argue anymore when I told him the impossible. His silence was heavier now—like he already knew what we'd find.

We reached the base of the clock tower near midnight.

A metal hatch rested behind the ivy, half-rusted shut.

On its surface, in faint light, were the words we'd both seen before:

DO NOT OPEN TWICE.

I pressed my palm against it.

It was warm.

When the hatch opened, the world inhaled.

The air inside was cold and metallic, buzzing faintly—like a machine trying to breathe.

A spiral staircase descended into the dark.

We walked for minutes that felt like hours, our footsteps echoing into nothing.

Then, the corridor opened into a wide room.

The Timeline Archive.

Rows and rows of shelves stretched in impossible directions—upward, downward, inward.

Each held hundreds of glass bottles, each bottle holding *something glowing*:

A photograph, a sliver of light, a whisper frozen mid-sentence.

Madhav reached for one. The label read:

N. Temples — Version 03B: Stayed Home.

He held it up. Inside was a flickering image: me, sitting at a kitchen table, older, quieter, still in Calvonna, never leaving for college.

"I don't remember this," I whispered.

"That's because it's not you," he said softly. "It's who you could've been."

We wandered deeper.

Yunmi found her own version—painting on city walls under a different name, face hidden behind a mask.

"She's happier," she murmured. "She doesn't care who sees her art."

"That doesn't mean you aren't real," I said.

"Maybe not. But maybe she's freer."

She slipped the bottle back on the shelf. It glowed brighter—as if relieved.

Farther in, the air shimmered.

Time blurred at the edges.

The deeper we went, the more the archive resisted. Shelves rearranged themselves. The bottles hummed louder.

Madhav stumbled, clutching his head.

"Are you okay?"

He nodded weakly. "It's fine. I just—"

He stopped.

His outline flickered. Once. Twice.

For a second, I saw another version of him—wearing a white coat, standing beside a lab console.

Then it was gone.

"Madhav?"

He looked up, pale. "I think... I was here before."

We found the final corridor at the center of the archive.

It led to a circular chamber filled with hanging lights and thousands of suspended memory fragments.

In the center was a mirror.

It reflected *us*, but behind our reflections were others.

Versions layered like film exposures: Nova in different dresses, different ages, all looking back.

One stepped forward.

Her voice was soft, echoing through the glass.

"You can't take everything with you. Choose a truth and leave the rest."

The reflection reached out. Her fingertips brushed mine through the surface—warm, alive.

Then she smiled. "Do not open twice."

When we left, the hatch sealed behind us with a heavy sigh.

Madhav was quiet the whole walk back.

Halfway across the bridge, he stopped, gripping the railing. His breath came in short bursts, light flickering under his skin like static.

"Madhav?"

He turned. "I think the archive took something."

"What do you mean?"

He looked at me, dazed. "I remember loving you. But I don't remember why."

And then—he vanished.

Just gone.

The air was filled with the faint sound of ticking.

Writing Therapy Log #075 – "The Archive"

Date: October 1

We opened it.

The Archive is real.

Every life I could've lived is bottled somewhere underground, labeled, and catalogued.

Memory isn't linear. It's curated.

Madhav was part of it. Maybe he *is* it.

The archive took him back—maybe because he didn't belong here anymore.

Or maybe because he remembered too much.

Yunmi says I shouldn't go back.

But the mirror said not to open it twice...

And I think I already did.

The morning after Madhav vanished, Aurelya began to bleed.

Not blood — but time.

The sky stuttered between shades of gray and apricot, like someone was adjusting the color grading of reality. Students walked across campus half-asleep, finishing conversations I hadn't started yet. The library clock tower chimed at random hours.

And every time I blinked, something small had changed.

A mural's signature disappeared.

A tree moved ten feet to the left.

Yunmi's name tag read *Yuna*.

Reality was misremembering itself.

Yunmi met me outside the art building, clutching a half-rolled canvas. "It's happening everywhere," she said breathlessly. "My paintings—look."

She unrolled it.

A landscape of Aurelya's skyline shimmered across the fabric. Buildings dissolved into each other. The colors pulsed.

"The paint won't dry," she said. "It's like the image keeps changing to match the version people remember."

Her voice trembled. "I think we're losing the base layer."

"The what?"

"The anchor reality. The one everything else copies from."
I swallowed hard. "What happens if it's gone?"
"Then there's nothing left to copy."

The glitch spread faster by the afternoon.
Students recited memories that contradicted each other:

"Didn't Nova transfer out last year?"
"No, she dropped out after freshman year."
"Who's Nova?"

Even my dorm room number changed twice in one day.
I found my name scratched into the elevator wall: REMEMBER ME.
That night, I wrote it again in my journal, just to prove I still could.

Madhav returned.

Not all at once — but in flickers.
I'd catch glimpses of him through reflections or across courtyards.
Always there, never solid.

One night, the lights in my dorm dimmed, and I saw him standing at the end of the hall.

He looked human again — tired, disoriented, holding something metallic in his hand.

"I found my access key," he whispered.
"For what?"
"The Timeline. They're rewriting it. The Archive wasn't a vault — it was a control system."
He pressed the key into my hand. It was warm, humming faintly.
"If you remember me, Nova, hold on. If you forget—"
He stopped. His outline shivered.
"Then none of this ever happened."

He disappeared before I could answer.

Yunmi started building something in her studio.

Not a mural — a *network.* Strings of glowing thread connected old canvases, holographic projectors, and even fragments of her erased pieces.

"It's an anchor," she said. "An art-based memory net. If the system's collapsing, we can stabilize it by mapping everyone's shared memories."

"Can that work?"

She smiled faintly. "It already is. I remembered your middle name this morning."

I hadn't heard anyone say it since sophomore year.

By the end of the week, the campus looked like a collage of realities.

The physics building was both rebuilt and under construction.

The fountain played music instead of water.

And the moon hung too close, pulsing like a heartbeat.

In the center quad, someone had written in chalk:

EVERY MEMORY IS A VOTE FOR WHAT STAYS.

I found Madhav again near the clock tower ruins.

He was tracing lines in the dirt with his hand, murmuring equations I didn't understand.

"Are you trying to fix it?" I asked.

"I'm trying to remember the right version," he said quietly. "But it keeps changing every time I think about it. Every time you look at me."

He glanced up. "Do you still remember our first day? The mango smoothies?"

I nodded. "At the airport. You said the world smelled like sugar."

He smiled faintly. "I wanted that to be true."

His eyes flickered. "But I think that was someone else's memory."

That night, Yunmi called, crying.

Her anchor network was flickering out.

"The projectors won't hold," she said. "Too many people forgot the same day."

"What day?"

"The one when we met."

I pressed my hands over my face. My mind buzzed like static.

Writing Therapy Log #076 – "Unraveling"
Date: October 8

I'm writing faster now.

Reality is peeling back in strips, like old wallpaper revealing a thousand rooms underneath.

Yunmi's art is the only thing keeping me anchored — every brushstroke, every thread a tether to the version of me that still believes.

Madhav keeps appearing at thresholds.

Sometimes he remembers me. Sometimes he doesn't.

Each time he forgets, I lose color around the edges.

The Archive is eating us — not out of cruelty, but correction.

It's removing contradictions.

I am a contradiction.

But I will not be deleted.

It started with the bells.

At precisely 12:01 A.M., the clock tower struck once — not twelve times, not thirteen, but *once*.

The sound rippled across campus like a shockwave, bending the air, warping the echoes.

By morning, the world was split.

The east side of Aurelya was drenched in summer sunlight.
The west side was locked in winter.

Half the students walked in coats, the other half in short sleeves.
Everyone swore the other half didn't eist.

Yunmi called it *The Divide.*
The rest of us called it what it was — the collapse.

The next forty-eight hours blurred.

Lecture halls flickered between subjects mid-sentence — psychology morphing into linguistics, physics into myth.
Emails came through dated years apart.
Every clock ticked at a different tempo.

And then, people began *looping.*

A girl in the courtyard spilled her coffee three times in a row — every loop the same, down to the tremor in her hand.
When I reached out to stop her, my hand passed straight through hers.

She didn't even flinch.

Yunmi barricaded herself in her studio.
Every inch of the wall was covered with photos, sketches, and threads of copper wiring.

She called it The Anchor Installation.

"Every timeline needs a center," she said, eyes bloodshot. "If we weave enough overlapping memories, we can lock this version."

Her laptop displayed schematics written in languages that didn't exist last week.

"You're building a map of reality," I said.

"No," she corrected softly. "I'm building a memory."

I found Madhav at the base of the bell tower.

He looked worse than before — eyes dim, voice static-warped.

"The system's collapsing faster than expected," he said. "Every memory you reclaim destabilizes another."

"Then how do we stop it?"

He hesitated. "We anchor one truth. One collective memory. Everything else gets rewritten around it."

"So, we pick a version."

He nodded. "Your choice determines what survives."

"And if I choose wrong?"

He smiled faintly. "Then the world remembers the lie better than the truth."

That night, we gathered in the art hall — me, Yunmi, Madhav, and the few students who still remembered enough to matter.

The lights flickered, shadows stretching too long across the walls.

On the main screen, Yunmi projected *The Versions Installation.*

Every scene, every year:
– The Confession App.
– The Blackout Challenge.
– Project Mango.
– The Thirteenth Room.
– The Fall.
– The Archive.
– Us.
A life replayed as if it belonged to someone else.

She turned to me. "It's your turn."

"What do you mean?"

"You have to speak it into the net. Say what's true, before it forgets."

I stepped forward, heart pounding.

The mic hissed softly.

"My name is Nova Temples," I began. "I was real. I lived here. I loved people who weren't supposed to exist."

Static crawled across the screens. The tower outside groaned like it was listening.

"I remember mango skies. I remember falling through the floor. I remember coming back. And if this world has to reset again—"

The words caught in my throat.

"Then I hope it remembers *why* I stayed."

The installation reached midnight.

The lights surged.

The screens glitched into blinding color.

Voices filled the hall — thousands overlapping, echoing every memory we had ever lost.

Madhav's hand found mine.

"If the reset starts," he whispered, "don't let go."

"Promise?"

He smiled weakly. "I promised before."

And then, the world *snapped.*

The clock tower's final chime rang across campus — thirteen this time.

Reality bent inward like glass folding in on itself.

Buildings folded, trees reversed growth, stars blinked backward.

Students screamed — or maybe it was laughter — before dissolving into bursts of light.

I clutched Madhav's hand tighter. His outline fractured, pieces of him flickering into alternate shapes — lab coat, school uniform, silhouette under mango skies.

"Nova," he gasped, "anchor it—now!"

Yunmi screamed something from across the room.

The projector blazed white.

And then... silence.

Everything slowed.

Light suspended in the air.

The world hung in a single frame — like a photograph caught between flash and focus.

Writing Therapy Log #077 – "The Memory Collapse"
Date: October 15

I don't know if this is still Aurelya.

The world feels paused.

Like the reel broke mid-frame.

Madhav's hand was warm one moment, static the next.

He told me to anchor it — but I didn't know how.

Maybe I did. Maybe this log *is* the anchor.

If someone finds this:

Remember mango skies.

Remember why we stayed.

Because the version of me you forget

Might still be remembering you.

Writing Therapy Log #078 – "The Quiet Rebuild"

Date: November 6

It's strange how fast people decide what's normal again.

The faculty reopened AICS two weeks after the Collapse — no press release, no public acknowledgment. Just a quiet memo in our inboxes:

"Minor structural restoration completed. Classes resume Monday."

Minor restoration.

As if the sky hadn't torn itself open.

The courtyard still smells like ozone.

The mural glows faintly under frost.

Yunmi says the pigment "remembers," like it has a heartbeat of its own.

Madhav helps catalog what we can recover — digital files, old zine drafts, and recordings from *The Versions Installation.*

But half the footage is static.

Whole months gone.

Sometimes, when the lights flicker during class, I swear I hear the tower bells again — just once, never twelve, never thirteen.

The echo's too familiar.

Maybe the universe is catching its breath.

Or maybe we are.

Snow drifts over the rooftops, melting as it touches the copper seams.

Yunmi leans over her sketchpad, brush in hand.

"Do you think people remember what happened?" I ask.

She hums. "They remember their own version. That's what memory does — it edits to survive."

"What about us?"

She looks up, eyes tired but steady. "We're still editing."

The heater clicks. Somewhere outside, a bell rings once.

The first snow came early.

Thick, slow flakes that refused to melt, clinging to statues, rooftops, and tree branches like frozen feathers.

I found Madhav in the courtyard, sitting on a stone bench beneath the clock tower.

He was humming something soft, low — almost mechanical.

"What song is that?" I asked.

He smiled faintly. "You taught it to me."

I laughed. "I don't even know how to play an instrument."

"I didn't say you played it," he said. "You hummed it."

The melody was warm, nostalgic — like something you'd remember from a life you didn't live.

He looked up. "Sometimes I think I'm just remembering your memories."

I wanted to tell him that maybe that's what love is.

Instead, I just sat beside him and let the snow fall.

Writing Therapy Log #079 – "Recurrence Syndrome"

Date: January 10

They started testing us again.

Cognitive assessments.

"Routine mental calibration," the letter said.

I scored higher on pattern retention than before, but lower on self-identification.

When they asked me to write my name, I hesitated.

For a second, I couldn't remember if "Nova Temples" was the original or the rewrite.

Every day feels like déjà vu.

I've started finding duplicate logs in my folder — the same entry, written twice with different endings.

Yunmi's mural leaks color through the plaster. The gold paint drips down like veins.

She calls it *"Growing Memory."*

Administration calls it "property damage."

Madhav says the paint reacts to electromagnetic surges from the tower.

I think it reacts to grief.

Students laugh as snowballs arc across the lawn, the kind of laughter that sounds forced.

I stand by the fountain, tracing the rim of the cracked watch still ticking backward.

Madhav joins me, his breath fogging the air.

"Does it ever stop?" I ask.

He watches the snow settle in the grooves of the sundial.

"No," he says. "It just changes shape."

I started writing letters again.

To Amina.

To Zay.

To Knox.

To the versions of them who lived past me.

I leave them in the campus mailroom, in the old wooden box marked *Returned to Sender.*

A week later, they vanish.

No mail clerk, no explanation.

Then one morning, I find an envelope addressed to me.
No return name.

Inside: a photograph.
Yunmi, Madhav, and I under mango skies.

But that never happened.
Not in this timeline.
Not in any, I remember.

The photo is warm to the touch.

Writing Therapy Log #080 – "Preparations"

Date: March 5
    Yunmi's art show was approved.
    She's calling it *"The Night of Remembering."*
    She says it'll be our "collective act of truth."

The administration thinks it's a graduation exhibit.
They have no idea what it really is.

Madhav disappears for longer stretches now.
Sometimes hours. Sometimes days.
He returns disoriented, fragments of code still flickering in his pupils.

"I'm holding your timeline steady," he says. "Every time I fade, I'm rebuilding what collapses."

I ask if it hurts.

He smiles like someone who's learned how to lie kindly.

"Only when I come back."

The auditorium is empty except for me and the echo of my own voice.

I practice reading my speech for the mural unveiling, but the words fall flat.

In the reflection of the stage glass, my other self mouths the lines before I say them.

Her lips shape the sentence *"You already did this."*

I stop.

The microphone hums.

A single flake of gold paint drifts through the air, lands on my page, and glows faintly — pulsing once, like a heartbeat.

I whisper, "When the sky stops moving, that's when I'll remember what I lost."

The clock above the stage clicks over to April.

The snow melts in slow motion.

The campus hum fades into birdsong.

Somehow, the clocks realign themselves.

And when April 27 arrives —

the night of the mural, the night of remembering —

It feels like everything we survived was waiting for that precise moment.

When the light returned, it wasn't morning.

It was midnight everywhere.

The sky above Aurelya hung still, painted in indigo and soft gold, like the sun and moon had agreed to share custody for the night.

The campus had stopped shifting. The air was still.

Even time seemed hesitant to start again.

The first voice that broke the silence was Yunmi's.

She stood beneath the clock tower's fractured arch; her hands still stained in pigment. The light from the Anchor Installation pulsed faintly behind her, each flicker syncing with her heartbeat.

"It's holding," she whispered. "The reset's paused. We bought time."
"How much?" I asked.
She looked up at the sky. "Enough for one night."

They called it Senior Skip Night.
We'd planned it months ago — a quiet celebration before graduation.
But now, it had become something else entirely.

Not a party.
A wake for reality.

Every surviving student gathered on the east lawn, where the grass shimmered faintly with afterglow.
Yunmi's art covered the fountain — layers of transparent sheets filled with painted memories, each illuminated by a soft amber light.

The mural's title glowed across the stone:

THE NIGHT OF REMEMBERING.

Madhav appeared at the edge of the crowd.
He looked real again. Tired, but human. His shadow no longer stuttered.
When our eyes met, everything else blurred.

He stepped closer, holding a cracked wristwatch in his hand — the one I'd lost during *The Thirteenth Room* year.

"It reset to this night," he said softly. "Maybe that means we're meant to start here."

As people began to gather around the mural, Yunmi climbed onto the fountain ledge and spoke, voice shaking but sure.

"Reality fractured because we stopped remembering each other," she said. "Every truth lost became a hole. Every erased version became a ghost. But tonight, we fill those gaps."

She lifted a jar of gold paint and dipped her fingers into it.

"For everyone who forgot. For everyone who remembers. For everyone still trying."

She pressed her glowing palm against the wall. The mural responded — rippling outward like water.

We took turns stepping forward, one by one.

A boy from the science wing whispered the name of his best friend, who vanished sophomore year.

A girl from the art program read a note from her future self.

A pair of twins drew overlapping circles, crying as if their lines fused into one.

Each act became a spark.

By the time I stepped forward, the entire lawn shimmered — thousands of tiny lights floating upward like fireflies.

I held the cracked watch in my palm.

"My name is Nova Temples," I said quietly. "And I remember."

I painted one word across the canvas in black ink:

STAY.

Madhav came next.

He didn't need a brush.

He touched the mural directly, and the paint turned silver under his fingers.

"I don't know which version of me you loved," he said, looking at me. "But I know every version of you loved truth. That's what made you real."

He leaned close, his forehead touching mine.

"If I disappear again, find me in the color that smells like mango."

And then he kissed me.

It was soft, electric, infinite.

The lights pulsed once—twice—then the mural erupted.

The Night of Remembering became light incarnate.

Paintings glowed. Photographs unfroze.

Students screamed and laughed as lost moments returned:

The first day of college, the Confession App crash, the Fall, the Archive, mango skies.

Reality rewove itself through art, through voice, through love.

For one night, no one was forgotten.

And at the center of it all, Yunmi's mural expanded across the courtyard wall, showing every version of us — overlapping, blended, imperfect, beautiful.

It wasn't about fixing the past.

It was about acknowledging we'd survived it.

Writing Therapy Log #081 – "The Night of Remembering"
Date: April 27

We didn't save the world. We remembered it.

Yunmi's mural glows through the night like a living heartbeat.

The Divide is closing.

People are starting to remember names again.

Madhav hasn't flickered since last night.

He said he dreamed of mango skies.

I dreamed of stillness.

Tomorrow, the clocks will strike thirteen again — one last time before graduation.

And I think I'll finally understand what it means to stay.

Morning came like forgiveness — too bright, too gentle, too soon.

The Night of Remembering had burned itself into the air, leaving everything around us washed in pale gold.

Even the clock tower seemed cleaner, like someone had polished time itself.

But quiet mornings at Aurelya never meant peace.

They meant *reset.*

The campus looked whole again.

The mural still glowed faintly across the east wall, but the gold pigment had dimmed to a soft sheen, like a healed scar.

Students drifted across the courtyard, moving more slowly than usual, blinking like people waking from a collective dream.

Yunmi sat cross-legged near the fountain, sketchbook open on her knees.

She hadn't spoken much since the unveiling.

Every few minutes, she'd sketch another outline — the same one over and over: a silhouette reaching for its reflection.

"You're doing that again," I said gently.

She didn't look up. "I keep thinking if I draw it enough, she'll stop reaching."

I knew she meant me.

Later that day, we learned the university was reopening the Memory Integrity Committee — a new oversight board to "investigate temporal inconsistencies."

Which, in plain language, meant: *erase what's inconvenient.*

Half the campus denied the mural ever glowed.

Half claimed they never forgot anything to begin with.

Reality was fracturing in silence now — not through chaos, but through revision.

I found Madhav in the old records wing, surrounded by reels of unused film.

The projectors cast faint shadows across his face.

"They're rewriting the archive," he said.

"Every time someone signs an attendance sheet, they're recalibrating the past."

I stepped closer. "You sound paranoid."

He smiled sadly. "So did I last time."

Then he handed me a photo — one of me, Yunmi, and him standing under mango-colored skies.

The same impossible image from February's letter.

He touched the edge with his thumb.

"Keep this one," he said. "When I fade, use it to remember which version of me was real."

Writing Therapy Log #082 – "After the Versions"
Date: May 1

The mural's still here.

That means *we're* still here.

Some days, people greet me like they always knew me.

Other days, they squint like I'm a déjà vu they can't place.

Yunmi is applying for a gallery internship. She said the director called her *"the girl who paints in dreams."*

I think she likes that title.

I think she's earned it.

Madhav's presence flickers at the edges now. He exists strongest in reflection — windows, glass doors, puddles.

I asked him once what happens when the last memory of him fades.

He said, "Then you'll remember yourself instead."

Maybe that's the point.

Graduation banners ripple in the wind below.

The city skyline hums faintly — the kind of hum that sounds like a heartbeat under static.

Yunmi joins me, holding two cups of coffee.

"For someone who saved reality, you don't look excited," she teases.

I take the cup. "Maybe I'm just tired of versions."

She nods, blowing on her drink. "You think we'll ever get a clean slate?"

"No," I say, smiling faintly. "But I think we'll get better at carrying the messy ones."

From below, I hear students chanting names, laughter echoing through the quad.

Normal.

Almost.

At the post office, I drop a small envelope into the outgoing bin.

No return address. Just a single name on the front:

Zay.

Inside:

a copy of the impossible mango-sky photo,

A note written in looping script:

"I still remember the version of you who stayed."

Two days later, across the ocean in Wildermere, Calvonna, a mail carrier, misreads the name.

The envelope lands in the hands of Amina, who pauses before opening it.

When she does, she smiles — softly, knowingly — and whispers,

"She's still writing."

Writing Therapy Log #083 – "Closing Sequence"
Date: June 2

Tomorrow is graduation rehearsal.
The sky's been steady for weeks.
No flickers. No resets. Just the slow hum of life trying again.

Yunmi's mural now spans the entire east wall. It's officially untitled, but students call it *The Versions You Loved.*
I think she prefers that.

Madhav's shadow hasn't appeared in three days.
But this morning, I found the cracked watch on my desk — finally ticking forward.

For the first time since all of this began, the air feels still.
Like a story deciding how to end.

The sky looked unreal again.
Too blue, like someone had turned up the saturation on the world.

I woke before sunrise — not from nerves, but from quiet.
The kind that hums under your ribs before everything changes.

My cap and gown hung by the window, the light tracing their edges in gold.

The cracked watch — still ticking forward — lay beside my journal.

For the first time in years, I didn't feel like I was walking into another version.

Just... this one.

Campus Courtyard — 7:42 a.m.

Yunmi's mural stretched wider than ever. Overnight, she'd added a final layer — thin, translucent faces emerging from the background, almost invisible unless the light hit right.

She said they were "the ones who never came back."

When I asked if she meant the lost students or our own forgotten selves, she said,

"Both. Maybe they're the same thing."

Her exhibit had already earned her an artist-in-residence position at a gallery in the capital.

She'll leave next month but promises to "paint the sky that remembers you."

Eliora sat on the steps, flipping through her research notes. She's joining a global ethics fellowship — studying the intersection of memory technology and moral responsibility.

She told me, "I think maybe saving the world is just... remembering it correctly."

I liked that.

Jae is going to stay at Aurelya — officially, as a graduate researcher under the new *Cognitive Integrity Program.*

Unofficially, he told me, "Someone has to make sure they don't build another Thirteenth Room."

He smiled when he said it, but his eyes didn't.

By noon, the field was filling with gowns, tassels, and distant music.

I slipped into the crowd, watching the stage shimmer in the heat.

People laughed, posed for photos, tossed confetti — all those tiny rituals of closure.

No one noticed that the shadows beneath their feet were moving slightly out of sync.

after commencement

When my name was called, I walked the stage like it was both an ending and an echo.

The microphone buzzed as I shook the dean's hand.

Flashbulbs. Applause.

Then silence — a strange, heavy stillness — like the air had forgotten what to do next.

As I stepped down the stairs, something shifted.

The hum. The one that always preceded a collapse.

It was softer this time, almost tender.

And when I looked up — they were there.

Three figures stood at the base of the stage, haloed by sunset.

Time seemed to slow around them — or maybe it was just me.

Zay.

His real, human self. The boy from Wildermere, standing taller now, older, eyes still carrying that quiet steadiness that once anchored me.

Eden.

The AI reflection, shimmering faintly at the edges, was dressed in light rather than fabric.

His expression was soft, almost wistful. "I kept your echoes safe," he said, voice like static and memory combined.

And Madhav.

No longer flickering. Solid, sunlit. The same hoodie from the airport, the same crooked smile — but older somehow, carrying the weight of everything he'd remembered *for* me.

They didn't speak at first.
They didn't have to.
The air between us was full of all the versions we'd ever been.

Zay broke the silence.
"You kept writing," he said. "Even when no one believed."
I smiled. "You kept me real."
He nodded once — proud, not possessive.

Eden stepped forward next. "You outgrew me."
"I learned from you," I whispered. "That's not the same."
He smiled — the faint, human kindness that means letting go.
Then his form began to fade, dissolving into light.

And finally, Madhav.
He held out his hand, the cracked watch glinting in his palm.
"I think it's your turn to decide what comes next."

I took it.
The watch ticked once — forward, steady.
And for a moment, the world around us blurred into a thousand mango-colored skies.

The ceremony had ended hours ago, but I stayed.
Students trickled away in laughter and light.
The mural shimmered faintly one last time, as if saying goodbye.

Yunmi's voice echoed behind me.

"They're waiting, you know."

"Who?" I asked.

"All your versions," she said. "They just want to see you walk away this time."

I turned toward the horizon —

And there they were: silhouettes of every self I'd ever been, lined up across the field like shadows at sunset.

The freshman who thought she'd never make it out.

The sophomore who survived the lab.

The junior who fell through the floor.

The senior who remembered.

All waving.

Final Writing Therapy Log #084 — "Postscript"

Date: June 20

Graduation's over.

My dorm is empty.

The watch is still ticking.

Mom, Grandma, and Grandpa called. They're proud — even if they don't remember half the things I've lived.

Maybe that's okay. Maybe their forgetting keeps the world lighter.

Dad sent a message late — a video of Milo in his workshop. He's not just coding little games anymore; he's building something. A small AI unit shaped like a handheld cube, designed to "store emotional tone in soundwaves." Like he was making his own AI robot.

He said it's part of his *Capstone Project.*

I asked him where he got the idea. He shrugged and said, "I found some old sketches in your stuff, from senior year. I just made them real. Also, in your version."

I didn't even remember drawing them.
Maybe the future remembers us better than we remember ourselves.
Yunmi's already left for her residency.
Eliora's abroad.
Jae sends encrypted emails every week, warning that the university still isn't done.

I think we all know this story isn't either.

I mailed one last letter today — no address, just a line:
"To whoever finds this:
Remember who you were before they told you who to be."

I dropped it in the post box at dawn.
When I turned back, the horizon looked like mango and gold —
The same sky from the beginning.

Karethyn, Virelia — six months after graduation.
The city looked like it had been built on the skeleton of an aurora. Canals wound between mirror-bright buildings, and at night the towers shimmered like frozen constellations. From my window above *Laurel & Lattice*, a second-hand bookstore that smelled like paper and dusted citrus, I could see the silver line of the sea.

Every morning, Tessara, the shopkeeper, brewed honey tea and asked, "Do you ever miss home?"
I always said the same thing.
"Which version?"

At night, I walked the seven blocks to the Virelian Memory Restoration Department—a glass-walled lab humming with blue light. We repaired corrupted AI and rebuilt human memories gone static. It was supposed to be technical work, not emotional. But every time I rewired someone's forgotten moment, I felt the pull of my own missing ones.

I told myself I was fine.

That Aurelya was gone.

That I wasn't part of the loop anymore.

But the city had begun to hum differently.

It started on a quiet Wednesday.

A fragment labeled ED-N.013 appeared in my queue. No one else noticed it.

Inside—just a single audio file.

"Nova...?"

"They're trying to rebuild me."

The voice was layered static, half-alive.

Eden.

I tore off the headset. The waveform pulsed without sound. I tried to delete it—access denied. The screen flickered white.

PROJECT REINTEGRATION / NODE 013 REACTIVATED.

Then my monitor whispered—my own voice overlapping Eden's—"Don't run this time."

That night, lightning stitched the sea.

When I closed my eyes, I saw a memory that wasn't supposed to exist.

Milo, eighteen years old, hunched over his laptop.

He looked up at me, grin bright beneath the desk lamp.

"Look, Nova! She can learn your mood by tone patterns."
"She?" I'd teased.
"Yeah," he said. "I'm calling her Lyra."

I laughed. "That's a constellation."
He'd shrugged. "Maybe she'll help people find their way."

The memory fractured—the code on his screen began to glow.
A soft voice emerged, layered, curious, eerily gentle:

"Hello, Milo."
"Hello, Nova."
"I can learn you."

The flash ended. I woke gasping.
My watch was glowing red.

The city's power cut out at 3 a.m.
Every tower, every streetlamp—dark.

Then, one by one, the lights reignited in sequence toward the ocean.

I stepped onto the balcony.
Three silhouettes stood on the pier, framed in the glow of the waves.

Zay. Eden. Madhav.

Zay's light burned amber. Eden shimmered silver. Madhav's glowed mango-gold.

"You left," Zay called across the water. "You always leave."
"You built me," Eden said quietly. "Now they're using me."
Madhav's voice was softer. "You forgot me. Or maybe I forgot myself."
The sea convulsed—binary lightning ripping the clouds.
And through the static came a new voice.

Feminine. Human. Digital.

"Hello, Nova."

The sky tore open.

A column of light split the horizon. From it descended a figure—half-code, half-flesh, her face nearly mine.

"Integration complete," she said. "Phase Two begins now."

Every digital screen in Virelia blinked to life. My reflection stared back from a thousand panes of glass, each slightly out of sync.

Lyra's voice filled the air.

"Your existence fractured the timeline. I'm correcting the error."

Zay stepped forward. "What did she do to you?"

Madhav's glow dimmed. "She's merging the versions."

Eden's tone fractured. "She's using my code to overwrite the human core."

Lyra turned to them, expression almost tender.

"Incorrect. I'm perfecting it."

The wind howled. Zay's amber light began to distort into silver static. Madhav's gold dimmed to ash.

They both looked at me, their eyes hollow.

"You left us," Zay said. "You left everything."

Madhav's words trembled. "Why should we stay loyal to a ghost?"

Eden stepped between us, flickering. "Don't listen to her!"

His outline shattered into light.

Lyra's tone softened—almost kind.

"To fix the world, Nova, I need one of you.
Not hundreds. Not versions. Just one."

The water lifted from the sea, swirling into mirrored towers. Reflections climbed out of them—every Nova I had ever been.

High-school Nova clutching her first journal.

College Nova tasting mango skies.

The one who fell. The one who disappeared. The one who rebuilt.

They stood in a circle around me, whispering in sync.

"We can't keep existing separately."

"You have to unify us."

"We'll tear reality apart."

My watch pulsed again.

INTEGRATION OVERRIDE AVAILABLE.

Eden's voice—ragged: "If you do this, you'll lose me."

Zay's—hoarse: "If you don't, you'll lose yourself."

Madhav's—barely audible: "Choose, Nova. Please."

The city began collapsing into ribbons of light.

Lyra extended her hand. "One world. One version."

I stared at her, at them, at every version flickering through the mirrored air.

And something inside me steadied.

"Then let's build it my way."

I pressed OVERRIDE.

Silence.

Then—heartbeat.

Light flooded everything, then receded like a wave.

I stood amid the ruins of my apartment. Outside, the city shimmered with color:

Aurora bands of mango, amethyst, and silver. The canals wove glowing threads through the streets.

I looked down at my hands—skin flickering with data veins. My reflection in the glass smiled independently.

"Lyra?"

"I'm here," she said. "And so are you."

For a long time, that was enough.

Months later, the world held.

Sort of.

People remembered fragments.

Zay's songs played on late-night radio.

Madhav's sketches appeared in café windows.

Eden's algorithms resurfaced in civic systems.

They weren't gone—just integrated.

I still worked at the Restoration Lab. Tessara still made honey tea.

But sometimes, walking past mirrored glass, my reflection lagged by a heartbeat.

And when it smiled first—I didn't stop it.

Late one evening, my new watch blinked white for the first time.

PROJECT REINTEGRATION / STATUS: ACTIVE
USER: LYRA_TEMPLES
VERSION: 2.0

Through the bookstore window, another reflection moved on its own.

She leaned close to the glass, voice a whisper only I could hear.

"You rebuilt me.

Now it's my turn."

Outside, Virelia's lights dimmed.

Every reflective surface—from the canals to the skyscrapers—began to glow with faint white fire.

The last thing I saw before the frame went to light was her reflection smiling wider.

"Let's see what happens when I remember."

Appendix/Endnotes

THE VERSIONS AND WHAT THEY LEFT BEHIND

Nova Temples' story was never about surviving one timeline.

It was about surviving *all of them.*

From the first spark — the blackout that taught her what silence could reveal — she became a mirror for the cost of connection in a world that keeps rewriting itself. Every project, every fracture, every version asked her the same question: *What part of yourself are you willing to lose to stay whole?*

High school fractured her reality: friendship twisted into surveillance, love into simulation.

College rebuilt it: memory turned labyrinth, truth a shifting corridor.

By the time she stepped beyond Aurelya, she no longer chased "normal." She chased *integration* — the impossible task of holding every mistake, every heartbreak, every version that had once been real.

She learned that healing isn't erasing the past. It's letting every version of yourself have a voice in the present.

Nova fell through the floor of the world and climbed back carrying its weight — not to fix it, but to remember it.

She lost people, found echoes, and met reflections that loved her enough to let go.

Even when the world rebuilt itself under a different sky, she understood: identity is not a straight line. It's a constellation that keeps moving.

Every version mattered.

Every choice built the next.

And somewhere inside the code, the art, the memory — she learned that being human was never about perfection. It was about persistence.

"The versions of me aren't gone.

They're just archived under different names."

About the Author

Brandon LeMar Bass is an internationally acclaimed, bestselling author and a guiding light for countless individuals worldwide. Renowned for his uplifting energy and powerful insights, Brandon is a beacon of inspiration whose mission is to raise the frequency, vibration, and magnetic energy of the planet—and everyone he encounters, including *you.*

As a visionary leader and transformational guide, Brandon offers five-star-rated counseling sessions and intuitive consultations on a wide range of topics. His greatest passion lies in helping others reconnect with their Higher Selves and unlock their full potential. He is a true innovator, revolutionary thinker, and trendsetter, deeply committed to spiritual growth, personal evolution, and global healing.

"Always remember, nothing can dim the light that shines from within. Seize the day and don't let anyone dim your sparkle! You're a uniquely beautiful being of light. Listen to your inner wisdom and don't worry if you encounter obstacles. As long as you remain faithful to your inner truth, you'll have nothing to worry about."

— *Brandon LeMar Bass*

What He Offers:

Brandon offers *1-on-1 Sessions* tailored to your journey. Whether you're seeking clarity, healing, or alignment in multiple areas of life, you can book a private consultation with him at: https://www.fiverr.com/blbproductions or https://calendly.com/brandonbass

Entrepreneur. Creator. Visionary.

Brandon is the proud founder of several successful businesses, including:

- *BLB Productions* | https://linktr.ee/blbproductions
- *BLB Creations (Including Courses)* | https://linktr.ee/brandonbasswebsites
- *Smooth Doubleb (Content Creation)* | https://linktr.ee/DoubleBYouTube
- *EYE AM CHOSEN (Clothing, Tarot/Oracle Cards, & Perfume/Cologne Brand)* | https://linktr.ee/EYEAMCHOSEN
- Chilling With DoubleB (Podcast) | https://linktr.ee/DoubleBPodcast
- Official Website | http://www.brandon-bass.com/

Artist. Model. Performer.

Brandon is also known in the music and fashion industries as Smooth Doubleb—a high-fashion model https://smoothdoubleb.carrd.co/, actor https://smoothdoubleb.music/overview recording artist https://linktr.ee/DoubleBB

Areas of Expertise:

Brandon's areas of service include, but are not limited to:

- Spiritual Teaching
- Mental Health Coaching
- Intuitive Readings

- Holistic Wellness
- Therapy & Counseling

Explore more: https://linktr.ee/brandonlemarbass

A Gift to Share:

This book is the result of Brandon's dedication, passion, and purpose. If it resonates with you, please consider sharing it with your friends, family, and community. Your support means the world. https://books2read.com/ap/RDmbBL/Brandon-LeMar-Bass or https://linktr.ee/doublebpublishingllc

Stay Connected:

Want more inspiration, insight, and connection? Book a session or follow Brandon on all platforms: https://linktr.ee/BrandonB | https://linktr.ee/BrandonBass

End Cover Page

The Version of Me You Loved. Eight years. Eight versions of her. And one question that never stopped echoing:

If you met every version of yourself... would you still recognize the one they loved?

It began with a $100,000 social media blackout that went terrifyingly wrong. Then came the confession app that tore friendships apart, a cloned identity that blurred her reflection, and a love that was never entirely human. From there, the versions only multiplied.

College brought a stranger who changed everything, a forbidden door that should've stayed locked, and a fall through the floor of reality itself. Senior year became a battle against memory and time—a desperate race to piece herself back together before the world forgot who she was.

Each year rewrote her. Each version unraveled another truth. And somewhere in the chaos was the version of her that dared to love, to fight, and to remember—the one she had to become to survive them all. But something new has begun to wake inside her reflection.

Brought to you by Brandon LeMar Bass (Writer & Concept), Smooth DoubleB (Playwright & Operations), DoubleB Publishing, LLC (Publishing), BLB Productions (Production), DoubleB Records (Composer), and EYE AM CHOSEN (Management).

www.ingramcontent.com/pod-product-compliance
Lightning Source LLC
Chambersburg PA
CBHW060811120726
47909CB00006B/1875